010

EAGLE
SONG

ALSO BY JAMES HOUSTON

Eskimo Prints
Ojibwa Summer
Songs of the Dream People
The White Dawn
Ghost Fox
Spirit Wrestler

EDITOR

Lyon's Private Journal 1821–23

ILLUSTRATIONS
BY THE AUTHOR

JAMES HOUSTON

EAGLE SONG

◆◆

AN INDIAN SAGA BASED
ON TRUE EVENTS

McCLELLAND AND STEWART

The Canadian Publishers
McClelland and Stewart Limited
25 Hollinger Road, Toronto M4B 3G2

Canadian Cataloguing in Publication Data

Houston, James, 1921-
    Eagle song

ISBN 0-7710-4258-2

1. Nootka Indians — Fiction.   2. Indians of North
America - British Columbia - Fiction.   3. Jewitt, John
R. (John Rodgers), 1783-1821 - Fiction.   4. Thompson,
John - Fiction.   I. Title.

PS8515.0868E23   C813'.54   C83-094135-5
PR9199.3.H675E23

Designed by Joy Chu

Published simultaneously in the United States by
Harcourt Brace Jovanovich, Inc.

Printed and bound in the United States of America

To Arthur A. Houghton, Jr.
with admiration and affection

When I was young, I have seen streams of blood shed in war. But since that time, the white man came and stopped up the streams of blood with wealth. Now we are fighting with our wealth . . . we do not fight with weapons; we fight with property.

Statement of a Northwest Coast nobleman,
Fort Rupert, B.C., 1895

Old
Sitka
(or New
Archangel)

ALASKA

North
Pacific
Ocean

Queen
Charlotte
Sound

Miles
0   100

Map
of the
NORTHWEST COAST
of
NORTH AMERICA
1797

NOOTKA
QUADRA
&
VANCOUVER'S I.

OREGON
TERRITORY

A. Karl / J. Kemp

SWAN GUN

 SPRING came blowing gently to us from the southern ocean. We could smell it, warm and salty on the breeze. We could see it in the new green featherings on the cedar trees. We could hear it high above us as the geese came flocking north to seek their summer nesting places. Yes, spring was coming to us once again.

I went wandering along the river toward evening and stood alone in the salmonberry patches that, together with an ancient pair of masks, a sacred song, and a dance that only she was privileged to perform, had been a small part of my wife's inheritance. Stopping to look out over the inlet as it steamed with mist, I tried silently to remember the words of her song, feeling certain she was close, that she could hear me if I sang them deep inside myself, even though she had been dead these countless moons. Then I walked back to the Eagle house and slept that night as soundly as a child, never dreaming of the dreadful things that were about to happen.

On that same night I was awakened by a scattering of gravel as human feet came dashing up across our beach. There was a sense of panic in those footsteps that set our house dogs barking so savagely they woke the guard.

The otter hunter and his son came stumbling through the entrance to the Eagle house. "A ship! A ship has come!" they gasped as they came running through the shadows to our end of the house, raising a cloud of gray ashes around the fire pit between Maquina's sleeping place and mine.

"*Tyee*, it passed us . . . just out there . . ." the old man wheezed, "not long after dark. They must be searching for fresh water and some place to rest themselves. They're just in off the ocean."

"We followed them," said his son. "We heard them drop

their big iron hook . . . right by the island in the small bay of Abooksha."

"We could see their shipsmen up against the night sky. Young boys they were, crawling all along the wing bones, folding in the feathers." The otter hunter knew that those were woven sails, not feathers, but he still preferred our older way of thinking and of talking. He picked up an armful of cedar driftwood and flung it on our fire, then, squatting, blew a glowing nest of embers into flames.

A blend of high-pitched women's voices and the gruffer sounds of men came to me from the vastness of Maquina's house. Another of our fires flared up. I heard one child, then another, start to wail. Good, thought I, the otter hunter's yelling and children crying and those yapping dogs will set this household moving soon enough.

"Is that ship near the point?" I called out to the otter hunter.

"Yes, yes. She's right in tight," he answered eagerly. "Me and the boy, we watched four shipsmen lower a small boat. They were carrying a lantern. We saw them rowing to the beach, towing a thick cord behind them—about as big around, it was, as a pretty widow's thigh." He turned and grinned at me. "Two of those shipsmen finally got their rope tied around a tree while the other pair went and filled up their barrels with fresh water from the stream. Only took two small barrels for drinking. That means they'll be staying here awhile . . . hoping to trade otter pelts with us, or maybe . . ." He narrowed his eyes and hunched his shoulders, turning suspiciously toward Maquina's sleeping place. "Maybe those shipsmen came here not so much for trading . . . as to go against us. They probably heard what happened down the coast last autumn. Did you hear me, *Tyee*? They may be looking for revenge!"

Some in our house coughed nervously, but no one answered him.

"Maybe," the otter hunter called up to Maquina, "just maybe they got that ship roped tight between her iron hook and that big cedar tree so's they can hold her steady sideways in the tide, pointing her big guns straight down toward this village."

That thought got me moving off my mat, and fast. For the most hateful memory in my life is of cannonballs ripping through house walls, sending long cedar slivers flying like daggers through the air, and of women running, bleeding, screaming, dying. I never want to see a sight like that again.

The otter hunter and his son went hurrying out to tell the other house chiefs what they themselves had seen. I watched our fire pit blaze up brightly, sending the night's shadows scurrying out the roof hole. Opposite me, in his apartment, I could see our village chief, Maquina. He was sitting up now, naked, his eyelids drooping like a sleepy child's.

Maquina is my brother-in-law, which is both a hindrance and a help to me. He is not quite as old as I am, but he has lived a lot. Here he was in the predawn with five stripped-down young women packed in tight around him, two of them on his left side and three on his right. Naked they were, only partly covered by the widest sea otter sleeping robe that anyone had ever seen, and all of them quivering. Now, doesn't that sound manly? But exhausting! Can you imagine taking on that crowd of younger women single-handed?

My younger sister, Fog Woman, is Maquina's real and proper *hacumb*, his head wife. Just from what I've told you, you'd be right if you guessed that on that night my sister was away, traveling, staying with her relatives some distance south of Wolf Town. Those younger women act a whole lot differently when she's around.

My apartment in the Eagle house is at the favored corner of the end wall directly opposite Maquina's. His place, like mine, is completely open in front so both of us may benefit from the heat and light that come from the single fire pit that we share. Our painted storage boxes are piled high to make side walls for both of our apartments. This we do to give us some privacy from our nearest neighbors. Living next to Maquina is Long Claws, the master of feasts, and I have the impossibly curious war chief, Man Frog, and his nosy wife living next to me. They both have families. This leaves Maquina and me facing each other with a clear view into each other's household.

When my sister, the *hacumb*, is away, there's always something interesting happening over there. Sometimes I glance through the firelight, and his place looks as lively as a bull sea lion's rock at moonrise. I mean, when he's with all those girls, the lot of them are always laughing, weeping, eating, singing, arguing, or just wildly mating with my brother-in-law.

Maquina can stand all of this because he is a big man and very strong, but I am the first to admit he does have curious ways. Those five or six young women who squirm beneath the otter skins with him, they spoil him very badly, yes. There are usually one or two or three of them kneeling around him, plucking out his beard with their keen-edged little clamshells, ceaselessly combing his hair and working it into many long thin braids and tying the ends with lucky otter teeth.

My brother-in-law, Maquina, never fails to interest me, first, I guess, because he is by far the highest-ranking person on this coast, and second, because he is like no one else I've ever known. He is changeable as the east wind, sometimes imaginative and joyful, sometimes full of stormy gloom. Of course, my sister, Fog Woman, does not really like her husband lying with that ambitious horde of semi-highborn females who think of nothing but to raise their rank to *hacumb*. She more or less pretends she doesn't know or care about them. She told me that's the only way a *hacumb* keeps her sanity. For my part, I never say a word to her about the impossible scenes I witness across our fire pit when she is away.

My sister once told me, "My husband keeps those young girls around him to drive away the winter dampness, and also to impress the likes of you!"

"Do I hear a jealous woman speak?" I laughed.

"Brother," she said, "my husband is no better and no worse than you. He, like you, Siam, is simply growing older."

I'd advise you listeners not to pay too much attention to my sister's way of thinking. If you want to know the real truth about Maquina, hear this! I'll tell you all about him. He's not old! Take that from one who knows him better than any man alive. He's got some good about him, but on some days it can be very difficult to find.

Even as a child, Maquina was not brought up to be kind and thoughtful of other persons. Oh, no, on the contrary! He was raised by his two parents to be the ruling *tyee*. Because of that, my brother-in-law tries to stand much taller than any other man along this coast. Fortunately for him, he is a tall man with a lean body and a proud, tight-drawn face with cheekbones that thrust forward like a pair of goose eggs underneath his smooth brown skin. His nose is hooked, and his dark eyes are hooded in a way that makes him seem as much like an eagle as a man. Maquina's carefully plucked mustache curves downward, giving him a grand, cruel look that makes one sense the grinding power of his strong white teeth. I sometimes stare at him and wonder how many seasons it will take for sun and wind and cold north rain to carve Maquina's face into that same stern visage as his father's, a person whom my father claimed was the only man he ever feared.

The Maquinas have held high rank here for much longer than any human can remember. On his father's side he inherited the name Maquina and became high chief of our village. On his mother's side he also holds a chief's rank among the Moachat; they are those clever Deer people living south of here.

The long family lines of the Maquinas have grown powerful through feasts, marriages, births, deaths, raids to the south for slaves, and, more recently, wily trading with the foreigners. Grossly exaggerated tales of the Maquinas have spread all along the Northwest Coast since early times. It is said that foreign shipsmen trading north or south of Wolf Town have all heard of the Maquinas, but only a few of them have ever seen one. Shipsmen like to lump a lot of smaller tribes together, calling us all Nootkans. That is a word we Yoquot do not choose to use.

In his own house, Maquina was famous as a deathlike sleeper. On that night when so much began to happen, I saw him half sitting, resting in his elbows, his naked shoulders hunched around his neck, staring straight ahead at nothing. I could not tell whether he was just relaxing among those smooth-breasted younger women who pressed in all around him or if he was actually planning what he was going to do about the unseen ship that now lay near us in the darkness. My brother-in-law is a pitifully slow thinker, especially when he's been disturbed before dawn after a strenuous night beneath the otter robe. Later, toward evening, when one sees Maquina fully awake, excited, laughing, shouting, singing, boasting, dancing at a feast, or boldly ordering his canoe onto the back of a bowhead whale, you would never believe this was that selfsame man.

My thoughts about Maquina faded as I watched Kawskaws —she's my Hupa servant girl—coming up from our fire, bringing me a steaming trencher of delicious-smelling clam broth. She smiled wearily as she bent forward and slid the wooden bowl to me, carefully staying just beyond my grasp. Oh, yes, I could sometimes catch her, but I could never really tame her. I like a woman who has a dauntless spirit. I like a younger woman who will bite!

I'll tell you more about that Hupa girl a little later, and about my son. First, let me caution you. Do not listen to any of the gossiping women in this house, and certainly don't listen to my sister, for even she does not know the truth of how I got Kawskaws and what that girl does and does not do for me and for my son, Toowin. We blow out the light in my apartment because we know my sister is a better watcher than sleeper.

Maquina laughed and clapped his hands together and shouted across the fire to me, "I saw you miss that Hupa girl. Your sister's right! Siam, you are getting old!" He nudged his five girls, and they stared across at me and giggled sympathetically. "Your sister will be mad because she wasn't here for the first day of trading with this ship. I warned you both that the whites would come again before the early salmon run."

"That's true! We heard him tell you that!" Spuck, the boldest girl from the Thunder house, called out to me. She probably knew she was the one that I liked the best.

I sat sipping calmly on my fish broth, keeping one eye on Maquina's place and my other eye on the Eagle house entrance.

Maquina wearing
his Eagle headdress.

I knew full well that this was going to be no ordinary day.

Reluctantly, Maquina rose, pulled a dark-blue blanket around his nakedness, and strode down to the fire pit, where I joined him. We could hear a lot of hacking and coughing from the next two apartments, which, like ours, stood open to their own house fire. Soon Man Frog and Long Claws came down and stood nearby.

Let me warn you about this curious pair of very minor noblemen who sleep next to us just beyond our protective walls of boxes. Together they try to sit far too close to Maquina. If I allowed it, they would gladly crowd me out. Man Frog is Maquina's war chief, but we only rarely go out raiding now that the trading ships have come to us. Long Claws is in charge of feasts and dancing, and I'm glad to say we do much, much more of that.

We were not long gathered round our morning fire before Red Tongue appeared. He is Maquina's chief talker. A middle-ranking nobleman of less than my age, he, like me, is without a wife, but for very different reasons. Red Tongue lives in a small apartment near the center of the Eagle house, where he can watch our single entrance and report to Maquina everything of consequence that happens there. Some persons in the Eagle house call Red Tongue by a more familiar name, Pillalang. This special word for him means the one who holds the talking stick.

Red Tongue is tall and lean, long-necked, but with a head shaped like a spruce cone. He has cold, quick, crafty eyes. Most visitors to Wolf Town find it impossible to imagine Red Tongue's age. Certainly he is a few seasons younger than Maquina, and definitely much more dignified. You won't find stray village girls lying around in his apartment. No, that cunning man is dedicated to passing on Maquina's thoughts. That's what a chief talker does; he boasts and echoes a *tyee*'s words. That I find very boring!

Yes, Red Tongue's main mission in life is to speak out strongly for Maquina at potlatch feasts and all other notable occasions. For that reason, Red Tongue carefully keeps his own thoughts and wishes always hidden. It is often said of Maquina's chief talker that he is a splended listener and a clever, self-less talker, a man of influence, who, like his father, has learned to walk quietly in the shadow of the so-called magnificent Maquinas.

I have never considered Red Tongue to be a friend of mine, nor would I wish him to be my enemy. Because of his strong position, Red Tongue is always careful of every word he says. I find it impossible to hold a worthwhile conversation with a man like that.

"Here he comes again," Maquina snorted, as the heavy-footed otter hunter once more galloped down the center of the Eagle house straight toward us.

This time the old man was drooling with excitement. "I met two hunters . . . from the Whale house . . . they're just back." He gasped for breath. "They paddled . . . out toward Abooksha. Their house chief, Matla, he went with them. Yes, they waited down there . . . listening . . . said they heard a shipsman's voice . . . call out words they could not understand. They saw a lantern glowing in . . . the fog. I tell you, those foreigners are getting ready to do something . . . not good, but bad, to us," he said suspiciously. "You'll see, *Tyee*, as soon as it gets light."

Maquina sat picking his teeth with a short stiff halibut bone and staring at the elaborate painted designs on the boxes that separated his apartment from that of Man Frog. Maquina sat as though he had not heard the otter hunter. A sudden down-draft of sharp-smelling cedar smoke set Maquina hacking and then sneezing. That finally woke him up. He started waving his hands and telling us how he and he alone would do the trading aboard that ship. By the time he finished talking, the vent hole in the Eagle house roof had turned early-morning gray.

I went back up to our apartment and shook my son, Toowin, awake. It was not easy. When I told him about the ship, he sat up, very tousled, but excited. He was eager to go out and see that ship. I threw my best Chilkat cape around his shoulders to try and give him a noble look and urged him to hurry down and join us. I wanted Maquina to view Toowin as a fine young man rather than a shaggy-looking speechless child. After Toowin's mother died, his aunt took him, but sad to say, she died just like her sister. After that, I got young Kawskaws as a servant, and between us we did our best to try and raise him. Lately, we both agreed, Toowin was improving—slightly.

I went down to the tide's edge, which was almost hidden in the fog, and listened, hearing nothing save the crying of sea birds and the sucking lap of water at my feet. Slowly I drained off that delicious clam broth that I had stored up in my body, returning it respectfully to the sands from whence it came. After that, I squatted in the little river's mouth and scrubbed myself and sang a sacred song until I felt right enough to face the day.

Turning back, I looked at Wolf Town. Is it any wonder that our beaches are strewn with so many different kinds of cedar dugouts? We are sea hunters. Except for the narrow strips of beach we occupy, land does not mean anything to us. If we clear forest trails, they grow in much too fast. We like living close beside the water. These bays and inlets are our surest ways to travel. Almost all our food comes from the sea, the rivers, and the tide-washed beaches. We take little from the land, but we would die without the sea and all the riches it provides us.

Wolf Town is a jumble of huge rough houses recklessly thrown together that stretches all along the high beach. The wide-split cedar roofs and wall planks of these shelters had turned silver gray, weathered by the salt and sun until they blended with the colors in the steep pebble beach. Not all of these were painted with house symbols. Maquina's dwelling, which I share with him, was in the middle and was by far the largest house in all of Wolf Town. It was a building so long a boy could not fling a stone from one end to the other, and it was at least half that wide. I had not counted since we came down here from our winter village up at Tahsis, but there must have been at least one hundred persons—nobles, lots of commoners, and slaves—who slept beneath our Eagle house roof. The other eight houses might have each slept seventy or eighty persons, maybe more, but there was not a one of them as large as ours.

Our house was decorated with an enormous design of the Thunder Eagle clutching the Whale, painted in black and red and stretching almost across its whole front face. Our neighboring house was painted with the crest of the Wolf, another with the huge heraldic image of the Killer Whale, another with that of a double-headed sea monster. A scattering of our tall wooden welcome figures stood along the beach before the houses. They had been carved to stand higher than a man, most of them with arms extended. There were, of course, some taller grave posts supporting ancestors' bones in funeral boxes. There were also a few simple potlatch figures to commemorate some highborn persons' coming of age or marrying or taking a whale. One totem standing near the Whale house was a hatred figure, the carving of a rival chief insultingly placed upside down and his crotch being gobbled by the Wolf because he had failed to pay his potlatch debts.

All sizes of dugout canoes had been hauled up along the beach. Most of them had been charred a handsome black, oiled on the outside, and painted ocher red within. Some of their prows carried handsome crest designs. The most impressive were the big fifty-man fighting canoes and the much smaller eight-man whale canoes. After that were the slender white seal canoes, otter canoes, fish canoes, women's canoes, even small children's canoes, all of them different sizes, serving our every purpose, for as I said, we are a people bound to water, not to land. Even our enemies are eager to trade canoes from us. They readily admit that our craftsmen shape them to ride a hard sea and go faster than any other dugouts in this world. Sea Spear, Maquina's largest canoe, is the only one of its kind among the dozen villages along this coast.

When I went back inside, the whole Eagle house was buzzing with excitement. On this first day, Maquina was the only Wolf Town person allowed to deal directly with these foreign shipsmen. Because we wished to look grand but not warlike, Maquina decided that his big canoe would go out alone to begin the trading. Maquina had sent word that Toowin could come with us. This was the first time that his uncle had given my son such a privilege.

Every man chosen to go out to the ship was busy painting himself or being touched up by one or several women. They were decorating their faces, and arms, and hands, and shoulders, spreading on the precious mixture of red ocher, making that more impressive by adding broad black eyebrows and family crests upon the chest.

Toowin faced a trade mirror on himself while Kawskaws whispered and smoothed paint all over him instead of me. That's the way it's been in our apartment lately. I had hoped that Kawskaws would be free to paint a Bear crest on my left shoulder, for she was very good at that. I wanted the Bear because it is my namesake. In my fourth winter my mother had declared that I would be left-handed. My father, welcoming this unusual fact, gave a small feast, with a few important witnesses, and I was renamed Siam, which means Grizzly Bear. Bears are usually left-handed, which one may easily see when they strike at salmon in fast water. Wolf Town people assured me that my new name, Siam, suited me, for, they said, I had the ambling gait and the inquisitive determination of a bear.

Male bears usually go and mark the boundaries of their forest by stretching tall and making deep claw marks in the trees to frighten off intruders. An old uncle of mine assured me that if I gazed into the eyes of a bear, I would discover a human spirit hiding underneath its handsome hairy cloak. That may well be true. Bears have been observed to dance like humans, and in certain seasons they show uncontrollable passions for their females. This, too, could be said of some persons living in this Eagle house. Even me. Animals and humans are not so different. Before she died, my grandmother told me she had grown tired of being a human and hoped that in her next life she would be a graceful soaring sea bird.

What with the dressing and eating and telling the women what to do, it was midmorning before our canoe and paddlers were ready. Maquina placed little trust in shipsmen and would allow no women out on that first visit, believing that some kind of violence might occur.

There was almost no breeze, and the fog lay heavy in our cove. This did not delay Maquina, who was now wide awake and eager to be gone. He strode through the Eagle house ordering those who were coming with us to stuff only a few trade skins into wooden boxes, and he warned us to keep them hidden from the whites.

The otter hunter called to us, "The morning wind is rising. The fog is drifting out to sea."

Wearing his best otter robe, Maquina led us down onto the beach. His sorcerer and drummer were with him. This sorcerer, whom I knew to be a treacherous man, carried a long painted wooden Wolf mask beneath his arm and was wearing a gray wolf-skin suit. He and the drummer were to do the dancing and make those familiar welcome signs that would calm any fears the foreigners might have. Maquina allowed the otter hunter to come with us because he had been the first to see the ship. Reluctantly, Maquina left his only living son, Satsatsoksis, weeping on the shore. He was only nine years old and could not come with us.

I wished that their ship had anchored closer so that the foreign shipsmen could see the splendid sight Wolf Towners made parading down to our mighty war canoes. I didn't care that every villager was down to see us off. It was the shipsmen we wanted to impress. We are proud people. Why would we not be? Wolf Town is probably the largest village in the world. There is certainly nothing grander this side of the mountains, east of us, or north or south along the coast as far as we have traveled.

We nobles, following our *tyee*, took only one step off the beach. Our second step was up onto the naked rump of the first slave, who was kneeling in the water. Our third step was onto the rump of the second bending slave, and finally onto the shoulder of a third. That trio formed a human ladder so that we might easily climb aboard. Then, in our descending order of rank, we took our places near Maquina, but well below him, for he had

had a wide plank laid across the dugout gunwale so that he sat high above us on a painted box. There could be no mistaking who was *tyee*. Man Frog and Long Claws sat near him, but not quite so near as me, for I am the usher of Wolf Town.

I watched with pride as forty of our warriors and paddlers leapt into the great canoe. I trembled at the sight of that. These days there are some who whisper that I'm getting too old for fighting, whaling, or for making children. They are wrong. My heart goes tum-tum-tum in my chest when I see our big canoes fill up with brave young sea hunters, singers, dancers, fighting men, whom I've known since they were clinging to their mother's breast.

Our paddlers were wildly eager to go out and see the ship, but Maquina, with one last proud gesture, ordered them to turn his great canoe slightly broadside to show their watching wives and children how grand Sea Spear could look with all our warriors in full array.

"You look fine," Man Frog's wife's called out from the shore, "but mind you, sit up straight."

"Great sea-lion turds!" her husband swore so few could hear. "Will that old Wolf bitch never cease complaining? I'm going to get a new young wife," he said to his cousin, Long Claws. "Help me start searching for one now."

Long Claws looked at him and then at me. He laughed. "You must be joking," he whispered. "I wouldn't dare!"

Urged on by the thought of trading and by sudden icy starts of cold spring rain, our paddlers stroked north through the fading morning mists.

"There it is!" gasped Toowin, whose eyes are as sharp as any falcon's. "You can just see its wing bones standing up above the fog. It doesn't look like any bird I've seen," he whispered.

By squinting my eyes, I could just make out its three tall masts and cross spars standing faint as fire-stripped cedars in a smoking forest. Soon I could see its bow spear and dark, whale-like hull emerging from the fog, and then, as we drew closer, the endless web of cords and lines that held its bones in place.

Maquina signaled his paddlers to dig hard into the water

and begin their rhythmic chanting as they drove our canoe boldly in toward this foreign vessel. Our paddlers stroked together, skillfully moving Maquina's high-powered Sea Spear across the wind-cut patterns of the inlet. We could see that our huge cedar dugout was much more than half as long as their clumsy water bird, our Sea Spear being narrower by far. While I was wondering what the shipsmen would think of our sleek vessel, Maquina raised his hand and brought it down sharply. His paddlers, obeying his command, drew broadside to this foreign ship at what we believed to be the long-range limits of their scatter guns. He looked at me.

"That's enough! Don't go too close," I whispered to Maquina. "Wait for them to make some friendly sign."

When he held up his hand to stop the paddlers, the sorcerer let the first welcoming flurry of eagle down go flying out upon the breeze. Then Maquina signaled his paddlers to move in closer to the ship, and immediately we heard a voice shout down to us in the trading language of Chinook: *"Peshak, peshak!* Bad *Mahka!* Go away, get out. Get out!"

More voices started yelling, and we saw crewmen hauling up the heavy boarding nets to protect themselves—from us! We could see shipsmen with blunderbusses go scrambling higher in the rigging. The men who lined the rail now carried short- and long-barreled muskets.

Maquina must have heard me snort. Turning, he leered at me and said, "I don't think they trust us."

"Throw out more eagle down," Red Tongue called back to the sorcerer.

"Now start the singing," Maquina ordered. "Let them know we come to trade, not fight!"

I looked sideways at my brother-in-law to see if I could read some mischief marked upon his face. His young women had done up his braided hair in a high topknot and covered it with soft white eagle down in a much more elaborate fashion than mine or the other nobles' with us. Maquina's face, like all of ours, was greased and carefully dusted red. In the midmorning light, the sprinkling of costly mica flakes made his proud face glisten in a splendid way. He wore a flicker's feather thrust through the septum of his nose. It took that common human look away from him. His eyebrows were one bold black zigzag stroke across his forehead. Oh, let me tell you, he and I looked grand!

"*Chahko klahwa!* Come slowly!" a voice yelled to us from the ship.

Red Tongue, who is most often wise and cautious, said, "We should allow our war chief, Man Frog, to be the first aboard that ship."

Hearing this, Maquina turned and looked scornfully at Red Tongue. Taking up his finely woven bulb-topped chief's hat, he placed it grandly on his head. He spread his arms like a great bird, welcoming these new shipsmen, letting them observe the rich luster of his full-length otter cloak, oh, so elegantly trimmed along its edges with costly squares of shining abalone. Then Maquina signaled his paddlers to move Sea Spear cautiously forward. Our drummer sounded out the paddle beat. It made me shiver with excitement to look up at the open gun ports and those protruding black iron cannon eyes that stared coldly down at us. Our sorcerer rose and did his stunning earthquake danc-ing in the bow and flung more eagle down into the air. I watched it shimmering white as snowflakes against the leaden morning light.

Maquina moved his right hand in a circle, then chopped downward, signaling the paddlers to stroke hard. They angled Sea Spear in a quick turning sweep that would bring us right beneath this vessel's stern. I was glad of that, for I confess that staring at those deadly cannons is not a thing I like to do.

These shipsmen were, as usual, secretive and flew no flag to tell us who they were. Nor did they cast out eagle down or give us any other signs of welcome. Instead, we heard a mixture of bare feet and stiff leather boots running nervously along their deck. A horde of shipsmen quickly lined the vessel's stern.

I looked up to see an unruly gang of savage-looking men hovering above us, their muskets pointed directly down toward our faces. Bravely we accepted this all in the name of trade. I am one who thinks whites are far too nervous and suspicious. My son, Toowin, he is different. He said some whites may well be just as good as we are. Don't you believe it, I told him. He had never even seen a big house torn to pieces by cannon fire.

I squinted up against the bleary noonday sky, keeping my eyes as well upon the scatter-gun men climbing in the rigging, who continued to point their weapons down at us. I could tell that being so close to them made Maquina feel excited. With Maquina such feelings can easily lead to trouble. He warned his paddlers to sit alert and ready until the whites made up their minds.

Above us we could hear nervous words all flung together but could not understand their meaning. Finally two shipsmen spread a small opening in their heavy boarding nets, and a rope ladder came hurtling down the side.

"*Saghalie! Saghalie!* Up! Up!" a voice yelled out in Chinook. "*Iakit tillicum saghalie!* Four people up! *Wake weght!* No more!"

Cautiously our paddlers eased the big canoe toward the ladder.

"*Yakwa*, this way," the rough voice shouted.

"Toowin goes up first!" Maquina ordered. "Have you greased yourself the way I told you?"

My son's voice trembled just a little as he answered, "Yes, Uncle. Yes, I have."

"If shipsmen up there try to take a grip on you, you wriggle like a fish and leap into the water. We'll try to pick you up."

I worried how my Toowin was going to jump through their heavy nets, but I said nothing.

Poor boy, he glanced back at me with a sick look as if to say good-bye, then started up the ladder. My thought was that I wished I'd taken Toowin and gone with my sister to visit our cousins down the coast and let my brother-in-law do all this trading. I held my breath in fear as I saw my son squeeze through the shipsmen's net and disappear.

We waited. Then, hearing nothing, Red Tongue started climbing, his face a mask of cold mistrust. I, being next in rank beneath Maquina, followed. I could feel him take the ladder right behind me. It swayed under our weight as we both climbed. My heart beneath my breastbone pounded tum-tum-tum as I, Siam, eased my head above the level of their deck, expecting at that instant to have my skull burst open with a heavy charge of shot.

 RED TONGUE and Toowin stood together, stiff and wary as a pair of gray goose ganders, surrounded by that barbaric-looking horde of shipsmen, most of whom were waving their muskets at them, or me. Poor Toowin, his eyes were wide with fear. No wonder! I myself might have ducked down behind the ship's rail, but Maquina's pointed hat came butting up against my rump. What could I do? I climbed meekly through their net and went to stand by Toowin, watching as Maquina came across the wide, clean deck. Everything looked very bad for us.

"I told you we should have sent Man Frog up here first," Maquina whispered to me.

We four stood with our backs to one another for protection, our right hands free and ready to reach under our cloaks for our long daggers, which we had strapped high across our chests.

This unfriendly gang of shipsmen that surrounded us were mostly tall, with hair of every color. Some of them had broken teeth, and all had pale, cold eyes. Most of them were bare-footed like ourselves and wore flat black round-brimmed hats.

One of these foreigners said something, and the others laughed, and many of them lowered their muskets.

I let out my breath, thinking, Maybe we will live through this. I looked over the rail at Man Frog and Long Claws, sitting peacefully with our paddlers in our big canoe, and I whispered to Maquina, "Yes, we should have sent the two of them for this."

Maquina sniffed when I said that. "I hate the way this big bird sways beneath our feet," he said.

I looked along the ship's enormous wooden deck. Smooth it was, and pale as a beach of sand. Everything aboard was clean, as though it had just been scrubbed by a giant wave. I mean, there was not one thing cluttering its decks except this hostile-looking band of shipsmen.

I have said that our big canoe was much more than half as long as this ship, which is true. However, each time you climb up from one of our sleek canoes onto the vast deck of these sea-going foreigners, you are shaken by the differences. I saw this vessel as though I were standing on its roof. Three dark holes cut into the planking made us realize that there was a house as large as ours hidden beneath this deck.

Three huge masts rose into the air, supported by countless lines and climbing ladders stretched like a morning spider web between the branches of a bush. The wide deck of this vessel was surrounded by a short, thick wall of wood so that the shipsmen could crouch behind it when attacked or save themselves from being washed away by violent waves. Hanging in readiness were four rowing boats that would allow these strangers to make their way to shore. Near the ship's stern I could see where one man could steer this wondrous vessel when its wide wings were set to make it fly across the water.

I could see a small house not far behind the middle of the ship where thin wisps of smoke arose and unfamiliar food smells made me guess that there these shipsmen did their cooking. It was strange to see a man prepare the food. We leave that task to women. These shipsmen must be awfully short of females, for we have never seen or heard of one who journeys with them. Some say they travel because they don't have any women and must make their children with any they may find. What makes us certain that is true is that all foreign shipsmen are so wildly hungry for our women. Perhaps on that first day it would have been kind of us to bring them out a few young slave girls just to wipe the anxious scowls off their faces.

We heard the harsh sound of a commanding voice, and the shipsmen quickly opened up a path. Through their middle strode a red-faced, heavy-bellied man. His hair had turned gray along its ruffled edges, and he wore a different hat and finer-looking buttoned coat than all the rest. I judged that he must be the chief.

Maquina raised his arms and spread his fingers wide to show he held no weapons, and this big man in the fine black coat made that same gesture. My guess was good. He was their master.

Beside the big man walked a dark-eyed, brown-faced man, who listened with alertness when we spoke. This short man wore the costume of a shipsman, but the jacket he had flung comfortably across his shoulders, as we do our capes.

"Do you think he is a Haida or a Tlingit?" I asked.

"Be careful what you say in front of him," Maquina answered me.

Red Tongue raised his hands, and I and Toowin raised our hands as well. Many of the shipsmen imitated our wordless greeting.

Seeing this more encouraging sign of peacefulness, Maquina ordered the paddlers to throw up a bark cord that was attached to a painted box filled with otter skins to trade. As he hauled it up on deck, Maquina called to our Eagle house men, telling them to climb up. But as the men in our canoe rose to do so, the heavy-bellied captain grew enormously excited. His face flushed angry red, and he bellowed foreign words that caused the musketmen to close their net quickly and aim their scatter guns straight down at our paddlers who were about to come aboard.

"*Clewtu! Clewtu!* Go away! Go away!" the brown-faced man yelled out, revealing for the first time that he was the master's talker. In his excitement he used his own northern dialect, which we little understand.

Maquina made a warning gesture with his hand, and our big canoe stroked quickly away and waited just beyond their musket range.

The ladder had been drawn up. Now we four were their captives. I noticed that the foreigners had mounted a swivel gun, which they leveled at the canoe, and musketmen moved in again close to the four of us. My thought was, This could lead to trouble.

Seeing that our canoe had withdrawn to a safe distance, the ship master relaxed a little and waved his men away. He leered nervously at us, showing all his teeth, and in imitation we showed all of ours.

Maquina turned his head toward me so the brown man could not see the movement of his lips. "I don't need to see their flag to know these men. If they were Spanish, they'd be dressed in finer clothing and have big red crosses on their sails. These are Boston men. See how quick and nervous they are? Did you hear them saying 'Yah' and 'yup'? See the patches on their clothing? These are frugal Boston men. You will see when we begin the trading."

Maquina was right, there was no mistaking these men. Two of their crew hurriedly set up a long, flat, waist-high wooden table, which is what they always choose to sit around; they could scarcely wait for the otter trading to begin. The Boston men don't waste time like the King George's men, who seem never in a hurry.

They brought forth six of those skinny-legged uncomfortable things that they have somehow learned to sit upon. We four were about to squat nervously upon them, as we had done before on other ships, when this master reached inside his coat and drew out his empty hand as though he held a dagger. In this wordless way we four were ordered to place our only weapons on the table. This Maquina refused to do until the master ordered the scatter-gun man above us to climb down to the deck. Only then did we give up our daggers.

The master and two shipsmen of some rank sat down with us, formally arranging themselves on the opposite side of the table. There was no place for my son, Toowin, so he squatted comfortably upon the deck beside us. One of the foreigners waved his hand, and a black crewman came and gathered up our four long daggers.

"I don't like that," Maquina scowled. "We should have

sent aboard Man Frog, the war chief, instead of us. Why didn't someone think of that?"

The red-faced master waved his hand, and his men bustled about, placing one small keg of rum and another of molasses in the very center of the table, along with two horn cups, which the master filled to the brim. One of these he slid across to Maquina, and the other he kept for himself.

My brother-in-law was cautious. He took up the cup and sniffed, then tasted it with the tip of his red tongue, then drank off half in one long gulp. "Rummmtaste ver gooo!" he lied in English, and he passed the rest to me.

I finished off most of the dark-brown drink and coughed. Then I gasped, for it set my gullet on fire.

Maquina picked up the little keg of molasses, sniffed it, nervous as a cougar, took a lick, a taste, and then a long deep swallow. This time he closed his eyes and sighed with honest pleasure. I did the same. It went down my throat as smooth as the oil of little fishes.

The shipsmen did not even touch the rich molasses, but they, like their master, gladly drank a second cup of rum. Red Tongue only touched his lips to the rum cup that was offered and did not drink at all, for like the rest of us he much preferred molasses. This was the first time that young Toowin had ever tasted rum. Tears came to his eyes, but to show himself a man, he said it tasted fine.

I looked up through the web of ropes and crossbones at the bleary sun that watched us through a distant bank of fog. No shipsmen now remained above us, and they had laid aside their weapons. My heart stopped going tum-tum-tum, and I relaxed—but just a little.

The master, he was nervous. He would often sit up in his chair and, half rising, crane his neck to see if our canoe was creeping in toward his ship. When he had satisfied himself that everything was safe, he would let his huge bulk sink back into his chair and continue to stare enviously at the rich guard hairs on Maquina's otter cloak and mine.

"I guess they've just come here to trade," Maquina said to

Red Tongue in our quick Wakashan dialect, which we believed could not be understood by the northern man, who remained beside us, listening to our every word.

The master whispered quick low words to his two helpers, then licked his lips and started drumming with his fingernails on the tabletop. Finally the master leaned back and whispered something to the ship's talker, who told Maquina that the master was ready now to speak about sea otter skins.

Maquina is wonderful at languages. He can say a little bit of the Spaniard's talk, and Frenchman's, and Englishman's as well. He liked to surprise all these foreigners by calling them *Amigo*, or *Monsor*, *My Deeeer Siiir*, or *Meester El Capeetan*. Maquina answered this master by pointing at a short belt knife worn by one of the shipsmen. "Looong knive ver gooo! We want a very long strong dagger," Maquina said forcefully in Chinook to the sharp-eyed ship's talker. Maquina spread his fingers. "Tell your master we want the long ones with four ribs and channels down the blade, those that cause fast bleeding. We hate those mean little white man's rattail knives that bend between our fingers like soft lead. You tell him," Maquina said, "tell him to save those little children's knives for trading with the bad men in the north!"

The ship's talker scowled at this insult and did not translate.

Maquina glared at him, "Wolf people want bright, strong daggers, do you understand me?" He held out his arm beneath the interpreter's face and pointed. "We want blades that reach from my elbow to my thumbnail. Tell him leave plenty of iron on top so that our artisans can make the Wolf head and set in teeth and abalone eyes. We will be glad to trade two good otter skins for a dagger blade that is shaped like that."

When the ship's talker had explained that to the master, Maquina raised his arms as though he held a musket and shouted, *"Sukwalal*, gun . . . gun." He also said, *"Polallie,"* the Chinook word for gunpowder, which most here understand quite well.

The master showed his teeth again and nodded his head so

hard his jowls trembled. He spoke to his tall, lean first man, who hurried away. Again the master filled the cups. He and his two most important men drank the rum while we four gulped the rich molasses. Oh, it tasted fine!

Suddenly we heard a high, sharp clang-clang-clang that made us jump. The master stood up and led us forward. Beside the first mast we observed a pile of reddish cut stones formed into a square fire pit that was glowing red. Beside the blazing fire stood a lean young man with copper-colored hair, gray eyes, and a ruddy face. This boy appeared to be about the same age as my son, Toowin, maybe seventeen or eighteen winters. He held a short iron hammer in his right hand and was talking to a younger black boy, who worked a curious wooden leathern thing with his feet so that it blew out wind with a powerful farting sound. That quick noisy wind going puff-puff caused the fire inside the stones to burn the hottest red that I have ever seen.

The ship's talker pointed at this bright-faced young ships-man with the hammer, and he said, "This boy, his name is John J. He is going to make for you a beeeu-tee-ful looong knife." He measured from his elbow to his fingertips.

"Jon Jay?" Maquina said, and looked at me.

I nodded and repeated that name, Jon Jay. We both liked the way that strangely pleasant name made us move our lower jaws and blow air through our teeth.

We watched the copper-headed boy intently. With tongs, he laid a bar of iron inside the fire, and when he brought it out, that iron was glowing yellow hot. He placed this on a cold flat iron beside the fire pit, and he struck it with his hammer. Clang! Clang! Clang! Sparks flew, and we four leapt back in surprise. The shipsmen laughed, and so did we.

This boy with the curious-colored hair kept pounding on the iron bar, reheating it, then striking it again, until the iron was flattened. Then he took a bright iron hammer and started to shape the fiery redness into exactly the kind of long blade that Maquina had described.

When this young dagger maker was finished, he smiled at
Maquina and at me and at Toowin. Then he plunged the hot
knife blade into a pot of water, and it hissed and sent up clouds
of steam. When he took it out of the water, the iron had turned
blue-black.

He caught the blade in a pair of iron jaws that were attached to a wooden block, then, making a nasty screeching sound
with a heavy iron file, he worked skillfully back and forth until
we could see a bright shining edge appear along both sides of
the iron blade. He turned a wooden handle that released the
powerful jaws and handed the new-formed dagger to Maquina.

Marquina felt the edge and handed it to Red Tongue, then
he to me. I let Toowin touch the blade. We were overwhelmed
at the sharp edge the dagger maker had achieved so quickly.

"Father, it is as I told you," Toowin whispered to me. "That
boy's not old, and he's a foreigner, and yet he knows as much
as anyone I know from Wolf Town."

What a foolish thing to say.

I passed the dagger on to the master, then stood there wondering what my father would have thought. He firmly believed
that the first shipsmen had found their bright iron daggers hanging like never-melting icicles on the northern edge of the world.
My father would have thought it magic that bright iron knives
could be pounded out in such a fiery way.

Maquina gladly opened his box and brought out two prime
sea otter skins—of course, without their tails.

You must remember that folks living on this coast admire
true artistry and craftsmanship beyond all reason. Here before
us stood a young, yet skillful dagger maker, exactly the kind of
artisan we most admired.

The master examined the workmanship, then handed the
long knife back to Maquina, who tested its point by driving it
deep into the ship's hardwood rail. It did not bend. "This is a
good blade!" he murmured to me. "But what I really want is
that boy!" Holding his left hand low so the crewmen could not
see, he spread his fingers quickly three times and then one finger

more. "I'd trade fifteen, maybe even sixteen, otter skins if I could own that boy. Imagine all the daggers he could make for us. Oh, yes, he would be well worth buying!"

"You mean sixteen skins with their tails as well?" I asked him in amazement.

"Yah, yah!" he answered in imitation of the Boston men. "Yah, shoooor! For a boy like him I'd let them have the otter tails as well."

The only exchange on that first day was two otter pelts for the dagger maker's splendid knife. The real trading would have to wait until next day.

With the changing of the tide, the deck beneath our feet took on a slow rolling motion that made my stomach feel uneasy, and only Toowin drank some more molasses. I watched the sun begin to set. Great flocks of orange-beaked puffins passed us in such numbers that the shipsmen called out in surprise. A cold east wind blew out of the snow-filled mountains and set me shivering as it cut icy patterns through the blue-green water.

"Let's leave now," I whispered to Maquina.

He looked at me and then at Red Tongue, widening those large night-animal eyes of his. *"Chalat seeklat tur wah,"* he said in his quiet yet commanding voice, telling the ship's talker that we now wished to return to shore.

I was relieved when I saw the master order his shipsmen to untie the net. Maquina hailed Sea Spear, and our paddlers brought it in to us.

Red Tongue was the first through the web of rope and down the ladder. Maquina followed. I went next, and Toowin, being youngest, was the last. As we passed outside their net, a hand reached through and returned the wrong dagger to each of us.

"If they ever come ashore," Red Tongue told Maquina, "we will take their muskets and their swords from them. We should never allow these whites to do things that they deny to us."

When we were seated once more in Maquina's big canoe, we heard a shout from above, and looking up, we saw the small molasses barrel and a sack full of hard bread come hurtling down through the hole in their net. It landed just behind me in the canoe.

"What a crude and clumsy way to give a gift," said Red Tongue.

We looked up at their faces, trying not to show disdain.

Maquina shouted up to them, *"Wik, wik, chamasish!* Yes, yes, that tastes good!" He smiled at all of them. *"Quart lak. Tomolla klootchman,"* he added, assuring them that he, Maquina, would bring otter skins and young women on the following day.

Jon Jay, the dagger maker, and the black boy were standing apart from all the others. They waved and called, "Good-bye, good-bye," and my son, Toowin, waved back, and using their language for the first time, called, "Gooo-bye! Goo-bye!" That made me feel quite proud of him.

Our paddlers were surly and did not sing as they paddled in toward our village, for they had been forced to sit cramped for almost half a day, staring at this ship's open gun ports. Nothing had given them any cause for joy.

It was early evening. The tide was low, and our long curving beach looked strangely out of shape. Clinging mussel shells made the exposed outcrops of boulders glow iridescent blue. These dark wet rocks seemed to glare out at the foreign ship like the hostile heads of underwater monsters whose hair was formed from rotting twisted ropes of kelp and seaweed. Noisy pairs of gulls swooped in against the ravens, threatening them in an endless argument that ranged across the shining tide pools. Nervous flights of shore birds skimmed in and ran along the beach, searching for bits of sea life with their quick, thin beaks.

Old men and our women and children came crowding around us as we landed. They were not impressed with the small amount of molasses and the hard bread that we brought back with us, and they were not surprised when they heard Maquina say that he planned to take some young women out with us the following day.

That night we people from the Eagle house feasted on

steamed octopus arms and molasses mixed with hot smoked salmon. What a meal! We sat on painted boxes around our eight separate house fires and talked to numerous visitors from the other houses, telling them all that had happened to us out on board the ship.

I felt exhausted from the day's events and went early to my sleeping mat. I looked out through my peephole in the Eagle house wall and saw that it was dark. The ship had moved. The faint yellow lights of two ship lanterns could be seen shining in long narrow paths across the still black water.

Not to be outdone, Maquina ordered two large bonfires built upon our beach. But he had them placed well off to one side of our village beyond Matla's Whale house in case, as had once happened, some drunken shipsmen fired a cannon at our welcome light.

I slept soundly all that night, untroubled by my usual dreams. When I woke, daylight had appeared again, and many excited men and women in the Eagle house were already up, preparing to go out to the ship.

Sometime in the night, my sister, Fog Woman, had come back from her visit to our cousin's village. I was delighted to see Maquina's wife return, for she has good trading sense when it comes to our dealing with the ship masters, and she can influence her husband more than all of us together. Maquina pretends to be somewhat scornful of women, but I tell you that he is in many ways advised by them. Yes, you might say that he is subtly ruled by women, as are many other husbands here in Wolf Town, though none would admit that such is true.

Fog Woman has been Maquina's wife for more than twenty winters. They have had one daughter and three sons together, but sadly only the youngest of their children, a nine-year-old boy named Satsatsoksis, stayed alive.

My sister has grown a little heavy around the middle and has lots of wrinkles by her eyes and deep lines descending to the corners of her mouth. She rolls and toes in badly when she walks. Naturally, she is no match in appearance for those five slim-waisted, heavy-breasted girls who warm Maquina's bed when she's away. But in all thoughtful ways she is vastly their superior. Fog Woman was born with a good nature and very high intelligence. Everyone knew that even when she was a child. By the time my sister had seen eleven winters, she knew almost all the great legends from both our mother's and our father's houses and could weave a cedar-bark hat better than most adult women. My father used to ask her very difficult questions and pay close attention to her answers. That proved to be a useful training for her.

As a young woman, she was smooth-skinned and handsome. I remember how delighted Maquina was when their marriage was arranged. At first she remained as she had always been, full of laughing, loving ways. But as she had children and lost them and began to help Maquina compete in the potlatching and feastings with other rival chiefs, I could see my sister change and rely more on her wit and cunning. Then, as Maquina began taking younger women into bed with him, as was the custom, Fog Woman used her high intelligence to rise above them.

My sister is very careful not to show this house that she has power over her husband. Maquina would react oh, so violently to that! But in a hundred subtle ways she controls him and rules most of his decisions. Sometimes she even tries to rule me. My sister's power extends not only over the salmon rivers, clam beds, and precious berry patches she inherited, but far beyond her household. She quietly determines, for example, whether Wolf Town warriors will or will not raid far south into California. She often determines exactly who in Wolf Town will be allowed to marry whom. Great dugout canoes have been built and sometimes given away at potlatch feasts because she thought it prudent.

Oh, I have watched her carefully over all these years. I know how she achieved her strength. First, she and Maquina used to whisper affectionately in the bed at night. But after those five younger girls came crowding in on her, my sister planned a brief meeting with Maquina, which occurs each day before the sun is high. No one dares disturb them as they sit beside each other on two painted boxes. During those all-important conversations by the fire pit, every action that might affect the life of Wolf Town is discussed—with one exception, the sacred art of whaling. That most manly of all pursuits his *hacumb* wisely leaves entirely to her husband and his sea hunters. Maquina will continue to be the one to cast the first harpoon at a whale. Yes, like his father and his grandfather, that remains the *tyee*'s privilege.

I went and squatted near Maquina at the fire. When Kawskaws brought the broth, my brother-in-law asked me if I was going to take her out for trading. He grinned when I scowled, for he always wants to remind me that he had heard that I bought Kawskaws as a slave. Maquina knew full well that neither I nor Toowin would lend our gentle Hupa girl to any shipsman, not even for the finest thing that they might have to trade.

I like the look of Kawskaws. She wears her blue-black hair in two thick braids. She has light-blue tattooing in the shape of two delicate ferns that extend outward from the corners of her mouth, so faint they are difficult to see. Those ferns seem to wave as in a breeze each time she smiles. I like everything about Kawskaws. I feel certain that she had been born with rank, though she was now a commoner in our household. She learned quickly to be thoughtful of my needs and Toowin's, but in truth she belonged only to herself.

Kawskaws had been captured in a raid upon her inland river village, quite far south in a country that our paddlers say is much too hot because it has little rain and rarely snows. This girl was freezing cold and nearly naked when they brought her up this way to sell. I made the standard offer for a female slave—three times her length in strung dentalia shells—and she was mine! I cannot tell you why I did this, but I do know that the instant I saw her I had the strongest feelings for that girl. My Toowin also liked Kawskaws right away. I never told my paddlers who she was, and certainly I do not treat her like a slave.

Among our people we do not allow any close relationships with slaves. Perhaps this was the reason that I arrived in Wolf Town pretending that she was a Hupa commoner whom I had

Kaws Kaws dressed in the
Hupa Style offers broth.

hired from her father, who had traveled north. I said he had agreed that she could work for me and help bring up my son.

When I told that to my sister, she gave me a sly smile, and Maquina leered at that long-legged girl and whispered to me, "Tell her she can come over visiting me. There'll always be a place beneath my otter robe for her."

I didn't laugh when he said that.

After Kawskaws came here, it didn't take her long to make a costume for herself. I was surprised. She used only cast-off Yoquot things of ours, and yet she fashioned them into wonderful-looking Hupa garments, different from our clothes in every way. She gathered ordinary small colored shells from the beaches and strung them to form strangely handsome patterns. That Hupa girl wove herself a clever round spruce-root hat that fitted on her head as neatly as a small tight bowl. It looked fine on her.

Kawskaws is a Chinook word describing a tall, beautiful, long-stilted bird we call the dancing crane. I gave such a name to that Hupa girl because of her graceful smooth-legged way of moving. I suppose the strange dance steps she sometimes performs for me and Toowin are common enough among her own people, but we Wolf Towners all too rarely see such graceful movements.

Once when everyone was outside waiting and hoping for the fish to come, I went inside our house and saw Kawskaws naked to the waist and dancing in a southern way that I had never seen before. She flung up her hands, warning me not to disturb her. She told me later that she was doing a Hupa Salmon dance, her gift to all of us. She said it had to be performed inside a house to be sure the souls of the salmon could not see her, but would come all unsuspecting to her wooing. That same night the big silver fish came splashing up the dark waters of our river. I told Maquina about her fish dance, and he was indeed impressed.

One autumn, when we journeyed to our winter houses up at Tahsis, Kawskaws told me she had a sacred Deer dance that she had been taught as well. But that dance, she informed me, must be done outside in the forest, and only during certain phases of the autumn moon. Even Maquina came to watch her. I am sorry to have to tell you that although she performed her White Deer dance most beautifully, our hunters went out and returned without so much as a single haunch of venison. Kawskaws wept when she heard that, but my son, Toowin, gave her some lovely loon feathers he had been saving, which she made into a clever necklace. Wearing that soon cheered her up. I guess it is such kindnesses that made her spoil young Toowin so.

My son, Toowin, was the only child of mine who survived. Poor Toowin. He lost his mother before he even knew her. I tried to bring him up with the good help of his aunt, who cared for my son as well as any woman could. But she too died, when he was only twelve (or was it thirteen?) winters. A bad time for her to go, just when Toowin was struggling out of his childhood but was not half-ready to become a man. Her death left Toowin so miserable he would scarcely speak. I tried to do what I could for him, taking him halibut fishing, making bows and arrows. Nothing seemed to help. My sister, Fog Woman, was busy with her own young son and with her duties as a *hacumb*. She told me that I couldn't remain a widower, that I should take another wife. I didn't need one after I bought Kawskaws. She soon showed her loving nature, taking good care of Toowin and of me.

But when the Boston men appeared, I still worried about Toowin. He was going into his seventeenth winter now, and still he overslept and mooned around this Eagle house, begging Kawskaws to oil and massage his limbs. I didn't really know what I was going to do about him!

On this, the second day since the ship had come, Maquina had his face painted with a Whale crest design, using much red and very little black, in honor of his mother. Before he left the house, he admired himself in an oval silver-mounted looking-glass that he had traded from the King George's men. Then, carrying his finest bulb-topped hat and otter cloak, he set out for the beach.

Almost every household had supplied one or more young

slave girls. There were at least a dozen of them crowding together excitedly. They had all bathed that morning and were
told to wait in a row outside the Eagle house entrance. Their
owners had lent them woven hats and decked their necks with
beads to make them look like the daughters of important people. None of these slave girls had their necks or shoulders colored, nor did they wear face designs. It was well known to us
that foreign shipsmen dislike girls with nicely oiled and painted
faces. They like their women scrubbed plain. Shipsmen greatly
favor girls who are not much under ten but certainly never over
twenty winters.

Kawskaws was not going out aboard that ship. I made sure
of that. I sent her back along a river path, accompanied by a
wise old woman. There they would smoke some spring salmon.
I warned Kawskaws not to come back until our canoes returned
that evening. "I've never been out on a ship," she said, and gave
me that sly smile of hers before she did what I had ordered.

I could feel the excitement of the young women behind me
as we moved out toward the ship. As I joined the others in the
big canoe, I wondered if Kawskaws wanted me to protect her
from these women-hungry foreigners, or if she, like some slave
girls, would have been glad to go and for a few beads and buttons lie with some shipsmen in the unfamiliar darkness, swaying
in their hammocks beneath the vessel's deck.

"*Klootchemup-elip!* Young sisters up first!" the shipsmen
shouted gleefully when we drew near enough to hear them.

Our slave girls climbed up onto the ship's deck and began
to cry out the words they had been told. "*Kamosuk-too, tsil
tsil, phelth!* Beads, buttons, cloth!" they called. "*Mesika tikegh
ayahwhul tenas totoosh?* You want to borrow young girls?"

Because of their hunger for these slave girls, the shipsmen
set aside their caution and allowed all of us aboard. Still, as
each of our men came in through the ship's net, he was made
to throw off his garments while two shipsmen examined him
from head to foot. All weapons were taken from us before we
were allowed to walk their deck. They whistled and stamped
their naked feet, crowding excitedly around the young slave girls.

You could tell that these foreigners had been too long on the ocean.

Fog Woman came up after the Wolf Town men, and she was followed by the wives of Man Frog and Long Claws.

I counted the crew on all my fingers and my toes and started around again.

"*Sak-aitz atelpoo.* I see only six and twenty or seven and twenty," Red Tongue whispered to me. "Not so many as we thought."

One shipsman held out his hat while another drew out a handful of little flat skin squares with red or black markings on them. In this strange way of gambling, the dozen slave girls were swiftly divided up. Then each ran hand in hand with a whooping crewman somewhere down beneath the deck.

The master stood watching, impatient for the last nervous girl to disappear. Then he walked over to the table and chairs, which were still on the deck. Half a dozen small wooden kegs of rum and molasses were laid all along the center of the table. Behind the table stood a tall thin man resting his hands on large round rolls of woolen blanket cloth, one a lovely red, the other indigo blue.

"Take only the red!" I heard my sister whisper to Maquina. "I hate that miserable blue."

Maquina grimaced, then pretended he had not even heard her.

A male slave of Maquina's, one of those tight-faced little nut gatherers from far down the coast, humbly shuffled toward him, carrying a painted box. Maquina took from it a sea otter skin of the poorest quality. He shook it out and held it in a clever way, causing the light to catch the tips of the shining guard hairs. He made it look like a prime skin, though its tail was missing.

"What you want for that one?" the ship's talker asked in English.

Maquina held up his arms again and said, "Glun . . . and plowder."

"*Nika tikegh opoots atla!* He want the tail before you get the gun!" the ship's talker shouted for the master.

"Oh, you want the tail?" Maquina asked. "We forgot the tails," he said, avoiding the master's baleful gaze. "Later . . . we bring you . . . tail, *amigo*. We bring you plenty of tails."

The master gave an order, and soon a shipsman, a long musket in each hand, hurried to him. Two animal horns filled with gunpowder and two small leather sacks of shot were slung round his neck. The master and the tall thin shipsman sitting beside him started whispering to each other, holding their hands before their mouths.

"There's nothing subtle about the way they deal with us," said Maquina. "Look at them, making secret plans even as we watch them."

Although we did not see him, we could hear the dagger maker's hammer ringing somewhere deep inside the ship.

Finally the master held out all his fingers toward Maquina's face and said, *"Tahtlelum!* Ten good skins I want for these two muskets."

Maquina shook his head, and both of them sat sulking, staring at each other. Then Maquina pointed at one small barrel of rum, hoping it was molasses. Finally the master nodded in agreement, and the price was set: five sea otter skins for each musket, with a little barrel of rum and some shot and powder all thrown in. Also on that day Maquina fixed the price at four fathoms of red blanket cloth for a single sea otter skin. My sister urged Maquina to demand six fathoms of the blue for a skin because she didn't like that color, and finally the master angrily agreed.

What a trade! I could scarcely believe how many wonderful things this master was willing to give away for a single otter skin. When I was a young man, I had been with Maquina's father aboard the first Spanish ship that arrived, which people here believed at first was some kind of giant bird. At that time the very sight of any piece of iron or copper almost drove our house chiefs wild. We had known iron that had come from far to the west, even the slightest scrap of that was precious. In those days we would gladly trade one prime sea otter skin for one small iron chisel, and when the shipsmen had no more sharp chisels, we would trade a fine sea lion pelt for a single ship's nail. Now everything was different. The coming of the Spanish and the Boston men and the King George's men had changed all that, for we had come to understand that these men were all against one another and would give more and more to get our sea otter skins from us.

Maquina took another long lick of molasses, then said to the ship's talker, "Tell your captain that's a lovely coat he's wearing, and a nice hat, too."

I think the master might have guessed that this would happen. His chair creaked under his great weight as he turned and signaled a helper, who went back and rummaged among their pile of trade goods until he found a large red silk-covered box. The master grunted as he rose from his chair and grandly presented this gift to Maquina.

My brother-in-law held his breath as he opened the box, then gasped as he showed us the splendors it contained. It was a shipsman's uniform, but far better than the simple one this master wore. Oh, my, yes, this ship chief's costume was deep blue in color, had huge silverish buttons, and goldlike medals on its chest. It had bumblebee-yellow facings and a wide watery-blue sash. It was by far the most beautiful uniform any of us had ever seen. Yes, there were britches and shining boots, and snow-white gloves as well, all arranged neatly in that glorious box.

"Oh, tell him this is very fine," Maquina said, holding up the swallow-tailed coat against his chest, then trying on the gold-trimmed three-cornered hat. He stripped off his otter cloak and handed it to Fog Woman. He hung the master's coat across his shoulders.

"It looks just right," I said.

"Don't worry if the arms are too long," my sister told him. "I'll shorten them for you."

"Forget the boots," said Red Tongue. "Give him back the boots. You don't need those at all."

"I had a pair once," said Long Claws. "They were a misery on my feet."

"You're right," Maquina snorted. "I can't stand those stiff things around my toes. But I could cut the feet part off and just wear the handsome upper legs."

We all agreed that was the best idea.

The next to receive a gift was Red Tongue. He was given a short bolt of brightly printed calico cloth. It was a miserable little gift. These Boston masters give a worthwhile present only to the highest-ranking chief.

Now Maquina waved his hand grandly toward Red Tongue and said, "Give him your cloak. He's been generous with us."

Believe me, Red Tongue was reluctant to remove the otters from his back and give them as a present to that Boston master. The enormous difference in the worth of that valuable cloak of otter skins and the miserable bolt of calico Red Tongue had been given should have greatly shamed the master, but instead he laughed and clutched the costly otters to his belly as though there was a living woman hidden in them somewhere.

"This sea otter robe is good," the little ship's talker said, "but we need much, much more than this!" He laughed as though he were talking to small children. "You people go away now," that squint-eyed little seal turd said. "Come back tomorrow. If you want to have our beeeu-tee-ful daggers, guns, and rum, and blankets, you bring us lots and lotsa otter skins. And *next* time, don't forget the tails!"

With those words, the second day's bartering was ended. Man Frog and the other owners gathered up their slave girls. Some of these girls were a little drunk, and all looked overused, but none seemed hurt in any outward way that we could see.

As we left the ship, our daggers were once more returned to us. Maquina looked completely splendid in his gold-trimmed hat and long-tailed coat. I laughed aloud with pleasure when I thought of our next feast and of the jealousy his rival chiefs would feel when they saw our *tyee* dressed in this gorgeous costume.

When we were in the canoes, the ship's talker shouted to Maquina, "Tomorrow back you come, and don't forget the tails!" And as we began to paddle away toward our summer village, the ship's talker called out to us again: "Don't you forget them little sea beasts' tails!"

"Why did you make me give that captain my otter robe?" Red Tongue aked Maquina.

"Because I'm saving mine to buy that young dagger maker."

"I hate to hear you talk like that," I heard my sister whisper to her husband. "You know that captain will never trade a useful boy like that—not to you."

But Maquina smiled at me and Red Tongue as though he had not heard Fog Woman's words.

 FOR three days in a row, Maquina went aboard the ship with Red Tongue and Long Claws. Matla and his people went beside them in the big Whale house canoe. Twice he took Toowin out, but I did not go with them. The master had said he wanted fish. I stayed ashore and made sure Kawskaws and our old slave woman were splitting and smoking fast enough so that I could take six, eight, maybe ten boxes of fish out to trade. This ship was going north and needed food because they would be afraid to go ashore among those dangerous people who lived up there.

Of course Maquina did not take our sea otter tails out to the ship. We are not stupid! We always save those tails to trade separately on the very day when the shipsmen plan to sail away. Only then do we go out there seductively waving those tails in our hands. They stop pulling up their anchors and trade anything they have left to get them.

Each morning when Kawskaws brought my soup up from the fire, she first blackened the tip of her small finger with charcoal, then impressed a small black mark on the cedar plank above my sleeping place to remind us both of how many nights this ship had remained anchored up the inlet. When Kawskaws made her sixth mark, we had more than a hundred nicely smoke-dried spring salmon in eight big bentwood boxes, and I decided on that day to go with Maquina and trade the salmon in two lots of four, that being our most fortunate number.

Maquina called out, "Siam, bring your fish and come out with me. Tell Toowin to come with us as well. I'll trade your salmon for you."

As we were being paddled out toward the ship, my brother-in-law asked me to sit up high on one of my boxes packed with fish. He sat on the other one, looking handsome in his sea otter cloak. He was in a splendid mood. Maquina laughed and sang, and taking up a whalebone salmon club, he joined with the paddlers in drumming out the rhythm of their chanting.

"Everything has changed out there," he said proudly, pointing toward the ship. "We are all good friends now. You'll see. The captain will ask me down into his cabin to drink rum with him. Oh, yes, I'll take you and Red Tongue and maybe even Toowin with me. That captain and I have become like brothers. He'll be glad to have these fish of yours. I wish we had more skins to trade. It's been an awful hunting season. I don't know where the sea otter have all gone. They're not out there swimming in the kelp the way they used to be. The otter hunter says we've killed too many, but I think there will be a lot back here next winter. If you get the chance," he said, "let someone show you deep inside the belly of that ship. It's crammed full of every wonderful thing that we desire. I hate to think of this captain sailing away from us and taking all those trade goods up north to barter with those savage people, but he knows we're almost out of sea otter skins."

When we arrived, the hole in the ship's net was gaping wide, and instead of hostile men with scatter guns climbing in the rigging, we could hear someone playing a banjo up on the deck. When we climbed up high enough to see over the ship's rail, we learned that that fast music was made by the dagger maker. Oh, what wonderful things he could do!

Only one man stood beside the opening in the net. He smiled as he demanded that every man throw off his cape to prove we bore no weapons. The slave girls had been judged harmless by the shipsmen, and they were never made to strip for weapons.

On this day, Maquina himself carried a present for the master: a dozen plump sea ducks that were delicious in this season. Fog Woman had caught them, for she knew a clever woman's way of netting ducks, which she does every springtime. Maquina gave these birds to the master, and I showed him my first four boxes packed with fine big fish. He was delighted and, without haggling, gave me all I asked for them.

When I produced the next four boxes, the master laughed,

then made us understand that he was oh, so fond of salmon, and that he also loved both shooting ducks and eating them. To show his gratitude, he gave me free the last three fathoms of the red wool blanketing on the roll, and he gave Maquina a large animal's horn full of gunpowder and a bag of lead shot in exchange for the ducks. They were fair gifts, but Maquina, receiving his, displayed as much awe and gratitude as if a neighboring chief had given him a freshly stranded whale.

The master laughed again, beckoned us down into his cabin, and sat us round his table. Young Toowin was invited also. We admitted to the master that we had almost no more sea otter skins to trade, but assured him we would soon have others from our neighbors not far along the coast.

The ship's talker said, "Tell us where your neighbors live, and we will go and trade with them." The Boston master smiled innocently at all four of us.

"Oh, no," Red Tongue answered, his face a mask of false distress. "My chief says our neighbors to the south are as dangerous as those northerners you seek. We would never be the ones to send you to such people."

The master shifted his great bulk so that he faced Maquina. "When will you get more sea otter skins? That's what I want to know."

"*Kunjuk, kunjuk,*" Maquina answered him. "Ver sooon, ver sooon."

Everything was going perfectly. We four were invited to feast with the master and several of his highest-ranking shipsmen. "Be careful not to eat the thing that they call cheese," Maquina warned me. He wrinkled up his nose. "It's the most disgusting stuff a human could ever put inside his mouth!"

We sat cross-legged on his chairs and ate chunks of my smoked salmon and drank hot tea, the cups half full of sugar, and we all smiled and laughed or knocked our knuckles on the table to fill in the moments when we could not understand one another.

It was hot and cramped down in that cabin. Every wall was painted a sickening yellow, and many strange things gave off revolting smells. I don't know why shipsmen would tolerate such a miserable way of living—probably because they have no women of their own. Maquina laughed and said he didn't mind the smells as much as I did, and Toowin didn't seem to care. He laid his head upon the master's table and went sound asleep. Above us, up on deck, we could hear the dagger maker busily hammering out iron dagger blades to trade with us. Maquina tried to repeat the rhythm of his hammer by pounding his fist against the table, and soon the master joined in. It was an awful din against his ear, but still it did not wake my Toowin.

When Maquina drinks rum, his tongue goes waggling loose and he starts to slur his words. It is then that he always breaks into rich, expressive hand signs accompanying many foreign words. Oh, yes, this master could easily understand him, partly, I suppose, because he was honking like a goose, whistling and making quacking sounds, pointing and flapping his arms. Anyone could tell that he was talking about geese, swans, ducks—countless numbers of them.

This red-faced master, who had, I think, been drinking earlier that morning, continued downing cups of rum with us. Suddenly he heaved his huge bulk from the table and started rummaging through his closet. "There it is," he shouted, and took from a green-lined leather box the finest looking musket I have ever seen. It was not a clumsy, rough gun like the muskets used for trade. Oh, no! This was a wondrous weapon that reflected like a clear night sky along its gleaming double barrels. The stock was made of a rich, dark polished wood with a grain that swirled like the water in a pool. Its two steel hammers were handsomely carved, each with its flint held in place by a small piece of red-dyed leather. On the silver side locks of this breathtakingly beautiful weapon some artisan of fine eyesight and incredible skill had deeply engraved a tiny dog and an even smaller pair of birds and several dancing rabbits. The butt of this most perfect musket was beautifully bound in glowing brass, as was the tip of its long slim ramrod.

"Oh!" breathed Maquina when he first saw it, and he jumped up from his chair and knelt upon the table.

The master cocked both hammers and aimed the double-barreled musket toward his rear window. He squeezed each trigger, making first one and then the other fall with a lovely, sharp click-click! I was glad that musket was not loaded, and very surprised to see that the first small click woke Toowin, who leapt up from the table, wide-eyed with alarm.

The master laughed and handed the new musket to Maquina. Our *tyee* hugged it to his breast.

I do not believe that the master intended to give that splendid weapon to Maquina. But the rum, I think, had made him overgenerous. Seeing how much Maquina desired to own it made the master turn deep red and belch with pleasure. He took the musket from Maquina, stood back two paces, then held it out unsteadily. Showing all his teeth, the master said, *"Mesika!* Yours!"

Maquina gratefully took the musket, then reached down to where we had piled our garments. Taking up his long sea otter cloak trimmed with costly southern abalone shells, he said, "She yoors! *Yahka mesika!* Goo *el capeetan!* Tank yooo, *amigo!* Yooo ver gooo man!"

The master hugged his otter cloak. It was easy to tell that these two high-ranking chiefs were overwhelmed with each other's generosity. The master poured one more cup of rum, and we all started patting one another on the shoulder in the Boston shipsman's fashion, laughing and singing as though we had all been born and raised together in the Eagle house around one fire.

I was all for sleeping right there on the master's table or on his bed or floor. But Red Tongue, who is always spoiling things, said he felt like throwing up. I believed it, because his face had grown deadly pale. One look at Red Tongue got the master moving. He hurried all of us up to the deck.

The fresh air made comrades out of me and Toowin. Together we started singing a song we had inherited. Carefully we helped each other down into the waiting canoe. The swaying ship and ladder and our singing made that very, very difficult. I was the only one to miss my footing, but our paddlers were below to catch me. No serious harm befell us after that.

Maquina stood swaying on his plank, clutching his new musket above his head and calling up, "Tank yooo, *el capeetan!* Tank yooo, sooh much, *amigo!*"

When we got home, my sister, Fog Woman, was awfully mad at Maquina and at me. "It was the rum," she screamed, "that caused you two to give away his best cloak for one stupid gun. You've got two guns already," she yelled at Maquina, which only proves that women cannot tell a really splendid musket from a pair of poor ones.

Next morning my head throbbed and my throat was dry as sand. Maquina felt no better, but nothing else would do except that we accompany him to the lake behind the village, where he assured me he would lay low lots of swans with his new musket.

To test the musket, Maquina insisted that I be the one to fire both barrels. I was nervous of this, and it caused me to miss the first swan, but I got the second one. Then Red Tongue tried it, but only wounded one. My brother-in-law sent a naked northern slave out swimming to retrieve it. "They're tough-skinned. They don't mind cold water," Maquina assured us, "even though they shiver like a dog while waiting for the wind to dry them."

A pair of big white swans came winging over us. Maquina fired the musket twice, disturbing not a feather. That made him hopping mad.

"This gun needs more powder," he said, and he poured far too much down the barrels, then rammed in a huge quantity of shot.

I did not dare to warn him because it is always a mistake to tell Maquina that he is wrong about anything. It often causes him to sulk for days.

We crouched in the canoe until a flock of swans came low toward us from the south. Maquina rose and fired both barrels. The gun leapt back and all but knocked him in the water. My brother-in-law let out a roar when he heard the paddlers suck in their breaths to keep from laughing. Then Maquina noticed

that the right hammer of his glorious musket had been blown
off. He cursed the ship master and flung the beautiful weapon
into the bottom of the canoe, then sat head down, chewing on
his knuckles. Red Tongue and I both tried to reason with him,
but he refused to answer us. Finally I made a silent signal to
our paddlers, meaning they should take us home.

That night I heard Maquina say that the new musket from
the master was no good. My sister, she said it served him right
for having given away his best otter cloak, the one he had sworn
he was saving to trade for the dagger maker. That made Maquina so mad that he stopped speaking altogether, to my sister
or any others in the Eagle house.

Next morning I rose early and went and sat near Maquina
by our fire. He was still silent. I don't think he had slept at all
that night. Both Red Tongue and I tried to cheer him up by
saying that he need only show the broken musket to the master,
who would surely give him a new one or have the clever Jon
Jay replace the missing hammer. Maquina disdainfully refused
the rich clam broth my sister brought him, nor would he touch
the rich young sea lion meat she offered.

Suddenly Maquina broke his silence. "I want to go out
there, now," he said in a cold, harsh voice.

I don't know what Toowin had been doing during the night.
I shook him hard but could not rouse him, so he did not come
with us.

We three were, as usual, the first to board the ship. Throwing off our capes before the shipsmen could demand it, we gave
up our daggers.

Maquina lowered a twisted cord of cedar bark and had the
broken musket tied to it by one of his canoemen. He pulled it
up as though it were a dead and rotting fish. The shipsman who
had searched us snatched the gun from him before it touched
Maquina's hands, took the flint out of the one good hammer,
and checked to see that both flash pans were empty. Maquina
ground his teeth with rage.

Seeing that the gun was harmless, the young shipsman carelessly tossed it back to my brother-in-law, who at that moment

caught sight of the master coming up the narrow passage from his cabin near the stern. Maquina moved angrily toward him. I watched both of them with care, for I have always had a lively curiosity about rival chiefs and how they act one to another. I followed closely beside Maquina, positioning myself so that I could observe their eyes and the expressions on their faces.

Maquina pointed at the musket's broken hammer and thrust it rudely toward the master's face, shouting, *"Peshak, peshak! Bad, bad!"* Then in English he said, "This glun . . . no gooo!"

The master's eyes narrowed, and his puffy jowls trembled and turned mottled red, and his heavy hairy eyebrows drew together in a frightful scowl. Oh, what a sight he was!

"Peshak? Bad? You say *bad?"* the master shouted at Maquina. He tore the weapon from Maquina's grasp, then, not knowing what to do with it, he turned and flung it into the dark passage that led down to his cabin.

The slave girls who had been left aboard had seen it all. Some of them started giggling nervously at the open anger displayed by these two rival chiefs. Maquina's body stiffened with rage. He turned his head and stared into my face, and then at Red Tongue, ignoring the master and the gang of shipsmen and the slave girls, who crouched not far from us along the deck. Maquina began to shake. With his left hand I saw him reach up and massage his throat and breast bone. His heart, like mine, was surely going tum-tum-tum.

Maquina's face was just as frightful as the master's; each was like the Eagle's mask. My brother-in-law's right hand went searching underneath his goat-wool cape, feeling for his missing dagger. Can you imagine, he, Maquina, treated by this cruel-hearted foreigner as though he were a slave?

"John J.! John J.!" the red-faced master shouted as he and Maquina glowered at each other.

The young dagger maker came bounding out of the ship's hold and ran directly to the master. That angry, heavy-bellied brute pointed toward the steep steps leading to his cabin, and the dagger maker hurried down and returned carrying Maquina's broken swan gun.

The flush-faced master pointed to the missing hammer post. The dagger maker examined it with care. I do not know what Jon Jay said in answer, but anyone could see that his words greatly displeased the master, who threatened to strike the dagger maker with his fist, then started wildly cursing him.

Maquina laughed and made a rude gesture toward the master, then turned and called to me in triumph. "Siam, you listen and tell others. This dagger maker tells the captain . . . that musket weak—it broke itself. He says . . . I didn't break it!" Maquina looked straight at the master and shouted, "*Yooo hear? Yoor shipsman say . . . Maquina not the man . . . who blake this glun!*"

Those slave girls started giggling once again.

My brother-in-law angrily flung his goat-wool cape wide open to show us that he had no dagger to avenge the awful insult that he had just suffered from this master, then whirled around, rudely turning his back on the master and sending his cape fringe swaying in the rudest way he could.

Still, we all knew that Maquina had not succeeded in insulting the master. Stripped of all his weapons, surrounded by armed shipsmen, my brother-in-law stood helpless as a child. To make matters even worse, the red-faced master laughed crudely at Maquina and gave him a rough push on the back, then turned and stamped off to his cabin and noisily slammed the door.

One word from Red Tongue silenced all the female slaves, but that did not stop the shipsmen's jeering. Believe me, I was oh, so grateful that my young Toowin had stayed asleep and missed this ugliness.

Maquina, still pale with rage, called out to his paddlers in a terrifying voice, "Get me off this stinking sea bird's back! I never want to see these hateful foreign lice again."

Acting as quickly as we could, Red Tongue and I ordered the paddlers into the canoe and herded all the frightened young girls down the ladder. They needed no urging from us, for Maquina had growled at them in a voice that sent them scurrying through the net, their faces drawn in terror.

My brother-in-law was the last one off that ship's ladder.
He dawdled purposely, showing he had no fear. As Maquina
entered the big canoe, he stepped down hard onto the neck of
the slave girl who had first dared to laugh at him. She bent,
taking his full weight without complaint, fearing that if she cried
out, he might have her drowned. Maquina I had seen in many
different moods, but never one as black as this.

Our daggers came clattering down into the canoe, flung
from above by shipsmen not caring if they fell into the water or
sliced into human flesh. Our paddlers stroked angrily away.

Neither Red Tongue nor I could summon the courage to
speak one word to Maquina during the journey back to our
village. We both hoped that our utter silence would convince
him that none of us would go ashore and gossip about the
dreadful insult and the final shove that my brother-in-law had
suffered from that accursed master. But deep inside, our instincts told us our silence would not help. Maquina knew that
all of us had seen him horribly insulted. During the coming winter, many witnesses would carefully reshape this happening into
a legend, a legend always told behind his back. It would provide
the main entertainment at feastings all along the coast. Children
who heard it would remember and tell it to their grandchildren,
and so it would go on and on forever. In this way, great chiefs,
and even their families, had sometimes been utterly destroyed.

Maquina was so upset on the following day that he refused
to rise up from his sleeping place. His ferocious silence had
frightened away all his younger women. Now only my brave
sister dared to remain squatting calmly by him.

When I went down to the fire pit, Maquina made a violent
gesture toward me, meaning I should come to him at once. He
made me place my ear close to his mouth so that neither my
sharp-eared sister nor Man Frog nor Long Claws nor their wives,
whom we knew sat slyly listening on the other side of their
partitions, could hear his words. "I am never going out to that
cheese-reeking ship again," Maquina whispered through clenched
teeth. "But still I wish to know exactly what is happening out
there, and when that heavy-bellied brute plans to sail his foul

ship out of my inlet. Usher, be my eyes and ears for me," he said. "Go to the Whale house and get old Matla. Take his canoe and paddlers with you. He's got a tight tongue in his head."

When I went back up into my apartment, Kawskaws was massaging oil on Toowin's thighs. "I'll come with you, Father," said my son.

"Oh, no you won't," I answered, as I searched through boxes trying to find my better bulb-shaped hat. "I don't like what's going on out there."

I got Matla, and we went out exactly as Maquina had ordered us to do.

"I wonder why he sent you and me instead of Red Tongue," Matla said. "I mean, to do his spying for him."

We took only the fifteen-man canoe. In it also was Matla's eldest son, named Hoiss, and ten strong paddlers, no other nobles, no wives, just a few slave girls to make everything look normal. We sat on empty boxes, for of course we would not dare to trade without Maquina. It was a clear blue spring day, and I was glad to get away from Maquina's wounded feelings as he lay sulking in the Eagle house.

Matla is, I believe, the fiercest-looking man I have ever seen. His skin is brown as underwater wood, and his heavy hunched-shouldered movements remind me of a bull sea lion. On occasions such as these, he wears a pair of long, curved beaver teeth that protrude cruelly upward from the hole pierced through the septum of his nose.

Young shipsmen gasped at the sight of Matla as he climbed through their net. I followed him, then came his son, Hoiss, and other young paddlers from the Whale house. All of us gave up our daggers before the shipsmen had a chance to demand them.

After that, I stood with Matla on the deck. The young men with us leaned awkwardly against the rail. Shipsmen wandered past us as though we were not there. We waited in silence as the morning sun moved two hands higher. It was unusual for shipsmen to act like this, as though they did not wish to trade with us. It could only mean that yesterday's trouble with the musket had made the master very angry. I was right.

The master came up out of his dark cabin and stood blinking in the sunshine. When he saw me, his lips curled back in disdain. He turned away and yelled, "John J.! John J.!"

The dagger maker came running up from that other place belowdecks where he cleans the muskets and pounds iron when it is raining. Jon Jay was carrying a powder horn and shot pouch and the same beautiful musket that had been given to Maquina.

The master snatched the weapon from Jon Jay. "Look you . . . good . . . not broke!" he bellowed at us in Chinook so badly spoken that even fierce old Matla started chuckling. The master glared angrily at Matla, then yelled out something that brought his brown-faced ship's talker running to him from their cooking place, his mouth still full of food.

The dagger maker looked at Matla and at me and smiled and blinked his eyes to show his friendliness toward us. I smiled back at Jon Jay, because on this whole ship he was the only one I cared to know.

The master stared red-faced at us as he carefully measured a small amount of powder down each barrel, then wadded it and poured in shot and set it with the ramrod. He took a small brass horn from his side pocket, shook some fine-grained powder into each flash pan, and closed them. He checked the flints and raised the musket menacingly.

We stepped back, fearing he might fire at us.

The master drew both hammers back, then snorted as he turned away. Leaning out over the ship's rail, he pulled the triggers. His shoulder jerked back twice as first one barrel discharged, and then the other. We watched two sprays of shot go lashing out across the water. He turned, still frowning, and held the smoking musket out to me.

"*Mahse, mahse.* Thank you," I said to the master, for I was grateful that he had not shot us and was giving me Maquina's musket, which I would take to him, so settling all the troubles.

"*No-no-no!*" the ship's talker said. "The captain's not going to give you that lovely swan gun, nor will he give it to that useless *tyee* sulking on the shore."

The master sneered at me and set the beautiful musket well

beyond my reach inside the narrow wooden passage that led down to his cabin.

Some of the young shipsmen who had been watching started hooting like owls and laughing openly at me and old Matla and at his son, Hoiss. Two of the crewmen walked rudely to the opening in the net and jerked their thumbs toward it, ordering us to go.

As we walked by the noisiest shipsmen, one of them put out his foot and tripped Matla's son, sending him sprawling to the deck. Hoiss jumped up, his face a mask of hatred. He stepped close to the one who had tripped him, a young, thin, bearded shipsman no older than himself. Hoiss was unarmed, but the foreigner drew his short sea knife and threatened to slash Hoiss's throat.

The two of them stood staring at each other, their faces only one hand's length apart. Oh, I was glad that my Toowin was not aboard. The tall, thin second chief ran up the deck and stamped with his hard leather boot on the bare foot of the shipsman, then snatched the short knife from him. The other crewmen watched angrily but did nothing.

Old Matla said one quiet word to his son, and young Hoiss obediently turned away and followed the two of us through the net. As the net man handed the long daggers back to each of us, he let young Hoiss's slip and fall into deep water. Many of the shipsmen laughed insultingly. That new dagger blade had cost two prime sea otter skins. Matla's son went pale with rage.

"You don't come back!" the ship's talker shouted out, pointing straight at Hoiss.

I sighed with relief when all of us were once more in the big canoe and had pushed off from the ship.

It was evening when we reached shore. I asked Matla and his son to come up to the Eagle house to support me in my answers to the questions that Maquina would surely put to me. Carefully we told Maquina all that had happened out aboard the ship. I had to admit that I had not learned how long the ship would stay. Young Hoiss was still so angry that he left us and stood among the cluster of paddlers near the entrance to the Eagle house. I could hear them talking excitedly about the insult Hoiss had suffered and whether he would dare go back aboard the ship. My son, Toowin, was standing with them, grim-faced, agreeing with every fiery word the paddlers had to say.

Maquina listened to them also. Their wild words seemed to make him lose his gloom. He sat up and said to Matla, "Am I hearing right? Is this all true?"

Tears came into fierce old Matla's eyes as he remembered the insult that his unarmed son had suffered. Matla struck his forehead with his fist and shouted, "Yes, it's true! If we had had our knives, we would have helped him kill those men!"

Just as it was growing dark, Matla spoke to Hoiss, who left the others and followed his father to the Whale house. It was the ninth night since that ship had come to rest at Abooksha.

It is unusual for any event such as marrying, dancing, or feasting to occur in our village unless the persons who are heads of other houses have first received Maquina's full approval, so I was surprised when a little later Kawskaws came excitedly and told me that someone had lit an enormous beach fire just beyond the Whale house. I got up and went outside. When I saw the leaping flames and heard the angry sounds, I was astonished.

Maquina and my sister and Red Tongue and almost every other person from the Eagle house came out and stood watching the flames, then we went together to the Whale house.

In the glaring light from their beach fire, I saw almost every person from the Whale house clutching long yew-wood staffs. They all began together, beating out of time, striking incessantly against the heavy cedar planking of the Whale house walls. They sent up an angry wordless chanting. The entire building acted like a drum and caused the sharp noise to echo and reecho in a deafening din that made me clap my hands across my ears. The shipsmen could not have failed to hear that violent sound as it went rolling north to them across the silent waters of the night, nor could they have failed to see the huge red glow of that tremendous fire and the angry sparks it hurled into the blackness.

The heat and the rhythm and intensity of the beating on the house increased. The young paddlers who had been with us that day started yelling and shrieking, and the women from the Whale house joined them in a frightful chorus. In all my life I had never heard such a furious, mindless uproar.

I turned and looked at Maquina. Although he had not joined in the yelling, a strange look of satisfaction had spread across his face. I could see old Matla moving between us and the firelight's glow. He had blackened his face the way Whale people always do in times of anguish or of death. Hoiss's face was glistening with seal oil and charcoal mixed with mica dust. He was dancing slowly with a score of young men, banded together for the first time in their lives as warriors. Oh, yes, my son, Toowin, was there, dancing as dangerously as any other one among them. His mother's Moachat dance steps were not at all in time with the sticks that were pounded frantically against the Whale house, but he didn't seem to care. The black faces of the young men danced past us, slow and stiff. The men held their arms akimbo, twitching their elbows toward their spine ends, as they imitated the jerking movements of those fearsome animals one sees only in dreams.

The elders who pounded on the house walls, then the women and the children, were the first to tire from the violence of their angry protest. Finally, most of the villagers went back inside their houses. But a few of the young men continued to pile wood upon the huge beach fire and did not let it die away.

Next morning, Kawskaws came and woke me with some salmon chunks and eggs of herring. She pointed nervously toward Maquina, who was striding up and down the center of the Eagle house, calling out orders to everyone and looking like himself again. That caused me to worry, for Maquina was not one to forgive insults. I did not like the way this day was beginning, and so instead of waking my poor Toowin, who was worn out from all his dancing, I left him sleeping like a child.

Maquina stopped his nervous pacing and called up to me, "Siam, they are filling all their barrels with water. I believe that ship will be leaving very soon."

My brother-in-law already had our women packing two large bent-cedar boxes full of fresh-caught salmon, as well as one white-bellied halibut too large to fit inside of any box, four large swans, and half a dozen black-necked geese.

"Come with me," Maquina said. "I am taking these out to trade with the captain."

I could scarcely believe the good sound in his voice.

He looked at me and smiled. "We want that captain to come back to trade with us, don't we?"

My sister answered before I could say a word. "I don't care if that captain goes or stays," she said. "I warn the two of you, be careful! I didn't like that fire last night, or all that noise, and I don't trust our young people or those shipsmen."

Ignoring her, we went outside and saw that Matla's big dugout from the Whale house had already left the beach and was now headed straight toward the ship. Maquina, Red Tongue, and I, paddled by eight of our men in one of our middle-sized canoes, followed them.

When we climbed aboard that morning I did not like the feelings that were given off by our Whale people or by the foreigners. The salt air was damp and still, and I could smell the sweat that comes with human nervousness and high excitement. It was a smell that I remember from the potlatch feasts when the fires are oiled to make the dance house hot, a time when rival chiefs are present with their sly-eyed women and their children, who stare at you as though they believe the stories that Wolf people come from breeding with their dogs. The dance house was always overcrowded then and steaming in the winter rain. Those feelings, like the feelings on this ship, were bad. I was oh, so glad that Toowin was not here.

Like all the others from the Whale house, Hoiss came aboard wearing a wooden mask. Some of the masks had round mouth holes especially carved so that through them they could blow mournful blasts on their woodwind whistles. At first all their notes were slow and measured, sad as death. But soon that sound lost all its gloom and turned into the dangerous, angry sound that one hears at warriors' feasts before they go out raiding.

The shipsmen gathered closer to the dancers, curious about the trembling, fast-muscled movements of their feet and hands and the swift, birdlike thrusts of their masked faces.

"I'm surprised to hear this," Red Tongue said to Maquina. "Did you tell them they could do this dance?"

Maquina turned away and did not answer.

If I had been Maquina, I would have made those dancers cease. He knew as well as I that such displays of warlike hatred most often lead to trouble. But instead of stopping it, Maquina stood back, watching the impetuous young men, his dark eyes glittering, his mouth half open, his chest heaving as though he was trying to catch his breath when running.

 I WISH that my sister, Fog Woman, could have come aboard with us that morning. She would have calmed Maquina and urged him to stop the young men from such dangerous forms of dancing. I was astonished that the shipsmen did not understand the deadly warnings in our paddlers' movements. They laughed scornfully when our young men from the Eagle house joined the Whale house dancers. With backs bent and arms held low, elbows beating like angry ravens' wings, these young hotheads stuttered out forbidden words in Wakashan that I was glad the shipsmen could not understand.

Old Matla did not sing with all the paddlers. No. But as he watched them closely, I saw him shuffling his feet, his fierce face more frightening than any painted wooden mask.

Throughout this most menacing Raven dance, the master must have been asleep down in his cabin. When he did come up, his jowls were stubbled gray, and he looked as wide-eyed as any owl when he saw Maquina and the dancers circling on his deck.

Maquina strode straight to him and made his generous gift of salmon, halibut, and fresh-killed waterfowl. The master seemed delighted that his offense to Maquina had been forgotten. He gasped at the weight of the heavy swans and admired the long-necked geese and the plumpness of the ducks. *"Mahse, mahse,"* the master thanked him loudly in Chinook. Maquina nodded back at him and smiled. I sighed with relief as I saw these two main sources of our troubles declaring peace with each other.

The master called his ship's talker and listened as Maquina made it clear that great rafts of swan and geese and ducks had that morning arrived in the lakes behind Wolf Town on their long flights north to nest. Maquina explained as well that there

were countless salmon schooling in the estuary of a nearby river.
My brother-in-law assured him that if some shipsmen went there
with gill nets and fowling guns, they could supply the ship with
all the fish and fowl that they would need for their coming
voyage.

The master was very pleased to hear those words. He told
us that after the midday meal, he would send out half his crew
and one of the ship's longboats. He asked Maquina if he would
send some men to guide them. This my brother-in-law agreed
to do.

I was delighted with the good feelings that had so quickly
been resumed between this heavy-bellied master and Maquina.
The ship's talker told us that they had already stored enough
fresh water and wooden spars aboard the ship. He said because
we had no more sea otter to trade, the master had decided to
sail north the next morning on the tide.

The master smiled and told his talker that he wanted Maquina, me, and Red Tongue to go down into his cabin and join
him in the midday meal. This we did most gladly. But I must
tell you that I was sad to see old Matla left out there alone upon
the deck among a scattering of our young paddlers, female
slaves, and idle shipsmen. Matla was a ranking nobleman, the
Whale house chief. He should have been included in the master's feast. Yes, I think everything might have been quite different if Matla had been asked to eat with us.

The master's tall, thin first man drank only one cup of rum
because he said it made him want to sleep. The master drank
two full cups of rum, as did the three of us. We tried to turn
our noses so we could not smell the awful cheese that had been
set upon the table.

Laughing and singing in the nicest sort of way, the black
man who cooked for the shipsmen brought in Maquina's gift of
geese all steaming on a large iron platter. Maquina stood up
and honored the master with a chief's departing song. It sounded
fine to me, even though Maquina got the words mixed up.

We drank another cup of rum, then using the master's short,
blunt food knives and our fingers and our teeth, we tore the

four hot geese into pieces and devoured them. Their melting fat ran clear yellow down our chins. They were delicious! When we finished eating all the salmon we could hold, the cooking man brought in another steaming dish. This one the master called suga puddee. Unlike the white man's ghastly cheese, this was the best-tasting food that I have ever put inside my mouth.

After the feasting was over, the master, as a present, gave us each a short clay pipe. He cut up shares of plug tobacco, and we squatted on our chairs and smoked hard until the air smelled awful and turned blue. Red Tongue choked, turned pale, and had an awful fit of coughing. We all hurried up on deck. The fresh air did smell good.

The tall first man, who drank so little rum, was up there waiting for us. He already had the longboat lowered in the water, its small sail rigged, and two fishnets and six muskets neatly laid out in the bow. It was agreed that four young men from Wolf Town would go along to guide them to the river and the duck lakes. The thin man took eight shipsmen with him in their long-boat, and the others followed in a smaller yawl. You could tell that those men were all eager to do some fishing and some wild-bird hunting.

Just at that time I saw the red-haired servant to the master and the black boy who worked the leather puff box for the dagger maker lowering the littlest jolly boat and throwing in a pile of clothing. I could not imagine why.

Maquina, who this day was not painted, looked flushed in the face and a little unsteady on his feet. He grandly told the master in half-English and half-Chinook that he was going back ashore to fetch an even better gift to give him before the ship departed. The master looked very pleased.

Maquina belched and said to me, "You stay here and watch these young people. I don't like the bold way they are acting. If they want to do fighting dances, you warn them to hold back until they've heard that such dancing has been agreed upon by me."

"Yes, I'll be glad to tell them that," I told Maquina.

I watched my brother-in-law and Red Tongue right behind

him making their way down the ship's ladder. Each stepped too heavily into the canoe.

Matla, looking very sullen, remained on the rear deck, and I went back there to talk with him, hoping I could make him feel a whole lot better. But whatever I said seemed to make him worse.

Nodding violently toward the master's back, Matla said, "These shipsmen, they know nothing. All of them are bad. The worst! I don't know why we let our young people go near them."

"You mean those girls?" I said, nodding toward the slaves.

"Of course I don't mean them. They're nothing," he snorted at me. "I mean our paddlers and young men of rank, like my son, Hoiss. And your son, Toowin. Where is Toowin?"

"Sleeping," I said. "Worn out, I think, by some woman and by too much dancing."

"That won't hurt him," Matla said. "Lying with your Hupa girl and doing lots of dancing, that will give him strength." I didn't like the sound of that, but I said nothing.

"Hoiss, my son, was insulted yesterday," said Matla. "He was kicked and had his dagger thrown away." This father groaned in anguish. "What's Hoiss going to do to make that right in the Whale house?"

"He should do nothing," I said to Matla. "These are foreigners. They don't know how to treat a person. They're here only to trade. It isn't as though Hoiss was insulted by someone from another village. No. These shipsmen are ignorant. They are leaving tomorrow. Maquina orders us, 'Do nothing,' and I say the same!"

Old Matla grunted when he heard that. We two spoke no more, but leaned against the rail, staring idly out toward the islands. My eyes closed, and my head nodded just thinking of the rum and yellow goose fat and lovely suga puddee and smoking all that strong tobacco. When I looked up, I could see the longboat moving away from the ship, heeling as it caught the afternoon breeze. Its short sail bulged with wind as it headed around toward the lakes.

"We should have sails like that on our canoes," I said to

Matla, and although he was angry with the whites and me, he grudgingly agreed.

When I glanced south toward our village, Maquina's dugout had already turned in to the shore. What interested me was that the master's red-haired servant and the black boy who helped the dagger maker had rowed a tiny boat onto the beach at Abooksha and were busy dunking the master's clothing in a small, fast-running creek.

"What are those two doing?" Matla asked me.

"I don't know," I answered him.

Soon I saw white froth like storm-blown spume, and I said, "Oh, yes, I do know. They are scrubbing out the master's clothes with that greasy yellow stuff they use."

Matla snorted when I said that. "They must be filthy brutes," he said. "We never wash clothing in the Whale house. If they're truly dirty with sweat or food-stained, we just throw them to the slaves and have the women make us new things."

"We do the same in the Eagle house," I said. "These shipsmen, they do everything in different ways. But then, they've got no women."

"Rude, crude bastards, they are," Matla said with vehemence. "They're not born of women. No one I know has ever seen one of their women. I don't believe they've got any. That's why they're always trading valuable little things so they can lie with ours. Imagine them," he exclaimed, "feasting with you and leaving me squatting out here alone, without so much as a swallow of fresh water!"

I couldn't blame Matla for being angry with them.

Then, looking at me slyly, Matla whispered, "Me and you— we don't have to do a thing. No. Our young lads who got insulted, they'll know just how to do it."

I didn't like the sound of that, and I looked back quickly along the deck at all the paddlers. But they were doing nothing, just resting, like we ourselves, or squatting on their haunches, warming themselves in the last weak patch of sun. The slave girls were not far away near a gang of young shipsmen, who stood cross-legged, talking together and pipe smoking and seeing who could spit the farthest out beyond the ship's rail.

The soft and springlike morning had all but disappeared. A southwest wind was driving heavy banks of clouds in from the ocean, and across the inlet rain was falling. A whole line of shipsmen now stood idle along the rail, looking out across the water at a towering blue-black thunderhead that was forming. To my amazement I saw that they were pointing at a strongly colored rainbow that had just appeared. I warned Matla of it, and we two swiftly turned our backs so that we could not see it.

"Imagine those foolish louts, all of them still staring at that dangerous rainbow," Matla gasped.

I agreed with him, for as everyone knows, even glancing at a rainbow is a most hazardous thing to do. I shaded my eyes from that calamitous sight but stole a glance at our masked dancers. They, like our slave girls, were looking in the opposite direction, but those foolish shipsmen kept pointing and staring straight toward that rainbow and spitting tobacco juice into the sea, which is our provider. That is to us a doubly certain way to court disaster.

Feeling chilled perhaps, some of our young men rose, blew their mournful whistles, and resumed their menacing performance. It was easy to tell that the shipsmen had grown bored with both our dancers and the slave girls. They were tired of all of us—any little child could have seen that in their faces. The only one I observed who still watched the dancing was the dagger maker. He was standing quietly by the hatchway with his arms folded, studying the twitching movements of our young men. I could tell by the pained look on his face that he did not like their jerking actions or the somber hooting of their whistles.

A young warrior wearing a blackened Wolf mask with freshly painted tear stains streaked white beneath its eyes leapt out from among the others and went hopping across the deck toward the dagger maker. This dancer was naked except for his wooden mask and gray wolf mane, which swished across his back. On his chest an Eagle crest was painted. He crouched before the copper-haired young shipsman and made his muscles tremble, as in our legend of the angry demon emerging from the forest cave. He increased the harsh wind notes of his whistle in time with his frantic body movements.

The dagger maker frowned at the unfriendly boldness of the dancer and turned away from him. A big shipsman, older than the rest, with hair cropped short and blue tattoos of animals on both his muscular arms, looked disdainfully at our masked dancer, then followed the dagger maker down inside the hold. I didn't blame either of them. What that young dancer did was wrong. I would not suffer that rude shaking, hopping, trembling nonsense so close to me, nor would I allow that death-dirge whistle to be blown in my face!

It was not long before we heard the rumbles of the fart box wheezing down below and, a little later, the dagger maker's hammer ringing with a steady beat. Its sound went straight against the rhythm of the angry dancers, and not long after that their movements stopped abruptly. Below the deck the iron went on ringing like a high, clear bell, as though that joyful hammering sound had somehow fought and won against the whistles of our young men.

I looked out over the water beyond the group of dancers and saw the black Eagle canoe leave our village cove. "Here they come back again," I said to Matla, pointing to the canoe that carried Red Tongue and Maquina. "I wonder . . . if the master will like the gift so well that he will give Maquina back his musket?"

I saw young Hoiss break away from the dancing and stare out toward the returning canoe. I told Matla that the rainbow had now disappeared.

Someone gave a warning owl hoot from behind a mask, and every one of the young slave girls leapt to her feet. To my amazement, each one of them flung back her cedar cape and drew out a dagger concealed in a sheath between her breasts. I saw the one who had had her neck stepped on thrust a dagger handle out at Hoiss. At first I do not think the shipsmen saw those long blades pass between the slave girls and the strong young dancers.

Atlin wearing
Wolf mask and
skin boots his
wooden whistle.

I was about to shout when fierce old Matla bumped my hip and growled, "What's happening is *their* doing, not *yours* or *mine!*"

I bellowed out my warning, but not soon enough.

Matla's son rushed across the deck and caught by the hair the shipsman who had tripped him. Raising his right arm, Hoiss drove his long dagger downward. I saw it go in beside his victim's neck where it would meet no bones and pierce downward through his heart.

By that time, all our excited slaves were screaming and running in confusion, and our young idiots, still with their masks on, were cutting, crouching, hollering, hacking, leaping, stabbing, and shouting. Shipsmen were writhing, falling, and deep-red artery blood was spurting everywhere.

Matla locked his powerful arms around me and forced me hard against the ship's rail. I tried in vain to struggle away from him as the slaughter went on and on and on.

The master must have heard the noise, for he came charging up his cabin stairs. He held the precious musket in his hands. He had taken only a few steps on the deck when I saw him slip in the blood and stumble heavily to his knees. The swan gun went slithering across the deck. A young masked man leapt astride him, clutching the master's bulging sides between his knees to steady himself as he, with two hands, drove his long dagger between the big man's collarbone and shoulder blade. Even as the blood came gushing from the master's neck and mouth, two of them took off his head and flopped his heavy body overboard.

At the worst moment of all, when everything was going wrong, I saw the young man, Jon Jay, stick his head up out of the hold. I gave a violent twist from Matla, who may have willingly let me go. I ran toward the dagger maker, shouting, "*Mahkh! Mahkh mi-mie!* Get out! Go down!"

He heard me, and turned his head. At that moment a masked dancer dived at him and grabbed the dagger maker by his copper-colored hair. The paddler was one who had not got a dagger from the slave girls but had run back to the cookhouse and snatched up the ship's wood ax. This he brought down viciously against the side of Jon Jay's head. Blood spurted against the warrior's hands, and as he tried to haul Jon Jay from the hold, his grip slipped and the dagger maker went plummeting out of sight.

I heard Jon Jay's body go thump-thump-thump against the ladder rungs, and then there was a heavy thud as he landed in the blackness down below. Can you imagine a blood-lusting young fool killing a clever artisan like that?

I ran at the one who had attacked the dagger maker. My heart went tum-titty-tum-titty-tum as I drove my knee up hard into his groin. He fell down screaming, rolling on the deck. If I had not known his mother well and liked her, if my friend Matla had not been his uncle, I believe I might have taken up that bloody ax and killed him. That young idiot deserved it.

"It's all over now," old Matla shouted to me. "There's nothing you can do."

Matla's words were true. There was nothing I could do. Every single shipsman was down in a steaming pool of blood. The slave girls stopped their wailing and stared along the deck in utter disbelief. The very shipsmen they had lain with in the early morning now lay grossly slaughtered—every one of them.

"You wait until Maquina sees all this," I cried out in anguish to Hoiss and his companions.

No words of mine could stop them from casting all the headless bodies over the ship's side.

"That won't change anything," I shouted. "Maquina will settle with you hard when he sees what you have done."

"He won't mind so much," said Matla. "This whole ship belongs now to the Whale house—yes, and everything that's in it is ours! I'll give Maquina that precious musket the captain gave, then took back from him. And he'll get back the otter robe he gave the captain. We'll give some gifts to him—and to you as well. I'll see to that myself."

He sounded like a new *tyee*. That was such an overwhelming thought that I said nothing more. I just stood there with my knees trembling and my heart pounding hard against my chest.

Maquina's canoe was coming in toward us when I heard Opoots say, "What about those two over there?" He was pointing toward the servant and the young black boy, who hadn't heard a thing. They were still squatting on the beach at Abooksha, scrubbing out the master's clothing.

Two of Hoiss's followers slipped over the ship's side and, kicking like a pair of frogs, swam in toward them. I did not see exactly what happened when those two reached the shore because I was watching Maquina's canoe as it drew closer, and I was trying to imagine the questions he and Red Tongue would ask when they beheld the slaughter and how I should answer them, remembering that all of these young killers were relatives of theirs and mine. When I did look again at the beach, I saw that the master's servant and the black boy had disappeared and our two youths, their daggers in their mouths, were swimming back toward the ship, each carrying something heavy. I saw that the little stream had turned dark red at its mouth and the master's shirts and his gray underclothes were drifting slowly out to sea, surrounded by whorls of dark-red blood.

At that moment Maquina's canoe lightly touched the ship's opposite side. He and Red Tongue were coming up the ladder. Old Matla followed me over to the opening in the net. The young men stood well back, as nervous as a flock of sandpipers.

I know that when Maquina and Red Tongue raised their heads over that ship's rail, they did not suspect the grisly sight that met their eyes. When Maquina saw the bloody heads severed from the shipsmen's bodies arranged side by side like a crescent moon upon the back deck, he made a low inhuman sound, blowing out his nostrils as though to purge himself of this impossible sight.

"Who told you to do this?" Maquina shouted, and he bared his teeth at Matla.

Red Tongue stared wide-eyed at me.

"Who did this?" Maquina nodded toward the row of shipsmen's heads, then glared at both of us.

I spread my hands and let my cape fall open, showing him I possessed no weapon and was not stained with blood. I was surprised to see fierce old Matla do the same.

"The boys did it," Matla answered in a rasping voice. "They did it because they sought revenge for that captain's insults made on you and them!" He looked straight at Maquina. "You saw one of those young whites trip up my son Hoiss, insult him, and fling his best knife down in the water—lost it for him, that's what they did!"

"That happened days ago," Maquina shouted. "Do you mean all this slaughter, all this blood, is because that loutish son of yours fell over some young shipsman's foot and couldn't catch his knife?"

"He's my first son," Matla said boldly. "They dishonored him. I saw a shipsman laugh right in his face."

"For that—he caused all this?" Maquina said in absolute disgust as he waved his hand toward the severed heads.

"The other shipsmen's boats, they're coming back," Red Tongue whispered to Maquina.

"Good!" said Maquina, and he pointed to Hoiss. "Now, what do you think is going to happen when they see what you've done to their friends? They have swan guns, and most of them are carrying pistols in their belts. I believe they will try to kill every one of us for the wrongs these few young idiots have done."

Hearing that, some of the slave girls started wailing, and the young killers from our village clutched their knives and crouched in silence, staring at the oncoming boats.

I, Siam, was worried. When the shipsmen see all this and start their shooting, I wondered, shall I jump over the side and try to hide in the lee of one of our canoes, or shall I take the chance against their musket balls and try to frog-kick to the shallows off the beach at Abooksha. Once on the beach, I could use the forest trail to Wolf Town. I could warn Toowin and Kawskaws and the others to flee before the foreigners sailed down to fire their cannons at the village.

The sail of the longboat was still up, but it flapped idly in the light breeze. The boat was being badly rowed toward the ship, and the smaller yawl was coming in behind it awkwardly.

"Stay where you are," Maquina growled at the young killers.

There was nothing any of us could do except watch the longboat draw nearer and nearer. When it came close, broadside of the ladder, it turned clumsily, and we could see that its opposite bow was stained bright red with blood. Paddlers from the Whale and Thunder houses were doing their awkward best to handle the unfamiliar shipsmen's oars. Atlin and another of the Whale house lads were sitting looking upward, tense and nervous. Each held a shipsman's musket and was pointing it upward toward the deck.

Young Hoiss ran to the ship's rail and shouted down to the paddlers in the boats, "Don't shoot! All the whites up here are dead."

Maquina's own nephew, Isinikah, called back proudly, "We killed off every one of them who was fishing with us."

"We too! We did the very same!" Hoiss shouted down to them, and he held out his blood-soaked hands in triumph.

Isinikah and another youth reached into the bow to gather up one of the salmon nets and, with all their strength, lifted it high for us to see. It was jammed full of gory shipsmen's heads.

Maquina turned away in anger when he saw the gruesome contents of the gill net. His mouth started working, and his fists were clutching at the rail as his arms were shaking, but no words came out of his mouth, for he could see that he had lost control of the young men of our village. It was a time for him to be very bold or very careful.

The eager warriors from the longboat came rushing up the ladder, proudly dragging their frightful load of heads. I could imagine the fear they must have felt when they saw Maquina scowling at them, speechless, his face a mask of rage.

The young men, seeing that Maquina possessed a knife, avoided him, and they avoided me and Matla also. On the back deck, they silently lined up the twelve new heads with the thirteen severed heads already there.

Young Hoiss stood in the center of the deck, staring at them and counting each one on his fingers. It took him some time, but finally he whirled around, wild-eyed, and said, "That's not all of them! There's more!"

"There's no one left alive," I yelled at them.

"Where's the dagger maker's head?" demanded Hoiss. "It isn't there."

"You're right," said Opoots. "His head is not with all the others."

"He must be down there among the hammocks where the others used to take us," said one of the slave girls, who was trembling and weeping and had turned her face away so she would not have to see the shipsmen's heads.

Perhaps because Maquina was now standing staring at him, old Matla shouted at his son, "Forget about the dagger maker. There's been too much killing here. Look at all those heads— heads that had to pay for your one damned dagger."

Matla's son ran toward the hold, almost butting into Maquina, who blocked his path. Maquina did not draw his knife. He did not need to. Hoiss let his dagger fall clattering to the deck as he leapt backward, for he greatly feared the look upon Maquina's face.

My brother-in-law reached out and slammed the hatch closed and stood upon it. "Don't you dare to try and harm him! If that dagger maker is still alive, he's mine," he bellowed.

"It's too late," I told him. "They've already harmed him. Someone hit him with the cook's ax and broke in his skull. He's dead."

"Who did that? Who killed him?" Maquina demanded. He was trembling from head to foot with anger.

Although I knew, I did not answer him, for if my brother-in-law killed that highborn person's son in retaliation, it would tear our village to pieces, setting blood relations feuding violently against one another.

"Never mind," Maquina said. "I'll find that out in other ways. Who will come and stand with me?"

I strode to his side, as did Red Tongue, and I was not surprised to see old Matla come immediately and join us. He too was thinking of his Whale house and our village. This quick vengeful killing by the young had shaken us older men. We felt a need to stand together against these cold-eyed children.

The ones who had done the killing were wondering when they would get the chance to wash the blood off their feet and legs and arms and hands, wondering what their fathers and their mothers and their young wives would say to them when they got home.

"We four are going to open up this lid," Maquina said as we stood down off the hatch. "If any one of you comes one step nearer than you are, we'll kill you. Do you understand me?"

No one answered.

We raised the heavy hatch cover. It was pitch black below and quiet as a grave. Maquina nodded to me, and I climbed carefully down the ladder. The blood on the steps was turning sticky.

My bare foot touched the dagger maker's hair. He was lying at the bottom, crumpled over in a way no living human would ever choose to lie. I shook him gently and was surprised to hear him moan. I propped him up from behind and locked my arms around him. His head lolled lifelessly against my chest. I could lift his weight, but I knew that I could never carry his body up those slippery stairs alone.

"Matla!" I called. "Will you help me?"

In a moment he came climbing down the stairs. Old Matla is easily the strongest man in Wolf Town. He got his left arm around the dagger maker's legs and his powerful right arm on the ladder. Together we eased him up out of the hold and laid him gently on the deck.

I believe that every one of those young killers was taken aback by the sorrowful sight they saw before them. The dagger maker's forehead was split wide open, and his face was pale as death. His whole limp body was soaked from head to foot with blood. We could hear an irregular gargling in his throat. His chest heaved slowly as he struggled hard to keep his life.

"It's too bad," old Matla said, as he looked at all the young men. "Why did you have to kill him too?"

Hoiss stepped forward and peered down at Jon Jay. "He's not dead yet!" said Matla's son. "But I and all the others here, we'll take care of that!"

 OLD MATLA slapped the dagger out of Hoiss's hand. "You shut your mouth," his father warned him.

Maquina frowned fiercely at Hoiss. "Get me some fresh water so that I can wipe the blood off his face," Maquina ordered, then watched to see how quickly this new leader of the young men would obey him.

One of the slave girls from our Eagle house started to run back to the cookhouse to do Maquina's bidding, but Maquina shouted, "Not you! I ordered him to do it."

Hoiss hesitated for only a moment before he strode off to the cookhouse and returned with water and a rag. Maquina took it from him and bathed the dagger maker's wound himself. Jon Jay's right eye was puffed out and swollen closed. His bloodshot left eye observed us with suspicion.

"Go down into the captain's cabin," Maquina said to Red Tongue, "and bring up that tobacco box, and tear a longer rag that I can tie around this poor man's head."

Red Tongue came back quickly with several large leaves of dried tobacco, which we know will quickly stanch most bleeding. Maquina laid three leaves over the long wound, a deep gash running from the dagger maker's hairline to his eyebrow. By tightly binding a calico rag, Maquina drew the edges of the wound together.

"He should be paddled in to shore," said Red Tongue. "The women could take care of him."

"I want a healing song sung over him. He needs to be away from these, these . . ." Maquina searched for a word that would aim all his anger at these murderous young paddlers.

We Wolf Town people do not like to let a wounded man lie still. We believe the worst thing is for them to lose the feeling that they are alive. Red Tongue and I took the young dagger

maker under the arms and sat him up, and although his head
bled a little on the sides, it did not seep through the tobacco
leaves and rag. I waved my hand before his good left eye.

"*Wauwau*, yooo talk," Maquina called to him. "Speeek
yooo to me, speeek!"

Jon Jay nodded his head painfully and said some of his
own words back to Maquina. He turned his one good eye and
looked at our blood-spattered young men, most of whom were
his age. Instead of looking back at Jon Jay, they moved nervously away.

Beyond their legs Jon Jay saw for the first time the line of
shipsmen's severed heads arranged upon the rear deck. His muscles tensed in horror as he recognized the master in the middle.
He strained to see the heads for one long moment, then fell
back and lay against me, sobbing quietly. The tears ran down
from both his eyes.

I put my arms around him, trying to comfort him, thinking
of my son, Toowin.

Maquina started weeping too, a sight that not one of these
young men had ever seen before. That frightened them far more
than all Maquina's threats and raging. I could see some of them
edging away from him toward the net hole that led down to the
canoes, believing that it would be wise to get as far away from
him as possible, but knowing they dare not leave until he commanded them.

Still weeping, Maquina turned to all of them and said, "This
dagger maker, if he lives, is mine. He'll stay in my household,
and he will be harmed by no one." His voice rose in a dangerous way. "Understand—I will kill any one of you who dares to
harm him."

The young men murmured, "Yes, we understand you."

"Now, you two, get those heads off this deck!" Maquina
shouted.

Young Opoots and Atlin pulled up their capes to hide their
faces, fearing the dead men's sightless eyes might somehow recognize them. They let the heads splash into the sea and sink like
stones. Without being told, the paddlers filled buckets and in

the shipsmen's fashion dashed salt water across the bloody deck. The rain that had begun again helped to wash it clean.

As it grew dark, the northwest wind rose, moaning through the high wing bones of the ship. Young Jon Jay shook and trembled. His body was covered in sweat. If we spoke to him, he tried to answer. Yes. He stayed alive.

Red Tongue went and looked at the enormous links in the iron anchor chains in the bow and at the long thick rope hawser still tied from the ship's stern to the nearest tree on the island of Abooksha. A thin, cold rain began to fall with force.

"What are we going to do about this ship?" Red Tongue asked.

My brother-in-law did not answer him, but stood up and looked around. I sensed that for the first time he was thinking, This whole ship underneath our feet belongs to us! No, not to all of us—but to me, Maquina. He would have to make us recognize that fact. Maquina stared down into the dark hatch, allowing his thoughts to move slowly over the mountains of trade goods packed within this vessel's hold.

"We cannot leave this ship out here to rot," Maquina said. "The next foreigners would come on board, then ask us, 'Where are all the shipsmen?' How would we answer them? Could we say some of our young fools just murdered them? Oh, no. We have to try and take this ship to shore," he said. "Do you think it could be taken to the village?"

We looked up into the confusing web of endless lines and mighty masts and crossbones.

"That north wind's blowing straight to Wolf Town," Red Tongue said, "and the tide is high."

"It would be a good time to do it," Maquina answered, "but . . . we don't know how."

"It's getting dark," I said. "If we're going, we should go now."

Maquina knelt down and gently raised the dagger maker's head. He pointed toward Wolf Town. "Jon Jay," he said, "you hear me?"

Jon Jay nodded painfully.

"*Nesika illahee kopa?* Can you take ship . . . over there?" He repeated his words carefully and pointed south toward the village.

The young dagger maker winced, then nodded, saying in a weak voice, "Yes." He struggled to sit up. Maquina and I helped him to his feet.

The north wind was rising, forcing the ship to jerk against its anchor chains. The thick rope to Abooksha had pulled so tight that we could not untie it. Old Matla got the cook's ax and chopped it from the stern. The wind and tide together swung the ship out from the land, causing it to roll beneath our feet with a sickening swaying motion.

Jon Jay was too weak to climb, but he kept pointing up toward the big mainsail. We had all admired the quick and agile way that shipsmen climb when ordered aloft to take in or let out the white wings, for climbing in that way is something that we have never tried to do.

Maquina started shouting like a ship master and pointing upward in the twilight. Because they feared Maquina, those young murderers began climbing awkwardly into the rigging. I could understand why they would be afraid. I myself could scarcely bear to watch them. Oh, how glad I was that Toowin had stayed ashore.

Maquina held his ear close to the dagger maker's mouth, then shouted whatever he imagined to be Jon Jay's orders high up into the wing bones of the ship, bullying our young men on to greater dangers. I waited, looking upward, until my neck grew cramped in the cold night wind.

It took a long time before they managed to loosen one edge of the big mainsail so that it came flopping down. This so surprised young Hoolhool that he yelled and fell down into the water. We had to throw a rope to him. It seemed to take forever before the others were able to crawl all along the largest crossbone and untie the center and then the other side of that huge wing. When they finally released it, the wind was gusting, causing the loose sail to make a rumbling sound like thunder. Jon Jay had to tell them how to catch the ropes and tie them.

The worst part was yet to come. We had no idea how they raised the huge iron anchor. That was something we had never seen them do. Jon Jay pointed at a round wooden thing up near the front of the ship and showed Maquina where the strong wood handles were hidden. Our men jammed these into the holes and then Jon Jay whispered to Maquina, who bellowed, "Mamook! Mamook! Work! Work! Walk around the hat!"

The sixteen paddlers on board and even the slave girls started pushing as they all walked round and round. We could see the anchor chain winding in. The young men snorted out with pleasure because it seemed so easy, and they looked up at the huge sail they had let down and thought, It is not so difficult to be a shipsman. I heard Opoots laugh and boast that he could make this huge bird fly anywhere out on the ocean.

It was easy enough to take in the slack chain. Only then did the truly heavy work begin. Before we got that anchor up, I was pushing, and Matla, Red Tongue, and Maquina were pushing, all of us together using all our might. Jon Jay was holding his poor head in his hands and calling out, "Mamook, mamook. Work, work," as though he was the master of every one of us instead of being Maquina's new-found slave.

At last the huge iron anchor was up and dangling. We had a terrible time holding it, and Maquina could not understand the dagger maker's words, and Jon Jay was much too hurt to help us. Finally, Matla climbed out and made one of our good strong whaling hitches around the anchor, and it held very well.

All of us lay against that turning hat, gasping, sweating in the cold night wind, trying to regain our breath, when suddenly we were aware that the huge ship was drifitng underneath our feet. At first she was moving just a little, but then she was going faster and faster. The square sail bellied out like a gigantic cloud above our heads. It was fortunate for us that the northeast wind continued blowing down the inlet toward our village. But we were still in trouble, for Jon Jay was too weak to guide the ship, and we did not know how to do it.

Jon Jay lay upon the hatch, so exhausted that he could not speak. Maquina and I put our arms around him and raised him up and gently carried him toward the vessel's stern. Jon Jay tried to take hold of the wheel, and we did all we could to help him, but he could not make his arms obey his thoughts. To- gether, we three struggled to keep that ship away from the rock- bound coast, where we could see the white surf breaking. My heart went tum-tum-tum as we fought to keep her going straight toward Wolf Town.

I tried to keep it in my mind that this huge ship with all its cargo did not belong to any foreign master, but to us. I had been beneath this same ship's deck. I tell you it was jammed full of everything that anyone could ever want! There were great bulking canvas bales with who knows what inside, and long, strong wooden boxes, and endless coils of shipsmen's ropes, and barrels and barrels of rum and molasses, sacks of sugar, copper nails, and bars of iron, gunpowder, boxes of lead ball, rolls of blanketing for countless bright-red blankets, blankets, blankets! Imagine! All of it was ours—if we could only safely steer this ship ashore.

Now I could hear the noisy waves and see them breaking white across the reef, which told us that the tide was falling fast. We helped Jon Jay turn the wooden wheel. That kept us clear of the reef. The north wind was strengthening at our backs. To our right we could just make out the faint gray line of beach before our village. We steered toward it. It was coming to us very fast—yes, far too fast!

Beyond the beach, I could see faint streaks of light through the cracks in the cedar planking on our houses. Someone was trying to light a fire in the protection of the rocks. The wind made yellow sparks go showering toward the sodden forest.

"Our Eagle house is there," Maquina called out forcefully as Matla tried to steer the ship toward the Whale house. There was no mistake about it: this ship now belonged entirely to Ma- quina. It was his!

Jon Jay leaned painfully against the wheel, and we helped him head the huge ship straight in at the Eagle house. We were going too fast.

"Baaad! Baaad!" Jon Jay called out.

At that very moment the ship lurched, and I heard a great grinding sound beneath us as we ripped across rocks in our violent thrust against the shore. The northwest wind filling the wing drove us onward. I could hear and feel the ship's bottom tearing open. The surging tide was behind us, and it seemed to me that the ship's great spearlike bow was going to pierce straight through the Eagle house.

At that moment the ship came to a shuddering halt, and we were all flung forward. Instantly two of the three masts broke and collapsed. The mainsail's lower ties were torn loose, and the sail went flapping straight out like a giant's flag.

Men, women, children, came racing out of the houses and saw the black outline of the great ship, with the huge white surf boiling all around it, canted over on our beach. At first they were aghast and silent, then they set up a high wild chanting, their words tumbling over one another with excitement.

"Where are the shipsmen?" a woman screamed up to us.

"Gone! All dead and gone!" the young paddlers hollered back at her, their prideful voices distorted by the howling wind and crashing surf.

A man named Stone Hammer helped me down the tall ship's side. I hurried up the beach, looking for my son, Toowin, and for Kawskaws. They found me in the darkness among all the men and women who were running toward the ship. Children were screaming, dogs were barking, and there was confusion everywhere around us. Women were scolding others, and old men were calling out advice. It was like an unbelievable nightmare that made me want to go back and touch my hand against that monstrous ship to see if it was real.

I did go back, and Red Tongue and I, helped by old Matla and my sister's servants, carried poor Jon Jay up into the dryness of the Eagle house. Fog Woman insisted that we gently place him onto a pile of cedar mats in her apartment. In the firelight we could see that his head was bleeding badly, and he could no longer speak or hear our words. Surely he would die that night. Old Matla's wife, who had been given a healing song at her puberty feast, came over from the Whale house and sang it over the dagger maker.

I felt stunned by all the terrible things that had happened in one day. I went to the Eagle house entrance and peered out. Even in the darkness I could see that the huge mainsail had been torn to tattered ribbons. The northwest wind shrieked in across the inlet, moaning around our houses, bending the giant cedars that stood behind our village. The rain came lashing against the walls, rattling heavy roof boards, as if to warn us that the ghosts of all those poor dead shipsmen would soon enough come sneaking up our beach to wreak their vengeance on us.

When the women fully understood the killings that had happened on the ship, they gathered inside, whispering by their fires, then together they began hammering on the walls with their long yew-wood staffs, trying to frighten off the headless foreigners' ghosts.

After this ear-shattering ritual, some of the greediest Wolf Town folks struggled out across the spray-lashed shore to try and go aboard the stranded vessel. But Maquina and Red Tongue had already sent our house guards out to protect Maquina's treasure ship, which now lay on his beach.

Flinging off his soaking cape, Maquina came naked to us where the dagger maker lay. Fog Woman and her female servants were crowded round Jon Jay, warning all others away. Red Tongue and Matla had both cautioned them that some vengeful young fool might try to come and stick a knife in him. Maquina helped my sister remove Jon Jay's bandage, lay new tobacco leaves across his wound, and once more bind it tightly.

Toowin squatted by my side and watched them. My son wore a sulky disappointed look upon his face.

"I'm glad you were not out there with us," I said. "All of it was terrible!"

"I'm not glad," Toowin answered. "Why didn't you wake me? I missed everything, sitting around in this house with the women while all the exciting things were going on out there."

I threw a bad look at Toowin. "If you had been there, you

would have stood with Maquina and me and with Matla against those crazy killers."

"How do you know that? I wasn't even there," said Toowin.

I could hear the bitter disappointment in his voice.

"I don't know what I would have done," he said. "But . . . I agree with Hoiss. That half-dead shipsman lying over there . . . if he stays alive, he could cause this village trouble."

"Do you mean to say," I gasped, "that you would go against Maquina and your father?"

"I didn't say that," Toowin sighed. "I'm not talking about you. I'm talking about that shipsman. You and my uncle sound like you're with that foreign shipsman, not with us."

"I'm always with Maquina," I whispered angrily. "And so are you! Don't be a fool!"

Toowin turned down the corners of his mouth and did not answer me.

Next morning as soon as it was light, I rose and looked through my peephole. Yes, it was no dream. The monstrous ship was there. Kawskaws brought me cold white halibut steak that had been steeped in oil the way I like, but I did not even taste it. My thoughts were only on the ship that lay upon our beach.

There were small crowds of Eagle house families gathered around our eight fires, and I could hear a low but steady hum of voices.

"Is Maquina awake?"

"No," said Kawskaws, looking over into the apartment across from ours. "He's still asleep."

"You go and wake up my sister and tell her I said she should shake him, wake him, and tell him that the two of us should talk about the things that are inside the ship before all the other house chiefs come to demand their share."

I ate the last of the halibut as I watched Maquina rise, pull his faded blanket around him, and stumble down to our fire. I waited until I thought him properly awake before offering my advice. "Share what's in the belly of the ship with all the other houses." I said that because I had not liked the way those young idiots had acted on their own, and it was important to keep the peace in Wolf Town.

The violent storm the night before had blown our cove clear of fog. Low-flying clouds scudded down the north inlet or were torn to pieces by the updrafts from the mountains.

In spite of the previous night's excitement, my sister had once more regained full control of the Eagle house. I could hear her commanding our slaves to pile wood on the fires, instructing them in the proper way to shift the roof boards to better vent the acrid-smelling smoke. All along the house I could see many women bunched around their fire pits preparing food. My sister's servants had a huge fish soup boiling in an iron trade pot and dozens of large salmon already steaming in her cedar boxes, for she was concerned that we had been without food since all this trouble happened. Fog Woman herself, appalled at the appearance of the dagger maker, knelt gently to wipe away the blood that was once more trickling from his wound. She was making soft affectionate sounds as though he were a newborn child.

In the evening, my sister came and spoke to me again. "I have heard from others what happened out there on the ship," she said to me. "I guess it wasn't Matla's fault or yours. If there is one thing that disturbs me, it is that gang of cocksure paddlers from the Whale house—yes, and this house, too. They'll be the death of all of us," she said in an angry, rising voice. "My husband's far too easy with them. Imagine those louts murdering all those shipsmen without his or my approval!"

"Silence, woman!" Maquina growled as he strode toward us down the center of his house. "You'll see how little we will give those miserable dagger slashers when it comes to sharing those trade goods."

My sister sniffed, but did not choose to answer him.

On this, the second night after we had brought the ship onto our beach, I looked across the fire and saw my sister spread a fresh-made cedar mat. With her women she eased the dagger maker onto it and carefully covered him with a warm Salish

Matla the whale
house chief sits
upon his box.

dog-hair blanket. Maquina stretched out in front of Jon Jay to make sure he was protected. Fog Woman lay down beside her husband and spread a pair of new red blankets over both of them.

The bold girls who always laid tightly packed around Maquina when my sister was away had disappeared. They said later that they were more than grateful not to be in Maquina's bed on that night, for they had heard from our young men that if the dagger maker was not dead, they planned to kill him before morning. The girls scorned the paddlers, saying they would not have the courage to go against Maquina. What dangerous talk!

I could hear those girls whispering to a young guard in our household before they settled down in an empty apartment and waited, sitting up in the darkness to see what was going to happen. I stayed by our fire until dawn, which may have prevented Hoiss's paddlers from carrying out their threat.

Maquina was not yet awake when I later roused myself and went down to the fire again. Fog Woman had been there ever since I had left at first light, seeing that the food was being properly prepared.

She took some steamed otter hams up to the young dagger maker, but still he would scarcely eat.

"He needs those little black mussels to make him well," I told my sister. "I'll send Kawskaws to get them, and Toowin can go with her. He knows just where to find them."

For five days the young dagger maker remained too sick to go out onto the ship that still lay like a huge dead whale upon our beach. Maquina would let none of the young men aboard. Having long since lost his claim, old Matla, like the other house chiefs—all men of reason—supported Maquina in that. But Hoiss and the paddlers, still feeling the ship was theirs, became so angry that they would not even look at us.

With each strong tide, more sand and gravel built up around the broken ship's hull. I do not believe that I would have ever grown used to the sight of that foreign hulk embedded in our sands. The bleached and broken masts were angled over like partly fallen trees, and almost every wing bone had been driven at odd angles by the violent jerking that had torn her bottom open. Her sails now hung in tattered ruins. Many of the countless lines were cut and hung dangling or lay like twisted lengths of coarse brown seaweed strewn across her deck. The ship that had once seemed so dangerously alive and vital now lay dead.

To our great surprise, on the sixth morning Maquina rose while others slept and woke me and Red Tongue, and sent for old Matla, who was now our best supporter. He told me to wake Toowin, whom he allowed to follow us. Together we went cautiously inside the ship, knowing that it must be alive with foreign ghosts.

Sand Shark, the old man who was chief of the Thunder house, followed us like a trembling shadow, though he had not been invited. That's what greed does to a human. Sand Shark, who had lost one eye to a sharp paddle in a close canoe fight, was then so frail and ancient that he had to be assisted by his grandsons. The farthest he ever ventured from his sleeping place was to the box beside the fire pit in his house. But that morning the very thought of the treasures hidden in the belly of this ship caused him to come staggering after us. Sand Shark knew how important it would be for him to view the trade goods if he ever hoped to have the Thunder house lay claim to any portion of them. The trembling chief looked ready to fall down when Maquina, ignoring him, pushed back the hatch. The old man had to call out to both of his young grandsons to help him down the ladder.

It was dark down there, a haunted place where one would never go except for greed. Cautiously Maquina and Red Tongue produced a tinder box which they blew into flames. They lit four torches that had been soaked in seal oil. These did not smoke or sputter but gave off an even yellowish light.

In the shadows we could see huge piles of boxes all around us. There was a lot of water in the hold, more than knee deep in many places, but of course that didn't stop the old Sand Shark, aided by his grandsons, from following us. He was into everything.

"What's this? What's that?" he called out. "I want to know what's in every one of them!" old Sand Shark croaked.

"Open one up for him," Maquina ordered.

Matla took the cook's small ax and chopped down hard into a crack in one of the tight-nailed boxes. With his great strength, he easily pried it open.

"*Sukwalal!* Muskets!" Matla exclaimed, pulling a long one out for us to see. "This whole box is packed full of greasy muskets. New ones!"

"I want them," said Sand Shark. "They can be a part of my share."

"What's in the next box?" said Maquina, ignoring the Thunder house chief.

"*Weght sukwalal!* More muskets!" Matla shouted as he pried it open.

Maquina pointed to another box far away from the first two, and Matla said, "*Weght weght sukwalal!* More and more muskets! This ship is full of muskets," Sand Shark gasped. "I want my honest share of them."

"*Kloshe!*" Maquina whispered to me. "Good! I believe that all of these are musket boxes. How many in each box?"

Matla counted on his fingers. "*Hyo-hyo-mooh.* Ten and ten and four."

"I never knew there were so many guns in all this world," Maquina sighed. "Can you imagine how many sea otter skins we will get when I trade these with the people living north and south of here?"

Like me, Toowin just stood speechless, staring at the impossible piles of treasure.

With his short knife Maquina sliced open a big canvas-covered bale, and out of it bulged fathoms of rich red wool blanket cloth.

"Oh, look at that," said Matla. "Wait until the women know how many blankets we have here!"

"What's in those barrels?" I asked Maquina.

He tipped one and said, "*Hyas till.* Greatly heavy. No rum in these barrels. Break them open."

The powerful Matla was ready with the dead cook's ax. "Copper nails!" he shouted. "*Ikt tukamonuk!* Hundreds and hundreds of big copper nails."

"And those barrels over there?" Maquina asked.

Matla moved to examine them. "I'm not hitting these with an ax," he said, and laughed with glee. "Listen, I believe these have got rum inside them. *Ikt*, one. *Inokst*, two, *llone*, three." He counted on his fingers up to ten. "*Kwaist!* Ten!" And then he started again until he reached twenty. "*Moskt tatollelums*, twenty! And maybe many more. Did you ever believe the shipsmen would have that much rum?"

"Never," Maquina said. "They were mostly very mean about giving out the rum." He looked worried. "And the molasses?" he asked. "I hope they didn't use up all the molasses."

"They must have gunpowder," said I. "Powder and shot, lead bullets. We should find all those soon."

But search as we did, past sacks of flour and useless, sickening white salt and half a hundred ghastly stinking wheels of pale dead cheese, we could not find any powder or shot. We all knew that was very, very bad.

"*Hyas peshak!*" Red Tongue said as a joke, using the Chinook we use when speaking with the foreigners or any of the other tribes who cannot understand our language on this coast.

I was so excited by the impossible amount of all this treasure spread before us that for a time the dreadful slaughter of the shipsmen went completely from my mind.

I was passing by the huge pile of canvas bales that held the blanketing when suddenly I saw a shadow, perhaps, that jerked away beyond my sight. I turned and saw that Matla was staring in the same direction.

"What was that?" I asked him.

"I don't know," he answered as we quickly drew our daggers from their sheaths.

I turned around nervously to Matla and said, "I am feeling the nearness of the souls of those poor headless men. Their heaviness is pressing in on me."

Maquina shuddered and said, "I feel them everywhere."

"What I saw was real," Matla whispered to me.

"Probably the shadow of a ship's rat," Red Tongue said, and shuddered. "I hate rats."

"There is food down here and rats," I said. "Yes, I can smell them. Let's get out of here and send others to bring all these things onto the beach."

"Follow me," Maquina said. "I'm leaving."

Some distance behind us I could see other lights come wavering toward us. The first torch was held high by Hoiss. A dozen young men followed him.

"Who told you to come down here?" Matla called out to his son.

When Hoiss did not answer his father, Matla bellowed, "Don't touch a single thing inside this ship unless Maquina tells you to. Never mind this pile of trade goods. I wish it wasn't here," he called out to his son. "Every man and woman and newborn child is going to suffer because the lot of you did such a stupid thing. You'll see. What do you think the foreigners are going to do when they see this giant bird of theirs lying dead, half-buried on our beach, with only one of their shipsmen left alive? The foreigners will be fighting mad. You'll see when they start firing their cannons, blowing our houses into flying splinters."

"That one shipsman who is left alive," Hoiss shouted to his father, "he's the one who will tell the other foreigners everything that happened. He is the one who must be killed."

It was a good thing that Maquina did not hear those words, for he and Red Tongue had already left the ship.

I held back with Matla, for I was not sure whether Toowin was still down there. I waited in a shadowy part of the hold by myself, watching young Hoiss and Atlin and Opoots and the others with their oil-soaked torches rooting boldly through the boxes and the barrels and bales as though they had a right to be there and to have a full share of this loot. Even as I watched them, they separated, prying and hacking into everything. Young Hoiss must have seen or heard something that disturbed him, for he too had drawn his dagger and held his torch out cautiously before him as he peered into the shadows. I watched him edging forward through the knee-deep murky water.

Suddenly I blinked my eyes, for I could not believe the tall pale specter of a man that I saw standing in the shadows pressed against the bales. As Hoiss's torchlight caught this ghostly vision, I could make out a hard, square face with short-cropped hair and wildly staring eyes.

Hoiss took one more step forward, and I called out, "There is an evil thing before you!"

Yes, I tried to warn him, but it was too late.

This ghastly figure of a man lunged out at Hoiss. One of its huge square hands gripped him by the right wrist and twisted downward till Hoiss screamed and dropped his dagger. The other hand reached up and grasped Hoiss's left hand and, bending it backward, forced the flaming torch into his groin. Suddenly this wide-shouldered monster with inhuman strength flung the powerful young Hoiss down into the dark water and stamped on him.

In a moment, six of Hoiss's companions flung themselves at his attacker. Smothering him against the bales, they pinned his powerful arms behind his back and held their dagger points against his belly, chest, and throat. It took all their strength to force him to his knees.

"It's a shipsman! A live shipsman!" Hoiss gasped as he struggled to regain his feet. "Hurry," he shouted at them. "A dagger—I need a dagger now!"

 WITH his knife lost in the dark swirling water, Hoiss was helpless. He screamed with rage, begging for a dagger.

"Don't you dare harm him!" I bellowed at Matla's son.

I do not think those mere words of mine prevented another killing. It was their fear of Maquina that caused the others to refuse to loan Hoiss a knife.

I could scarcely believe what I saw before me—another white man still alive. I leaned forward in the trembling torchlight and peered at that wild kneeling creature. I reached out and touched him to make certain he was real. "Do any of you remember seeing him before?" I asked.

"I do," Opoots said. "Look at his arms. He has those same blue tattoos. He is the one who sews tears in the sails."

"I'm going to kill him!" Hoiss screamed as he bent searching for his dagger in the knee-deep water. "Cousin, lend me your knife!" he called out in a pleading voice to my son, Toowin, who to my horror I saw splashing toward Hoiss, offering him his dagger.

"Don't you dare!" I growled at Toowin. "Maquina will decide about that shipsman, not any one of you!" I yelled. "Take him to the Eagle house."

"Your father's right," said Atlin, thrusting himself between Hoiss and Toowin, sounding for the first time like my favorite nephew, which he is.

Hoiss was bent double, soothing his scorched groin with his left hand and holding out his right hand, still begging Toowin for his dagger. I could hear the powerful shipsman gasping on his knees, pinned by five men tight against the bales. My thought was, Let's get everyone out of here while this last foreigner is still alive.

"Take that shipsman to Maquina," I demanded. "Don't any

of you dare to stab him. Remember, I am close behind," I warned them. "My eyes and Atlin's are watching every one of you."

My nephew, Atlin, frowned at me, annoyed, I suppose, that I had made him seem to side with me against his friends. Toowin splashed past and walked near the paddlers, not wishing to be seen too close to me, his father.

I moved through the water as noisily as I could to remind them constantly that I was at their back. In this way I forced Hoiss's paddlers to leave the ship with their new-found captive unharmed except for one deep cut across his nose. My task in calming them was made difficult by their prisoner, who was strong and unruly and did not seem to care about his life. They had bound his hands behind his back, yet whenever one of them came near him, he made savage sounds within his throat and kicked out violently with his right foot.

I yelled at him to stop, but he would not or could not understand what I was saying. Can you believe that any human with both wrists tied behind his back would be so recklessly insane as to kick at those young hotheads, who already had their daggers drawn and were aching for an excuse to take his life?

I sighed with relief when we finally got that tattooed man onto the beach. At least I could tell Maquina he was still alive when I got him into the light of day. When they saw him, women and children came rushing around us. They stared in disbelief at this tall, burly white captive, his upper clothing torn away, who walked among us ramrod straight.

Hoiss was trying to herd his followers toward his father's Whale house, where he certainly would have killed this man or claimed him as their slave.

"Take him to the Eagle house," I commanded. But even then I had to grab Hoiss by the arm and force them all to turn in that direction.

This made Hoiss so angry that he dashed into his father's house and leapt out a moment later to confront me with a dagger in his hand, so that it looked for a moment as though I might have to perform a violent trick I know to defend myself, one I myself did not wish to do to Matla's foolish son. Toowin told me later that the two of us, glowering while standing nose to nose, were a wild sight to behold. Finally Hoiss wisely turned away.

But my troubles were not over. I had to help those reluctant paddlers push the strong man through the entrance to the Eagle house. Finally they did my bidding with such force that our prisoner stumbled to his knees. In an instant, he was up again, roaring and cursing and trying like a mountain goat to butt them with his head.

Maquina snatched up the heavy whalebone club that was called the widow maker and rushed halfway down the Eagle house. "How dare you come into my house with your knives drawn from their sheaths!" Maquina roared at Hoiss and all the others.

I watched with interest as they hung their heads and quickly hid their daggers underneath their garments or tossed them outside the entrance.

"They found this white man hiding in the ship," I told Maquina. "I said you were the only one who would decide what should be done with him."

The dagger maker, who had been lying on a mat near Maquina's sleeping place, rose painfully. Holding his bandaged head and walking sideways like a crab, he staggered toward us. The right side of his whole swollen face was blue and greenish-black in color, and his right eye was still partly closed.

Maquina looked at Jon Jay. "Who? *Klatsta?* Who is this man?" he asked.

The young dagger maker pointed to the thick leather needle pusher on the prisoner's belt and made a sewing motion with his hands.

"*Mamock tipshin*, sail sewer," Maquina said, using the Chinook words instead of ours.

Then Jon Jay touched the deep cut on the big man's nose, and in a soft voice spoke rapidly to him. The tall man's only answer was to nod his head.

Jon Jay said, "Thompson," and he said again, more carefully, "Good man—his name, Thompson."

Maquina thought a moment and then called out to all those listening, "See this new man . . . Tom Sin . . . He, too, belongs to me. Anyone harming these two shipsmen will become an enemy to me. You tell all the others what I say. *These two men . . . belong . . . to me.*"

Everyone who lived inside our Eagle house answered loudly, *"Kloshe, Tyee, kloshe,"* showing the others they approved.

The young men from the other houses did not answer him.

Maquina showed his teeth as he shouted at them. "Did you not hear me?" and he took the whalebone club in both his hands.

Only then did they answer. *"Nawitka! Ah-ah!* Yes, indeed!"

Maquina told me to cut the cords that bound the big man's wrists and ordered a servant woman and Jon Jay to lead the new man to our fire and feed him. Maquina did not offer this sullen giant of a man a place to sleep in his apartment, nor did I, for we both felt some fear of him. That night and later Maquina had him sleep in Beaver Seeker's household. Beaver Seeker was a respected whale hunter, a silent man whom Maquina trusted very well.

It is only fair to tell you that, much as we wanted to, we never learned to know or love this unsmiling strong man even one small part as well as we came to cherish and admire the dagger maker. Even with his painful head and half-closed eye, Jon Jay from the start would try to smile at us and understand our words and ways. As if that was not enough, we soon discovered that he could whistle far more tunefully than the birds. But Tom Sin, this new, grim-faced foreigner in his middle age, was not at all like Jon Jay. He did not trust us and seemed disdainful of our women and our children. He wrinkled his nose at the rich smoked-fish smell inside our houses. There was little that he liked. I never imagined I would see a male slave who would dare to go openly against his master and remain alive. Well, this man, Tom Sin, did that—not once but many times. Maquina admired bravery and courage above all other things, and this new man had both those qualities in incredible abundance—so much that I myself did not believe he would survive.

One of the Whale house slaves told Kawskaws that young Hoiss rose in his father's house and made a warning speech against this large and surly foreigner. Hoiss was the first to call Tom Sin *Mamook Pukpuk*, fist fighter. A few here continued to call him that until the very end.

The removal of the trade goods from the stranded ship began in earnest about midmorning on the seventh day after it was run aground. Maquina, Man Frog, Long Claws, and I from the Eagle house, Matla from the Whale house, and Sand Shark from the Thunder house, we were all right in the middle of everything, giving separate orders and sometimes arguing with one another, each trying to make certain that we got more than our share of the booty. Maquina had Jon Jay and the big heavy-fisted Tom Sin, standing on either side of him, as advisers. Both these shipsmen were armed with a pair of pistols tucked into their belts and a navy cutlass that had been taken from the master's cabin. There was little about those two foreigners that would make you think them slaves. They knew that Maquina was their best protector, and so they carefully guarded him.

When we were down in the hold, those whites advised Maquina as to exactly which barrels and bales and boxes he should take for himself and for the Eagle house. Jon Jay could do this more quickly than Tom Sin by studying the marks on the outside instead of opening every one of them. They also told Maquina which barrels and bales and boxes he would not want and should therefore try to push off on to other unsuspecting house chiefs. Knowing exactly which to choose gave Maquina a very great advantage. For the others there were many difficult decisions to be made, and that took time.

Except for the sputtering light thrown by our pine torches, it was pitch black down inside the ship's hold. Both Tom Sin and the dagger maker became nervous and started shouting boldly when anyone with torches went near the barrels of gunpowder, which they had reluctantly showed to us. Oh, yes, there were many, many good-sized casks of powder and countless smaller boxes full of lead shot of several different sizes.

The salt water had done some damage to many bales and boxes, seeping into the wreckage as it rose and fell on every tide. Maquina tried to urge old Sand Shark and Matla and the chiefs of half a dozen other households to take the salt-soaked bales and boxes, because, he argued, the good things in the ship rightly belonged to him.

The young paddlers from the other houses still complained when they heard that. "It was us, not you, who did the killing!"

"A fair share of all these things belongs to us," said Matla's son.

Maquina pretended not to hear him.

Hoiss grew bolder. "If you, *Tyee*, had been there," Hoiss said, "you say you would have tried to stop us. If that had happened, all this cargo would have sailed away."

Maquina would never have tolerated such insults before this ship was taken. But so eager was he to carry off much more than his share of all this loot that he paid only slight attention to the hotheaded grumblings of the younger men. Ignoring them seemed to me a truly dangerous thing for him to do.

All that day there was nothing but a steady stream of men, women, children, slaves, every one of them straining, hauling, carrying the unevenly divided treasure off to various houses. As usual, some of the women were the hardest workers of them all.

That night we in the Eagle house were so busy and excited by our enormous share of the treasure that we forgot to open the molasses or the rum. Young Jon Jay and my Kawskaws did the counting, for those two proved to be best at that. Kawskaws made her curious marks upon a board, and Jon Jay made others that we could not understand. Fog Woman helped both of them with her accurate, quick finger counting. Imagine three very different counting systems that in the end came out exactly the same!

Can you believe me when I tell you that after several days of hard work, that ship's hull was no more than half unloaded? By three good and careful counts, we had gathered into the Eagle house three thousand seven hundred and twenty fathoms of beautiful red and not-so-beautiful blue wool blanketing, all new and still in rolls, uncut. We had six hundred and forty-eight looking-glasses, lovely ones, some set in shiny iron and some in bright reddish-painted wood. We had nine good-sized wooden barrels all filled with beads of many colors. When the women saw those, they slapped their breasts, and some fell down, overcome with sheer delight. We had six large wood boxes filled with folding iron knives having antler handles and brass ends. These we did not really admire, but they made good presents for the children. We had seventeen big barrels with liquid in them. The women hoped that they would all contain molasses, but most men said they hoped for rum. That made the women fuss and scowl at us.

Best of all, Jon Jay and Kawskaws assured Maquina that we now had eight hundred and forty-two new muskets. Can you imagine that? Some were short sea muskets of a kind that hold a dagger on the end for fighting, and some were bell-mouthed scatter guns. Two hundred others were long-barreled swan guns. There was none so nice, of course, as that beautiful double-barreled musket that had started all the trouble between Maquina and the poor dead master. I tried not to think of him again for fear his ghost would come and stand moaning near our entrance after dark. Along with all those muskets, our share was sixteen barrels of gunpowder, which Jon Jay and the big man, Tom Sin, had insisted that we set apart in the farthest corner of the house and protect with a wall of dampened sail-cloth against any chance of fire. Besides all these wonderful things, we had three big boxes filled with bright new sharp-edged cutlasses, thirty and six in each, the kind that highborn shipsmen carry, with blades as long as a woman's leg, curved like the thin bright edge of the reborn moon.

Maquina roared with pleasure, as did I, when we opened three of the last iron-bound boxes and found inside them four and twenty flintlock pistols. Big, strong, new ones they were, with brass butts and brass-tipped ramrods and fat, well-shaped handles made of very pretty hardwood.

Maquina and I, and Red Tongue too, had all been wildly

angry at those young men for slaughtering the ship's crew. But slowly our worst feeling subsided. Soon I found myself forgetting that bloody moment of slaughter on the ship's deck. Yes, we spoke of nothing now except the vastness of this treasure that lay spread out before us: muskets, looking-glasses, beads, pistols, molasses, blanketing, bolts of brightest calico, rum, nails, and swords—everything any man could ever wish for—all arranged by our delighted women in neat straight rows or fan shapes.

It seemed impossible to us that there could be so much wealth in all the world. I went to the Whale house and to the Thunder house and all the other houses just to feast my eyes on all their loot spread out in similar array. I could see that it had been unevenly divided—they had all the hammers and we had all the nails! But nevertheless it was easy to see that Jon Jay and Tom Sin had advised us splendidly. The other houses, in their hurry, had chosen boxes of small fish hooks that were too small, rusting iron scissors, moldy calico cloth, round sacks full of useless mildewed rope, and, to our delight, those dreadful blocks of cheese, while we in the Eagle house had almost all the dry boxes full of muskets, bolts of blanketing, barrels of rum and gunpowder—all untouched by salty water. We in the Eagle house were in no way envious of the others' share.

We were only laying plans, hoping to do as well, when we started next day to unload the last half. Old Matla, his son, and others may have had bad feelings, but they were perhaps afraid to reveal them within Maquina's hearing. I myself believe the reason they were silent was because Maquina walked everywhere carrying that now repaired and beautiful double-barreled musket. He went aboard the ship flanked by Jon Jay and the threatening-looking Tom Sin. Who would have dared attack my brother-in-law?

Maquina ordered his Eagle house men to unchain two of the ship's cannons and drag them up onto our beach. These Maquina had placed one on each side of the Eagle house, their round iron mouths gaping menacingly toward the sea. He also ordered them to remove the dagger maker's forge and all his tools from the ship onto the shore. Meanwhile, Jon Jay and Tom Sin went down into the master's cabin. I did not go with them, for it was a gloomy place and I had a gnawing fear that we would meet a headless gang of blood-soaked ghosts. But Jon Jay was not afraid. He came up carrying a small flat wooden box that made Maquina suspicious until the dagger maker opened it and showed us all that it contained. It had nothing but a bunch of thin white skins sewn between two black boards, a little bottle full of dark liquid of the kind that squid shoot out, and several blue-stained goose quills. Maquina laughed and said Jon Jay was welcome to them. I did not know it at that time, but the innocent-looking items in that box were far more dangerous than all the gunpowder that a dozen ships could carry.

On the eleventh night, to celebrate our great good fortune, Maquina invited all the Wolf Town people to a feast, which began with our eating old ship's bread and some vile-tasting salted meats, which, like all the dreadful cheese, we flung out to the dogs. After that we satisfied ourselves with molasses and our own delicious hot smoked salmon lightly slicked with the precious oil from small pressed fish. There is nothing better-tasting in this world than well-slicked salmon—except, perhaps, that poor dead black man's lovely suga puddee.

I watched Jon Jay gladly cast aside his hard cracked bread in favor of our salmon, but Tom Sin continued chewing at it, always with his back half turned as though he did not wish to see us. When the two foreigners were filled with food, they lay back, whispering to each other. I know they must have thought of us as persons very superior to themselves, clever in so many ways. Still, I wondered what they were saying together, what plans, if any, they were hatching in their heads.

Next day at dawn, I saw the big man go quietly to the edge of Maquina's apartment and wake Jon Jay. Together they went out wandering. Curiosity made me rise and follow them along our beach just as the morning fog was lifting.

The two foreigners stopped and examined the white boat that we had taken from the ship, a boat with a small sail that could be handled by two persons. They found a water barrel that had been left behind by other shipsmen, rinsed it carefully, then filled it with fresh clear water from the little falls and hid it in the white boat. They stood whispering together. Could they be thinking of escape? I thought not, for the only way they might do that would be to go out onto the ocean. Even in their white boat with its sail, that would be a very foolish thing to do.

Maquina told me on the morning of the following day that he had had a dream that other shipsmen had come to seek revenge. That warning drove him into sudden action. Without waiting until everything was unloaded, he sent out every active Eagle house man to mutilate the ship. That's the way Maquina acts. He is a nervous and impetuous man. He ordered us to use cutlasses and daggers, to slash away all the rigging and the lines. That made it easier to bring down the two tall broken masts. The one standing mast and the long bow spear we planned to cut off with iron tools brought up from the ship's belly. One was a long-bladed two-man saw with straight rows of sharklike teeth, which we had seen the shipsmen use on shore to bring down trees. Atlin and Skag got on either end of this strange tool, and imitating the shipsmen's forward and backward motions, they started on the mast. It wasn't easy. They kept buckling the saw blade, and laughing at themselves, they would begin making ragged new cuts. You could see that it would take at least a day or more. Finally, Tom Sin snatched the saw away from them in disgust and got Jon Jay to take the other end. They spit on their hands and, together, made that saw go smoothly, biting through the dry wood so quickly that when the mast fell, it surprised us all and would have killed poor Man Frog if he had not hopped away. Grim-faced, Tom Sin and Jon Jay quickly cut the front and rear masts into pieces and sawed off the bow spear.

Matla tried desperately to chop away the steering wheel with a broad-bladed ax that he had found belowdecks. When he could not do this, he unpinned the rudder, causing it to fall and lie useless beside the ship. That made him feel a little better. What had been a tall ship now looked like nothing but the black and rotting carcass of a whale half-buried on our beach.

Maquina had the young men go out in three canoes and cut large masses of kelp. They towed these in and tied them over the hull so that seen from the sea, what remained of the ship appeared to be nothing but a pile of weed-covered rocks. "There," he said to me. "We will use the belly of that ship as our storehouse for all those things that are left inside."

As proof of how truly useful dreams can be to warn a human of the things that are to happen, only a few evenings later two foreign ships came bearing up the sound toward us. Anyone could see that they were eager to anchor near our village.

"There they are! The dream ships!" Maquina shouted, and he flew into utter panic. I had never seen my brother-in-law in such anguish and distress.

"Siam," he shouted to me, "what am I going to do?"

"Pile everyone into the canoes," I said. "Let's fade away, let's disappear. We can go up into the Hisnitt Inlet where no ship would dare to follow, set up our summer fishing camps at Coptee a little early. Come on, let's leave this murderous, haunted place!"

"We can't do that," he shouted. "What would we do with all the treasure that is still in the belly of the ship and stacked up in the houses?"

"Leave everything!" I advised him. "Run now and save our lives."

Maquina thought about that for a moment, and then he laughed at me. "This is my place, my village. I'm not going to run away and hide from any miserable shipsmen. Let them learn to hide from me. Hurry, someone load the guns!" he shouted, imitating the bold gestures of the ship masters we had seen.

Maquina got first twenty and then more than forty men down onto our beach, all carrying scatter guns and muskets, which he ordered Tom Sin and the dagger maker to help us load. The sailmaker looked like he wanted to kill every one of us, but young Jon Jay understood that they dared not refuse Maquina. He laughed and tried to cheer Tom Sin. The dagger maker even sang a little as he underloaded all the muskets. I myself believed that he was on the way to being one of us completely.

When all our guns were primed, Maquina took a pair of pistols from their boxes and had Jon Jay load them for him. Then Tom Sin charged another pair for me and loaded two more for himself and Jon Jay. As I looked at our brave musketmen lined along the village beach and felt the solid weight of those two pistols in my hands, I myself believed that we could fight off any enemy who came to us from land or sea or sky.

It was almost dark when the first ship drew so close that we could hear harsh orders being shouted on the deck and see boys scrambling upward in the rigging as they started to take in their sails not far off our beach. When he saw that, Maquina was the first to fire both his pistols out toward them. *Poof, bang!* Then I fired mine. *Poof, bang!* What a lovely kick and yellow stink of gunsmoke! I let out a triumphant yelp of pleasure. This was war!

Taking that as their signal, more than forty of our warriors and paddlers started firing off their pieces and letting out the wildest whoops we use when raiding or for frightening off our enemies' attacks. The sun had sunk into the ocean, and against the darkness of the forest, the incoming shipsmen could see our muskets flashing all along the beach and the heavy leaden balls skipping across the water but falling short of them. What a sight that was for us—and a shocking surprise for them. We could hear them cursing us across the water. "Bloody fuugging Injuns!" they hollered. We shouted far worse insults back at them.

My brother-in-law loudly ordered the sailmaker to load and fire both cannons. The big man frowned and stubbornly refused to charge the heavy guns with ball. Finally he did take up the smoking fuse and set one cannon off. Jon Jay fired the other. Each made such a tremendous flash and ring of smoke and echoing *Boom! Boom! Boom!* that most of our women and children fell down flat—the mothers in stark terror, the children in surprised delight.

The awful thunder of our cannons and the exploding noise of our second round of musket fire must have discouraged those two ships from coming any closer. The nearest master answered us by discharging three cannonballs and two lengths of chain shot, which we heard go smashing harmlessly through the branches of the cedar trees not far beyond our houses. After that, those vessels turned and fled just as darkness fell.

What a wonderful bit of fighting that had been! A really different style of fighting, I told Toowin, but with no serious losses among ourselves or them. After such an exciting evening, I found it difficult to go to sleep. I told Toowin as we laid down on our mats that white men's ships quite often journey two together.

"Why is that?" he asked me.

"Ship's talkers have told us it is because any good-sized vessel likes to have some company when it is sailing far away in unknown waters. If one ship alone is caught by storms or tides and is driven onto reefs, then all aboard are lost. But when two ships travel together, there is always a chance of one ship rescuing the other's crew if they are wrecked, and even salvaging the trade goods from within its belly."

"That sounds right to me," said Toowin.

"Well, don't be too quick to accept such reasoning. I myself believe they travel two together for a very different reason. Two ships go together," I warned Toowin, "so that chiefs along this coast dare not attack them. When a ship is traveling alone, it is sometimes possible for reckless ones like Hoiss to carry out some violent trick, and in a moment win a single vessel over. But it is almost impossible to take two of them. Imagine if that grounded ship upon our beach had had a companion vessel anchored not far off its side. When the other shipsmen sensed that there was trouble, they would have turned all their guns against the attackers. Neither Hoiss nor any of those paddlers would have reached our shore alive."

"I never thought of that," said Toowin.

When I awoke next morning, Maquina was already down at the fire pit talking rapidly to Red Tongue. That was unusual, for Maquina was not an early riser. When I went to the fire, I could see that Maquina had already worked himself into a state of great excitement. His jaw muscles were jumping underneath his cheeks, and he was tugging so hard at his mustache that he sometimes winced with pain.

"Oh, yes," I heard him say to Red Tongue, "I know they'll be back! They'll tell other shipsmen there's been bad trouble here, that we fired many guns at them. *And cannons!* They'll ask themselves were we got two *cannons*. When they think about that, they'll come sailing up here all together, firing heavy guns and seeking blood revenge from us. Who told those two shipsmen they could fire my cannons? That spoiled everything. Those captains must certainly know that we have caught a ship!"

Maquina, like all the rest of us, was jumpy for several days. But gradually his nervous feelings faded. Still, even though the ships did not return, Maquina had our treasures carried back and hidden in a forest cave we use for keeping important persons' bones. In there we covered all our treasure with woven cedar mats or repacked them in their grease and boxes, for the rains and dampness on our coast eat iron more quickly than they do the needles fallen from a winter spruce.

Kawskaws helped change the tobacco that was bound to Jon Jay's head. She told me his wound was healing very well. I myself was growing used to seeing those two strangers wandering along our beach or lying near our beds. We were none of us surprised to see the dagger maker squatting by our fire with Tom Sin, both of them staring up in disbelief at our enormous home. We know, of course, that our Eagle house is the largest dwelling in the world. This spring place of ours must have seemed oh, so wonderful to Jon Jay after being cramped up on that ship. He must have wondered at sixteen families living comfortably together under one huge roof.

When Kawskaws asked Jon Jay about his family, he told her that he had a living father but no mother. I was not surprised. Those shipsmen are always hungry for our women because they have no mothers or women of their own.

Jon Jay, like all of us, enjoyed staring up and admiring the thousands of small candlefish spitted through each eye, sus-

pended on wandlike poles between our long roof beams to dry
out slowly in the semidarkness. I hoped that Jon Jay enjoyed as
much as I did the delicate perfume of those delicious little fish.
Our grand way of living seemed so much more spacious and
refined than the miserable, foul-smelling quarters that those men
suffered aboard their ships, not to mention the stale, revolting
food that those shipsmen seemed content to eat. Yes, we knew
that Jon Jay and the sailmaker were truly fortunate to stay with
us and share our good life, even though Tom Sin seemed surly
and unappreciative of these benefits—at least, until after his
troubles with Maquina came.

I told Kawskaws and Toowin that we should all spend more
time with our own thoughts and affairs and less time observing
the strange movements of these two foreign shipsmen. As it
turned out, I was right. There was a greedy fool who lived among
us, a commoner who had taken the name Stone Hammer just
to change his luck. This Stone Hammer, a wanderer who could
not keep a wife, was living off his relatives in the Thunder house.
The simpleton promised a new red blanket and some beads to
a girl if she would let him lie with her. Late one night, when
the tide was high and the moon had sunk behind the trees, Stone
Hammer crept across our beach and climbed aboard the shipwreck, easing past Maquina's sleeping guard. He lowered himself down the hatch and partly closed it after him. He opened a
small tinder box that he had brought with him and blew the
embers into life. With these he lit his oil-soaked torch. Then he
started moving through the knee-deep water, searching among
the shadows for the bolts of blanketing and the casks of colored
beads. He could not find them, and he said later that he was
afraid down there of ghosts or perhaps another living brute like
Tom Sin lurking in the shadows.

What Stone Hammer did find was a large rum barrel with
a horn cup sitting up on top. He didn't know how to open the
barrel. But with a small trade ax that he had brought with him
for opening the bead casks, he started prying and suddenly the
whole top of the barrel collapsed. Stone Hammer looked down

and could see his face reflected in the dark pool of rum when he held the torch above his head. Stone Hammer bent and sniffed to make sure that it was safe to drink, and as he did, his torch touched the powerful rum and sent blue flames flickering across its surface. Stone Hammer panicked and tipped the barrel, splashing its contents over some bales of tarred rope and across the water in the hold, sending the blue flames dancing crazily around him.

Stone Hammer said later that he tried to kick and splash the blue flames out, but instead he made a roaring fire inside the upturned barrel. That miserable thief became so frightened that he flung down his torch and ran stumbling back through the knee-deep water until he saw the patch of light above the open hatch. He hauled himself up the ladder, kicked the sleeping guard, and ran up to the safety of the Thunder house.

He tried to lie with the girl, but she scorned him, only half believing that he had tried to get her beads and a blanket. Because Stone Hammer greatly feared Maquina's anger, he told no one else about the blue rum fire that danced inside the belly of the ship.

Kawskaws woke me with a violent shake.

I was shocked when I saw people running down the whole length of the Eagle house. Through its entrance could be seen the glowing-red flames. I jumped up from my mat and ran across to wake Maquina and my sister.

By the time we three got outside, we could see that it was far too late to save the burning wreck. The whole hull was hidden in a billow of dark smoke and a roaring seething mass of wind-fanned flames. I felt like weeping when I remembered that at least half of all our treasure was still inside that ship.

"How did it happen?" my sister screamed at me. Before I could answer, she put her hands up to her face to protect it from the heat and wailed, "I cannot bear to think of all those lovely new red blankets burning and the copper for the bracelets melting."

Some people tried to go close to the ship, but Tom Sin and the dagger maker ran out in front and drove them back, yelling,

"*Coolie, coolie!* Run, run! Plowder, Plowder! *Boom! Boom! Boom!*"

Even as I watched them shouting, a vast blanket of bright-yellow flame blew upward, lighting the whole night sky. This was followed by a sudden gust of wind and then a tremendous roar louder than all the shipsmen's cannons in the world. I was knocked backward by the blast as I saw the whole front of the ship's hull blown to pieces. Burning bits of wood went whirling high into the air then rained back down upon us or fell hissing into the waters near the shore.

I, like every other person, lay where I had fallen, waiting in fear to see if all the gunpowder had exploded. Like Jon Jay and Tom Sin, we were cautious, afraid at first to go near the burning ship. There was little we could do but sit and watch our Wolf Town treasure disappear in smoke and flames.

Just before dawn, it began to rain, and when the light of morning came, there was nothing but a smoking skeleton with a sagging deck and black protruding ribs. I looked at Maquina and my sister and at the other house chiefs, but we could find no words of comfort. All was gone.

I felt tired and started walking up toward my mat. I saw Jon Jay sitting by the path. He had his knees drawn up beneath his chin in that curious shipsman's fashion. I could see where tears had washed clean channels down his sooty cheeks. Kawskaws and Toowin were squatted protectively beside him.

"Has he been crying?" I asked Kawskaws.

"Yes," she answered. "Yes, he has been crying. Wouldn't you," she said in a quavering voice, "if you had seen all your best friends stabbed to death and then you had to sit and watch the only house you had burn up to nothing?" Kawskaws sobbed, "Jon Jay's got nothing now, nothing at all. He's just like me. I've got nothing either, except . . . maybe you, and Toowin."

I didn't try to answer Kawskaws, for I could see that she was weeping and acting like every other woman. Toowin gave me, his father, a hard look as though the burning of the dagger maker's ship was all my fault.

I moved past Tom Sin, who laughed in a cold way, then

gave me a silent look as if to say he didn't care that his ship and all its treasure had been blown up and burned beyond our grasp.

I went inside the Eagle house, and I lay down on my mats. But still I could not sleep. I felt bad. Not because of the enormous treasure we had lost. Oh, no. I myself was thinking of poor Kawskaws and of Jon Jay, two young people who had lost their way back home because of us.

POTLATCH

THE BURNING of that ship, like the killing of its crew, changed everything. Perhaps it was a warning, telling us to move. We were eager to go—we waited only for some good-luck sign. That came when the new crescent moon appeared with a star not far above its delicate upturned horns.

When our women saw this message in the sky, they started calling out, "Get ready! Everyone help load the canoes. We are moving. We are leaving on this tide!"

Oh, I was glad to hear those familiar words of theirs—our women are usually the ones who decide when we will break camp and move.

When our two shipsmen realized that we were going, they hurried to the beach with our sharp-eyed children. The dagger maker and Tom Sin made a last search through the rain-soaked ashes of the shipwreck, rooting for any useful things that they might find.

To my surprise, they discovered quite a lot: heavy iron ship's bolts twisted by the heat, partly melted copper spikes, iron hoops from barrels, the wood of which had been burned away completely. All of these blackened bits of metal, together with gray bars of iron that would be pounded into daggers, Jon Jay piled into our oldest dugout. Our women came down and looked at this miserable pile of salvage from the fire. They shook their heads in disbelief as they remembered that half of all our treasure had disappeared in flames.

Our moves never happen quite as quickly as the women wish. Despite the rain, my sister and Man Frog's wife and Long Claws's wife, like so many others, were ordering servants to carry down and pile their household boxes into the big canoes, which were already pushed out in the water. Maquina was away with Red Tongue and Matla and a gang of paddlers taking the two cannons around the burial cave and covering them with cedar mats.

Jon Jay and Tom Sin seemed amazed by our seemingly careless actions. Certainly there is no ceremony about our leaving. The same tasks happen in all the households. First the women start gathering and tossing our sleeping mats and cooking boxes and our long food trenchers outside the Eagle house. Everyone, even the smallest children, helps carry household things down to the canoes. Men take short knives and cut the lashings holding the wide cedar house boards. As the boards are lifted off, they expose our eight still-smoking fire pits and the thick house posts and long ridgepoles that form the frame. We bundle all these roof and wall boards down into our largest dugouts, for they too are moved.

"I'm glad to leave this Eagle house of ours," my sister said with a sigh. "The winter rains will come and clean the floors for us." She looked back nervously and said, "I hope the winds will blow away any other things that may be creeping around."

I knew she meant the souls of those poor shipsmen, but she was afraid to speak their names. Oh, yes, I too was glad that we were moving early, for this place seemed to have turned against us. I wanted to be somewhere that I could look out over water without seeing that burned-out wreck before my eyes. I would be glad to escape to our summer salmon camp at Coptee, where I knew the entrance passage was so treacherous and shallow that no foreign ship would ever dare to follow us.

At the very moment of our pushing out from shore, old Sand Shark's daughter came over from the Thunder house. She told Maquina that her father could not rise from his mat and was too ill to travel with us.

There was nothing we could do to change our going. Every house in Wolf Town had been stripped of its roof and walls, and these had been bundled into canoes.

"Keep some boards. Build him a little house," Maquina said to Sand Shark's sons. "Keep his wife and daughter and that slave woman here with him. You can follow us to the salmon camp as soon as he is well enough to travel."

When we finally pushed off from shore, the rain ceased, and the whole inlet lay mirror still, reflecting the gray sky. Our two shipsmen in their white-painted longboat were rowing. Four of our young men had joined them. Into this boat they had placed the ship's iron anvil, the puff-puff box, a sturdy leather sack containing Jon Jay's hammers, tongs, files, and pincers, and his rolled-up leather apron. Also, Tom Sin carefully stored the six iron lamps that he had taken from the ship's cabin.

As we moved out into the deep waters of the inlet, we looked south to the ocean and saw a pod of feeding whales. Of course, that made us glad. We did not try in any way to harm them. No, we did the opposite of that. Maquina rose up in the bow of his canoe and called out to them, saying, "Great whales! We are your countrymen. We respect you. Swim away now, but return later to these waters and share your beautiful flesh with us." Some of our most sensitive women said they saw the great whales turn beneath the water and heard the first deep-sounding echoes of their sacred song, assuring us they would return.

On this journey, this escape into the north, there was nothing I could do but sit resting my back against a roll of cedar bed mats, so I decided to enjoy each small island as we passed it, admiring the perfect reflection in the water. These rocky islands were partly covered with moss that was turning new-spring green. The trees on them were like small wind-twisted dwarfs battered by countless storms. The nearness of our big canoes caused a herd of sea lions to raise their heads and bark out warnings to one another before they slipped into the safety of the water. The women called out greetings to the females, assuring them that this was not a day of hunting. I drew a deep breath and felt truly glad to be alive and on the move again.

There is a quiet beauty here. The sea spreads out like a giant hand reaching inland with watery fingers, forming deep inlets and channels. There are small hidden beaches and, creeping through the forest, little rivers where the early salmon run. In any season, our coastal inlets are lonely places haunted by the ghostlike laughing of the loons and the sad crying of the gulls. On these soft mornings, the giant cedars with their feath-

ery green branches are often misty gray, their tops lost in the
fog until it is burned away by the warm sunshine of midday.
When the tide runs out, black rocks are exposed amid a twist
of giant roots and driftwood logs. Warm ocean airs come and
gather into distant thunderheads, breathing out the rich salt
reekings of the sea. The big moon tides will guide the salmon
back into the rivers where they were born. Even on clear, flat,
calm days like that one, it is easy to imagine the violent storms
with pounding surf that will come gnawing at this coast in winter. But we will be long gone by then from our summer bays,
for we know a better place to hide from winter storms.

The big freighting canoes that had been lashed together with
boards between them to carry even greater loads were paddled
by our Wolf Town slaves, who needed constant urging so they
would not fall too far behind us. The sky took on an ominous
look, but there was still no wind. Jon Jay and Tom Sin, with
four others, had started out beside us in the white boat. They
had taken down the short mast and tightly furled its sail. Big
Tom Sin was rowing the longboat from the cross bench near
the stern, setting the stroke with his long oar and cleverly working a small rudder with his big bare feet. The second oarsman
was my son, Toowin, and in front of him Jon Jay, then three
strong young men, one from the Thunder house and two from
the Whale house. Though Hoiss and some of those other hotheads nurtured their hatred for the shipsmen, others, including
my Toowin, admired them greatly in spite of their strange habits. I could see that each of them in that boat was eager to learn
this new foreign way of paddling with a square oar while sitting
backwards. Having not too much to weigh them down, they at
first put on an impressive burst of speed and proudly stroked
past all of our canoes. But they soon tired, and little by little
our long dugouts drew up and passed them.

We stopped to rest and eat cold chunks of halibut and
greased cakes of berries. When we were moving again, I watched
the white boat draw abreast of us. My son, Toowin, missed a
stroke while showing Jon Jay the first blister on his hand.

Maquina called out to them, "We will sleep tonight in the sheltered cove on Puffin Island."

I sat contented, looking at the pale eye of the sun as it started sinking toward the ocean through banks of heavy clouds. A wet breeze rose and sprayed patterns out across the water. I looked back and saw that the white boat had fallen so far behind that it was almost out of sight. Not long after that, my sister pointed out that they had raised their small yellowish triangle of a sail.

I was amazed at how quickly the white boat overtook us, even though our paddlers were stroking hard, determined to keep ahead of this new sailing craft. Tom Sin sat in the stern, now steering with a sweep oar, looking straight ahead as though we were not there. Jon Jay and Toowin, like the others, had laid aside their oars and were leaning comfortably against the white boat's windward side. Their little sail was bellied out, carrying them swiftly past us. Toowin and Jon Jay were both smoking short clay pipes. They smiled and waved good-bye to us, as did the other three. I had a feeling that Toowin and the young ones with him had all somehow become foreigners, that they would grow up using sails and guns, smoking pipes, playing banjos, dancing in hard boots, speaking other languages—and never, never return to us.

When our paddlers, their faces strained from overwork, pulled into the lee of Puffin Island, I could see that two large fires were already burning and that the white boat had been drawn up onto the beach above the tide. They had removed the mast and sail, with which they had erected a clever tentlike kind of shelter I had never seen before. Jon Jay was laughing with Toowin and the others. He played a cheerful welcome song for us upon his banjo.

When I beckoned, Toowin did come over and help me and Kawskaws and the others build our shelter. I was not surprised when he hurried back and made his bed beneath the yellow sail with the two foreigners. I suppose he did not wish to miss his studies of new foreign ways. Before I went to sleep, I could hear him singing and laughing and talking over there. I didn't know what language they were using, but it was not ours and it was not Chinook.

"Don't worry," Kawskaws said. "He'll come back to you and me tomorrow . . . or the next day. He won't always stay with them."

In the morning we set out again, and by evening we could see the mouth of the river and the remnants of our salmon camp at Coptee. Two white-headed eagles wheeled above us, waiting for the fish to come. Scarcely anything was standing to remind us that exactly like these eagles and the salmon, our people had been coming here for countless generations.

The light was fading as we passed through the salt chuck at the river's mouth. This we did with great respect, paddling oh, so gently, hoping that some of the Salmon people were already gathered there, waiting beneath the waters. We wanted them to remember us, and trust us as the thoughtful friendly folks we are.

At dawn next day, the oldest woman from the Otter house, who held the river rights to both the Coptee River and its rich berry patches, sang her own song to the salmon. Our men cut slender sapling wands and wove them carefully into our long basket weirs, repairing winter's damage. Skillfully they prepared the clever tunnel shapes that we hoped would receive our share of the migrating salmon.

This summer fishing village is much more ramshackle than our winter house frames up at Tahsis. What do we care? The weather is pleasantly warm, and if any rain comes through the roof at night, one can simply roll over and find a drier spot to sleep. We are glad to have holes in our house walls so that we can peer out at the river and observe all movements on our beach. We are a people who only rarely place a foot inside the forest. The few trails that we make there soon grow choked with alder and deadfall and disappear. Our food, our light, our way of traveling, all these good things come from the open rivers, the beaches, the estuaries, and most especially from the sea itself.

Both men and women helped slaves cut flimsy poles, stand them upright in the earth, and with twisted cedar-bark cord loosely lash our wide boards to them. The slaves once more arranged our flat board roofs and lightly weighted them with stones. Next we set our smokehouses in readiness—with all the usual advice one hears from my sister and the other women. Our young people went out and carefully watched each tide as it came sweeping up the river. At first they did not see a single salmon. That was not surprising, for we had come to this camp early, for other reasons of our own.

Both my sister and Kawskaws cautioned the two shipsmen while others warned our children to be oh, so careful to do nothing that might possibly offend the salmon. It is well known that throwing stones toward the water or harassing those dear fish in any other way is the cause of earthquakes, lightning, and disaster and will result in the Salmon people leaving the river and going away from us forever.

At the salmon camp, Fog Woman ordered some of her women to rearrange the sleeping mats and boxes to accommodate Jon Jay in their apartment, for she still wanted him protected by Maquina, while Tom Sin hung his hammock in the apartment of Beaver Seeker. My sister indicated to Jon Jay that he could sit next to her on a handsome painted cedar box she gave him, which would now be his alone. She advised him to keep his spare clothing in this box. His sleeping place was right against the inner wall, which she said was safer from attack. I believe she was also trying to keep him separated from Maquina's flock of younger women when she herself was overnighting near the upper-river smokehouse. As it turned out, that distance she arranged was not wide enough. I thought, Sleeping those young girls so close to Jon Jay will surely lead to trouble. I was right—it did, but not in the way I had imagined.

I had almost forgotten about the one-eyed old Sand Shark, who had been too ill to travel with us, when one of the smaller Thunder house canoes paddled by his sons came cautiously into the river's mouth and landed at our camp.

"He's dying," Sand Shark's daughter told Fog Woman. "He

made us bring him now. He said he wanted to leave from here
with all of you around and with the Salmon people close beside
him."

That night I picked a handful of ripe berries and went to
the Thunder house to say good-bye to that old man. He opened
his only good eye and looked at me and my small gift. He let
me put one in his mouth, but I guess he was too sick to swallow
it. He moved his lips, trying to tell me something urgent, but he
could not make his poor weak voice come round the berry. What
could I do? I just sat there and held his thin frail hand to try
and comfort him.

I've often joked and sometimes spoken badly of Sand Shark.
When we were both much younger, I had thought him something of a rival. As an adult, Sand Shark had been a quiet nobleman among us; he had never given a feast that I found worth
remembering. But now that he was leaving me, I knew I would
miss his poky habits. Yes, like myself, old Sand Shark was one
who had grown up before the coming of the whites. We had
known good days together, days that would never come to us
again.

"Good-bye, friend," I whispered to him in his ear, and in
answer, he clung to my hand as though he did not want to
leave.

Next morning, when I awoke, Kawskaws said that old Sand
Shark was gone. Before he went, his daughter told my sister, the
roof boards had been opened wide so he could use the stars to
travel by.

His young wife, his daughter, and their slave woman
mourned him very loudly. His sons helped prepare for their father's funeral. Sand Shark had given his grandson a beautiful
small canoe, and now his grandson gladly gave it back to be
used as the old man's coffin. The canoe was just exactly right
in length to let him lie with his knees only slightly bent. On the
outside, this dugout had been charred black by fire, then polished bright with seal oil. Using clever ovoid forms, the Sand
Shark crest had been carefully painted on its high-curved prow.
The canoe inside had been stained with rich red ocher and

rubbed with salmon oil that the rain would not wash away.
Black is the color of death and red the color of life. But since
these two colors were used in equal portions, they subtly can-
celed out each other, which was exactly as it should be.

When old Sand Shark's women and his friends had finished
mourning him, Maquina followed the dead man's wish by cutting a small eyehole in the river side of his burial canoe. The
old man's richest cloak of sea otter skins was affectionately
wrapped around his body before he was laid out with his head
turned so that he could see through his observation hole. Sand
Shark had his chief's hat on his head, his feast bowl in his left
hand, his old-fashioned whalebone dagger laid across his chest,
and his right hand free to use the rattle. Gently his daughter
covered him with her finest woven-cedar mat.

When all of that was done, the Thunder people pulled away
the side wall boards from their summer house and bore him in
his small canoe to their chosen cedar tree.

"Is he nicely arranged in there," Maquina fussed, "so his
good eye is looking out the hole?"

"Yes," the Thunder people said. "Oh, yes! His good eye is
at the hole."

Maquina brought forth a wooden carving of a life-sized
human hand. From that red hand dangled a hollow bird-shaped
wooden rattle filled with small stone pebbles. Maquina ordered
Jon Jay to nail the wooden hand and rattle to the outside of the
small canoe.

I helped many others slowly haul on the twisted-cedar cords.
We gently raised Sand Shark's black canoe, drawing it evenly
upward until it rested in the protective branches of the cedar.
When that was done, the supporting cords were tied tight around
the tree.

We were especially careful that the old man's eyehole would
have a clear view of the river down toward its mouth. Yes, I
myself had heard him promise at the winter feasting that he
would watch the river for us and tell us when the Salmon people first came upstream from their lands beneath the sea. He
said that he would try to warn us with his rattle.

Sand Shark's son performed for the first time the masked
Thunder dance which he had inherited from the old man, weeping and slowly pounding his feet on the moss-covered earth to
purify the ground beneath the burial canoe that now hung above
his head. The sorcerer struck his tambourinelike drum, accompanying his women's farewell song.

Kawskaws had made fifteen small black marks on the plank
beside my sleeping place by the time the salmonberry moon of
summer was showing half its face. Still, none of our underwater
kinsmen had come into the river. When the summer moon was
in full face, a huge tide came sweeping up our river. I awoke to
the screaming of Sand Shark's daughter, his young widowed
wife, and that strange red-handed slave woman who was to cause
us such a lot of trouble.

"Did you not hear it?" they wept, as the three of them ran
into our house just as dawn was breaking. "Did you not hear
him sound his rattle from the little black canoe?"

"We heard it," the young wife cried with joy. "He told us
he would do it, and he did!"

"We heard him shake that rattle very, very loudly." Sand
Shark's daughter laughed and wept. "Oh, yes, he shook it—four
separate times we heard those pebbles!"

"It means the Salmon people are coming now! He must
have seen them," his wife said. "That's what he was telling us."

The slave woman stared at her red-dyed hands and feet
and, sobbing to herself, said not a single word.

Because I was sound asleep, I regret to say, I myself did not
hear the old man alert us with that rattle. Kawskaws and Toowin
both were certain that they had heard it. Kawskaws asked Jon
Jay excitedly if he had heard the rattling. To my surprise, he
looked at her and said, "Yes, maybe." When she asked Tom Sin
if he had heard it, he scowled and shook his head.

Oh, I am certain he shook it. Yes, it was not so surprising.
Sand Shark had sounded his rattle, triumphantly signaling to us
from the other world. The proof, if any need be given, is that
when we went down to the river, we could see the Salmon peo-

ple thronging through the dark waters. Countless shoals of them, their bright sides flashing like heavy silver icicles, thrust their way joyfully up into the sparkling freshness of the river, washing the sea salt from their sides in the clear waters flowing down from distant mountains.

"Maquina must feel relieved that the Salmon people have come to feed us once again," I told Toowin, who was preparing a double-tipped harpoon.

Taking countless numbers of these fish was easy, and we did so with respect and gratitude. Then we relaxed again, each household knowing that their winter baskets would be tightly packed with the pungent brown-smoked flesh of salmon. Having this abundance of food would free us in the coming winter to enjoy the more important parts of life.

You may find it strange when I tell you that at his death old Sand Shark willed his favorite slave, that red-handed woman, to my brother-in-law. This gift seemed odd because Maquina already possessed more slaves than any other person in our village, and certainly he did not need another.

"I don't want her," I heard Maquina saying to his wife. "Slaves like that cause far more trouble than they're worth. Why not give her to your brother, Siam? He needs another woman!"

My sister laughed, but she would not agree. "That woman's said to be wise," my sister told him. "She might help you forget the problem of that wrecked ship lying on your beach and your troubles with the whaling. She is an inland woman from the mountains," said my sister. "The people in the Thunder house swear that she causes dreams."

"Has she a good voice?" Maquina asked her. "Those mountain women are supposed to be fine singers."

"Let's listen to her," my sister said, and she waved her hand, beckoning the short, thick-set slave woman to them.

From across the fire I observed the slave's heavy tattered winter garment made of black bearskin. The woman hunched forward and with her blood-red hands raised the skin protectively until it covered her head. I could see that she was naked underneath the bearskin. The outline of her strong face was hidden in the shadows cast by the shaggy pelt, but the glint of the fire from the pit was reflected in her watchful eyes.

"*Shintee*, sing to us," my sister ordered.

That strange slave woman flung back her bearskin, and with staring eyes she pointed her blood-red forefinger at Maquina, at my sister, then at me. She began her mournful wail, which we found powerful and haunting, though all her mountain words were strange.

When her singing was finished, Fog Woman said, "Yes, she is a good singer. That 'Wah, Wah, Wah, he, wa, ha' repeated again and again makes my head nod. Tell her to go away. I want to sleep."

"You tell her," Maquina yawned, as he stretched out beneath his otter bed robe. "She doesn't understand a word I say."

I, too, felt the strongest urge to go to sleep. And when I did, I had the strangest dream. That I will tell you later.

At Coptee there was a young widow who had married into the Thunder house. Her name was Cheepokesklickeryek, that rich-sounding name meaning copper rings. This childless woman of fewer than thirty winters had roving eyes and lived secret lives that scandalized Wolf Town. She was disliked by all our women, young or old.

The copper widow, as she was called behind her back, had come to us from a distant village. She did not become one of us, though she had quickly learned our language and spoke it with the soft, slurry river accent that all adult men find interesting and women are so quick to ridicule.

It is somewhat unusual for a highborn family to reject the suitable daughters of those in their own or nearby villages and then arrange a marriage match from far away. However, such family ties do sometimes make new trade alliances and cut down the likelihood of feuds and murderous raiding.

This marriage had had a swift, cruel ending when the young husband took a fish bone in his throat and choked to death in the middle of a winter feast. It was hoped by all the women in the Thunder house that the copper widow would remove herself to some other village or return to her father's house. That first summer passed and then another, but still she remained among us, sleeping in the Thunder house.

The copper widow was the most hot-blooded woman I have ever known. She openly rejected all our women. She would scarcely speak to them. She lived only for our men. She talked easily and intelligently with them or rubbed up against them. A few men were almost always near her. She drew them to her like a bitch in heat.

Not long after her husband died, I was visiting my cousin in the Thunder house when this young copper widow came up to their fire. My cousin's wife immediately rose and, without speaking to the widowed woman, strode angrily away. The young woman stared at me, then came around the fire in a way that made me watch her every movement.

"What a handsome Chilkat cape you wear," she whispered in her soft and slurry voice. "I have never seen one patterned just like that."

She did not look at the cape but straight at me as she ran her hands over the breast of my cape. My cousin smiled knowingly and stuck out his tongue at me.

"It must be a warm cape," this young widowed woman said, as she ran one hand tenderly beneath my cape and along my naked back in a way that made me shudder with delight. Then, without warning, she hooked her fingers like a bird's talons, and digging in, she raked them down my back. Because my cousin watched me closely, I dared not change my expression. But when she withdrew her hand, I could feel small rivulets of blood go trickling down my back. She licked her lips and without another word turned and strolled away.

I scarcely slept that night for thinking of that crazy woman. Why had she raked my back? The pain was nothing really. It was the tender upward motion of her hand that made me shiver, and the rolling motion of her hips beneath her *kotsak* when she turned and left my cousin's fire. I slept very badly on the second night as well, and brooded through the day so much that both Kawskaws and my sister asked if I felt ill.

I believe all this happened to me because the moon was entering the waxing quarter, which is known to have a powerful effect on animal and human copulation. Certainly Maquina too could feel it. He arranged a canoe and sent Fog Woman off to visit an ailing relative, and I, for the first time, insisted that my son, Toowin, go with her.

That night I waited as long as I could before I told Kawskaws to go to the Thunder house and ask the copper widow to come and visit me.

Kawskaws remained squatting by our fire, staring at me with those dark eyes of hers as though she had not understood my words. I told her more forcefully a second time. Still she hunkered down and would not move. That made me mad!

"I bought you and I swear I'll sell you to the worst brute I can find," I said in a low voice. Those were the worst words I ever said to Kawskaws, and I felt ashamed.

"Don't have anything to do with that woman," Kawskaws whispered. "Do anything you want with any other women, but keep away from her."

"Go and get her," I said angrily, and Kawskaws rose and left my fire.

After I combed my hair and put a little red and black paint on the Moon side of my face, I subtly arranged my boxes so they cast a long dark shadow across my sleeping mats.

It seemed to take forever, but finally I saw the copper widow come drifting through the shadows of the Eagle house. Kawskaws was not with her.

Cheepokesklickeryek came and sat boldly on the high box next to me beside our fire.

"Well, look who's out wandering tonight," Maquina called down to us in a joking way.

The copper widow quickly turned her head and smiled up at Maquina. If he had said such a thing to any other person, those girls of his would have squirmed around beneath the otter robe in fits of giggling. But now they all sat up, alert and silent, watching the copper widow with eyes of cold mistrust.

"Come, I have something to show you," I said to her.

The copper widow
displays Siam's
gift to her.

She followed me closely up to my apartment.

"Sit here," I said, and from a secret place removed an exquisitely carved ivory pendant that had once belonged to someone who was very close to me.

The widow took it in her hands and held it out beyond the shadows to admire it in the firelight. Then she let down her *kotsak* and dangled the pendant for me between her beautiful breasts.

"Let me put it on for you," I said. "It's yours."

She smiled and drew me down upon my mats.

"Brother-in-law, I can't see you," Maquina called out, "but I think I can guess what you must be doing."

The copper widow raised her naked legs above the boxes and boldly waved across our fire toward Maquina.

He snorted enviously, but all his girls remained completely silent.

My heart went tum-tum-tum when the copper widow wrapped her nakedness around me, and three times we did different things in ways that I had never known before. Then I slept—only for a little while. When I awoke, she was gone but the lush smell of her still clung to my sleeping place and the feel of her thighs refused to leave my mind.

"Look at your poor back," said Kawskaws when she brought hot morning broth.

She tried to hold the looking-glass for me, but I didn't want to see.

"It's all scratched bloody by her fingernails." Kawskaws curled her lips. "How can you have anything to do with a woman who would tear your flesh like that?"

"I don't know," I said. "But I know one thing—that you are going to go as soon as it is dark tonight and tell that woman to come here to me again. And this time," I told Kawskaws, "I don't want to waste precious time in arguing with you!"

It was Fog Woman who finally removed the rag that had held the tobacco leaves against the dagger maker's head wound. All of us could see that it was healing, but that ax stroke had left an angry scar that we knew would never go away. Jon Jay, after he saw the wide red gash in a looking-glass let Kawskaws arrange his copper-colored hair so it hung down, covering most of the wound. The swelling had gone from around his right eye. Its blue-green color had turned brown, then disappeared. Still, whenever I looked at his wounded face, I was painfully re-minded of that blood-soaked afternoon at Abooksha.

Though the young dagger maker towered over Fog Woman, she would often forget herself and lead him about by the hand like a small child, for she was trying to teach him our language and our true Yoquot ways. When he came to us, Jon Jay knew only a little of the Chinook language, yet suddenly, to our amazement, he was able to use it and could speak quite easily with us. By squinting his eyes in the firelight and studying the thin white skins with lots of squiggles on them, those harmless-looking things that he had brought up from the master's cabin, he could say all sorts of words, even if he sometimes used our phrases backwards. Still, we were often able to understand him, and he sometimes understood us.

First, he said my name, "Si-am," then made an imitation of a bear. Second, he pointed at Maquina's otter skin robe and said, *"Quart lak."* He aimed as though he held a musket and called out, *"Momook poh."* He pointed at Fog Woman and said, *"Klootchman."* He reached out and touched Kawskaws's breasts and whispered, *"Totoosh."* Every word he said was good Chinook.

I asked him to let me hold that magic piece of skin, and I studied it with care, turning it one way and another, even rat-tling it near my ear. But no matter what I did, it would not speak to me, nor would it speak to Maquina or any other per-son at our salmon camp.

It was Kawskaws who thought to have Jon Jay give his magic skins to big Tom Sin, for he was very poor at speaking or understanding words we spoke. The sailmaker took the pa-per and held it, frowning at the little marks. Jon Jay turned it upside down for him, but still Tom Sin, like us, caught not a single word from it. This important difference between these two foreigners was very difficult for us to understand.

One day when our smoking of the salmon was almost finished and my sister and her women were away at the weir on the upper river, picking and drying berries and packing them in boxes, a seal hunter from the south came to our camp. He was the first that year to see the whales.

"*Kwadis!* Whales begin their passing!"

He did not need to say those magic words a second time.

Maquina forgot all about the salmon—about every other thing except the whales! Reluctantly he barred all of those hot-blooded young girls from his bed, and he even sent Tom Sin upriver with a slave to warn my sister, saying she should remain there, for Maquina said he greatly feared that her return might sexually excite him. I doubted that, but still, no man can be too careful in such matters if he plans to go and hunt the whales. Lying or even hand-playing with any woman is absolutely taboo for any man who wishes to go out and seek the big ones—that is well known here! "If you keep away from that copper widow and that girl of yours," Maquina called across our fire, "then you can come with me."

"What girl?" I asked him angrily.

He only laughed when I said that.

As I got my own boat and equipment ready, I could hear Maquina every morning hollering across the beach dunes where the river joins the sea. He himself had selected the strongest, wiliest paddlers for our two whale canoes. His swift dugout had been painted black with a fresh Eagle design upon its bow.

All the equipment for both canoes was spread neatly on our beach so we could easily inspect it. Maquina ordered that new sealskin floats be blown up to make certain they were airtight. He demanded of the women endless coils of strong new sealskin lines and a new pair of extra-long harpoon shafts. He wanted everything at once.

Jon Jay and the sailmaker joined in the all-male excitement. Those two came and examined every part of our equipment carefully. Because he still found it easiest to speak through Kawskaws, Jon Jay went and got her and his thin white skins. Maquina warned her away from the beach, for down there we allowed no women. When I came up with Maquina from the beach, Jon Jay spoke to Kawskaws carefully in Chinook, mixing in as well a few words from our language.

Kawskaws nodded when she understood him, then said to Maquina and me, "This dagger maker says he wants to make a strong iron end . . . for your harpoons. He says it will be very good . . . and knife-edge sharp . . . to go into the whales, you know?" She nodded toward me and added, "He says, too, he wants to go . . . hunt the whales . . . with you, Siam. Yes, he . . . and you, together."

Maquina stared at me angrily and then at Jon Jay. "You tell that boy we have been using heavy sharpened shells to pierce the whales since humans were first created by the Raven and came crawling from the giant Clam." He continued in a loud voice that all could hear. "You tell this dagger maker we don't need his iron points to take the whales. Tell him that iron offends the whales. You tell him all those words from me!"

"Yes, I'll tell him," Kawskaws said, "but . . . he wants to know if he can go with you two high men out to hunt the whales?"

I looked at Maquina, who was frowning but had not said yes or no. So I said quickly, "Yes! You tell him, yes! He is welcome to come and hunt the whales with me." The truth was that neither Maquina nor I had managed to take a whale during the past four springs or autumns, but, of course, we had no need to tell Tom Sin or the dagger maker that!

When she told Jon Jay he could go, a look of pleasure spread across his face. On the following morning, early, I heard Tom Sin set the puff box roaring as he raised their fire, and soon I heard the dagger maker's hammer striking iron on iron.

Maquina left careful instructions with all the women, cautioning that while he was away they keep their legs clamped tight together and do nothing that might break any taboos and spoil the whaling for us. Then for a second time, he sent Tom Sin and a slave upriver with a warning to my sister, telling her to make sure that she and any women with her think only the kindest thoughts about the whales. I too told Kawskaws to sing gentle Whale songs while bathing in the morning and evening while we were gone away, for I had begun to think that Maquina and I were jinxed.

On the fifth day, Maquina placed his bulbous woven whaling hat upon his head. I got mine. We were ready to go. We had long enough abstained from women. We were pure. No other thought but whales now filled our hearts and minds.

On the morning of our leaving, Maquina more or less forced old Matla and Red Tongue to go down with both of us and squat naked in the ice-cold water of a mountain stream. With hemlock branches twisted in our hair, we all scrubbed and cleansed ourselves to show the whales that we were pure. Together we sang ancient and respectful songs to those great creatures of the deep and promised we would put the blue duck feathers on their back if one of those mighty giants would give itself to us.

Our two canoes with twelve of our strongest paddlers and Jon Jay left in midmorning, and by evening we had reached the whaling grounds. We tied our two canoes together, ate little, and slept out on the restless ocean far beyond the sight of land, a risk good whalers have to take if they wish to be in the best position for the lazy early-morning rising of the whales.

Hunters must be oh, so careful later not to let women hear what happens on the whaling grounds, so, listener, remember, tell women nothing of these words you hear from me.

We were gone for three long days and nights and returned to the beach on the fourth morning. Maquina was in a mood so black, he would not say a single word. Let me explain the reason.

At dawn the first day, not long after we cut our two canoes apart, a large sperm whale rose and blew not far from Maquina's dugout. His crew, paddling quietly, took our *tyee* up behind it, almost onto that great beast's back. Maquina called out the magic words as he drove his long harpoon straight into him. My heart went tum-tum-tum when I saw the white spray fly and the long line go whipping out as the whale raised his huge tail flukes and smashed them on the water. Regrettably, the clamshell point broke loose. The whale dove.

Maquina showed only a little anger, then, for we two are used to losing whales. We were not disheartened, for many other whales were there waiting for us, and we had shunned the pleasures of our women for almost half a moon.

Maquina got a second perfect chance when his crew took him silently onto a second whale. He made an enormous thrust. All his paddlers saw the clamshell twist and shatter before it even cut through the huge creature's skin and blubber. Even from a distance I could tell that my brother-in-law was raging mad.

I brought my canoe up alongside his and, speaking quietly, said, "Maybe we both should have taken this young dagger maker's offer and let him make a pair of whale irons for us."

Hearing the words *kwadis chickamin*—whale irons—Jon Jay proudly reached into his sack and brought two out and offered one to each of us. Maquina got so mad at Jon Jay and at me that he turned his head and refused to speak a word. That's how my brother-in-law gets sometimes. I was fed up with him. When we returned to Wolf Town, he told my sister that we missed the whales because Jon Jay had brought those offensive points onto the whaling grounds and the whales could smell the iron. Did you ever hear of an excuse like that?

I honestly don't know how my sister stands him. She says she doesn't like it when he's lying with all those other girls, but I told her that his temper grows far worse when the whaling causes him to drive young women from his bed. I told her I thought sleeping alone turned him into nothing but an evil-tempered brute! She thought that over for a little while—and did not seem to disagree with me.

The night after we returned, I found those two sharp whale irons lying underneath my sleeping mat, where Jon Jay must have placed them. Did I throw those cursed harpoon points away? I did not! I saved them for a better day. But I didn't tell my brother-in-law.

I thought a lot about the copper widow. She had brought with her to Wolf Town one male slave and two female slaves, all three a wedding gift from her father's house. After her young husband died, they continued to care for her while she lived on in the Thunder house and moved wherever it moved. That house chief was responsible for her safety and well-being while she lived beneath his roof, but that did not prevent his wife and the copper widow from hating each other very much. Hatred was not reason enough to make Cheepokesklickeryek leave the food and comforts of the Thunder house. Oh, no! The disdain of other women did not bother her. She had known it all her life.

I myself cared nothing for what other women thought of her. That night the widow came to me so quietly she did not even wake my light-sleeping sister, and before morning she was gone again, leaving me with that hot, musky smell of hers and just one bad bite on my neck, which I easily covered up with ocher paint.

Bad luck came to punish Maquina for his whaling tantrum. At high sun on the following day, we saw a strange canoe coming up the inlet. It had clumsy lines and was badly paddled by a gang of northern Black Fin people, crude distant neighbors whom we mistrusted most of all. Of course, these northerners were singing one of their outlandish songs and murderously stabbing their sharp red-painted paddles into our sacred salmon waters, eager to be the bearers of bad news. They had a winged sorcerer, wearing a coarsely carved Raven mask and a laughable feathered suit, dancing like a mad thing in their bow. Those Black Fin often potlatch with the Kwakiutl and affect some of their costumes and many of their styles and manners because they think them elegant.

The Black Fin halted their canoe at a safe distance off our beach. Then their chief's talker shouted out, "Our chief, Tall Hat, is going to give a potlatch feast. You, Maquina, and your most important people are all invited." He paused to let that thought sink into us before continuing. "Begin your journey to us at the end of the November cleansing moon, before the young sister moon comes into crescent."

Maquina nodded bleakly, and Red Tongue asked the Black Fin talker if he wished to come ashore. Coldly he refused our invitation, saying it was late, as he ordered his paddlers down the inlet.

I thought of those Black Fin sleeping on some wet gravel beach beneath their upturned canoe rather than accepting our coldly formal hospitality to them.

That night I tried my best to explain the northern clans to Toowin and to Kawskaws, who did her best to interpret for the dagger maker. "The people dwelling in the north, beyond the limits of our Nootkan country, live in very different ways. They have gathered into separate clans, whereas we have houses. Among those people no person is allowed to marry any other person within his or her own clan. Also, they have the habit of having a father's children follow in the line of their mother's clan, taking their mother's crest, be it Eagle, Raven, Wolf, or Bear."

Toowin scoffed at that.

"It's not funny," I told him. "If you had been born among northern people, you would have been brought up and trained by your mother's brother or some uncle in her clan, not by me."

"I would have hated that," said Toowin. "Why wouldn't you have trained me?"

"Because," I told him, "I would have known nothing of the secret societies within your mother's clan. I would not have known how to train you. How could I, myself a Bear, have taught you how to live in the Raven or Eagle clan?"

Jon Jay and Kawskaws said nothing, but Toowin nodded, and I think it is just possible he may have understood me. You can never tell with a son that age—you can't tell what they learn, or even if they're listening!

As I went to sleep, I could hear Maquina raging at my sister, saying that she or some of those younger women must have broken some taboo, done something wrong, which had caused the whales to throw off his harpoons and refuse to give themselves to us. As if that was not bad enough, he shouted, he was now forced to attend a hated Black Fin potlatch feast in the most dreadful house in all the world.

A GOOD SIGN came to us when the meat-cutting moon of autumn appeared and an all-white female deer with pale-pink eyes was seen. But along with that good hunting sign came the direct warning of dangerous events about to happen. A great, rich-hued double rainbow appeared in burning colors, arching itself across the whole sky near the mouth of the salmon river. Of course, I swiftly turned my back, as did all others, trying oh, so carefully not to look at it. I had the feeling that it was long past time to leave this place, and yet we stayed on, uncertain.

Even though we sang to the white deer and acted quickly to guard against that ominous warning in the sky, I slept not at all well, for my night thoughts were riddled with visions of those violent happenings from our recent past. When I closed my eyes, I imagined I could see little moving serpents of red blood come shivering toward me across my sleeping mat. Finally I gave up all hope of sleep and, rising, made my way out of our house.

The night wind came gently moaning through the giant cedars, creeping like an unseen spirit all along our beach, spreading smokelike fog that rose across the dark, still waters just before the coming of the dawn. I sat alone, not far from our house entrance, staring out over the river as night faded and the Dog star flashed its bright message to me from the west.

I heard the whispering tree, sighing at first, then speaking words slower and clearer than I had ever heard it utter in the past. Whispering trees like ours are oh, so rare. This one stands no farther from the northeast corner of our summer house than a man can cast a stone. We Eagle people planned our dwelling to be within listening distance of this tree. Some Wolf Town folks have never heard it speak—nor will they. Not everyone's ears are attuned to forest sounds, so busy are some with living out their lives as human beings. They do not care what other shape they once possessed, nor do they think about the future form their soul will take the next time they appear.

As I looked both ways along our salmon river, I saw nothing strange and heard no more, and yet I had the certain feeling that many foreign eyes were watching me. Those were my own night thoughts, quite different from the words that came drifting to me from the whispering tree. I looked beyond the Thunder house and saw old Sand Shark's canoe protected among the cedar boughs. I hoped that he was resting, knowing that I watched the river well for him.

Even though we had almost half a moon of sunshine days without a drop of rain, I knew that this middle season was about to run away from us. I could smell it in the air and see it in the cold blue of the autumn sky. I was about to lose my favorite time of year.

On the following night, I heard men and women talking outside our house. Going out, I looked into the night sky and saw long fingers of pale light probing through the stars. What a marvelous sign! This first herald of the winter season set us moving on the very next day.

We unlashed and stripped the boards from our house supports and once more piled them on the platforms we rigged between the big canoes. We now had with us a huge pile of baskets and bentwood boxes filled with dried salmon. Our women helped their female slaves pack household things: the large quantity of smoked fish, food dishes, skins, tools and daggers, masks, ceremonial costumes of all sorts. Everything in boxes, so protected from the rain, was piled into the big canoes. There were grease boxes, clothes boxes, berry boxes, boxes of every size resting among rolls and rolls of cedar house mats and piles of hunting gear. Children and old folks and slaves and dogs were all laughing, calling out, or barking with excitement at the very thought of moving. Oh, how good it felt to be leaving the waters where that menacing double rainbow had appeared! How fine it was to be on the move again—protected by that white deer's lucky traveling sign!

When all my boxes and my gear were stowed in my big

canoe, I left Toowin and his older cousin, Atlin, in charge of it
so that they could have the feelings of responsibility. I turned
and walked away beside Maquina. Together we climbed into
one of his overcrowded canoes and watched critically as his
slaves, waist-deep in the icy water, eased it gently outward from
the shore. I looked back at our salmon camp and saw it as a
deserted place of gray wood skeletons, poles tilted at odd angles, smokehouses now open to wind and weather. I wondered
if old Sand Shark was watching us through his eyehole in the
black canoe.

Tom Sin and the dagger maker had more of our young men
eager to row the white boat than there were places for them.
This time the white boat was quite heavily loaded, but they were
favored with a good southwest wind, so they raised their sail,
and it was not long until they were all but out of sight.

"My Toowin is sad not to be with them," I said to Maquina.

He laughed and said, "But if he were with them, you would
be sad, for Toowin might persuade them to keep on going over
the ocean until they reached the distant river of the Chinamen."

I didn't laugh when my brother-in-law said that, for it was
all too true. Toowin was becoming like a brother to Jon Jay.

With so many persons and weighty things to carry, it took
three days for us to travel north to Tahsis. I welcomed every
moment of that journey. Each day I felt as though a huge stone
had been lifted from my back. At last the vivid image of that
bloodstained deck was fading from my mind.

During our passage up the long fiord, we had the great
good fortune to sight a small whale stranded in a tidal pool. It
blew noisily and thrashed the water, not yet dead. I believe the
white deer had left that whale there as a gift to us.

After the sorcerer's appropriate ceremony to this splendid
creature, Maquina, being *tyee*, took up a killing spear and respectfully ended its life. We enjoyed an enormous feast and slept
there that night. Naturally, we did not move the next day. On
the following morning, amidst the screaming of countless sea
gulls, we cut and piled as much meat and blubber into our ca-

noes as we could safely carry and hid the rest, to be picked up later by our paddlers. Our dogs, like our slaves, had such well-rounded bellies they could scarcely crawl into their places in the dugouts.

It was just like old times traveling up the long arm from the sea. Anyone could tell by the look on the faces of Tom Sin and the dagger maker that they were impressed by the sight of the enormous trees that stood watching us from the mountains and overhung the very edges of the cold blue waters of Tahsis Inlet. I too was thrilled to see that high country once again. It made my soul start singing deep inside me.

As our paddlers stroked up into the clearest reaches of this narrowing inlet, I tried to see Tahsis freshly through Jon Jay's and Tom Sin's eyes. In some ways that country appears as though a band of round-headed giants had thrust their green-haired skulls up through the shining arms of sea. Here and there tree-covered mountainsides had been stripped bare when heavy rains had caused enormous slides that had plunged downward, carrying earth and trees away, exposing scowling gray rock faces. In the blue distance, every mountain wore a white chief's hat of snow that day. I wished to be in no other place than this.

It was midmorning when we reached the end of the inlet and touched our bows onto the beach at Tahsis and saw our familiar house posts and beams and sleeping benches, all washed bone clean by rains. We ordered the boards carried up to them. Against the enormous house posts we pegged our wide split cedar planks, placing them close together so the winter's cold and dampness would not come whistling in to freeze our bones and choke our throats with smoke. Our work was far from finished by nightfall, for we are careful with the building of our winter houses.

Slaves laid the roof boards all in place, weighing them with many heavy stones. We knew that according to the winds or rain or snow, the women would endlessly demand that someone reach up with long poles to readjust the smoke holes. Then they would pile and repile our storage boxes to help hold out the dampness and the cold.

Maquina's apartment was far grander than all the others, for in this Eagle house his servants erected a wide cedar screen against his side wall. It was not just to keep the wind out. No. This screen displayed a powerful heraldic painting in red and black of the Thunder Eagle carrying the Whale up to the mountains, where it dropped him and created Thunder. Through this screen Maquina had pierced several small openings that would allow him to peep out and observe any animal or human movement that might occur along the inlet.

Cedar mats are not enough to make a bed in Tahsis. I, like all the others, use trade blankets and winter sleeping skins that I can wrap around myself. In cold and windy weather, slaves are ordered to stay awake all night to keep our house fires burning. I am not one of those thin-blooded humans who abhors snow and freezing weather. I like Tahsis best of all. It is our most elaborate home, our place of winter feasts.

Exhausted from our journey, the careful rebuilding of our winter village, and overeating of the whale meat, we lay about for a few days listening to the pleasant drizzling sound of the early-winter rain, and in the darkness enjoying the wind songs of the mountains that stood all around us. We are like those big blue flies: we like to lie abed and muse to ourselves when our food boxes are full and it is raining.

When we were rested, Jon Jay and Tom Sin went outside and stood near the entrance to our Tahsis house, staring upward at the round white-headed mountains. I wondered if they were sorry to have no chance of seeing shipsmen passing. Yes, we were far inland from the sea, hidden in a narrow fiord where no white man's ship could travel.

It was unusual for Jon Jay to try so desperately to make me and Kawskaws understand him, and strange that he could not. We believed that what he was trying to ask us was whether we would ever return to our place beside the sea. Of course, we could not answer him, for in this life who knows whether we will even live to see the following day?

I could see that the young dagger maker was in awe of our four enormous house posts that were so long ago driven deep into the earth. They are almost twice as large around as the largest mast aboard his ship and are shaped like four ancestor creatures. A carver's adze strokes had left the long roof beams uniformly fluted all along their smoke-darkened length. The ends of these huge beams are carved with Wolf and Eagle faces that seem to wink with their inlaid blue-green abalone eyes and move their mighty teeth and beaks in the flickering firelight.

Late autumn came, and with it black-necked geese and the last flights of swans returning south. I looked forward to roaming once more along the flat frost-rimed beaches and to hunting the deer and elk that come out of the mountains when it snows.

Maquina had insisted that the dagger maker take all his armorer's tools with him, first to the salmon camp and then to Tahsis. Jon Jay had his hammers and his tongs, one large and one small iron anvil, his box of files, the all-important leather puff box, as well as other things. Tom Sin helped Jon Jay build an outside workplace not far from Maquina's dwelling. I must admit that it was as well built as our winter Eagle house, although in a totally different manner. We were amazed to see the way in which Jon Jay and the sailmaker put sides on their workplace. First they took their sharp-toothed saw and cut short round pieces from a cedar log, not longer than an elbow from a wrist. Then placing these round sections upright, Jon Jay would hold a cutlass while Tom Sin struck the blade a powerful downward blow with his hardwood billet, causing the cedar to split along the grain into thin shakes. They covered their workplace with a split-cedar roof and had the two weather sides well shingled against the autumn rains. In no time at all their work was done, which only goes to show that there are new and different ways to do almost anything.

Those two men seemed to enjoy working together. It was not long before we could hear Tom Sin's puff box squeezing and wheezing and the dagger maker's hammer ringing and his brave young voice singing in the clear chill air.

Jon Jay was now accepted—even loved—by almost every person in our village. That was, I think, because he sang and smiled and laughed with us in such a friendly way. He could not stay angry with us about the killing, and I believed he was glad to have found a way of life so superior to the one he had known before he came to live with us. He seemed to love the people of Wolf Town, especially old people and the younger children. He would take the smallest nail and hammer it bright and shape it for the wrist of a young child, who would run with delight to show it to his family, who would in return give those foreigners a well-smoked salmon or some woven cedar-bark mats to sit upon.

It was a happy thing for me too that the dagger maker had brought with him some good-sized copper nails. They were so soft that he took his hammer and, without even heating one of those pretty metal spikes, pounded it flat into a handsome bracelet. This he most carefully shaped and fitted to my wrist. When he knew I liked it, he took a file, then sand and ashes, and rubbed until it glowed. Then he closely examined the Bear crest that Kawskaws had earlier painted on my chest. Taking up a tiny pointed tool of hardest iron, he cleverly engraved the same Bear crest deeply into my bracelet. He took charcoal from the fire, mixed it with just a touch of grease, and rubbed until each line stood out most beautifully.

When I proudly showed that copper wristband to Maquina, he became insanely jealous! He said the dagger maker belonged to him and that I would have to pay him, Maquina, for all of Jon Jay's work. Well, I could see the sense in that. So I rooted through the odds and ends I'd kept and gave him two good-sized southern abalone shells that I found in a basket that had been finely woven by my dear dead wife. Maquina was well satisfied with that exchange, but to soothe his feelings Kawskaws and I went to the dagger maker and asked him to make a better bracelet for Maquina. This Jon Jay was able to do because he begged from Tom Sin a large silver coin, which he had hidden in his belt. Tom Sin reluctantly gave this to Jon Jay, who carefully hammered it into a wide, thin bracelet for Maquina. Jon Jay made many fancy marks and curls upon it, and in the middle he deeply cut a portrait of Maquina wearing his Whale chief's hat. This Jon Jay gave to him only after he had polished it as bright as any looking-glass.

Maquina was delighted. To show how pleased he was, he loaned Jon Jay the beautiful double-barreled musket that the dead ship master had given him, then snatched away. Jon Jay and the big man borrowed a small dugout canoe and for the first time went hunting by themselves. We heard them fire the musket five, six, seven times. We did not hear the eighth. They came back with a deer, two fat swans, nine sea ducks, and a thin blue heron, all of which they gave to us. They also had a loon, which would bring bad luck if any human dared to eat it. Tom Sin looked his usual gloomy self, but you could see by Jon Jay's red-cheeked face that they had both enjoyed their expedition. Certainly they knew they were no longer slaves in our house.

That night, after the women had skinned the birds, Jon Jay and Tom Sin speared one of the plumpest swans and roasted it over our fire pit, burning it in their own special way. Then tearing it in half, they devoured it between themselves.

Early on the following morning, when our house people were still asleep, I heard the big man pass our fire, then go to Maquina's apartment and wake the dagger maker. Together they went outside, and to warm themselves, they ran for some distance along the beach. Then walking back, they kindled up their hardwood fire, and from my sleeping mat I could hear Tom Sin working the puff box forcefully with his strong right foot. It was not long before all of Tahsis woke to the clanging of the dagger maker's heavy hammer. Then he took up the lighter one. Yes, I could now easily tell by listening—the light hammer as it struck his anvil had a high and joyous ring that would almost always start him singing and make me want to tap my fingers on the box beside my bed.

I drank the blue-mussel soup that Kawskaws gave me and ate some herring eggs before I flung my cape around my nakedness and followed Red Tongue and Maquina to the forge. Jon Jay was pounding out a heavy copper bolt into an arm-long dagger that Maquina had ordered him to make. I could see that it was going to have a splendid shape and balance.

Clang-clang-clang went Jon Jay's hammer, and squeeze-puff-squeeze-puff went Tom Sin's box. The sparks flew, and their stone hole turned from fiery red to yellow to white, so hot that you would not dare to look at it or place your face too close. When this splendid dagger was finished, Jon Jay rubbed it smooth with fine wet sand, and after that Tom Sin polished it with ashes. That made it shine along its deep-grooved blade like moonlight on the water.

Maquina showed the gathered house chiefs and other nobles the reflecting finish of the copper blade, and he said to them, "Can you imagine why those ignorant young brutes from all your houses wanted to destroy my clever dagger maker? Could any one of them create a blade like this?" he shouted as he waved the beautiful dagger in the air. "Gain tight control over those foolish hotheads or they may be the death of you."

I agreed with Maquina's thinking, and so did Kawskaws. I'm not so sure about Toowin. He was still rebellious against his elders, even though he was now a close friend of the dagger maker and would not want him harmed.

The two shipsmen did a curious thing with the white boat. They used it like a ship. By that I mean, they did not pull it up on shore but left it floating on the water, anchored with an iron hook about three stone's throws off our Tahsis beach.

Maquina was amused at this new way and said to me and Red Tongue, "Let them leave it out there."

We often watched them use a small canoe to go back and forth, leaving the canoe tied to the anchor rope when they wished to use the white boat. I noticed that my son, Toowin, almost always went with them. Of course, Hoiss and his friends were never asked to go, and I am sure that kept their anger burning.

One evening, the otter hunter and his son saw a foul thing happen. They came and told me right away, but I did not tell Maquina. No! The damage had been done, and I did not want my words to cause more trouble. The otter hunter said that he and his son were coming in late from hunting when they saw it all. Young Hoiss and the others had quietly pulled their seal

Jon Jay forges a long dagger for Maquina.

HOUSTON 3DT

canoe up beside the white boat. They got inside, and using two of the ship's iron augers, they started drilling holes in the bottom of the white boat, working as fast as they could in the bleary moonlight. When the white boat was almost filled with water, they jumped back into their canoe and kept on drilling through the sides with both augers until only the white boat's gunwales remained above the water. Those spiteful wretches must have drilled twenty holes, each big enough so you could easily stick your big toe through any one of them. That's the way we found the white boat in the morning, with only its bow above water.

Big Tom Sin and Jon Jay went paddling out to see the damage and came back trembling with rage.

"*Iktah mamook klawhap?* Who made holes?" Tom Sin had Jon Jay shout out in Chinook.

The old otter hunter, who was tough and honest, called back to them, "Hoiss and Opoots and the other boys—they did it!"

When the sailmaker heard Hoiss's name, he whirled around and marched straight to the Whale house, his curved cutlass hanging out behind him, swaying stiff as a mean dog's tail.

I myself never wish to miss the exciting things that happen in our village, so I hurried after Tom Sin, following him inside the entrance to the Whale house.

Tom Sin stopped and bellowed, "Hoiss! Hoiss!"

The hard tone of his words seemed to make the roof boards rattle, and his iron sword, as it came slithering from its sheath, gave off as bad a sound as I have ever heard.

"Hoiss is not here," a woman's voice called nervously from somewhere in the shadows of the house.

Of course, Tom Sin did not understand, but he went inside, searching for Hoiss down the whole length of the Whale house. Yes, I kept going along right after him, and if Hoiss or his friends were in that house, they must have been crouching up behind the house posts or hiding under the sleeping mats with some woman lying on them for protection. Jon Jay did not come into the Whale house.

When Tom Sin went outside, the dagger maker was standing beside Maquina, whose face was flushed with anger.

"That was my white boat," Maquina shouted at old Matla. "You tell that cocksure son of yours or any of his helpers that if I see any one of them before the next moon rises, I'll have hot stones rammed down their throats! You tell them that!"

Old Matla turned away without a word and stalked into the Whale house.

Tom Sin and Jon Jay took the small canoe and went out to the white boat again. I saw Tom Sin reach out with his cutlass and angrily slash the rope that still held the ruined vessel to its mooring, and it drifted away—one more ship's thing gone.

When I went back inside the Eagle house, Maquina was raging around our fire while my sister tried to calm him.

"I'm glad they drilled those holes and sank the white boat," Fog Woman said to my brother-in-law.

"Why do you say that, you crazy woman?" he shouted.

"Did you not know that those two shipsmen kept a barrel of fresh water in that boat, and a box of dried salmon, and an ax and rope and knives? I believe that when the winter storms were over, they would have tried to use the white boat to sail away from us and find another ship."

Maquina growled at her, then settled on a box and became very thoughtful. I myself believe that what my sister said was no longer true—at least, not for Jon Jay. He was becoming one of us. I was sorry that Hoiss and his friends had ruined something that gave Jon Jay so much pleasure. That was very wrong of them.

Jon Jay was trying hard to learn more of our language and improve his trade talk in Chinook so he could speak it well. He was clever and could easily remember almost any word. On his white skins he often made many-hooked squiggles that helped him to catch and hold most words we taught him.

Some nights, when a mood for learning came upon Maquina, he used to shout at me, "Siam, come over here with us and bring that long-legged Hupa girl of yours."

I didn't like the sound of that. Still, she came with me. I sat on a high box with all of them in his apartment and listened as Maquina asked the dagger maker to teach us important words in English so we could all of us speak together. Jon Jay seemed more than pleased to do that for us. Kawskaws stayed squatting humbly in the shadows. She wasn't really with us, but Kawskaws listened carefully, and could quickly understand many of Jon Jay's words.

Fog Woman listened as well—the only difference being that Kawskaws stayed silent while my sister, like any highborn *hac-umb*, asked too many questions, which for the most part the dagger maker rarely understood. Fog Woman did not hesitate to laugh at her own mistakes or ours, but I must say that my sister was always kind and thoughtful to Jon Jay.

Maquina improved his way of talking like a shipsman while I, for the first time, started to learn, mixing their foreign words with trade Chinook and throwing in a sprinkling of our own Wakashan. I learned to say "He bloke de moosket blarrel," and I know my Boston shipsman's accent was just perfect, though not so good for the Spanish or the French.

Kawskaws learned to say that, too, but she could not get her tongue around the beginning of "bloke" as perfectly as I could. That poor Hupa girl said "broke." She also said "barrel." She could not pronounce "blarrellll" as richly as Maquina or I.

Jon Jay was very polite to Kawskaws and did not try to correct her mispronunciations. He smiled or even sometimes laughed when I spoke and was most encouraging. He was a lovely teacher. It made our learning of the Boston shipsman's language such a pleasure.

After any lesson, when I went back to our apartment I would repeat to Kawskaws all the shipsman's words that we had learned. I was surprised at first that she could remember so many more than I could, and except for her saying "boy" instead of "bloy," she could pronounce many words exactly as Jon Jay had said them. Yes, Kawskaws has sharp ears, and she is quick to learn. Perhaps that is not too surprising. I have heard mothers tell their small children legends in this house, and later those children can repeat every single word perfectly.

But the big man, Tom Sin, did not even try to learn our language. He usually just lay on his back, gently swaying in his hammock in Beaver Seeker's apartment, his hands locked tight behind his head. He stared up at the thousands of winter candlefish we had hanging to dry on thin wands from our roof poles.

Yes, Tom Sin never tried to learn from us. Anyone could see that he cared nothing for our way of life. I often watched Tom Sin. I saw him staring up at the smoke hole, his eyes following the sparks that flew up into the night sky. I had the feeling that he was trying to see far out beyond the house. Tom Sin was dreaming with his eyes wide open. His body was lying here with us, but his mind was somewhere wandering, sailing on some distant ocean . . . one that I, myself, shall never, never see. Still, I hoped he too would come to embrace us as the dagger maker had, though I knew it would take Tom Sin longer, for he was not so quick or open as Jon Jay.

My familiar spirit is the Grizzly Bear, and it is well known that such bears are very curious. I suppose it was for that reason that one day I noticed Jon Jay doing something sly when he went outside the Eagle house. He glanced around to make sure that Maquina was not watching him, then made his way cautiously down to the far end of our beach. Why, I wondered, as I saw him edge his way and disappear behind the prow of my old whale canoe.

One of Maquina's younger women, the one named Spuck, was truly beautiful to look upon. Kawskaws had once whispered to me that this highborn girl felt like an outcast because she was allowed to sleep in our Eagle house only when my sister went away. Kawskaws said that she had seen that same girl one star-filled night lure the dagger maker into a beached canoe. Kawskaws said Jon Jay had eagerly jumped inside and lain with her. I was curious to know whether even in the daylight Spuck would come to him again.

I conveniently remembered that a paddle of mine was missing, and I went down to the beach to search for it—but really to see what Jon Jay was doing. He was there, sitting with his back against the bow of my dugout, the two small black boards open across his knees. He was exposing the thin white skins to the sun's heat, hoping, I guess, that it would dry the reddish berry juice mixed with charcoal that made the marks. He sharpened his quill then quickly started to scratch more tiny running marks.

There was nothing wrong with what Jon Jay was doing as far as I could see, but I myself had heard Maquina tell the dagger maker that he was not allowed to make squiggles on the thin white skins unless he had been told to do so. Maquina said that shipsmen's skins with marks upon them have sometimes been carried by one man to another who may be far away. That second shipsman can study the marks and understand their meaning as easily as we can understand the lines and dots that are tattooed on a women's face. Our tattoo marks indicate only a person's rank and family and whether one is married. But the shipsmen's marks can do much more than that. Their marks can inform them of countless complicated things about the past, or what is happening now, or even about events that have not happened yet—though that sounds unbelievable. Maquina asserted that those simple-looking marks that Jon Jay made could be very dangerous to us all. He had said that even years after the last bones of those shipsmen had crumbled and washed away and their burned-out ship had disappeared, other white men could come here and open up those two black boards, and if Jon Jay's squiggles were about that terrible day at Abooksha, they could understand exactly who had spilled their fellow shipsmen's blood. You may find that difficult to believe, but both Maquina and Red Tongue had assured me it was true. We talked about making some such useful marking system for ourselves, but for some reason we never did it. The dagger maker had been warned that he would surely get in trouble with Maquina if he went on making squiggles, but being Jon Jay, he chose to do it anyway.

That day when I went looking for my paddle, I saw Jon Jay not with Spuck but with Tom Sin, who was walking up and down the beach not far from the dagger maker. Like a nesting sandpiper, he pretended to be looking for clams or something else to eat, but I know now that he was guarding Jon Jay.

I watched as three young men led by Hoiss came walking along the beach, making straight toward the dagger maker, who sat in the shadow of the whale canoe. They were coming the way young men do, jostling and pushing one another and joking about some young girls from other houses.

Tom Sin watched them for a moment, and when he could see that they were coming too close to the canoe, he held himself stiffly erect and marched toward them in such a swaggering way that they saw only him and not Jon Jay, who sat still holding the black boards and skins upon his knee.

As Tom Sin moved along the beach path, Hoiss, feeling brave because of his three companions, stepped boldly up and blocked the big man's path. Hoiss, like the others, was naked except for his short bearskin cover and a long dagger strapped high upon his chest. His only decoration was a hawk's-quill ornament, which projected a hand's span out from the opening in the septum of his nose. Hoiss stood leering at the big man, demanding that Tom Sin go around him.

The sailmaker stepped aside, and Hoiss did the same, still blocking his way. Yes, Hoiss and his friends made it difficult for Tom Sin to come to like us.

I heard a bitter growl come out of Tom Sin's throat, and I saw his huge right hand dart out and twist the feather quill in Hoiss's nose. Can you imagine how that must have hurt? Hoiss grunted in pain and dropped to his knees, but he was up in an instant, his teeth bared in rage. I saw all four of the young men's sharp daggers come glistening from their sheaths.

Tom Sin nimbly sprang back and at the same time whipped his cutlass from its scabbard. He slashed the air between himself and his opponents, back and forth it went, then downward at a deadly cleaving angle. Vengeful as Hoiss's feelings must have been, I could see he feared that slashing blade. All four young men lowered their knives as they cautiously backed away from the oncoming Tom Sin, who snorted at them in disdain.

Of course, Maquina heard about that trouble on the beach.

Hoiss halts
Tom Sin in
his walk
along the
beach.

He told me that he was worried about both Tom Sin and the dagger maker, fearing that those same wild hotheads might lay in wait on some forest path or on the beach at night, where they could so easily ambush and kill both shipsmen. For this reason, Maquina encouraged Jon Jay and the sailmaker to go about with a pair of pistols visible in their waistbands and to always wear a cutlass hanging from a leather strap across their shoulders. This they did at first, but Tom Sin soon set aside his pistols, saying they were too uncomfortable. When Jon Jay reminded him that he should wear them, I saw the big man grimace, and take a stiffened stance, his head back, his chest out, and both his powerful fists cocked out before him. That showed he was brave but stupid. Our young men are trained as hunters. If they want to kill a man, they will do that—by surprise, and always from an ambush when one least expects attack.

I had only half believed Kawskaws when she told me of that smooth-faced Spuck trying to lure Jon Jay into my canoe.

"She is right!" my sister said, agreeing with Kawskaws. "Brother, you have got to warn Jon Jay to keep well away from all my husband's women. He throws a temper fit when anyone steals a young girl out from under him. I know because I've seen it happen." She counted on her fingers. "Once, twice, yes, three times!" She giggled with delight. "Or was it four times, maybe five."

It was easy enough for Kawskaws and my sister to tell me to warn the dagger maker about these women, but how was I going to do it? Such a task would be difficult, and sad too, for there is no joy in depriving someone—and a friend, at that—of pleasure. It took me all that evening and some of the next day to work out, with help from Kawskaws, the proper words. Then I practiced them on her when no one else was listening.

That evening, I took Jon Jay aside and said, *"Tyee solleks tenas klootchman itlokum.* Chief very angry get . . . you handplay his young women. *Kumtuks?* Understand? *Keek willie Kapswalla yah wahtin.* Young girls of the *tyee* you do not secretly touch the crotch!"

But I got it all mixed up, and Jon Jay started laughing because he only partly understood me. I tried again, but by then I was nervous and got even more mixed up.

He kept saying, *"Keek willie? Keek willie?"* and searched through the squiggles on his white skins. "What does Cheepo-kesklickeryek mean?" he asked.

With that I gave up.

Then I heard Kawskaws speaking with her shy Hupa accent. "Young wives . . . of *tyee* . . . you don't hand-play the underbelly. *Kumtuks?* You understand?"

At first the dagger maker did not answer.

Kawskaws tried again and must have found a gesture or plainer way to say it, for Jon Jay smiled at her and answered, *"He ho, kumtuks.* Oh, yes, now I understand."

Then he softly said something else to Kawskaws. Those words made her smile a little, and her face turned red. She would not look up at me and refused to translate what the dagger maker said.

After that, none of the three of us were able to find more words that we would care to say about those girls. Jon Jay put away his squiggles, and we three started laughing. I noticed that he was looking straight at Kawskaws's face, and now she was not turning her eyes away from his, which most unmarried Yo-quot girls would surely do.

I sent Kawskaws to the Thunder house to bring the copper widow to me. Kawskaws came back and squatted by our fire. She was so upset she would not even look at me.

"Where is Cheepokesklickeryek?" I demanded. "Is she coming here?"

"No," Kawskaws answered. "She's doing something else. She says she does not want to come to you tonight."

I had some rum mixed with only a little molasses that I had planned to drink with her. But when I heard Kawskaws's words, I became excited and drank all that rum myself.

"Where are you going?" Kawskaws said.

"I'm going to get her," I shouted. "If you won't bring her over here, I will!"

"Don't go over there," she pleaded. "It will look bad in the

Thunder house, your going there so late. You'll be sorry," she called after me as I went out the Eagle house entrance. "You'll get hurt!"

It was raining lightly, and it was absolutely dark, and I had been in too much of a hurry to take a torch with me. When I neared the Thunder house, their dogs set up a furious barking. By the time I stumbled through their entranceway, dozens of men's and women's heads were up, watching me in curious silence.

I knew that the copper widow lived in the important part of the house. I went straight to her apartment. When I got there, I drew back in horror, for behind the boxes she was riding naked on top of her male slave. That brute lay upturned underneath her. He leered up at me triumphantly.

"Go away," she hissed at me, and I could see my ivory pendant swaying back and forth between her breasts. "I'm busy with this one tonight. Maybe I'll come back to you . . . some other time."

In Wolf Town any noble or commoner, male or female, who lies with a slave runs the greatest risk of execution. That so worried me that I scarcely slept that night. I didn't want the copper widow killed. I didn't want to lose her.

 THE GHASTLY moment that Maquina dreaded most of all had finally caught him. He made us all aware of that as we counted the waning faces of the early-winter moon. I, like Maquina and other important persons of our village, ordered that my finest cloaks, capes, hats, frontlets, ceremonial weapons, feathered nose pendants, paints, mica dust, and eagle down be carefully packed and safely bound into my journey boxes. The time of the Black Fin potlatch had come.

It was decided that Satsatsoksis, Maquina's only son, would remain at Tahsis with his aunt because, as my sister said, they wished to spare his young memory from the embarrassments this potlatch feast would surely heap upon his father's head. For that exact same reason, I decided that Toowin should not go. I told Kawskaws that that son of mine did not need his limbs massaged by her. I told her that Toowin looked lean and sinewy to me and urged her to make sure he got enough meat and fish to eat.

Maquina let Jon Jay know that he and Tom Sin would be coming with us. My sister offered to sew a tear in Jon Jay's shirt. But instead, the sailmaker took out his own bright iron needle and his finest thread. Sitting cross-legged in a most unusual position, he neatly repaired and patched both Jon Jay's clothing and his own, using curious lock stitches of a kind our women said they had never seen performed before.

"That is just one more proof," my sister told me. "Those poor creatures had to learn to sew because they had no mothers or women of their own. That is why shipsmen are always so hotly after ours, even when it is not wise—I hope Maquina never hears about Jon Jay and Spuck."

"If they have no mothers, how do they get born?" I asked Fog Woman. "Do they come out of eggs—like birds or fishes?"

But even she had no answer to that mystery.

Finally, Maquina had to admit that we were ready to depart. Toward evening, our two largest canoes left the beach at Tahsis and headed south along our inlet until we turned west into the passage that leads toward the Black Fin waters. All together—nobles, paddlers, servants—we were over seventy persons on the move. Because we were southerners going feasting with Maquina's northern rival, we tried to look impressive, and we did. Both his Eagle canoe and my Bear canoe had freshly painted bow designs.

Imagine us going to a potlatch witnessing with two white foreigners sitting high in our canoes. How strangely grand they looked, fully armed with cutlasses and pistols and wearing their shiny flat black shipsmen's hats and neatly tied kerchiefs. Those Black Fin would not be able to believe their eyes. I watched the dagger maker as he stared out at Sea Lion Rock and listened to the booming of the surf as it rushed in and struck the vertical gray stone face, then spumed high into the wintry air. Who was there alive who would not envy us the dark-green beauty of our mountain country and our inland waterways?

As evening settled, our dugouts cut silently through the water, which lay black and still, reflecting the faint silver ripples that fanned out from each canoe. Night fell, and low in the sky the Dog star came out and winked and blinked its single shining eye at us, as white frost shimmered on the sides of our canoes. It was not hard on the younger paddlers, who, though naked, warmed themselves by stroking hard. But for us who were being carried to the feast, it was utter misery. We dared not complain, of course, and yet without space to exercise our legs, the shivers ran along our spines. I tried thinking of lying with the copper widow. Yes, that helped a little, but still my buttocks grew cold as stones. I tried to think of blazing fires. That did not help. My fingers and my toes turned numb as ice.

This misery that we shared was exactly as Maquina planned. He preferred to travel in the blackness of the night. Of course, he too was aware of the cold as he felt it settle all around him. But seated on his box with his legs drawn up against his body and his thick sea otter cloak drawn tight around him, he seemed to suffer less than others. The chill salt air dampened his face, keeping him keen and alert. I knew that he must be carefully planning his entrance into that much-dreaded Black Fin village.

In the blackness before dawn, the stars came out above our heads in countless numbers, and through them northern lights appeared, wavering like ghostly fingers, sometimes fading, sometimes reaching upward in the immense bowl of the sky. I shuddered as I listened to the rhythmic swish-swish of the paddle strokes and forced my frozen thoughts to dwell on the old Black Fin chief named Tall Hat. Maquina hated and feared him more than any other soul alive, and yet for that very reason he had not dared refuse his feast. Maquina had no choice except to go and suffer who knows what insults during this potlatch, an event that could easily lead to trouble. This aging Black Fin monster could scarcely wait to squash Maquina with his wealth, to roll on him like a grizzly wallowing in a cache of rotting salmon—we Eagle house people would be forced to sit and watch it all. This would be Tall Hat's fourth large feast, his final strike against his greatest rival. Of course, Maquina needed all of our support. Yes, this winter witnessing, if all went well, would be a bloodless combat fought between two powerful chiefs.

No wonder we were silent as our two canoes traveled until it grew light, then landed in a sheltered cove. We stretched, relieved ourselves, and gathered near as the slaves made fires. We ate chunks of cold boiled halibut, smoked salmon, old duck eggs and dried herring eggs on seaweed. Then we slept. Even that delicious food and rest did not take away our gloom. Except for our two guards, we spent the warmest part of the morning and the midday fast asleep.

In the late afternoon, Maquina lay on his back, feigning sleep, knowing that many curious eyes were watching him. He could feel his kinfolk crowded close around him. They squatted nearby, wrapped in capes and blankets, searching his face for any twitch of anguish, any subtle sign that would betray his horror of the ordeal he was about to suffer. Fiercely Maquina held his jaw muscles in check so that his observers would not see them leap and lock like fighting crabs. I could imagine all his frightful thoughts, which must be piling one atop the other, demanding that his face contort with rage. But Maquina lay breathing quietly, appearing as serene as a sleeping child. He lay there gathering all his strength inside himself, preparing to brave the indignities dealt him by his old rival, Tall Hat.

Maquina opened his eyes so suddenly that he startled Matla and me and several noblewomen from the Whale and Thunder houses, who too quickly looked away. My brother-in-law removed the fine white frost that he had breathed upon his mustache. Red Tongue and I were the first to cautiously return our gaze directly at Maquina. Jon Jay and Tom Sin, both of whom were not squatting but sitting with their legs stretched out before them on the beach, gawked at the paddlers, who with Man Frog and Long Claws were already in the icy water of the salt chuck performing their first naked rituals for the coming journey.

I looked away from Maquina and listened to the mournful calling of the shore birds distorted in the mists, echoing back to us like the helpless cries of drowning men. I could see our sorcerer shaking his rattle as he hurried up and down the beach. I had expected this, for water birds that cry while hidden in the fog have often proved a fatal omen for sea travelers. Soon the sorcerer was rooting madly through his bag in search of powerful amulets to trade to Maquina and me. I saved mine to give later to Toowin, whom I thought needed help more than anyone I know.

We nobles climbed the warm-blooded three-man ladder of bare flesh and settled in our places. Tom Sin and the dagger maker rolled up their pants legs and, like the paddlers, waded knee-deep into the water and vaulted with agility into Maquina's big canoe. We moved out again to suffer the long, cold ordeal of night.

When morning came, Red Tongue ordered the paddlers to turn into a deep fiord. The two foreigners had no way of knowing it, but this was the last leg of our unwanted journey. I tried to put the coming feast out of my mind and enjoy the look of this unfamiliar country. Although we are bitter rivals of the Black Fin, I must admit that the approaches to their village on that frosted morning seemed to have a strangely dreamlike quality.

White-winged gulls soared lazily against the somber background of the tall green forest or sat bobbing like little chunks of ice on the lead-gray waters. The female gulls rose and wheeled, screaming their displeasure at the greedy adult males, who called back rudely sensuous invitations to debauch. Young gulls, fully grown but still wearing their childishly drab brown feathers, landed awkwardly, then joyfully rode the insurge of the tide.

Jon Jay and the sailmaker sat just behind Maquina in the huge canoe. I guess they must have felt as cramped and cold as we did. At times I saw Jon Jay shudder as he drew his thin cedar cape around him tightly. My sister, seeing this, felt down into a box and pulled out two blue woolen trade blankets. She handed one to each of them.

When we reached the narrows of the Black Fin Channel, the rising tide was moving very fast. We passed through, cautious of the fanglike rocks that jutted upward just beneath the boiling surface. At the end of the narrows, we saw ahead two good-sized canoes, which had gone through just before us.

"Otter Town people . . ." said Maquina, craning his neck to see their bow designs and if his southern rival, Wickinnish, was with them. He was not! Maquina let out a sigh of relief, for two such formidable chiefs at a single potlatch was more than even he could bear.

Maquina started tapping his knuckles impatiently against the side of Sea Spear until our paddlers picked up his quicker rhythm and increased their stroke. Slowly we drew up near the Otter Town canoes.

"She's there," Maquina whispered, and he leered at me and nodded toward a handsome girl who turned her head and stared back at us.

She was young and fine to look at—dark eyes with thick lashes, clear sun-browned skin drawn over wide cheekbones, and hair shining blue as a raven's wing. Her teeth gleamed white when she smiled at Maquina. Yes, I could tell he wanted her! But did he show that? No, not he!

Instead he turned and looked at Jon Jay, then pointed to the beautiful girl. "Sea Star is her name," he said in Chinook. "You want her? I'll buy her for you, dagger maker. She'll make you a very good wife."

Jon Jay understood his words and sat up high in our canoe to see this girl. She wasn't shy. She stared straight back at him.

Maquina nodded and spoke to Upquesta, a house chief from Otter Town and father of that girl. "I hoped that I would see you here," he said most cordially. "I wish to speak with you sometime during this dreadful Black Fin mishmash!"

The nobles in the Otter Town canoe smiled and nodded, for they no more than we admired the Black Fin. Our bow was now drawn even with the leading Otter Town canoe, and Sea Spear would easily have passed it. But the rhythm of Maquina's beat slowed down, as did our paddlers, and he allowed the Otter Town canoes to pull ahead of us. I had never seen my brother-in-law act so politely.

"Don't you think she would make a fine wife for my son, Jon Jay?" Maquina asked me in a voice that would allow those in the other canoes to hear him.

My sister stared suspiciously at her husband, and I must say I did, too, for this was the first time Maquina had openly admitted that he intended to adopt Jon Jay as his son. I myself had heard my brother-in-law tell those killers on the ship that he was taking Jon Jay as his slave, and now he was talking like an anxious father trying to marry off his son to a young noblewoman of wealth and power from one of the strongest houses on this coast.

"You don't fool me," my sister whispered to her husband. "She is exactly the kind of girl you like. You don't care about Jon Jay. You're thinking of her for yourself."

"Silence, woman," Maquina said, but in a voice so low that those in the other canoes would not hear him. Then with a loud command, he ordered our canoes ashore.

The girl and her father turned again when they heard that. Maquina smiled at Upquesta and his daughter. Jon Jay nodded his head toward the beautiful girl, and to my surprise she nodded back.

"Did you see that?" said Maquina. "She has admired me since she was a small girl." My brother-in-law looked at his wife and said, "Well, I can't help it if she likes me!"

Maquina chose a narrow hidden beach for us to land. We slept through the day and embarked as the winter sun sank early into its night place in the western ocean. We started out again. Unseen loons called into the silent gloom and were answered by others far away. A sharp west wind whipped up shivering silver patterns as it raced in heavy gusts along the inlet. With the wind at our backs, the paddlers made good time. Huge rafts of winter sea birds rose screaming above the beds of floating kelp, where female sea otters nursed their young and raised their heads the better to see us passing. Of course, we would not hunt here, for we were now in Tall Hat's country.

Sometime past the next midday, we reached the Black Fin Narrows and were swept through on the incoming tide. The paddlers turned the canoes and glided up the narrow bay between towering stone cliffs finely laced with early winter snow. Our painted prows sliced silently through the water, the paddlers stroking with a steady, tireless rhythm. We rounded a protective point of land and there, surprisingly close to us, saw the Black Fin village.

A guard, who had been set out by their war chief, saw our two huge canoes emerging from the fog, and he gave a clumsy imitation of a raven's cry. That croaking sound was passed along by others, warning the Black Fin that newcomers were arriving.

"Stop!" Maquina warned his paddlers.

They backstroked, then held steady as the women in the two canoes untied the boxes and hastily shook out all our costumes. Swiftly we nobles had our faces painted. Slaves helped us arrange our otter robes or long-fringed goat-hair capes and freshly twisted-cedar headbands or small helmet masks.

Fog Woman held a small looking-glass for Jon Jay while

he brushed his hair, and she retied his blue neck scarf and reset his hat exactly to her liking. Tom Sin scorned all primping except to set his black varnished hat at the same flat angle as Jon Jay's and roll back his sleeves, proudly exposing the elaborate blue tattooing on his heavy muscled forearms.

When Fog Woman put the looking-glass away, Maquina snorted, "Your sister helps those foreigners far more than she helps me."

"You look fine," Fog Woman said with a laugh. "I'm trying to help these two tidy up. The Black Fin will be shocked to see them with us."

Maquina scowled as he signaled his paddlers forward, then put his hand up to his forehead, shading his eyes, trying to block out his view of the huge plank houses emerging from the mist with the outlandish Black Fin Whale designs freshly repainted on all the house fronts. My brother-in-law avoided looking at the scattered line of big canoes already pulled up on the beach and the numerous glow of paddlers' campfires and slaves' lean-tos that edged the Black Fin forest, for it showed that an unusual number of important persons from north and south along the coast had been invited. Maquina hunched his shoulders, making his thick new otter cloak cover his ears in an effort to shut out the monotonous throbbing of their sorcerer's drum and the somber-sounding notes from the wood whistles and the uneven chanting of the greeting songs, which seemed to mock Maquina, daring him to come and suffer the humiliations that the Black Fin had so carefully planned for him. I saw my brother-in-law squint his eyes, trying to blur the nearness of those Black Fin totems. Huge coarsely carved wooden images they were, with folded wings and clutching claws and long tongues slavering down.

The Black Fin are different from our people. We speak to them best in the Chinook language. They are not like us. These northerners also hunt whales, but our canoes are vastly superior to theirs. Oh, yes, we are famous everywhere for our fast canoes.

I watched with morbid fascination as Black Fin slaves lowered the climbing log from the largest stilted house front. Maquina groaned again as we all recognized Tall Hat's grandson step fussily out of the big house entrance, ducking low to protect the crown of sea lion whiskers that topped his elaborate headdress.

Jon Jay sat up to look when he saw this boy, younger than himself, draw a magnificent Chilkat goat-hair blanket around his shoulders, then purposely sway his hips to make the fringe dance. The young man climbed down and marched toward the beach with mincing steps. His young ushers assembled around him, holding their arms akimbo to spread their splendid capes like sunning cormorants, trying to give an illusion of grandness to their dreary Black Fin town.

Maquina turned his frowning face away and looked across the water. I believe he was imagining the effect it would have if he suddenly ordered his canoes to turn and leave. I shuddered to think what my sister and every other person on this coast would say if he dared try anything like that.

"You be careful at this feast," my sister warned her husband quietly. "It could be dangerous."

Our two canoes moved in to make a landing on the beach. These northerners, who have taken on so many of our customs, do not lay out long cedar welcome mats as we do. They do not greet important guests in our more cordial southern fashion. Instead, they had these mere children waiting on their beach.

Tall Hat's grandson made a quick hand signal, ordering Maquina's big canoe into a chosen landing place.

Then suddenly they dragged from the crowd one of their short male slaves, naked except for a heavy twisted-cedar collar. He began to scream in terror. Two of their young ushers grabbed the slave and flung him down in front of our oncoming canoe. I saw them kick the slave's legs wide apart, and one raised a whalebone club to brain him at the very moment when our heavy canoe would pass up along his spine, using his body grease to slide Sea Spear up out of the water without damaging its delicate cedar hull. Seeing this, Maquina flung out his right arm, ordering his canoemen to change their course so that Sea Spear's knifelike prow swung away from the prone slave. Then, on his command, our paddlers drove the huge canoe at murderous speed straight in at this future Black Fin chief and his elegant crowd of ushers.

This caused everyone of them to lurch away, leaping backward, bumping into one another in confusion as they tried to save themselves from being rammed. Maquina allowed his Sea Spear to grind recklessly onto their rough gravel beach. Oh, but it was more than worth the risk of damage. I, Siam, was proud of him! Maquina glanced back at his wife and Red Tongue and at me in triumph, and we three widened our eyes to show him our delight. Certainly my brother-in-law had won that first small challenge in this game of wits and power, but inside ourselves we knew his troubles had not yet begun.

The Black Fin villagers now stood motionless on their beach, watching us with sullen scorn. Three of our strongest slaves leapt out of our canoe and once more formed a human ladder. Maquina rose from his high box and strode majestically down their backs. We high-caste people followed him. Jon Jay and Tom Sin showed their boldness and agility by leaping to the beach, and this first vigorous sight of those two armed foreigners drew gasps of astonishment from the Black Fin.

When our second canoe had landed and we had gathered close behind Maquina, Tom Sin and Jon Jay on either side of him, my brother-in-law led our people up into the village. The Black Fin walked somberly beside us. Neither party would have been willing to lose face by trailing behind the other, and neither they nor we would willingly have walked before the other, fearing that some rude, indecent insult might secretly be acted out behind their backs. No such thing occurred. What Tall Hat and his son had planned for us was far more subtle than a simple crudeness such as that.

The Black Fin usher climbed the ladder first but stood aside to allow our *tyee* to precede all of us into their big house. Maquina turned and went through the entrance backward to show his mistrust of Black Fin daggers at his back, twitching his rump as he moved through their entrance to show utter disdain for his old rival, who awaited him inside.

This potlatch was going to be a real ordeal. The only plea-sure left to us was to watch the faces of the Black Fin people in the house as they stared at our pair of stern-faced shipsmen. They must have tried to guess how these two foreigners had come to be with us. Had we bought them? Had they been ship-wrecked? Or, they wondered, had we possessed the bravery to go against ship's cannons and take them captive in a fight?

At all times Maquina kept the dagger maker and Tom Sin one on either side of him. They, like Maquina, went barefoot. Each wore a leather strap over the right shoulder to support his murderous-looking cutlass, and each carried a highly visible pair of pistols in his waistband. Although the Black Fin insisted that guests come to feasts unarmed, no one had the courage to chal-lenge Maquina's pair of foreign bodyguards.

As the early-winter night was falling, we, like all the others, were ushered near the central fire and shown our places. More than a hundred nobles had already gathered in the Black Fin house, each seated proudly according to his rank. Behind them squatted the commoners, warriors, carvers, weavers, boatmen, servants, children, concubines, and even slaves. To Jon Jay and Tom Sin, this Black Fin house may have seemed like ours, but to us it was different in oh, so many ways.

Maquina marched grandly forward, turning his head only to recognize his older sister from Kelp Rock, whom he had pur-posely not seen for several years. He did not so much as glance at her wizened husband. He did nod to an occasional neighbor-ing chief as he and my sister took their rightful places in the very center of the foremost rank, facing the chief talker of the Black Fin people, who stood immediately before them. Jon Jay was at Maquina's right hand, a significant position reserved for one's most favored child, and I was seated next to him. Red Tongue moved in beside Tom Sin, whom he did not like or trust at all.

Before Maquina, seated grandly in the place of honor, was

Old Tall Hat stares blankly at the guests arriving at his potlatch.

his old Black Fin rival. Tall Hat remained bolt upright, his face expressionless. Peering narrowly at all his guests arrayed around the fire, the old man's eyes stared dully from beneath their half-closed lids. The shadows shifted in the sunken hollows beneath his high cheekbones, as though he were trying to whisper something to his son beside him, the one called Molasses Eater. This gross brute of a man looked nothing like his father. He had small, treacherous eyes, sensuous lips, and greasy jowls that seemed to melt into his bloated body.

Maquina leaned forward, studying old Tall Hat carefully, searching for any sign of movement; and when he saw none, he nudged me and whispered, "He's not drunk, and he's not asleep. He's dead!"

"Dead!" I exclaimed.

So that was it! That was what had caused the frantic hurry. This old man must have believed that he was dying when he rushed his chief talker south to shout his invitation to Maquina. I peered thoughtfully at the old man. Yes, he was dead, dead some days ago. It would be hard for Maquina to absorb the knowledge that the soul had finally flown out of his most bitter rival.

Tall Hat's body sat in quiet dignity on a thick pillow of freshly cut strong-smelling cedar boughs placed there to mask the scent of death, which by then must have surrounded him. The old chief's body was draped in a full-length sea otter cloak spread over his crossed legs and covering the short post that supported his body. On his head he wore a woven spruce-root hat of northern style, wide-brimmed and topped with not four but five round cylinders, each one representing a potlatch he had given. His hat was painted with a bold Black Fin design. From the top ring, which represented this, his last potlatch, hung a cascade of white winter ermine skins, which hid the cords bound harnesslike around his shoulders, neck, and skull to keep his lifeless body from sagging forward against his copper shield.

"*Mossum?* Asleep?" Jon Jay asked me in a whisper.

"*Yahka memaloost.* He's dead," I answered.

The old man's face had been carefully decorated for the

feast, painted with a hundred thin red and blue lines, each line representing ten trade blankets of those colors. All of these and much, much more he had ordered to be given away. Even his own death was not allowed to disrupt his last great potlatch, his final triumph over Maquina, which would give his totem pole its topmost ring.

I tried to muster up some feeling as I stared at this vengeful old man who refused to go into his funeral canoe until he had finally put Maquina down. He was the only one who could have ordered this. Even in death he was determined to sit there witnessing his victory. I tried to imagine the last moments of this chief who sat so stiff and proud before us. I wondered if his soul was still attending this potlatch, peering now at me perhaps through dull glazed eyes.

I wondered too if Maquina could accept the fact that when this feast was over and all the old man's titles had been given, Tall Hat's son would outrank my brother-in-law and every other chief upon the coast. It is my duty, as the usher of Wolf Town, to know that. It is up to me to understand each noble's rank and position. Here, age means nothing when it comes to rank. The right to possess certain names, songs, dances, masks, the right to display family crests, means everything to us. At this feast, Tall Hat's son would be given many titles, many privileges. That is why all of us had been invited, for this giving had to be seen by many witnesses—how else could it be recorded?

Even I, Siam, Wolf Town's usher, sat there trembling as I imagined the mountains of gifts that must be hidden behind the great Black Fin house screen. Who would not shudder with awe and excitement at the very thought of feasting with one's enemies, especially when they were dead? I also knew that some day, in some way, Maquina would have to give a gigantic feast to outdo all of this. That feast would take all gifts given here, and much, much more.

Some slaves fed the one big central fire with half-dried logs, while others slowly pulled around to all the guests a huge wooden trencher carved into the form of an enormous sea otter. Jon Jay and the sailmaker poked cautiously into the food, each taking only the smallest portion, fearful of what might lie buried under the glistening slick of candlefish grease poured over old fish eggs, octopus, and seaweed. Like Maquina, I ate little because I wished to save my stomach for the awful ordeals that we knew lay ahead.

The evening dragged on and on with tiresome dances and that stupefying Black Fin style of singing and drumming. Old Matla fell sound asleep and snored. Red Tongue yawned, and Maquina allowed his head to nod and his eyes to close, letting the Black Fin know that he was bored with their pretentious myths and dreams of power. As we had expected, on this, the first of many evenings, nothing of consequence was given away. Jon Jay spent his time staring at the wide-cheeked girl from Otter Town, and she quite often glanced straight back at him. I thought of the copper widow and imagined I could feel her fingernails along my back.

When, mercifully, that night's performance was ended, Maquina rose with all the others, and we left the house, my brother-in-law leaning heavily on the dagger maker to show the fat Molasses Eater that even though he had been too cheap to serve us rum, the awful quality of their performances had partly paralyzed Maquina's body and may even have unhinged his mind.

Fog Woman nudged Maquina and said, "It's rather early in this feast for you to put on that sort of act. Save your insults for the bad times. That will surely come to you tomorrow!"

WHEN Maquina heard his wife make that remark, he staggered even more and refused to pay attention to any other word from her. He glanced slyly at his older sister but was careful not to speak to her. She turned down the corners of her long-jawed mouth and frowned and shook her head at him in disapproval.

The elder Black Fin usher offered us a house so newly built it still had the lovely scent of new-cut cedar. Maquina noisily refused it and chose instead to sleep his party in the oldest vacant house in the whole village. We stumbled toward it along unfamiliar paths, accompanied by the yaps and growls of unfamiliar dogs.

"This house smells worse than a foxes' den," Maquina grumbled when we were inside.

It remained dank and depressing in spite of the five soggy fire pits we relighted. Fog Woman had slaves push open the sodden roof boards around the smoke holes, making all of us miserable, as she tried to air that ancient house.

In the firelight that danced against the soot-stained inner walls, we saw some old dance paraphernalia: a broken Shark mask, some mildewed cedar robes, and badly painted storage boxes, most with shattered lids.

Maquina smiled when he looked at Red Tongue and me, then shouted in his loudest voice, "Is nothing sacred to these Black Fin monsters? Would you believe that anyone could live inside a tumbled mess like this?"

For the first time since this moon had appeared, my brother-in-law was delighted with himself. He sat there chuckling, knowing that the Black Fin would have someone outside listening. He imagined the shame their nobles must be feeling with their rival guest of honor sitting staring at the mildew of their moldering house ruin.

Not far from the damply hissing fire pit, Maquina huddled uncomfortably on our storage boxes, which his servants had arranged for both of us. Nobles, paddlers, and slaves sat or squatted awkwardly around us, afraid to trust the rotted planking of the sleeping platforms but more horrified at the thought of lying down on the moldering earthen floor. Three of our guards we posted at the entrance to this old house just to show our Black Fin hosts that we did not trust them, although Maquina knew full well that we had rarely been safer from attack in all our lives.

It had been a long, cold, tiresome journey in our canoes and a dreadful evening in their feast house. I wished that I had brought Kawskaws with me, and I tried to imagine what she and Toowin must be doing at this moment. That thought made me restless, and I set my mind to thinking once more of the copper widow. While trying, I fell into a blissful sleep.

I awoke alone with the rotting Black Fin house around me. I shuddered when I peeked through the wide wall cracks and saw that snow had fallen in the mountains and now clung wetly to the lush green feathers of the cedar trees. Jon Jay was sitting huddled in his blankets, drinking a steaming bowl of abalone broth that gave off a savory smell. Knee Scars, who wore the tatters of a cougar skin, sullenly came and gave me mine. Maquina was always slow to wake, and when he did, he sat until midmorning listening to the sad wood whistles repeating their first four magic notes that called us to the potlatch. Yes, the Black Fin were impatient to get at Maquina. That crass Molasses Eater, he could hardly wait.

"Oh, how I long to leave this ghastly village," Maquina groaned as he stared up at the wet smoke-blackened roof beams of the dying house. "I wonder what those six girls are doing back at Tahsis."

Scowling and complaining of the dampness stiffening his joints, Maquina spat a piece of fish spine into the fire, held his wooden bowl outstretched, and growled out for more broth. When the meal was done, he took endless time to paint his face—anything to delay our going to that Black Fin crest house.

Through the long cracks in the walls, I myself could see guests parading from the other houses and hear sly whispering and see them casting sidelong glances as they passed us.

"We should go now," Fog Woman said. "Remember, some here would be glad to crowd us from our proper seating."

Maquina rose and drew his otter cloak around himself. Red Tongue did not take his talker's staff, for we had agreed he would refuse to speak at such a gathering. Fog Woman placed a simple ring of newly pounded cedar bark upon her husband's head, and he paused while she brushed and straightened his otter cloak, the one that had been retrieved from the master's cabin.

"You look just fine," she whispered. "But remember, they will try to trick you and drive you mad today. Don't let anything they do upset you. Keep those two shipsmen near you. They make you look very dignified."

Instead of answering her, Maquina turned and led our party up to the Black Fin crest house, his red-painted face expressionless in the falling winter snow.

A crowd had gathered near the new long grave post. It lay face down in its wooden cradle so that it pointed like a giant finger out across the inlet, its carved crests hidden from our curious eyes. The old man's painted box that held his body had already been secured inside the hollow made to hold it. Wet snow covered the ground, making the village houses and the forest behind them look black in the morning light. The beach before the houses formed a long gray curve where the tide had come up and washed away the winter whiteness.

We waited silently. Jon Jay and Tom Sin stood with us, also watching, not knowing what was going to happen. Maquina remained aloof.

When their chief talker gave a signal, the Black Fin and their guests took hold of the many twisted-cedar ropes attached to the pole. All of these had been tossed over a trestle temporarily erected in front of the Black Fin house. As they pulled the ropes, the huge pole entombing Tall Hat's body eased forward along a shallow groove that had been cut in the earth to guide it. Now the many groups of people hauled harder on the lines, and the giant grave post began to tilt upright as it neared the hole.

"Wait! Wait! Hold it there!" Molasses Eater shouted. "Bring him up here! We're ready for him now!"

I easily recognized the slave who had been flung down in front of our canoe on the day we had arrived. He was brought up and made to stand beside the base of the huge cedar pole. He was very afraid to be there and had to be held in place by three strong men. Two held his arms, and the strongest one held him around the neck.

I was wondering what was going to happen to that man when out of the watching crowd of villagers and guests a young slave woman was thrust forward and her *kotsak* roughly torn off her body. When she saw the great pole tilted up before her, she too started pulling violently back against those who held her wrists. Then she began wailing and screaming. It was a horrible sound to hear.

The male slave was the first to be cast head first down into the dark hole in the earth. He struggled to his feet and was trying to climb out when suddenly the naked young woman was flung in on top of him, knocking him back to the bottom. They were both up in a moment, leaping, trying desperately to catch a grip on the crumbling wet earth at the edge of the hole. The huge cedar butt of Tall Hat's totem came grinding and sliding toward them, leaving a long black scar in the snow. As true fear came to them, their voices rose and blended together into a ter-rifying male and female sound. The pole tilted upright and hung there for a moment. Then its full weight went crushing down on top of them with a dreadful *thuuunk!* For one awful moment we could hear a broken whimpering filtering up out of the dark earth, and then everything was silent.

The villagers and guests stood back quietly. The falling snow hushed every sound. I waited, trembling, finding it hard to draw my breath. I watched strong men move forward and force heavy stones tightly against the base of the pole to hold it upright. After that, old women came and threw baskets of black earth around the totem, and a drum started slowly beating, and their masked thunder dancers and the earthquake dancers moved ponderously around the pole, packing the earth with the heavy pounding of their naked feet.

"I hate to see those two humans thrown away," my sister said in a voice loud enough for many there to hear. "That is not our custom. These Black Fin learned such madness from potlatching with that half-crazed northern chief!"

Molasses Eater was standing near us and heard Fog Woman's bitter criticism. He turned and, seeing the disdainful look on all our faces, glared at Maquina and his *hacumb* and demanded, "What is wrong with that? Those two slaves belonged to my father. Would you want to see your father go out of this world all by himself?" He shouted, "Those two slaves loved my father. They were glad enough to go with him."

"It didn't sound like that to me!" my sister yelled at him.

"I don't want to hear you!" He turned his back on us and, putting his hands over his ears, strode angrily away and disappeared inside the Black Fin house.

Jon Jay looked so pale, I thought he would be sick. It was not like that with big Tom Sin. He stood tall, looking scornfully at the dancers around the pole and at the crowd of Black Fin and their guests. The sailmaker, it seemed to me, was a man who expected the worst in others, and on this day he was in no way disappointed.

I heard a gasp come from the guests as they forgot about the bodies in the hole and looked up to examine Tall Hat's totem. Immense it was, standing arrow-straight. It revealed a splendor of interwoven crests, deep-carved with a skillfulness none of us had ever seen before. There was something spiritual about its deep-carved shadowed figures rising through the falling snow that made my spine tingle and my heart go tum-tum-tum.

I looked back at our Wolf Town people and saw Red Tongue wince and Fog Woman close her eyes. Beside me I heard Maquina grind his teeth. This was by far the grandest totem pole that any one of us had ever seen. It was wrong that such a splendid pole would stand here with these Black Fin people. It had been the old man, of course, who had carefully planned this pole, arranging each of his crests intermingled with his wife's all in their proper order, the most important at the bottom. Tall Hat would have specified the exact size and shape and cautious use of colors. At the top of the pole were five great potlatch rings.

Just seeing them made Maquina close his eyes in horror. "Who could have carved that totem?" he demanded. "None of these clumsy Black Fin wood slashers could create a pole like that."

We stared at one another and then back at the powerful, clear-cut cedar images on the totem, and we were silent. What could any of us say?

Maquina beckoned to his slave, Knee Scars, who had long ago been stolen from the Klamath. Turning his head so that none could read the movement of his lips, our *tyee* whispered to him. Knee Scars hobbled away and reappeared unnoticed beside a female Klamath slave belonging to the Black Fin *hacumb*. Soon Knee Scars returned and whispered into Maquina's ear.

My brother-in-law put his hand before his mouth and spoke to me. "See that lean man with the sloping shoulders standing over there? He's a Haida. He's the genius who carved this pole for them. Everyone here agrees the cleverness belongs to him."

Maquina stared at the narrow-hipped carver, who was dark-skinned from his constant work out in the sun and wind and rain. He was not tall, and he had a thin, slightly twisted face and large, sensitive, deerlike eyes. A small black beard sprouted just beneath his chin, which our young Wolf Town women would gladly pluck from him if they ever got the chance. His dark hair hung down in the fashion of the Haida. He had long, strong sensitive hands with fingers blunted by his work. He wore a spruce-root hat, wide-brimmed and decorated with half a dozen squarish southern abalone money pieces sewn randomly, and tall, trembling sea lion whiskers stood upright all around its flat-topped crown. He wore a short cedar cape and around his loins a deerskin scraped clean of hair and painted with a raven's crest.

"He is a slave. The Black Fin have given him the name Ax Hand," Maquina said. "He was captured from the southern Haida village of Koyah, a place famous for its carvers, but here among the Black Fin he is treated like an honored artisan. Old Tall Hat and Molasses Eater, both have promised Ax Hand that they will raise him to the status of a commoner among them because he carved that splendid pole for them."

Smiling falsely, pretending that we thought nothing of that glorious pole, my brother-in-law nodded right and left to all the other gathered chiefs, whom we had always known. They were being just as careful not to let the Black Fin see their envy of the old man's wondrous totem.

When the pole raising was over, we were led once more to our rightful places in the Black Fin house. The body of the old man, Tall Hat, had disappeared, as had the fragrant cedar bows and the post that had held him upright. In his place of honor sat his son, Molasses Eater, huddled beside his sly-eyed new *hacumb* and their son.

Neither Maquina nor I had eaten properly for days; now for some strange reason, seeing this old rival raised high up in his tomb caused both our appetites to come surging back full force. On cedar mats that had been spread before us, our Black Fin hosts placed piles of steaming clams, mussels, herring roe on seaweed, six or seven different kinds of fish, grease dips, mountain goat meat, elk, beaver, and berries of every kind. I was starving and could scarcely wait to eat. Many women hurried from the rear cooking fires, filling a food trencher half as long as a small canoe that lay before us. An endless delicious stream of food was being brought to all the guests.

"Well," Maquina said grudgingly, "there is one thing that the Molasses Eater knows, and that is how to overstuff himself—and others."

During this feasting, a long-winded Black Fin legend was recounted, with two clumsy dancers and some drumming and more endless chanting on this night. Quite a lot of guests fell fast asleep.

"Oh, I don't think I'm going to be able to stay until the end of this," Maquina said the next morning. "It's too terrible—one ghastly Black Fin boast that leads only to another. Let's pack our boxes and go home!"

"No!" my sister said in her most forceful voice. "We've got to see this to the end. I won't have our neighbors whispering that you ran away from these slave-killers."

The third evening was absolutely different. During the feasting there was more dancing, but it quickly turned insulting, at first subtly, but then with an increasing crudeness that drove our Wolf Town people into a wild and dangerous mood.

"Do you see that dreadful Sea Lion mask?" my sister asked her husband. "I swear that mask has purposely been carved to look exactly like you. And it does! It really does—especially the mustache."

"Well, that was not as bad as that coarse song they sang about him," Man Frog grumbled. Oh, yes, that song was aimed straight at Maquina.

"Or," said I, "that crude dance they are performing in imitation of Maquina's home life."

"I don't think it's funny," Red Tongue said. "Look at them now! I mean, having half a dozen of their masked dancers facing north, then howling and noisily breaking wind toward the south as a satire on good Wolf Town people. Judging by all the ruckus in this Black Fin house, they are making just the kind of cruel joke that delights their other guests and sets them into gasping fits of laughter."

Maquina knew it would look bad if we got up and walked out, so we sat and suffered until it ended.

In the mornings, the women gathered in small groups and exchanged gossip about all the scandalous happenings that had occurred along the coast. Then at night, I often heard them whispering to their husbands as they lay together underneath the mats. Sometimes sucking in their breaths with glee, they recounted the outlandish secrets of their neighbors. Most of the gossip about Wolf Town, my sister told us, was not only about women but about our dangerous capture of the ship and our foolishness in leaving two of the crew alive. What our neighbors did not seem to realize was the vast amount of trade goods that had been packed inside that ship. This fact Maquina was saving as a stunning blow to them.

On the fourth evening, the Black Fin chief talker ordered two blue-painted slaves with huge cedar collars on their shoulders to pull away the woven cedar mats that hid Tall Hat's mountain of potlatch gifts. A gasp went up from all the guests. We had expected to see a lot of gifts, but we had not expected this! Molasses Eater stared at Maquina. His little eyes narrowed like those of a cougar about to jump a deer. He still gave almost nothing to his guests.

Sea Star, the girl from Otter Town, was privileged for the first time to dance publicly in a mask she had inherited from her grandmother. The rhythm of the drumming and the song that went with the mask seemed to belong to some ancient time and perhaps some very distant place, for all of her movements were different, slower yet somehow more seductive than all the other dances. Or was it the girl that made it seem so? None took their eyes away. Maquina watched her like a starving man who sees food before him, and Jon Jay stared at her as though he was seeing a truly sensuous young woman for the first time in his life. I thought only of the copper widow. This feast was improving. Jon Jay looked worn out the next morning, and I wondered if he had slept at all that night.

The fifth evening, as we had expected, was the moment when Molasses Eater had decided to show his strength. Once again his huge pile of potlatch gifts was unveiled for us. A dozen slaves squatting among these Black Fin treasures stared rudely at the visitors. Pointing at four enormous piles of blankets, Molasses Eater had them distributed to the guests, giving as many as two dozen to each important village chief. When that was done, there was a pause, and everyone was silent, trying to imagine what would happen next.

Suddenly Molasses Eater hunched forward and, pointing

his finger at Maquina, called out to his slaves, "Give these few things to him."

The Black Fin *hacumb* screamed and clapped her pudgy hands in glee as the house slaves leapt to the task, crudely lugging painted boxes and armfuls of elaborately carved masks around the central fire pit to Maquina. The other guests sat back gasping in amazement as they tried to count the endless pile of gifts. They whispered to one another, wondering how far this new Black Fin chief would go.

As the slaves brought more and more to stack around Maquina, we, the highest guests, were forced to move to avoid the Black Fin slaves, who pushed rudely past us, heaping this unwanted bounty all around my brother-in-law as though they had been ordered to bury him in treasure.

Jon Jay and Tom Sin stood back in amazement, not knowing what to make of all of this. Maquina sat stiffly through it all, coldly ignoring the objects that were being forced against him. There were dozens of clever portrait masks, animal masks, split masks, whalebone salmon clubs carved and decked with human hair, drums and dance rattles, deep-carved feast bowls, rare ram horn ladles, gorgeous goat-hair capes, boxes of beads and wide brass bracelets. The polished blades of elaborate-handled Russian daggers traded from the northern Tlingit reflected in the dancing flames.

I craned my neck, looking for any bundles of sea otter skins, but there were none. All of those, I guessed, would have been used for trading to amass that awesome hoard of blankets and other foreign gifts. Let me tell you, we people from the Eagle house were truly outraged, for we had never witnessed such a crude gift-giving, or one so full of utter scorn.

Their drumming started up again, and one of their rude masked dancers appeared dressed in the costume of an old male eagle. It chased five naked slave girls all around the fire. In an instant every one of us from Wolf Town whirled in our places, turning our backs on Molasses Eater, his *hacumb*, and their son, drawing our cloaks and blankets over our faces to insult them. We howled like wolves and, leaping up, wiggled our asses in imitation of the black fin whales. We tried to overcry their drums and whistles, eager to blot out the image of their dancers' hateful satires of Maquina, screaming our proud chak-chak-chak, the warning cry of eagles. Our women hooted the death sounds of night owls. Even our paddlers and our slaves supported us by yapping out like mating foxes.

Of course, we were the losers at this feast, but we had not gone down without a valiant struggle. The evening ended on a totally different note, not boring as all the rest had been. We Wolf Town people had finally driven some life into this dreary Black Fin feast. But did they thank us for it? No. Maquina and all of us from Wolf Town laughed openly at the Black Fin as we gathered up our enormous pile of gifts and pushed our way outside their entrance.

On the last evening, when every other valuable potlatch favor had been given away, Molasses Eater did the very thing that we had dreaded most. He had his father's famous Black Fin copper brought out by four slaves and held high for all of us to see. It was shield-shaped and half as tall as a man. It had been cold-hammered out of heavy copper of the kind found only in the far north. This thick copper first belonged to a Bella Coola chief who had named it Nineteen Slaves, for that had been its modest value at that time. It was old now and had been given away at countless famous feasts, each time gaining power until now its worth was beyond all human calculation.

Maquina was very nervous when before our eyes a strong man was ordered by Molasses Eater to strike away its upper left-hand quarter. This he did with thunderous blows from a stone maul against an elk-horn chisel. We were horrified when a large piece broke away. This immensely valuable piece of the copper was carelessly tossed down at Maquina's feet.

That should have marked the end of the gift-giving, but to our horror it did not. The room was hushed as the new Black Fin chief pushed forward the great Haida carver, Ax Hand, forcing this final, impossible, unrepayable gift onto his chief rival. When he saw Maquina massaging his throat to keep his heart from jumping out, Molasses Eater leered at him and drank his mixture of rum and thick molasses, then drooled and giggled. This was his greatest moment of triumph.

"I free this clever slave to you. Will you make him free or not?"

We heard those near us whisper. "Maquina has been driven down. The Wolf Town chief is beaten. This Black Fin house has given him gifts so rare and valuable that they can never be repaid."

For us it was all over. Maquina left that Black Fin house with caution. He had the fiercely powerful Matla stride out before him, carrying his huge whalebone club, called the widow maker. Jon Jay and Tom Sin strode beside him, each with his cutlass drawn. Two Wolf Town warriors carried a thick yew-wood plank to shield Maquina's head because his lookout had warned him that there were men on the house roof shifting the heavy stones that might serve as either weights against the rising wind or deadly skull crushers aimed at himself or Ax Hand. Maquina used all this protection, not because he was afraid they would assassinate him, but to try as best he could to repay the insults that the Black Fin had heaped upon him.

Early on the following morning, we escaped that dreadful place. We departed with Ax Hand and all his carving tools and three big canoes. The third canoe had also been a gift. It was one of those clumsily carved Black Fin dugouts, which we would hide in the forest as soon as we got home, for we would be ashamed to have it seen upon our beach. However, we did need it now to lug home all this treasure, and it would serve later as a minor potlatch gift.

I saw Jon Jay look longingly at that wide-cheeked girl as we pulled away from the Otter Town canoe. Sea Star, like her mother, now sat luxuriously among their gifts of bright-red blankets. Her father, Upquesta, bowed his head to show sympathy for the awful defeat that had been dealt Maquina. As our long dugouts pulled apart, Upquesta called out to Maquina, "Come soon, friend, and visit me."

Cold white sleet fell in long diagonals as we headed into the south channel. Our paddlers battled valiantly into the headwind. Maquina, like the rest of us, sat hunched against the weather. His cloak of otter glistened with a hoary sheen of winter dampness. I saw my brother-in-law glance back several times to make sure that the carver, Ax Hand, was truly his. What a gift! Impossible to repay!

Maquina must have been thinking of the sly talk that would come later from all our people in Wolf Town and neighbors north and south along the coast. People would soon begin to speak in awe of the generosity of the Black Fin. They would say that Molasses Eater was just as fine a gift-giver as his generous old father. They would exaggerate his openhandedness and boast about the huge number of gifts he had showered upon them and upon Maquina. The paddlers would praise the free ear- and nose-piercing, along with the beautiful free tattooing. Above all, they would remember that Tall Hat's son, not Maquina, was the person who now held the highest rank on our whole coast. Later, the Wolf Town people would say they felt ashamed because Molasses Eater had proved that he, not Maquina, was the most lavish gift-giver in all the world. They would refer endlessly to this Black Fin feast, forcing Maquina to try to give a greater potlatch to defend himself. If he did not, the family line of the Maquinas would lose control of Wolf Town.

I heard my sister say to him, "I believe our two families could gather together enough food, enough trade gifts, enough carvings, to go against some other chiefs along this coast. I hate the very thought," she said, "of that crude wretch of a son having the right to sit above us at a feast. We cannot suffer that! Let's give an enormous feast for our son. Let's give him all our titles. Let's turn everything around and bury all our enemies in wealth!"

Maquina laughed. "That's just what I've been thinking." He wiped his hand across his brow, and it came away dull red with ocher paint. "First I will call in all the debts that we are owed. Then both of us will have to go out begging to our relatives. I dread the thought of asking anything from my sister."

Maquina looked at me, then closed his eyes and sighed. "Siam," he said, "the kind of feast I have in mind will take

every mask and song and title—everything that you and I possess. But if we do it right, my son, Satsatsoksis, will sit forever
far above that miserable Black Fin horde."

I agreed that to outdo the Black Fin Maquina would have
to give the costliest potlatch ever witnessed on this coast. But
still, I must confess, I did not like the way he said *"give everything that you and I possess."*

 IT WAS good to be back once more in Tahsis. In this winter season, I myself was glad to be hidden away in our deep inlet, protected from the lashing violence of the ocean's storms.

Climbing the narrow deer trail behind our village, I could see that in the mountains snow had fallen, turning each peak ghostly white. Along the high ridges and in the deep fissures the shadows were cold blue or somber gray. The ground was slippery in places, and the north sides of the trees were caked with sleet.

Thick mists came swirling around me. Walking through clouds, I listened to the moaning of the wind and the eerie creaking of the cedar giants. These trees made strange inner sounds, as though their tendons were paining them inside their bark. They, like Toowin, were growing, yes, still growing.

My pace slowed as I climbed, and my face grew wet with fog. The wind was stronger here. It tore the mists into long white shreds and sent them streaming. The big cedars nodded to the south. Below me in the valley I could see the trout lake.

The sky cleared in the east, and a distant range of mountains was revealed. High they were, alert as crouching animals, their backs a deeply shadowed white. Pale clouds of steam spumed from their mouths as the sky behind them glowed deep blue. These strange snow peaks seemed totally unreal to me, as dreamlike as the clouds that trailed along their spines. These were not like our nearer crags, where our sweating hunters climbed in search of game to eat. No, these distant ghostly mountains would surely fade and disappear if living humans dared to set their feet upon them.

Was I seeing into the other world? The very sight of these peaks gave me hope—hope that as I move beyond this life I would find a way to soar across the forests to those magic mountains. Once there, I could wander endlessly upon their slopes and at my leisure explore each one of those mysteriously shadowed gorges.

Huddling in my goat-wool cape, I squatted on my heels, enjoying the wind, for it felt like a woman pressing lustfully against my back. Above me and below me that invisible force had set the whole world into motion. The feathery green branches swished and swayed, flinging out fine powderings of snow.

The lake was covered with slow-moving patterns of waves. These began on the near shore and fanned outward, drawing for me the exact shape of the wind. Gradually each line of waves faded, then disappeared into the drifting phantom forms of snow that hid the far end of the lake.

I closed my eyes and may have slept a little, for when I looked again, the wind signs had all but disappeared. Beneath me the dark-green wooded country stood out sharply. From each hidden canyon white mists rose like camp smoke. The sun had completely broken free of clouds and painted the high country with its golden light.

I remained there while the day died gloriously all around me, watching far-off clouds as they moved more gently now across the world. I forgot all about myself, and Maquina, and the troublesome feast that we must give, until a sudden fit of shuddering took hold of me. I rose and made my way stiffly down the long trail. In my mind's eye I could already see the copper widow by my warming fire and smell the clam broth brewing.

She was not there, but Maquina was, sitting on his cedar box, and I could tell that he was feeling better.

"Siam," he said, speaking to me urgently as though he had been waiting for me to arrive, "if I arrange a marriage for my son, Jon Jay, to that young girl—what's her name?—from Otter Town, do you think her family would approve that? Would they see it as a friendly gesture by me? Would it help join our two houses, our two villages?"

Before I could answer, his words continued tumbling toward me. "They have skillful carvers over there in Otter Town. Do you think I could count on them to lend me customary potlatch gifts, wooden things of the kind we Yoquot use? I'll get laughed at if I give away nothing but half a shipload of greasy muskets and salt-soaked blankets."

I was glad to hear Maquina talking about arranging a marriage for Jon Jay. He should have a wife. My sister, when she heard her husband's thoughts, said nothing. I could tell that she was instinctively suspicious of his plans.

When the winter days began to lengthen, Jon Jay and Tom Sin kept busy pounding iron at their workplace. That work seemed to give them a hunger they could never satisfy. They learned to dig clams in our way and to collect mussels at low tide. Both men showed some restlessness, which seemed to increase with the changing faces of the moon. Of course, Tom Sin had always been like that, but Jon Jay had become almost one of us. Still, it seemed to mean little or nothing to Jon Jay that he had been adopted by Maquina. I wondered now if he would leave us even if he had the chance.

On cold gray winter mornings, Jon Jay seemed grateful to leave our house at Tahsis and search the beaches. Sometimes the whole inlet was still as ice. I used to watch him stop and study the black rocks rimmed with frost. On days when the fog drifted over the black waters of the inlet, Jon Jay would find shelter beside a driftwood log or warm himself by skipping flat stones across the water, or simply squat in our fashion, staring at the sky's reflections in the oily undulation of the sea. Sometimes a seal would raise its dark head and look at him, puzzled, perhaps, by the dagger maker's unhappiness.

One morning I saw Jon Jay shudder as he watched the winter winds whip the steel-gray inlet into swiftly changing patterns. An old male raven and a younger one soared together on an erratic current of air, their wings held stiff as they played unfriendly games of nerve and skill—rising, falling, tilting, using only the clever manipulation of their tails to control their perilous flight. Above them scudded heavy-bellied clouds weighted down oppressively with soggy snow that became visible only as it fell before the dark-green wall of forest. I had the feeling that Jon Jay, like Tom Sin, at those times was remembering some place very far away.

When Jon Jay and Tom Sin came to live with us, we learned a peculiar thing about shipsmen that we had not known. Those poor motherless creatures could let no more than half a dozen days go by before they had to scrape their lower faces. If they failed to do this, they sprouted a very nasty growth of hair. We Yoquot men are grateful that we are not so miserably afflicted. Oh, we have a few hairs, yes, but when these emerge, our women wrinkle up their noses and with clamshell pincers quickly pluck them out.

The dagger maker told me that ordinary knives and daggers are not sharp enough for shipsmen's faces. So those two borrowed a thin folding blade from their dead master's cabin. Between them they made a great evening ceremony of sharpening this special knife, first on a flattened stone, then on Tom Sin's leather belt. When this was done, they each rubbed seal fat into their faces, then commenced, one holding a trade mirror for the other. They bled a little, it is true, but when they were done, the good effect was more than worth it. They were smooth-skinned and handsome like ourselves.

Tom Sin was a person of the strictest habits. He wished to do everything each day at the same time and in exactly the same way. It was as though his ears could still magically hear that clanging ship's bell, the one that ruled those shipsmen's lives.

Summer or winter, Tom Sin used to rise most mornings from his hammock in the darkness and go marching ramrod straight along our beach just as dawn was breaking. At night he would climb into his hammock early and lie there swaying slowly back and forth, back and forth, staring up at the countless little eulachon fish that hung above our heads. He paid no attention to the things that we were doing. He didn't mind noise, people laughing, singing, drumming. No! He simply stared up at the smoke hole or went to sleep. That made me wonder what kind of house Tom Sin must have lived in when he was young and what strange kind of shipsmen he must have known.

Yes, Tom Sin was not at all like any one of us, and he was not like the dagger maker either. There was something very dangerous yet shy that seemed to crouch inside that big sail-maker, something that made all of us uneasy whenever we were near him. Only Fog Woman and her son, Satsatsoksis, seemed undistrubed by Tom Sin's ways. Several times I saw my sister smile at him and give him an extra ladleful of broth.

During that winter at Tahsis we had all the food we needed. It was safely stored in boxes or hanging from the house beams. Maquina finally ceased his unpleasant brooding about the shameful ordeal that his pride had suffered in the Black Fin village. When my sister went to our relatives' village in Nesook Bay to see a newborn child she had the right to name, no sooner was she gone than all Maquina's girls came flooding back to his apartment. That always makes Maquina mellow. It was like old times for me, looking across the fire to see my brother-in-law's famous otter robe undulating like a giant caterpillar and hearing all that high-pitched giggling and laughter.

Jon Jay—oh, my, yes—he was over there as well, not under the robe mind you, but lying on his own mat, propped up on one elbow eying every move. One night about midway through the wildest part, the dagger maker raised his arm and waved cheerfully to me, and I waved back. Yes, we two were always interested in Maquina's head-on approach to life.

Kawskaws was a person full of warm compassion. I know that she felt sorry for Jon Jay. I guessed that she could not stand the lonely look upon his face or the nervous way he flung those smooth flat stones.

I was standing quietly beside a tree when I saw Jon Jay coming along the beach. Kawskaws moved out delicate as a deer and stepped into my canoe. She stood there watching him. When he saw her, Kawskaws knelt down until only her eyes and rounded Hupa cap showed above the gunwale. When Jon Jay came up to the canoe, she disappeared entirely, and I guessed she must be lying down.

Jon Jay got into the canoe with her and he too disap-

peared. Everything was silent until suddenly the canoe jerked
over sideways, and I heard Jon Jay and Kawskaws laughing,
and then I could see the seal canoe was trembling from bow to
stern. I didn't know whether to laugh or cry, so I turned around
and walked away.

I did not wish to let my best thoughts dwell on young girls
jumping in and out of my canoes. So I was glad when it came
time for all the feasts and dancing, which were the essence of
our winter celebrations.

All went well until Maquina once more became erratic. This
usually happened to him just before the Tahsis ceremonies. During our eleborate Wolf Town rehearsals he would rage at our
dancers, forcing them to strive for absolute perfection.

"Oh, I am not like some of those northern chiefs," my
brother-in-law would shout out to his dancers. "I am not one
who goes stamping out onto a dance floor and slaughters a per-
former just because that dancer has made one wrong step. Oh,
no!" he bellowed. "I am a compassionate man! But remember,
we are preparing Klukwana! I demand that every one of you do
everything you can to make this winter ritual perfect. I warn all
you performers," he said menacingly, "I want this dancing and
the singing to come out in a way that will make me proud of
you. Anyone who spoils this feast can go and try to find some
other village chief to let you share his little cache of salmon."

My sister's canoe came hurrying back just in time to allow
her to join us in Klukwana.

Jon Jay looked at everything we did in wonder, for there
was a tremendous excitement that went throbbing through the
Wolf Town houses. But Tom Sin paid not the slightest attention
to our frantic preparations. I watched the big sailmaker crack-
ing the heavy knuckles on his hands as he continued to ignore
the bustle and confusion that was crowding all around him. To
try and cheer him up, I tipped back my head and let out a long,
beautiful Wolf howl, which I had inherited the right to do during this phase of the winter moon. I cocked my head and listened, hoping that a true wolf might oblige me by answering

from the forest. I have heard that female wolves and bears often
spoke to my grandfather, but I must admit to you they have
never answered me.

Kawskaws helped me try to explain all this to Jon Jay,
though being a Hupa from the south, she herself did not really
understand Klukwana, the feast between our familiar Wolf spirits and we humans dwelling in their houses. Of course, she did
not know how it began or how the wolves would come to our
winter village. Certainly Jon Jay had no clear idea of what we
were preparing for with such elaborate care. No wonder! Klukwana is such an ancient communication with the wolves that
we ourselves scarcely understand it. Some say that Frog, the
communicator, is the only one who knows how it all began, but
now he rarely speaks with us because, according to legend, a
beautiful girl who once lived among us got him very excited,
then played a nasty trick on him.

We have an old man here, one who holds the black stick.
He is famous for his knowledge of Klukwana, so famous that
some important Sheshant and Moachat, people of the Deer, this
winter journeyed from the south to join us to learn more of this
sacred feast. The Kyuquot came to us from the north. As soon
as the moon was right, our people sang a song to him to begin
the ceremonies:

> There he sits
> In the morning sky
> That new-horned animal
> The Moon.

Only then were the five fires in our Tahsis Eagle house extin-
guished and the wide roof boards readjusted to vent the one
huge fire that was built in the very center of an open hearth.
Maquina's largest painted screen had been placed across one
end of the house, in front of which he sat with his *hacumb*. I
carefully positioned our high-caste villagers and guests in proper
order facing them.

In the evening, when the fire burned low, Jon Jay and Tom

Sin, like our people, waited in expectant silence. From far away we could hear the heavy swish of wings as Raven, the creator, flew toward our house, his rough voice calling, "Cauk, cauk, cauk, cauk!"

Suddenly there was a frightening knocking at the rear end of the house, and in a moment this sound spread and shifted into a more violent pounding against all four walls. I, like others, held my hands over my ears, my shoulders hunched in fear. The dagger maker stared at us in great alarm, and Tom Sin stood up stiffly, looking all around, his big fists clenched, ready to do battle with those ghostly sounds. Imagine!

Four of our strong men rose and stood facing out from the dying fire. In the entrance to the house a frail old man appeared. His hair was gray. He wore an ancient portrait mask that hid his face, and a long black robe covered his body. He carried a carved staff and moved slowly like a phantom figure one sometimes sees in dreams. The black-robed man stopped just beyond the fire, and from behind his mask a quavering, cracked old voice called out to the strong men, "Build up that fire! I tell you, throw on wood!"

Our strong men whirled around and flung dried cedar logs onto the flames. I watched one of them furtively dump a seal bladder full of rancid whale oil on the fire. It burst alive, sending white tongues of hungry flames licking upward to the roof. Tom Sin sat down in disgust. I could tell from the expression on his scarred and battered face that he believed that we were going to burn the house down. We knew better! Our roof, like the moss-hung forest, was sodden wet from winter sleets and heavy rains. It would not catch fire.

An old widowed woman rose and called out in a high-pitched wail, and many women answered her with a steady whirring from their rattles. A heavy pounding came again upon the outer walls. Men groaned, women screamed, and children wailed in fright and clutched their parents.

Jon Jay and Tom Sin jumped to their feet when they heard a tearing sound, as some unseen power ripped the wall boards from the back of our house. Four figures came leaping through the opening. They wore painted Wolf masks and were naked except for shaggy animal skins that hung down their backs. They came shambling, howling, crouching, crawling toward us. Four times they made their way around our blazing fire. One tipped back its head and let out a fearful howl. It was answered by other distant Wolf howls echoing from the forest and the mountains. I felt shivers running all along my spine.

A rugged man-beast of the woods leaped out of the shadows. Upon his face he wore a grotesque hook-nosed giant's mask topped by a tangled mass of rain-soaked eagle feathers. This apparition hammered on his Thunder drum. The women screamed and shook their rattles at him, warning him away. Most of the watchers, joined by Jon Jay and by Kawskaws, squatted and made ourselves like the smallest animals, then leapt up very tall with arms outstretched, swaying to the east and to the west while the Moachat people moaned and whirled their short staffs and made their dangling deer hooves clatter. The crawling Wolf dancers, called by us the spinners, whirled like animals gone mad among our somber audience. What a sight that was! Even the sailmaker stood open-mouthed in wonder.

From behind Maquina's painted screen the Wind spirit appeared magically, snapping open, then quickly closing, its brilliant, many-colored mask. I could hear the rising rhythm of the Thunder drum, which reminded every one of us of great legends of our past when the angry Serpent's hiss turned into Lightning and the Thunder Eagle dropped the Whale among the mountain peaks. Who could forget the kindly young mother who foolishly gave her breast milk to the Caterpillar, nursing him into a frightful monster?

I myself could feel it as we humans gained our power from these helping spirits of ours, the wolves. The children in our house could feel the courage coming to them; their infant fears were disappearing. Their paths as adult humans would soon be cleared forever.

Above us from the shadows the Earthquake dancer roared until he set the women and the children screaming. Leaping down from a roof beam, he gave us his thunderous warning, his

feet pounding on the earthen floor. He flung wooden images of
the Salmon people into the air to remind us that we must be oh,
so careful to respect them.

Maquina rose and came toward the fire. On his forehead
was a small Wolf mask, which in this world he alone could
wear. Maquina moved in slow, rhythmic patterns as he sang his
ancient song:

> Aya ho, Aya ha,
> When searching through Wolf Town,
> Our future chief I found.
> Just big enough was he
> To sit in his canoe.
> Take care, high chief.
> Beware, young master,
> You whose town this is to be.
> Aya ho, Aya ha.

When he finished his song, my brother-in-law promised his son,
Satsatsoksis, that he would teach him that ancient song and pre-
cisely how it must be danced.

Once more the Wolf whistles began hooting and the Thunder drum resounded. Jon Jay, like all of us inside the house,
began leaping and swaying to the rhythm that took hold of every
one of us. I saw the big sailmaker staring straight at my sister,
who was smiling back at him. Now even Tom Sin was hunching
his powerful shoulders and moving his lips in time with hers,
trying to follow the chanting and the mystical passions of the
Wolf song. I heard low howling sounds coming from the sailmaker's throat, which only proves that no living person can re-
sist the powerful magic of Klukwana.

I was grateful when the riskiest part of the Wolf ceremony
was ended and the feasting could begin. I watched people in the
firelight wipe the sweat off their faces and their bodies. They
sighed with relief to one another. Yes, the dangerous part of
Klukwana was over for another year. Our lives would be protected.

I sat with the heads of seven other houses around a canoe-shaped trencher full of delicious clams and halibut and salmon soaked in the well-aged oil of candlefish. Jon Jay, dressed for this occasion in his best shipsman's costume, was sitting next to Toowin, not far away from me. I looked over and saw Maquina eating alone with his *hacumb*, as was the custom. I could not hear his words, but he was urging my sister to do something. There was no sign of agreement in her face.

Maquina beckoned Jon Jay and Kawskaws and, using her to help him talk, told Jon Jay that he wished to give him an important name. I thought that good. Why not give the dagger maker a good name that carries rank? I could see my sister, Fog Woman, did not agree, and that made Maquina angry. Maquina told my sister that he had adopted Jon Jay and would now act as his father. He had decided that the dagger maker was to have a wife. For that, Jon Jay would need a family name. My brother-in-law said he would make all the arrangements and pay the bride's price to acquire Upquesta's daughter, the girl from Otter Town.

When Jon Jay understood what Maquina was saying, he did nothing except stare at Kawskaws. Toowin jumped up from where he had been squatting. For just one moment, I saw him glare at Kawskaws with a crazy, jealous look upon his face. Kawskaws jumped up from where she had been squatting and ran out of the entrance. Toowin followed her. I saw the suspicious eyes of every matron follow him. Kawskaws was our servant, a commoner. It was the worst thing Toowin could have done. I later warned Toowin that it makes no difference whether a woman is highborn, a commoner, or a slave. When they're upset, they usually act in ways men cannot understand.

Maquina pointed at the dagger maker and shouted, "I am going to buy a proper wife for him!" Then my brother-in-law growled at me, "Women! Women! Women! I'll tell you about women—they're against us. I try to do a decent, honest thing by buying this new son of mine a wife. And what do I get for it? Bitter words from my wife and weeping from that servant girl of yours. I don't care what either of them says or does. Jon Jay's going to have that girl!"

We did not take a single woman with us on our journey south to Otter Town. Thirty of our strongest paddlers worked in Sea Spear and twenty-two in my canoe. Both were loaded with impressive boxes.

Maquina had Tom Sin go in my dugout, and Jon Jay went in his. It was the first time that I had seen both shipsmen fully dressed in Nootkan clothing. Maquina had ordered that, and my sister had arrayed them splendidly. Both wore fine new fur-trimmed *kotsaks*, and each had a tightly woven hat of a kind that is reserved for high-caste persons. Our two shipsmen now wore elaborate daggers strapped, as our warriors wear them, high up on their chests. Their faces were painted red and their eyebrows drawn in into one wide black line that zigzagged magnificently across the brow. They had white eagle down plastered grandly in their well-greased hair. I thought both of them looked truly fine.

Why all this manly pomp, this pile of gifts? Because we believed that we were going to a wedding feast.

Red Tongue steered the big canoe, and for a while I let Toowin try his hand at steering ours. We kept the paddlers' beat while we sang songs in rhythm with their strokes. We blessed the wind that pushed so steadily at our backs.

Only two nights we slept out. On the third evening, we rounded Salmonberry point and came in full view of Otter Town. It was indeed a handsome place.

They recognized us right away and must have guessed our mission, for instead of challenging us, they warmly welcomed all ashore with dozens of men to help us draw our canoes up on their beach. We were ushered up to their village and shown into Upquesta's large and well-built Salmon house. Beside him sat Wickinnish, who was the village chief of Otter Town. Wickinnish was a huge man and no friend of Maquina's, for there had always been great rivalry between them.

Only when Jon Jay saw the girl, Sea Star, appear did he

stiffen as he realized that perhaps he and the girl were really to be married. Married! That is, if a fair bride's price could be set and all the other fine details could be worked out between the fathers. Can you imagine my brother-in-law, that lover of young girls, deciding to play Jon Jay's father? I was eager to observe every move or sidelong glance that anybody made, for this was just the kind of human play that interests me.

First all the women left the house. Then the girl's father, Upquesta, invited all the other noblemen and house chiefs from his village to join us, and we sat down, six around each trencher full of herring spawn on a bed of seaweed steeped in rich fish oil and smoked salmon lightly steamed. I myself was not surprised when the great *tyee*, Wickinnish, came and sat by my trencher and not with Upquesta and Maquina.

After we had eaten all we could, the main events got started. Upquesta welcomed Maquina, and my brother-in-law had Red Tongue make a fine speech to the girl's father and mentioned some of what he thought would be a fair bride's purchase price. When he heard what Maquina intended to give, I saw Upquesta sit back in delight. Wickinnish pretended he was not impressed.

Then Maquina had his paddlers bring in all those new muskets, cutlasses, the kegs of molasses, rum, and gunpowder, scissors, looking-glasses, bolts of calico, and more red blankets and everything was grandly heaped before Upquesta. The box of square-cut money bits of southern abalone thrilled them, and last of all, Maquina displayed a beautiful pair of arm-long daggers made by Jon Jay.

As Maquina's chief talker, Red Tongue delivered a loud speech making much of the fact that Jon Jay was a very skillful dagger maker, bracelet maker, necklace maker—in fact, as it turned out, he spoke far too much of that.

After he had made his answering speech saying that he welcomed all the wonderful gifts and the marriage of his daughter to Maquina's son, Upquesta paused, then added, "I want my daughter to remain with us in Otter Town. Her new husband is most welcome here. I want him to stay and make daggers like this pair he made for me."

Well, until her father said that, everything had been going very, very well, and Jon Jay almost had a splendid wife. But right there all the marriage plans turned sour. Of course, I knew Maquina wasn't here to give away this new and valuable son of his. Can you imagine my brother-in-law giving up our splendid dagger maker to a minor chief of the Salmon house in Otter Town to add glory to his southern rival, Wickinnish? No, never!

There was a lot of excited whispering between Maquina and Red Tongue, who then went and spoke to their Otter talker, who whispered behind his hand to Upquesta.

"For two moons each year, he will come here with my daughter and he will make me daggers," said Upquesta.

"For only one moon he may come and make you daggers," said Maquina.

There was silence. Upquesta sulked a little, but finally he nodded in agreement.

Immediately the girl was led back through the entrance on her mother's arm. She wasn't nervous. Oh, no! She had an eager look upon her face. Jon Jay was so excited that he jumped up when he saw her, but because he was a clever dagger maker, his unseemly action was forgiven by the witnesses.

Big Tom Sin had not understood that the reason that had brought us here until he saw the girl dressed in her finest cloak with the small frontal mask upon her head. He frowned and looked at Jon Jay, then at me. I could tell he was not pleased.

Upquesta's chief talker said, "His daughter sits on many privileges. She has inherited masks and songs and crests and titles, berry patches and rich stretches of a salmon river. Any nobleman who marries her will himself become a man of higher rank."

Maquina nodded and said, "She will be like a daughter living among high-caste people. She will be well cared for underneath my house roof."

We drank with them some of the rum and molasses we had brought as a gift. When that was done, the girl's father gave his daughter and her new husband two young male slaves, and as well he gave the bridal couple every one of the gifts that Maquina had given him to make the bride's price—everything, that is, except Jon Jay's splendid daggers. Upquesta said Jon Jay could easily make another pair to protect his daughter and himself.

That was a sly remark. It seemed to pass unnoticed in this most successful marriage feast between these two important chieftains' houses. But that unfortunate slur by Sea Star's father referring to Maquina's troubles with the unruly young men in Wolf Town was reason enough for my brother-in-law to decide never to send Jon Jay south to make another dagger for Upquesta. Of course, that would have caused enormous trouble if those two chiefs had both survived.

Upquesta himself and the proud but weeping mother brought the wide-cheeked bride down onto their beach and handed her very gently into my canoe. When Jon Jay, not understanding our traditions, tried to sit with her, we were embarrassed and had to bar his way. The dagger maker was forced to sit high on his box beside Maquina in the big canoe. Tom Sin stayed in my canoe, but he never even glanced toward that girl.

The new bride quite properly refused to look at Jon Jay until we arrived at Wolf Town, and then our women warmly crowded around her and took her away to the Thunder House, where she had female relatives. Jon Jay did not see her once for ten long nights and days. That same thing had happened to me when I was first married. What a torture!

Kawskaws had become jealous and would interpret nothing for Jon Jay.

Just when the dagger maker had given up and thought he was mistaken about being married, the women brought Sea Star to our fire. She was dressed in her finest garments. Then, with Jon Jay they led her up into Maquina's apartment and sat her down on Jon Jay's sleeping mat and arranged around her all of their most precious marriage gifts.

I must say that I looked across our fire pit with considerable anticipation, for what was about to happen would be entirely new to me and would interest me far more than all my brother-in-law's wild thrashings with that ambitious flock of girls. I had a clear view of the marriage bed, and this I hoped would greatly further my study of foreign shipmen's ways, which had made them famous with our slave girls.

I was excited, and so was Jon Jay! He had no sooner laid down beside the sensuous Sea Star than I saw her strip away her garments and roll toward the dagger maker. At that very moment that accursed sister of mine came and rearranged their wedding boxes so that I could no longer see them. As if that was not bad enough, she blew out Tom Sin's two oil lamps and called out, "Sleep well, brother."

I heard Maquina groan, for, I guess, he too had a lively interest in the details of that night's goings-on, which, judging by the sighing, moaning, squealing, and the heavy breathing, would have been a grand sight to behold.

Jon Jay seemed a new and different person after he became a married man. He did not dress so often as a shipsman, but allowed his new wife to paint him lightly and wore a *kotsak* and his elegantly woven Whale hat, which had been given to him by Maquina. Instead of eating always with Tom Sin, he, along with Sea Star, more often came and sat with me and Toowin at our food trencher, joining in our conversations, dipping politely, like us, only with his right hand, licking his fingers afterward as neatly as a cougar.

Sea Star must have taught him many things that winter when they were underneath the mats. His Chinook was improving greatly, and Jon Jay was starting to mix in our own Nootkish language. Yes, two persons waking and sleeping together are compelled to talk. If they did not have a language between them, I believe that they would swiftly make a new one for themselves.

Jon Jay's wife from Otter Town got on very well with all our women except, of course, the copper widow. Sea Star was not shy. Why should she be? She had been brought up by the second strongest family in her village. Sea Star acted humbly to no one here except Maquina. To Fog Woman and me and Jon Jay, she was polite and pleasant. But most others she treated as though they had been born beneath her. Perhaps because of her beauty, no one seemed to take offense. There is something in our character that makes us admire high-caste women who are young and beautiful. Many girls in Wolf Town began to imitate Sea Star's delicate way of eating, the close-legged way she had of walking, the styles in which she had her servants fix her hair, and even the slightly different way she wore her kilt and open cape.

When my sister, the *hacumb*, was in charge of their apartment, Sea Star was always attentive to Jon Jay. But I noticed that when Fog Woman was away, that apartment became an entirely different place. Maquina's five young women would come drifting in, and he would shake out that great otter sleeping robe of his and, instead of coming to the fire to talk with me, would stay up there joking with all of them. To my surprise, Sea Star would always stay up there, laughing and singing with Maquina and his girls. Sea Star was as handsome in the face as Spuck, and she liked to sit on that wide robe of his, teasing Maquina and making deer's eyes at him, as though she was much closer to him than any of the others, who would soon be lying with him underneath the otter robe.

Jon Jay grew nervous of that gang of girls and would often come down to the fire and eat with me. There was little he could do. In some tribes not so far from here, the men beat their women, even bite their noses off. But we are not at all like that. Besides, our proud women like this wife of Jon Jay's would suffer no such treatment. Even a threat or strong insult is enough to cause most highborn women to gather up their marriage gifts and storm angrily back to the protection of their family. Such an act could cause family feuds or even violent raids between Wolf Town and Otter Town.

"When I was young," I said to Toowin, "we were not on good terms with the chiefs of Otter Town because of a young Wolf Town woman who had fled from them and come back to us. One day we met their warriors, each of us in a thirty-man canoe. At first we only traded insults with the Otter Town men. Then we drew in close together and fought with our spearlike yew-wood paddles. That was when old Sand Shark lost his eye.

A dozen of their men and a dozen of ours were drowned. You remember that," I said to Toowin. "Women usually stay behind to mind the children and the house, but their influence goes traveling with us—everywhere."

I was proud to have Fog Woman for my sister. After all, she was the *hacumb*, and a person everyone could trust. One winter afternoon when I was resting, I overheard her talking about her husband to the Salish woman weaver, who had married into our household and had brought that pack of little white wool dogs with her. I heard my sister's voice droning on and on, mixed sometimes with the gentle words of a weaving song. Fog Woman knew I was lying on my mat in my apartment just beyond the fire, but she must have believed that I was sleeping. Just seeing through half-closed eyes the way my sister leaned close to that weaver woman's loom made me cock my ears and listen.

"That's what I heard," my sister said. "Yes, I heard it from the women at the Black Fin feast. Don't you tell—but they all swear it's true. Those island women living just along the coast, they got themselves a real live Passioks tied up to a post. Yes, he's in the very center of their village."

"What's a Passioks?" the Salish woman asked her, as she squinted at the complicated pattern on her loom.

"Oh, you know!" my sister laughed. "A Passioks is French, one of those shipsmen who waves his hands a lot and says, 'Oui, oui, oui.' Yes, a ship's captain, on the day that the ship was leaving, traded the women a nice young Passioks for ten prime sea otter skins and a basketful of salmon.

"In the daytime, they tie that Passioks up to a post by the ankle—not too tight, mind you. They keep him on a long loose sealskin line so he can easily move around for exercise—but not too much exercise!" She giggled. "Those women give him all the food he wants: oysters, mussels, clams, thick salmon soup, all those sorts of things. Believe me, he must need it, for they tease him into lying with a different woman every single night!"

"Laaah!" The Salish woman chuckled. "That's interesting! But why do they do that?"

"Because they really care about that Passioks," my sister explained, smiling. "They told me they admire the slow and easy copulations of their Passioks. They say the Passioks becomes as passionate as a mink. He is very nice to have between the sleeping mats, they say."

"What's going to happen to that poor Passioks they've got tied up to the post?" the Salish weaver woman wondered.

"Oh, don't worry about him." My sister chuckled and handed her another twist of dog wool. "They told me that when their Passioks gets a little older, they are going to send him back home safe aboard a ship. They say they are going to trade him for another fresh one by giving two or three more otter skins. Don't worry. In the meantime, they say they are taking very good care of their Passioks. I heard that a number of them got together and sewed a lovely little tent for him. It's made of salmon skins to shed the daytime rain. They say they take turns keeping him warm and dry at night. It's not always easy for me being a *hacumb*," my sister told the Salish weaver woman. "Sometimes I think we could use a nice strong-backed young Passioks down here. Don't you say I said that!" I heard my sister whisper. "This talk is just between us two."

I was always interested in my sister's secret conversations. She realized that Jon Jay and Tom Sin might have remained slaves or become like the Passioks for our women. But instead, the clever dagger maker had truly become one of us, a nobleman in the Eagle house.

She looked over into my place to make sure I was asleep before she said, "Have you seen my husband when he scowls like this?"

I saw her give her favorite imitation of Maquina's glare.

"Have you seen him stare at our guests across the firelight with those eagle-hooded eyes of his? He even makes *me* shudder sometimes. Have you seen him wearing his eagle feather nose quill? It makes him look so dignified.

"I was the one who trained him to use that piercing, hungry bird stare that sets his rivals' teeth on edge. It was I who told him how to hunch his shoulders as though he was ruffling up his feathers like an angry bird of prey."

I saw my sister mimicking her husband's every gesture.

She continued, "I helped to teach him how to hold himself erect and motionless and then suddenly to turn his head, using that quick, observant movement of an eagle. That's the way his father moved. I saw him do it just like that when I was still a child. My husband's far from being any nice, soft-talking Passioks, but let me tell you, he's not always the stern *tyee* he pretends to be."

"Oh, I know he's not," the Salish woman said. "I've seen him sad and forlorn when you have to be away traveling to other places." She reached out and stroked the wide otter skin bed cover, saying, "He's so very lonely sleeping by himself."

"Sleeping by himself!" Fog Woman snorted. "You must be going blind!"

Of course, I was angry and jealous because of the copper widow. Who wouldn't be after all the things she'd done to me? She who spoiled even my poor night resting habits. The best thing I had found to make me sleep was to go out alone and make long walks on the beaches. On this evening the big moon tide was just receding, which sometimes leaves stranded interesting things that have been washed in off the ocean.

I had not gone very far from the house along the high beach when I heard my name called lightly from the forest. That gave me a nasty start, for I feared it was an owl warning me of my death. But no, it was no owl. It was the copper widow. I could see her standing slim and ghostlike in among the trees.

"Siam," she called again, and she laughed, then did some sensuous movements of a virgin's dance that especially she had no right to perform.

I just stood my ground and watched her.

"Are you afraid of me?" she called.

Angrily, I strode to her, remembering all the awful things she'd done to me. But before I could speak, she reached out and took both my hands, and leaning up against the tree, she drew me close to her, and I could feel her hot breath blowing up against my neck, then underneath my cape in a way that set me shivering.

"I need you," she said. "I want you now!"

I tried to utter all the harsh words that I had been saving up to pour on her, but when her hot tongue touched me, my words stumbled and got all mixed up. I didn't care. I put my arms around her, knowing she could feel me trembling. I said, "Come back to the Eagle house."

She said, "No, do it here."

I tried to draw her down, but she refused, saying, "The moss is wet."

She ground her hips against me.

So I had her up against that tree. She started biting, clutching, grabbing, trembling, turning that unwanted meeting into something as violent as a knife fight, something so shamelessly passionate, so unexplainable, that the thrill of it will haunt me to the last breath of my life.

Late winter is a time when households have been crowded together too long. Women get sharp-tongued and nervous, and men's tempers all too easily snap. The big man, Tom Sin, had brought north to Tahsis seven of the small iron ship's lamps that he had taken from the master's cabin before that fool, Stone Hammer, set Maquina's ship afire. These lamps were small in size, but of a clever shape that caused whale oil to burn in them with a clear, bright flame. He had reluctantly given one to Matla in the Whale house and another to old Sand Shark in the Thunder house. The remaining five Maquina had insisted were needed for our Eagle house.

To drive away the winter darkness, Tom Sin had hung four of these lamps near Maquina's sleeping place and mine. He suspended these lamps from ship's nails driven into our house walls well above our children's reach. When Man Frog and Long Claws asked why the lamps were not spread out, Jon Jay, with the help of Kawskaws, told them that we all wished to keep them far away from the place where our barrels of gunpowder had been stored.

Of course, Tom Sin placed no light near his own hammock, but I used to see him urge the dagger maker to go and sit beneath one small lamp beyond Red Tongue's apartment and make marks on those thin white skins. I don't think Tom Sin ever looked at the marks that Jon Jay made, for I am sure those squiggles made no more sense to him than they did to me.

The big sailmaker was very jealous of his iron oil lamps. By his stern gestures he made it clear to all of us that he was to be the only one to light them, snuff them out, or touch them in any way. Tom Sin lit these lamps each night exactly at the moment when the white wool dogs began their yapping to be fed. That was Tom Sin's way. Everything done exactly as the day before.

One evening as I lay watching Tom Sin fill his lamps, the usual crowd of children followed him. Our young ones played joyfully with Jon Jay, but I noticed that these same children had not lost their early fear—and fascination—of Tom Sin. He never smiled or fooled with them. My sister's son, Satsatsoksis, was the only child who was ever bold with Tom Sin.

On this evening, Satsatsoksis ran hard against the sailmaker's leg, causing him to lose his balance and spill whale oil on himself and into the small box where Jon Jay kept his flat white skins for marking. I heard the sailmaker let out a grunt of anger and saw him cuff Satsatsoksis with the back of his hand. It did not seem to be a hard blow, but the boy went sprawling onto our hard-packed earthen floor. Maquina must have seen it too, for I heard a roar from his apartment and saw him rush down. Kneeling, he picked up his son, who was stiff with fright.

"Bring me my musket!" Maquina bellowed out in rage.

My sister, Fog Woman, had also run to them and was now holding their son and trying to calm her husband.

"Do no such thing!" my sister cried out.

"Bring me a loaded musket!" Maquina shouted out again, and he held out his right hand, waiting to receive it.

Every person in the Eagle house froze in silence, knowing exactly what was going to happen.

The big sailmaker calmly continued to fill and light the lamps.

Maquina was glaring at Tom Sin's broad-shouldered back. Our *tyee* held his head thrust forward, his muscles bunched like a cougar about to leap upon a deer.

"Siam!" he shouted to me. "Bring me my musket, now!"

It is more than a little dangerous to disobey Maquina, but I held fast and did not move. I wasn't going to help him kill one of our last shipsmen.

However, others saw this as a way to avenge themselves against Tom Sin. Young Opoots leapt up and ran to the place where Maquina slept. Snatching up the beautiful double-barreled musket, he hurriedly placed it in Maquina's hand.

When he heard my brother-in-law draw back and cock both hammers, Tom Sin turned and scowled at him.

Maquina's teeth showed in his rage as he reached out and placed the twin muzzles of the musket so close they almost touched Tom Sin's muscular left breast.

I was horrified when I saw Tom Sin tear open the shirt he wore and thrust his hairy chest against the musket bores. Tom Sin's face flushed angry red. He bellowed harsh words at Maquina, words we could not understand.

The corners of Maquina's mouth turned down as he clutched the musket tight and pulled the trigger. The hammer fell, striking a flash of sparks into the pan. But nothing happened.

Tom Sin pressed boldly forward, roaring even louder at Maquina.

Maquina was about to pull the second trigger, but at that moment the young dagger maker came racing across the house toward him, holding a heavy flintlock pistol in each hand.

Maquina looked at him with an expression of surprise, for Jon Jay could so easily have taken Maquina's life, and I believe he might have done so had Maquina pulled that second trigger.

When Maquina lowered the musket, Jon Jay laid his pair of pistols on the floor and knelt with them safe between his legs while he examined Satsatsoksis. He smiled at Fog Woman and

Tom Sin lights a
ship's lamp in
the Eagle house.

Houston
SDT

the boy and spoke a few soft words to him.

My sister said to Maquina, "He's not hurt. Calm down, husband. Let's have no trouble. Come back with me and finish up your salmon soup."

Maquina turned and, stiff-legged, strode away from them. He swore in English, "Thees glod-damn glun no gloood!" and he aimed it at the west wall of the Eagle house and pulled the second trigger.

There was a flash in the pan and a roar and the yellow light of evening beamed through a ragged hole in the cedar planking. It was big enough for a man to stick his head through.

Jon Jay turned so pale, I thought that he would fall. Tom Sin stared at that ugly hole torn through the wall by swan shot and made not a sound of joy but one of triumph. That was almost the only time I every heard him laugh. His laughter sounded like the dangerous echoing of boulders pushed into a rough stone canyon. I think if that musket had had a third barrel, Maquina might have shot him.

My sister quickly took the smoking musket from her husband's hand, saying, "Come and drink your soup."

Tom Sin turned his back on all of us and marched to his next lamp, which he filled with the remaining oil and lit with a steady hand. It was as though being close to death was like an old, familiar game to him.

I went and sat with my brother-in-law to help him forget about his bitter contest with the sailmaker. My sister helped me, for neither of us wanted any conflict up at Tahsis after all our troubles on the coast.

"What are you going to do about that mountain of gifts the Black Fin gave you?" Fog Woman asked her husband, trying to make him think of something else.

"I'm going to give a feast," Maquina grunted, "a potlatch like no one on this coast has ever seen."

"What's going to be so different about *your* feast?"

"I'm going to think of splendid pieces for Ax Hand to carve. Together we'll make the cleverest things in all the world—masks with mouths that open, eyes that shut, as well as wooden birds that will fly about the house."

"Then you should get him started," said my sister. "He must be bored to death carving all those dull feast bowls and ladles you demanded." She sighed. "You have moved Ax Hand all around this house. Where do you have your carver sleeping now?"

"I've got him living down with Red Tongue until I find a better place for him."

"You must get him out of there," my sister whispered. "I don't know how any carver could live with that cold-hearted man."

"Artisans are usually very nervous, anxious persons," I agreed. "Living with Red Tongue will wither all his feelings, all his skills."

"That could be so." Maquina nodded. "Send Knee Scars for him. Have him bring that carver here to me."

Ax Hand came and stood beside our fire. There was nothing bold about him, yet nothing humble either.

"Living with those Black Fin people," said Maquina, "must have been an awful life for you to suffer."

Ax Hand did not reply.

"You must have had to stare at the loutish face of that Molasses Eater until his image was a horror to you."

Ax Hand nodded but said nothing.

"You probably remember exactly how he looks."

"Yes," said Ax Hand. "I remember him too well."

"I want you to make a portrait mask of that great glutton." Maquina closed one eye. "Yes, I want it to look exactly like him. You know, a low forehead, little porpoise eyes, a sea lion's heavy jowls, and with his lips all pink and puckered."

Maquina crossed his eyes, tipped back his head, and held his mouth as though he had gone mad. "See what I mean? I want you to make a clever portrait mask of him. Don't hurry. Get it right, then paint it very carefully. When you are finished with his likeness, keep it secret—show no one. Just bring that mask to me. After that, I'll have other important carvings for you to do. But for now, I want you to find a quiet place and work, work, work. Knee Scars can help you roughing out the wood for masks."

"Where is Ax Hand going to sleep?" my sister asked.

Before anyone could answer, Ax Hand said, "There's a pleasant young widow living at the other end of this house."

"Good! Try her," Maquina said before my sister had a chance to ask her name. "Let me know if she's worthwhile," Maquina added slyly.

Just as Ax Hand turned to leave, my brother-in-law asked, "Did you ever carve a whale?"

"Yes," said Ax Hand. "I've carved two of them."

"How big?" Maquina asked him.

The carver held his hands out at shoulder width.

"I was thinking of something much, much bigger," said Maquina. "Sharpen up your little axes and your knives."

 NO ONE in the Eagle house had ever seen Fog Woman sick before. She was violently ill now, vomiting and fainting. There was no mistaking that.

While we hunters had been away, Fog Woman had collapsed outside the house. Kawskaws, with others, had carried her inside and laid her on a mat and covered her with two thick goat-hair capes. My sister's women stared at Fog Woman's ash-gray face and wept, saying over and over, "Someone very bad and powerful has done that to her."

When Maquina returned from the deer hunt, he was not as worried as I was. "I know her. Your sister's tough," he said to me. "Takes more than rum or bad meat to knock that strong-gutted woman down."

An aunt of ours, an old widowed noblewoman who usually helped supervise the Eagle house, assured Maquina, "My niece has not drunk any of that rum or eaten anything unusual except a meal of ripe sea lion meat. Do you think that would have hurt her? It just may be she's broken some taboo."

I went with Maquina to have a look at Fog Woman. My sister's women had piled four more red trade blankets on her, but we could see that she was still shivering. I put my hand against her face and found that she was burning hot. She told Maquina she was freezing cold. Her eyes were bright with fever, and now Maquina was truly frightened. As we squatted together watching her, my sister drew her knees up against her stomach and moaned in pain.

I, like Maquina, scarcely slept, and the Salish weaver stayed close by her through the night. My brother-in-law and I rose when we heard my sister gasping, trying to catch her breath. Twice more before morning I saw Maquina rise and hold the whale oil lamp to look at his wife's face and to offer her some water. Later she must have been delirious, for she knocked the ram's horn ladle from the Salish weaver woman's hand. By that time, Fog Woman didn't even know that we were all beside her. That's how sick she had become.

I told my sister's women to take her son, Satsatsoksis, to a married niece of mine. She was not far away, having married into the Thunder house.

Maquina even asked Jon Jay if he knew any foreign way to help her. All the dagger maker could do was to lay his water-sodden kerchief across her forehead. Later he told us through Kawskaws that he would gladly go barefoot into the ponds and let leeches stick to his legs, then pluck them off and put them on my sister and let them suck her blood. Jon Jay's new wife, who was squatting by him, made a face as though she would be ill, showing her feelings about his frightful remedy. She said to me, "Have you ever heard a more revolting cure for sickness?" Yes, we all liked this young dagger maker very much, but we decided that foreigners probably knew nothing about saving the lives of human beings—they didn't even know that their own tobacco would heal a nasty wound.

On the following morning, Fog Woman was so much worse that Maquina called me over, and together we decided to send for help. We had three sorcerers in Wolf-Town, but only one was skilled at curing illnesses. We were told by his apprentice that he was making powerful amulets in a little spirit-catching house that was hidden in a secret cove. He had warned his apprentice to come nowhere near him and not to allow any animals or humans to disturb his solitude.

"I'll disturb him," Maquina shouted. "I'll go down there and bring him back myself!"

The apprentice trembled when he heard Maquina call out, "Siam, you're coming with me! I don't want to spend a night alone with that flat-headed spirit-caller. I don't trust him."

"Who else will come with us?" I asked him.

"Take the dagger maker—if he can bear to leave that new little wife of his." Maquina snorted as though she belonged to him and not to Jon Jay. "He's not afraid of soul-catchers; he doesn't even know what they can do. Tell him to load both his pistols carefully in case I decide to have him shoot this spirit-catcher. Knee Scars and that Walla Walla man can do the paddling for us. We'll go in that new small seal canoe of mine. Tell them to have it ready when we come down to the beach."

We departed in a hurry, but the winter light was short, and it was almost dark when our paddlers finally found the entrance to the hidden inlet. Maquina grunted with impatience as the Walla Walla bowman helped turn the sleek canoe. We headed in. I felt Jon Jay shivering with cold as we listened to the eerie croaking of a startled heron. We paddled around the island to the end of the short arm of water.

Jon Jay stepped out after me and Maquina onto the ice-cold tidal rocks, each of us searching uncertainly for a steady footing in the darkness. Knee Scars and the Walla Walla slave eased the dugout away from shore and paddled several canoe lengths out into deeper water, then held the dugout there with the sharp points of their paddles. They had both heard terrifying tales of this ghost-ridden place.

The house of the spirit-catcher was supposed to be at the very end of this small inlet, and yet we had the greatest difficulty finding it. No wonder, for his house was hidden like a small deserted tomb, lost in a thick, low tangle of dead devil's club and huge withered ferns and twisted moss-hung branches. Everything was winter-killed and sodden wet.

The dagger maker waited just behind me, staring through the oppressive gloom. The cloud-hung night gave all of us a damp and deadly feeling. Unseen things slithered against my legs as I moved my bare feet forward, cautiously touching cold, spongy moss that partly covered slimy rocks. I held my hands before my eyes as I imagined the sharply pointed spine bones of dead dog salmon thrusting themselves toward me in the darkness.

Suddenly Maquina grabbed me, warning me and Jon Jay to stay close behind him. Together we waded through icy pools of rain, searching vainly for the beginning of a path that would lead us to the soul-catcher's house. We stumbled this way and that in the shapeless blackness, sharing Maquina's anger and frustration.

Abruptly the outline of an apparition rose before us. Flinging his arms out with a cry of terror, Maquina brushed his nails across the cold flesh that covered jaws, a pair of leering eyes, a broken nose. He gasped with horror and pulled back his hand as though it had been bitten. Maquina's long dagger came slithering noisily from its sheath at the same time I drew mine.

"You wouldn't dare," a harsh voice whispered. "Warn your slaves to take your canoe out into the very middle of the inlet and wait there. I will call them later if they still have any reason to return."

I doubt that Jon Jay understood a single word of the sorcerer's gutteral speech, but I heard him draw his pistols to half-cock.

Maquina rammed his dagger back into its scabbard. "Watch your tongue, you night-floating shark turd," Maquina warned him. "I almost cut your liver out!"

"That would not be as easy as it seems," the sorcerer grunted. "Come with me, and bring that bear man and the little blade hammerer along with you."

Jon Jay cautiously uncocked his pistols and came stumbling after us. Certainly he did not know at all where we were going.

The only light inside the sorcerer's hut came from the half-dead embers of a small fire in its middle. I call it a hut, but it was a little better than that. As the sorcerer kicked the embers with his bare foot, I looked around and saw that his miserable house was in two separate sections. I could see that this place in which he lived was like the inside of an animal's rib cage supported by a single spinelike pole. The other part was like the inside of some unwholesome monster's belly. Skulls and bowels of sea beasts and the partly feathered, bony wings of long-dead herons hung down from the rib structure, which was covered with rotting skins and graying cedar mats that were meant to keep out snow and rain. The smell inside was dreadful!

Maquina held his nose, which made his voice sound strange as he explained my sister's illness. The sorcerer leered and drooled and chuckled at the three of us.

"They say you have a whole ship's treasure moldering in a cave."

Maquina nodded without speaking.

"The moon is in a position right for curing. I shall come south tomorrow with you, towing a spare canoe. If I make her well, will you let me fill it with the things that I desire?"

Maquina frowned at him but nodded in agreement.

"Sleep here," the sorcerer said, pointing at the foul mud floor. "I will collect my cures. We cannot leave until morning."

"Collect your cures right now," Maquina shouted. "I would not lie down in this octopus hole of yours for a hundred otter skins. We're going now! Siam, call in my canoe. And hurry! I want to leave this place."

"No wonder!" the spirit-catcher said. He jerked back a moldy elk skin curtain and held up his fish-oil light to reveal his secret room. In its very center was a crudely carved, black-painted wooden whale, and seated round it were three human corpses. Each held a harpoon line whose heavy shell barb was thrust into the whale.

Jon Jay flinched when he saw those three gaunt human skeletons, each with a bulbous chief's hat on its head.

"Next time out," the spirit-catcher snorted, "if you are generous with me, I'll see to it that you come home with a whale!"

"You cure my wife," Maquina shouted. "Later, we will talk about the whales."

It was morning before we got back to Tahsis. That lean-jawed spirit-catcher slept like a newborn baby all the way, his thick cloak of cougar skins drawn round him like a tawny shroud. Maquina woke him with his foot, and the sorcerer struggled up our beach, imitating an exhausted fisherman.

In his right hand the spirit-catcher carefully carried a small smelly salmon-skin bag. Over his shoulder he had slung a much larger woven basket. He warned Knee Scars not to try to help him, for even this second bag, he said, was much too dangerous to entrust to ordinary human hands.

When we entered our house, the sorcerer slipped in behind Maquina's painted screen. When he reappeared, women screamed and the dogs and children yelped and fled from him in terror, for he had utterly transformed himself into a ghastly shaggy creature. His face was covered with a skull-shaped mask that had a howling mouth and sunken eyes. Its hair was nothing but a tangled mass of jet-black cormorant feathers. The salmon-skin bag had been suspended around his neck. With it were hung sharpened quills, bird claws, and little twisted bones of rodents. The very sight and smell of him would make a grown man want to run away. Over his back was hung a mangy-looking black bearskin with its head axed open. One eyehole glared from either shoulder, and its front teeth served to clasp its snout together on his chest. The paws and claws swayed loosely as the spirit-catcher crept toward us.

Maquina and I had known this sorcerer well since all of us were young, and even though we desperately needed help, neither of us could take this spirit-catcher seriously. Yet everything was different with us now. When our sorcerer reappeared, he had utterly transformed himself. Seeing him in this new array, neither Maquina nor I now thought of him as anyone whom we had ever known. The youth we used to know had disappeared, and in his place was this gaping demon, dressed to drive away whatever evil had come to occupy my sister's body. His mask moved slowly in the firelight like some powerful inhuman form of life. I had the feeling that if we had torn the mask away, there would be nothing behind it that our eyes could see.

When the Eagle house folk regained their courage, they pressed in close around Fog Woman, eager to see the spirit-catcher extract the evil from her bones. The sorcerer pushed them angrily aside and squatted beside my unconscious sister. He peered into her half-closed eyes and bravely placed his ear close to her mouth, listening for any fiendish whisperings coming from within her.

Young children squealed in fright as this unknown beast

inside the howling mask spread his arms wide over Fog Woman's body, then waved one hand, fingers spread, above her tight-drawn face. Sensuously chanting, grunting, moaning, calling out magic words that none of us could understand, his long thin body started to weave.

Cautiously, so that he would not break the spell that he had so carefully woven round her, this bearlike creature slowly reached for his curing rattle. With nervous birdlike motions, he held the rattle belly up and shook it very gently. His hand trembled slightly, and at first those crowded round my sister held their breaths to hear the sound. Then the tempo of his rattling increased and could be heard above his chanting. This new animal crouched and turned its head up as though it sensed some strange thing moving through the air.

The spirit-catcher flung the rattle onto Fog Woman's breast, then fumbling beneath its shaggy hide, jerked out a hollow bone tube that hung around his neck. Our villagers lunged away in fright, covering their mouths and nostrils as the sorcerer sighted on them through the opening of his frightening little trap. He placed one end through the puckered mouth hole of his mask and blew through it noisily.

"Hear that?" he said. "It's working. Are you ready?"

He dangled the soul-catcher over my poor sister, moving it deviously from her feet up along the ample contours of her body. When the spirit-catcher hung above her face, it started trembling, then whirling wildly. That was what he had been waiting for. Now! With his left hand he pinched her nostrils closed, forcing her to open her mouth to breathe. When this happened, the whirling ceased. The sorcerer rushed to stuff tight the double entrances of the soul-catcher, using soft bark wadding to capture all her sickness, imprisoning it within the hollow tube. When this was finished, the sorcerer bent and listened to my sister's breathing. He drew back one of her eyelids and felt the blood pulse on the side of her neck.

His bearlike figure rose and stood, his back to us. Suddenly he crouched and spun around, revealing a huge, jawed mask far more terrifying than the one before. Thrusting out his trembling

The sorcerer works
his magic as he
shakes his rattle

arms he rotated slowly, vibrating his painted wooden rattle toward the four corners of the long, dark room. This, we knew, would drive out any sickness spirits that might remain within the Eagle house.

The sorcerer's two apprentices held green hemlock branches in our fire, and when they started burning, these two ran wailing through the Eagle house, filling it with acrid smoke. I do not know what it did to the spirits or to my sister, but it drove me and most other humans choking and coughing into the winter night.

Finally, when we dared go back inside again, we saw the sorcerer, now stripped of his two masks, sitting red-eyed and dejected on Maquina's sleeping platform.

"I don't think I got it," he told us. "I didn't see it flying out her mouth. Did you?"

Maquina shook his head, as did I.

Jon Jay tried to assure us that some bloodletting or a dozen leeches would do a whole lot more to cure her.

The sorcerer listened carefully and said, "That sounds like it might help her. I never thought of that. She's still very sick," the sorcerer reluctantly admitted.

"We've got to give her an awful shock," Maquina said. "She was like this once before. What shall we do?" he asked the spirit-catcher. "If you cure her, I'll give you a house perhaps. Or a good-sized canoe, or half a dozen slaves."

"Yes, I'd like all of those things," the spirit-catcher answered. "I think," he said, "a land otter may have crossed her path. That's one of the worst things that can happen to a human. Has she looked at a rainbow lately? Has she been sucking any old goose eggs?"

"Who knows?" Maquina said disheartenedly.

"Perhaps you're right," the sorcerer said. "She won't get well unless we give her some sudden kind of shock."

The sorcerer gathered up his tubes and rattles and his bag of amulets and went away. Big Tom Sin was the first to take the long pole and open up the smoke holes. That act alone may well have saved my sister's life.

That night the full force of his wife's sickness came down
upon Maquina. For the next five days, he ate nothing but a few
quick swallows of fish broth. Fog Woman lay before us slowly
dying. The sorcerer returned and worked his magic over her a
dozen times. Still nothing seemed to cure her. The young women
who always clung to Maquina when my sister was away now
feared to enter the apartment where his *hacumb* lay unconscious. But they came near our fire pit every day, widening their
eyes and smiling at Maquina, wondering which one of them
would replace Fog Woman as head woman of our village.

At first Maquina could not believe that his wife was never
coming back to him, even though she had gone beyond the point
of eating or of speaking. My sister simply lay there with her
glazed eyes seeing nothing. Her women swore that their mistress
could no longer hear or see the spirit-catcher's rattles as he tried
to scare the evil out of her. Sometimes I wept with Maquina. At
other times, we just sat together staring at our fire. Finally, as
the coldest winter moon was dying, Maquina devised a plan so
subtle that he would only whisper it to me.

"What shall we do?" Kawskaws asked me. "If your sister
dies, Maquina will go mad with grief, or fall upon his dagger.
Is there no way we can help him?"

"Yes, there is a way," I said to Kawskaws. "Go quietly and
give this message straight to Ax Hand."

Her dark, deerlike eyes widened when she heard the plan.

Next morning, Ax Hand came and said that in his dreams
he had seen my sister fully cured, seated once more before her
fire. "I am going to try and surprise her," he told me simply.

He did not reappear for three days. But the evening of the
fourth day, he returned bearing a large object hidden beneath a
cedar mat in the bow of my small canoe.

Kawskaws went down and met him on the beach. "You
don't have to be so secretive with me!" she called out to him.

"Will you go up and fetch Fog Woman's cape?" was his
answer to her. "Bring the one that has the Chilkat design, and
I'll want her wide-brimmed hat as well."

"You look very tired," said Kawskaws. "When did you last rest?"

"Never mind that," said Ax Hand. "Help me to get everything right, and then I can go to sleep. You could join me if you wish."

Kawskaws smiled but did not answer him. She hurried to the Eagle house. Inside, only a few women and slaves were still awake. The women huddled together, whispering in the shadows. Some distance from them, Maquina sat alone by the fire, waiting for his wife to die. Poor man, he hung there nodding, halfway between our world and the other world of sleep.

Ax Hand stood his heavy covered burden just inside the entrance. Looking up, he saw that the wide roof boards had been almost closed against the falling sleet, and the whole upper part of the house was gray with hanging smoke. He cautiously walked to our fire pit and spoke softly to Maquina. But my brother-in-law had by then nodded off to sleep. Then Ax Hand crept back to the entrance. With Kawskaws's help, he eased the covered carving so close it almost touched the fire. He stripped the cedar cape away and carefully replaced it with Fog Woman's woven goat-hair cape and her familiar spruce-root hat.

When Kawskaws saw the finished figure, she clapped her hand across her mouth and ran away, for the Hupa are superstitious people terrified of ghosts.

Cut Ears, the lowly underneath-the-house slave, was the next to see Fog Woman sitting by the fire. He bent, clutching his short hair in terror, for there before him sat the perfect living image of the *hacumb*, whom he believed was dead. He would have run out of the house if Ax Hand had not grabbed him by the wrist, ordering him to be silent and to pass a small bundle of dry cedar twigs. To accomplish this, Cut Ears had to approach this lifelike phantom, which now sat before him waiting to be served.

Cut Ears watched in awe as the carver laid the cedar twigs on the embers of the fire. Ax Hand then crept behind the sleeping Maquina, and when the twigs burst into flame, he clapped his hands together, imitating the sharp sound of a musket shot.

Maquina awoke with a sudden start and stared across the fire. He saw his wife, Fog Woman, sitting in her usual place, gazing calmly at him with just the hint of a faint smile on her kindly face. "Oh, I'm glad to have you back," Maquina called out to her. "Has all the sickness flown out of you?"

The dampness that had gathered caused her eyes to glisten, and the flickering firelight made her lips appear to move.

Maquina squinted his eyes and stared at her. "Wife of mine, is that really you?" he called again, fear rising in his voice as he perceived the frightening stillness of the figure. "Who are you?" he said, leaping up from the fire in wild alarm.

"She is someone from the forest," Ax Hand said, "a woman who has come to warm a lonely man."

"She is not . . . not a real person," Maquina stuttered out in fear. He crept cautiously around the fire. "Are you a ghost?" he asked. He forced himself to touch her before he would believe she was not made of flesh and blood.

"Magic man!" he whispered. He whirled and stared at Ax Hand. "Can you not bring one or the other of them to life for me?"

"Who knows?" said Ax Hand. "I have done all for now that I can do."

Maquina seemed not to hear the carver's answer as he stood staring at that perfect likeness of his wife.

Day after day, my poor sister continued to hang near death while Maquina stared across the fire. He fell more and more under the spell of Fog Woman's wooden image. Before it ended, Ax Hand told me he wished that he had never dreamed of carving that likeness of Maquina's wife. He had made my sister appear young again. Maquina would sit staring at this perfect wooden maiden, so fascinated that he rarely ate or slept. Sometimes he sang songs to it, or talked, or laughed, or wept with her, remembering old times.

For three successive days the rains drenched the trees, and the damp smoke hole remained almost closed. On the fourth evening, Maquina seemed to lose his reason. I heard him talking wildly to the wooden woman. "I want you!" he pleaded. "I care nothing for those young sluts. I want you, woman, you!" Maquina knelt and lustfully threw his arms around that perfect wooden image of my sister.

You'll be astounded when I tell you that I heard that carving sigh a word, then scream at him before it split in half. Oh, yes, I swear to you it did just that! In the intense heat and the gathering dampness, the wooden image split. With a high-pitched scream and then a woman's sigh of resignation, her cape fell open and her hat slid sideways as the figure tore itself apart and toppled from Maquina's arms into the flaming embers of the fire.

The exact tone of this ghostly *hacumb*'s scream was the gossip of the Eagle house and all of Wolf Town for days and moons and countless seasons. One woman asked another, "Exactly what did that carved spirit woman say to him before she tore herself in two?"

Another whispered, "What message did she call to him from that soul of hollow cedar?"

It was wrong, they said, to have a poor, sick wife who could look up from her deathbed and see a life-sized image of herself.

My brother-in-law suddenly raised his arms above his head and shouted, "Spuck! I heard that wooden woman sing out, 'Spuck!' Siam, did you not hear the wooden woman call out, 'Spuck'?" he asked me.

"Yes," I said, "I guess that splitting wood did say, 'Spuck,' or something like 'young Spuck.' "

"Yes," Maquina said. "It's true. 'Spuck, young Spuck,' is the very name it called to me."

"It's true. I heard it also," Man Frog's wife called out from the next apartment, where she had been listening. "Yes, 'Spuck, young Spuck! Spuck! Spuck!' "

Almost all the slave women agreed, "Yes, we heard it, too . . . saying, 'Spuck, Spuck, Spuck!' "

"What did you hear it say?" Maquina demanded of Fog Woman's Salish weaver.

"I guess maybe it did say, 'Spuck,' but I thought it was a longer name than that." The weaver woman sighed.

"Yes! Yes!" Maquina shouted. "Everyone in this household heard it call out some woman's name."

"Oh, yes," those near him nodded. "All of us heard it cry out some young woman's name to you!"

"Well, I think it said, 'Spuck'—where is she?" Maquina shouted. "Where is that nice plump-breasted little girl? You," he said to Knee Scars, "go over to the Thunder house and tell those two dear girls that I want them over here. No, wait! Red Tongue," he shouted, "put on your best robe and your frontlet. Bring your talking stick. We're going over there and speak to young Spuck's father. I may need to have a new young *hacumb*, I may need another wife. Quick!" he shouted to Toowin. "Go get the sorcerer. Bring him here as fast as you both can run."

When he arrived, the sorcerer and Maquina whispered together so that others could not hear. The sorcerer sat thinking, shading his eyes from the fire. He looked up quickly as a new thought came to him.

"The splitting of that carving means," he said, "that Fog Woman's spirit has spoken her last request to you through that wooden carving. It means she wishes you, her husband, to take a new young girl to be your *hacumb*!"

"Yes, that is certainly true. Many heard it," Maquina said. "That's what Fog Woman wishes me to do!"

At that moment the copper widow walked straight past me and went up to Maquina. "The word that wooden image called to you was 'Cheepokesklickeryek.' I am the one she chose as your new *hacumb*."

"Wrong! You are wrong," said a quavering voice from behind.

Turning in surprise, we all saw my sister roll over and prop herself up on one elbow. "She cut you dead, did she, poor brother?" She laughed dryly, then pointing a trembling finger at Maquina, she said, "This true wife of yours is not dead yet! Get that awful widow out of here! Kawskaws!" she called. "Bring me some of that octopus soup that smells so good. And you, husband . . . you! Imagine you thinking of remarrying before you've even raised me in my last canoe. You sounded out of your mind . . . when I heard you yelling the name of that child, 'Spuck, Spuck, Spuck!' But when I heard you speak that copper widow's name—well!" Fog Woman snorted contemptuously. "I saw that wooden image before it cracked and fell into the fire, where it belongs. That piece of yellow cedar, it didn't look at all like me!" she said in scorn. "Its eyes were set too close together, and its cheeks were far too fat. It looked old, you hear me, old and haggard, like my elder sister, who lives south of here."

Maquina looked at his wife and chuckled. "Have you been lying there playing dead all this time, just so you could have the pleasure of watching your poor husband grieve for you?"

"Oh, I was sick. There's no denying that, poor husband. But I was also curious to see which one of those young nips of breast meat you would choose to be your new *hacumb*." My sister took a gulp of the thick soup, and laughed. "Yes, as my father used to say, 'You Eagle house people never learn.' "

Maquina took his old wife by the hand. "It's exactly as your brother and I agreed. A shock like that was the only way to get you back. I'm truly glad to have you with me once again."

My sister smiled at him and shook her head. "I'm never going to die," she said. "I just can't trust you. Will you bring me some of that boiled deer meat?" she asked the Salish weaver woman. Turning to Maquina and looking accusingly at me, she said, "Open the roof boards, husband. Let's get all the smoke and strange female odors out of this house—of yours and mine. I swear that copper widow smells just like a fox in heat."

 IT IS well known that women have always caused us trouble in the Eagle house. One morning when we were down on the beach together examining a badly split canoe, Maquina said, "Brother-in-law, you worry me. That copper widow is probably the worst female either of us has ever known, and yet you won't let her alone."

I looked at him and said, "My sister told you to say that to me, didn't she?"

Maquina nodded his head in agreement. "Nevertheless, I think she's right," he added. "That young widow is changing you in ways I do not like. You walk around like a man half in a dream." He put his head close to mine and said, "Just between us, I too bedded with her not long after she arrived in Wolf Town. Almost every ranking person here has lain with her once, and maybe twice. You're the only fool who goes on and on with it."

"I can't help myself," I answered. "I haven't got a wife."

Maquina laughed and said, "That's no excuse. But if you do go on, don't have her wandering naked around your apartment when my wife is staring out at you across our fire. Brother-in-law, I'm the one who has to listen to your sister raving endlessly against that woman. Sometimes it gets so bad, I'm afraid she'll snatch up a dagger and go across and kill that woman as she rides on top of you."

"No, my sister won't do that," I said. "But I am worried about Kawskaws. She's a Hupa, and they can be oh, so unforgiving."

Sea Star woke one morning weeping and told Maquina that because of a bad dream she wished to go home and see her family. No, she said, she did not want Jon Jay to go with her. She said she wanted to go alone.

Fog Woman was much against her going, but Maquina,

paying no attention to his wife, immediately ordered up a whale canoe for Sea Star and sent her homeward in our grandest style. It is not unusual for a young wife to feel homesick. We all understand that when a gray and soggy winter gets a person in its grasp for four long cold-faced moons, it's enough to set even a hardened warrior screaming.

Ten days after Sea Star's departure, the first huge spring tide came sweeping up our narrow inlet. I went out with the hunters early and watched the rising waters as we searched the sky for signs. I warned Toowin that winter, just as it is dying, often sends back its fiercest spirits for one last wild attack. I sang for him an age-old song:

> You, up there in the sky,
> Don't you ever get tired
> Of having the heavy clouds
> Between you and us?

This storm began for us in the midmorning. We could see huge blue-black thunderheads scudding in toward us up the long fiord. They were moving much too fast. Then the whole sky darkened as though night was falling, though midday had not yet arrived. We could hear the wind sighing and moaning and the unseen surf breaking against distant points of land. High above us the wind whistled as it drove the heavy clouds against the mountains. Still no rain fell. The first great gusts of wind that came against the houses seemed almost warm to us.

Then the storm came on with a force more violent than any could remember. It came roaring straight up our long protective water passage and pounded our secret hiding place at Tahsis.

As the first sharp drops of rain came slanting in across our beach, I hurried to my apartment to get my cedar rain cape and my widest hat. The chief's wife from the Thunder house came running inside after me.

"Is Spuck here?" she asked Fog Woman. "Have you seen my daughter, Spuck?"

"No," my sister answered. "She went with Kawskaws up

the inlet earlier this morning." Fog Woman looked worried. "The two of them were gathering spruce roots. I loaned them my small canoe."

"Small canoe?" Spuck's mother said. "Have you felt the strength of the wind? Have you seen the surf that's coming in against our beach?"

Toowin came with us, and we stood in the Eagle house entrance. The rain mixed with icy hail came lashing in. The chief's wife from the Thunder house was right. Each wave was building up in a frightening way before smashing against our beach. White foam blew off each wave crest and came hurtling in like small white birds against the houses. What a storm!

"My husband is out there," Tunwata, a woman from our Eagle house, wailed as she pointed out across the inlet.

My heart went tum-tum-tum as I caught sight of them. There were two white seal canoes with four men in each, paddling hard toward us, trying to quarter the huge green headless seas that heaved monstrously beneath them. Only when the waves crashed into the beach did they break. I did not so much fear for those men while they were on the inlet, for they were wily sea hunters used to ocean storms. But I did not believe that they could ever bring those two lean dugouts through that tremendous tumbling surf that was tearing at the shore.

It was terrible to stand in the fierce downpour that soaked us to the skin, surrounded by their women, and watch helplessly, waiting for the worst to happen right before our eyes. Those men out there were used to heavy surf, but like me—like all men here—they understood the sea and feared it.

I saw them cautiously back-paddling, keeping the canoes steady, hanging just out beyond the draw, where they knew the waves would snatch them and drive them in against the shore. Oh, yes, Meetlak and Kapswalla, they were in firm control of their canoes. But they couldn't stay there. The wind was increasing all around them as the storm grew worse and worse. They dared not turn. There was no place else to go but straight ashore.

Meetlak was head man in the first canoe. They eased in

behind the pounding surf, then backed off quickly, trying to get their rhythm right. I could almost hear them counting—*sah-wauk*, one, *atla*, two, *katsa*, three—trying desperately to catch the thrust of the wave so they could ride in on its crest with the lucky number four.

They waited, and they backstroked, and they waited. I did not blame them. I myself would have been dead afraid to try it, and yet with the wind rising at their backs, they had no choice at all. They had to come ashore or drown.

Suddenly, I saw the stern of Meetlak's canoe rise as a huge wave came beneath its stern. In a single motion, all four men drove their pointed paddles into the water. These sea hunters tried with all their skill and might to ride that single wave to shore. The seal canoe rose with the surf and went shooting forward. I could see all four men straining with every muscle in their torsos as the dugout came hurtling in toward the beach.

The instant that their bow touched gravel, all four men vaulted out. Then, grabbing the sides of the slender canoe, they ran with it at full speed up our steep beach, shoving, lifting, carrying, running. I heard them scream and laugh in triumph. They were free of the deadly waves.

Some of the women and the children round me fell down, weeping with relief.

"Oh, they're young. They're good at it," I told those women near me. "That other canoe will be coming in just like that one, you will see."

Even as I spoke I could see the second group move their dugout to the back of the surf and start their counting. They seemed to have the rhythm—one, two, three. But oh! They missed the lucky number four. The wave that lifted them was like an angry gray-green serpent, roiling, boiling, spitting foam at its enormous crest.

As the second canoe came hurtling in onto the beach, the first man jumped just as the canoe bow struck, tipped sideways, and was smashed wide open, grinding him into the gravel with the sea's full force. Splintered shards of cedar were flung up on the shore and then sucked out again. I saw one of our seal hunters crawling on his hands and knees. A second lay face down as the next big wave gathered strength to come and suck all of them away.

Along with our young warriors, I started running hard toward them. Jon Jay and Tom Sin easily passed me. Hoiss and Tom Sin were the first to reach the crawling man. Together they dug in their heels and fought against the rush of water. They held fast and refused to let the big wave take him from them.

It was Jon Jay and Litka who caught and dragged the unconscious man to safety. The body of the third man, Quartlak, was beyond our reach. We watched as he was tumbled and rolled away from us, caught in an undertow so powerful that it was sucking heavy gravel from our beach. Behind me I could hear the pitiful wailing and screaming of the women as they saw Quartlak's body roll in the waves, then disappear forever. The fourth man we never saw. I stood helplessly staring at all four blood-red paddles as they drifted aimlessly away on the gray-green waters just beyond the thunderous surf. Yes, we who spend our lives on the sea, we are the ones who dread drowning most of all. We believe that the soul is carried with the body into that dark underworld beneath the waves. There the body and the soul cannot part, but roll endlessly, hopelessly struggling to reach a proper place to rest.

With true night came violent sleet and hail. The wind rose and howled and thundered against our roof until we knew the boulders could not hold the wide boards down. My son, Toowin, and Jon Jay and Tom Sin, together with almost every man within our house, stripped naked. The women slathered bear and seal grease on the men's bodies to help protect them from the rain. Rushing out, Toowin and Jon Jay climbed to the roof while big Tom Sin and the others gathered heavy stones to pass up to them. I, Siam, the aging usher, stayed inside to help Maquina make decisions.

No human could have felt relief inside that house on such a night, for with each new howling blast of wind we could hear the giant cedars near us sway and creak and groan. Along the beach we could hear some of them come crashing down. The grim-faced women clutched their children close to them. No one slept. All of us looked up and shuddered as we imagined the misery of the men who squatted up above us in the wintry darkness, gripping the heavy boulders, trying to save the house.

The otter hunter and his son came staggering through our entrance. *"Tyee! Tyee!"* the old man gasped. "A tree fell right through the middle of the end house. Yes, bashed it right in half. No one was killed, but some of their roof men got hurt. What a night!" The two of them went running out to tell the other houses.

Imagine a storm so noisy that a big house could be crushed near us, yet we did not even hear the roof beams crack as they fell in!

Just before dawn, the wind began to die, and one by one the shivering men crawled down off the roofs. The women rubbed their bodies, wrapped them in fire-heated blankets, and fed them steaming broth.

"I hate to think of Kawskaws and Spuck out all night in that," said Toowin, who was still pale and shuddering, his wet hair clinging to his head. "I'm going to find them."

"Oh, no, you're not!" I said.

Toowin looked me in the eye, then put on his cedar rain cape and hat, and as though I had not even spoken, he turned away from me and strode out the entrance. I watched him heading west, picking his way among this driftwood newly strewn along the beach.

I had the certain feeling that Toowin had lain beside not one but both of those young women. Instead of being angry with him, I was proud. His defiance of me was the most manly deed that I had ever seen my Toowin do.

Jon Jay bolted down his ladleful of broth. Then snatching up the old rain cape that my sister had given him, he ran after Toowin.

Full morning came to us as wind-torn and shabby as a half-drowned sea gull. I have never seen such rain. We could hear rock slides in the mountains. The small root systems of the enormous trees were soaked loose and slipped, allowing them to collapse against one another, causing a thunderous tumble, leaving giant gray rock faces that were frightening to behold.

The wind died as evening came, the sky partly cleared, and the new air that swept in from the ocean was icy cold. After a great storm one feels worn out and tired. But this time, not me. I was too worried about Toowin and Jon Jay, and just as much about those two missing girls. Besides that, I found it difficult to rid my mind of the image of those four blood-red paddles, still floating in my vision as I stared into the fire.

Not long after dawn, the Salish weaver woman screamed to me, for she had had her eye to the peephole since first light. "They're coming! I see them coming back along the beach!"

I looked out my own peephole and saw Toowin, Kawskaws, Spuck, and Jon Jay, one following the other in single file. I was overjoyed as I watched them heading straight for us! "We lost your canoe," Kawskaws gasped to my sister. "It was washed away from us. It's gone."

"That doesn't matter," Fog Woman said with great firmness. "I'm so glad to see you safe. You're wet," my sister said to them. "Stand in close by the fire. Bring soup," she called out to her women. "Cut Ears, do you hear me? Bring more wood!"

I saw Maquina staring suspiciously at Spuck. She stood shuddering close to Jon Jay, shivering and saying nothing.

When Fog Woman's servant brought broth to all four of them, Spuck alone refused it, and without even drying herself or saying a single word to anyone, she turned and ran out of the Eagle house.

Kawskaws and Toowin turned their heads and watched her go. Fog Woman and Maquina, yes, and I, we watched the remaining three. None of them seemed surprised that the beautiful, rain-soaked Spuck had fled from all of us.

It is as Maquina said. Our women sometimes bring us more trouble than storms and rival enemies combined. Even women who don't live in Wolf Town cause us problems. If you doubt that, listen to what happened at Tahsis just after that last winter gale had blown up our fiord and left all of us exhausted.

A few nights later I was sleeping soundly, when suddenly I

was awakened just at dawn. Fog Woman and Maquina were already sitting up.

"Listen!" my sister whispered.

We peered through the shadows of the house and were amazed that the sounds that had shocked us into wakefulness had disturbed not a single other person.

My sister and I hurried to the entrance and saw strange men wailing, moaning, painfully dragging themselves up out of the water onto the gravel beach in front of Tahsis.

Fog Woman ran back and told Maquina. "A canoe of enemy warriors has overturned down on the beach," she whispered. "More than thirty of them. Hurry! Hurry!"

When he heard that, Maquina was up in an instant, stark naked except for his long dagger in its scabbard, which he had slung across his chest.

We three crouched together at the entrance, peering out into the first gray light of dawn just in time to see the last of the men come struggling up out of the cold waters of the inlet.

"Serves the sneaking cod turds right!" Maquina snorted. "Must have come in on that surf all wrong and upset their war canoe. That will teach them to come raiding against my village."

"They didn't lose their weapons," I told her. "Look, their war chief is ordering them to build a fire."

"Those brazen fools! Imagine them daring to light a fire right on our beach. Wake up the warriors! We'll show them that fighting men live here!"

"That morning wind must cut right through them," Fog Woman said. "They're shuddering. Look at the hoarfrost gathering on their backs and along the slats of their wooden armor and on their fighting helmets. Those are northerners, Haida or Tlingit."

"It must be cold on the beach," I whispered.

Maquina said, "There are four white men with them. I find that strange. We have never seen shipsmen here in Tahsis. Nor have I seen any dressed like that before. Their war chief is pointing to our smokehouse. He's sending them to look inside.

Woman!" Maquina whispered, "bring Siam and me our heavy arrow shirts. Be quick! They're robbing us of all our salmon. Wake every man and warn the women. There is going to be a fight! Get Jon Jay and Tom Sin. I want them on either side of me—armed! Whites against whites—that's a sight I want to see."

"Wait! Wait!" Fog Woman said. "I never saw a fire that burned so coldly blue, and those men standing closest to it are still shuddering. See, one man is standing right inside the flames."

"We can take them best while they're still cold and wet and don't know what they're doing," Maquina said as he hurried back inside the house.

When his men heard that the enemy was already on the beach, every able-bodied warrior swiftly armed himself. They swarmed out—Jon Jay and Tom Sin with them too—fully armed and ready to do battle. Our war chief, Man Frog, led the whole attack. Maquina followed close behind him.

There was great confusion on the beach. Man Frog turned and gestured wildly at Maquina. "Where are they? Where did they go? We see no one here, no warriors, no enemy canoe."

Fog Woman, who had followed us onto the beach, shrieked, "They've got to be here. We three saw them—a northern canoe full of them with four white men."

"Where?" said Man Frog. "Show me where?"

"Right there," Maquina said, pointing a few paces out in front of them. "They were huddled all around that fire."

"What fire?" said Man Frog.

It was true: there was no sign of fire, no footprints on the tide-smoothed beach, no mark that anyone had been there. "I saw them stealing salmon from that smokehouse," Maquina said.

"I did, too," my sister added. "Armloads of them."

Long Claws and Man Frog laughed at her. "That old house is falling down."

"He's right," I told her. "Nobody has kept salmon in there for who knows how many seasons."

"I don't care about that," Maquina shouted. "That was no dream. I saw them. Siam saw them. My wife saw them. They were coming up out of the water. Yes, we three saw them all together. Did you ever hear of three persons sharing the same dream?"

"I never did," said Man Frog. "But I would rather think you shared a dream than believe you saw phantom warriors on this beach foretelling troubles yet to come."

The dagger maker and Tom Sin, both with a look of disappointment, slipped their heavy cutlasses back in their sheaths. I do not believe those two shipsmen ever came to understand that they, like the rest of us, had been out there chasing a red-handed mountain woman's power to control our dreams.

On the very next night, we three were again awakened. The following morning, the short, thick-set mountain woman came into the house carrying two salmon in a grease dish.

"I thought I asked you to keep that witch away from me," Maquina said. "I don't trust her."

"Did you see them again last night?" Fog Woman sighed.

"Oh, yes, I saw them. Of course I saw them," Maquina groaned. "Did you, too?"

"Yes," she nodded. "And my brother, Siam, saw them also." Fog Woman held out both her hands once, then again with three fingers held back on her left hand. "There were only seventeen last night. I counted them."

The red-handed woman listened very carefully, though I still do not believe she understood our language. She pulled her tattered bearskin around her shoulders and stood on one red-dyed foot watching us, her dark eyes glittering.

"Yes, there were seventeen," I agreed.

"I counted them as well," Maquina said. "Did you see the four white men?"

"No, two were gone," I said.

"What else did you observe?" Maquina asked me.

"Their wet capes were rotting on their backs. Their beach fire had black flames and gave off cold instead of heat. Did you see one white man lie down in the ashes of the fire?"

"I did," my sister said. "It seemed to me that they had all but given up, that they were dying. They moved as stiffly as old gray herons. Perhaps they are already dead."

Maquina shrugged his shoulders.

"Everything about those warriors on the beach seems to have happened long ago," my sister said.

The mountain woman smiled, sucked in her breath, and nodded.

"And yet," Maquina said, "something is different about their capes, their weapons, and all their crest designs. The whites were wearing long, straight swords of a kind I've never seen before and gray leggings and short, puffed-out pants and padded jackets and all that white ruffled cloth around their necks—like the Spanish men who came and made their houses."

Maquina interrupted himself. "How could we three have had exactly the same dream? That has never happened to any other persons here."

He stared belligerently across the fire at the nearly naked mountain woman, who suddenly held out her blood-red hands toward him, hooking them like claws.

"Get her out of here!" Maquina shouted to his wife. "Trade her off for candlefish, or give her to your brother. I hate a slave with power."

"I don't want her near me," I said quickly. "She was showing us ghosts of the past."

"Don't you two worry. I'll get rid of her." My sister sighed. "I'll have her taken safely back into the mountains, where she can easily find her own way home."

The red-handed woman smiled at us, delighted that the dreams she had conjured had made us do exactly as she wished.

We had all of us grown impossibly tired of winter. The roofs at Tahsis glistened from countless days of dreary rain. The trees near our houses, burdened by snow-sopped moss, adopted somber, drooping postures. Half-naked children tried to warm themselves by playing their one-legged hopping games inside the cold and gloomy houses.

Our women, like the men, had all turned surly, hating the confinement demanded by this sodden weather. They carped at the slaves and gave murderous looks to one another as they unpiled their painted cedar boxes, shook out our ancient cere-

monial capes and crested blankets, then folded them away again.
They oiled and polished the fine-carved yellow cedar helmets
and dance masks and wrapped up their best rattles and brass
and copper bracelets. Yes, the ceremonial trappings for the winter feasts and dances disappeared. That meant that our women
were more than ready for a change of season; they could scarcely
wait for the warmth of spring to come.

I thought a lot about Maquina. Was it his long siege of
worry about the nearly fatal sickness of my sister that had un-
nerved him? Or, as some of our house women have gossiped,
would our *tyee* really have taken that plump-breasted little
beauty, Spuck, or—for shame!—that dreadful copper widow to
be his new *hacumb*? Certainly those events seemed to have un-
done him. For a while it appeared to me that my brother-in-
law's powers to reason had blown away.

Finally, early one morning the wet winter flew away from
us, mercifully driven by the south wind. Oh, yes, we were very
cautious of those first warm breezes that bring us early spring,
for it is of course the most dangerous season of the year. The
trouble being that throughout the long dark winter persons hold
back their worst grievances, believing that their anger is brought
on only by the cold wet gloom and deceiving themselves into
thinking they will forget all hatreds when the warm days come.
But with true spring come wild feelings of exuberance, and
boldness too, and the sense that one can burst out of one's winter house restraints and at last shout to a passing canoe, "You
there, you floating louse's rectum, take my warning—come close
to me only if you dare!"

Also with spring come other passions of a very different
kind. You can see their signs in the ruffling feathering of the
birds, the excited, chattering chasing of the squirrels. You can
hear them in the nervous laughter of young girls. It is a most
unsettling season.

I had just come in from a long and tiring journey with Maquina in his big canoe. We found my sister, Fog Woman, by our
house fire supervising her women as they prepared our evening
meal. My son, Toowin, squatted near her, half-asleep.

Maquina and I each took a large hot bowl of clam broth and had just settled down to enjoy the warmth when through the shadows I saw the copper widow beckoning to me eagerly.

What could I do? I couldn't just get up and leave and go to her, and I didn't dare to ask her to join us and suffer my sister's scorn.

Cheepokeslickeryek waited only a moment before she moved boldly into our firelight. Without so much as a glance at Fog Woman, she walked over to the box on which I sat and leaned affectionately against me.

Oh, you should have seen the awful look that crossed my sister's face. She hated that poor widow beyond all reason. Most women chose to walk away when the copper widow came near them. But not my sister. No. After all, she is the *hacumb* of this village.

Maquina looked coolly at the copper widow as she ran her hot hand underneath my cape. But when I sat stiff and still, not recognizing her, she angrily withdrew her hand and quickly stepped away.

To my surprise Toowin leapt up and went and sat upon a box near me. Seeing this, Cheepokeslickeryek smiled and quickly moved to stand beside my son.

"Who wove this cedar cape for you?" she asked him in her soft, slurry river voice, and as she spoke I saw her slyly run her hand up Toowin's back.

He smiled, then sucked in his breath in pain. When my sister saw that, a look of fury spread across her face. The copper widow looked at all of us, then smiled triumphantly at Toowin and slowly walked away.

"Awhhh!" my sister gasped. "I've never known a woman I despised as much as that one! Toowin! You keep away from anyone who acts like that," Fog Woman warned her nephew.

Maquina pretended he had noticed nothing and, to ease the pressure, called for more broth and salmon. When my sister's women brought it to us, we were surprised to see that Toowin had already slipped away.

Yes, he was gone for two nights and the whole day in between. When he did come home, he looked lean and drawn and would tell me nothing. In some ways Toowin was never quite the same again. Kawskaws wept when she told me how dreadfully his back was scratched, but there was nothing she or I could do.

After that, what happened here at Tahsis on one fine spring afternoon was blamed upon the widow, which just shows how much our people despised her. Certainly it changed everything for me and my son, Toowin—yes, and also for Kawskaws and Jon Jay and even that bold girl, Spuck. How could we have guessed that the simple actions of these four could have caused such troubles? It was before the women thought it time to move out to the coast, and I wish they had not been so slow that spring.

On this day of which I speak, spring was shining all along the inlet, and new leaves were budding on the alder branches. The dagger maker was busy at the shipsmen's workplace, while Tom Sin was squatting cross-legged on the beach sewing a large, three-cornered sail for Maquina's big canoe. Toowin was helping Jon Jay by pumping on the puff box.

The dagger maker's hammer sent its joyful ringing through the village. I remember exactly when it stopped. Toowin told me later that Spuck had come running to the forge to say that she had seen the place high on a tree where a huge black bear had stood up and made deep scorings in the bark. Toowin wanted to show those scratches to Jon Jay because the dagger maker had never seen such marks and, also, because my son and I are known to be closely spirited with bears.

Toowin and Jon Jay followed Spuck along the narrow path that leads east until they came to the upper salmon pool, where Spuck showed them the bear claw marks. Toowin was very disappointed. He told me they were old claw marks from the spring before, and small, not at all worth looking at. He said he was surprised that a girl like Spuck could make a mistake like that.

They were hot from hurrying, Toowin told me later, and Spuck was the first to take off her clothes and go into the pool. Toowin said that Jon Jay was very quick to join her, I guess because it was spring and he was missing his young wife.

Even as I came along the path with Maquina, we could hear Spuck laughing in the pool. Toowin said the next thing he saw was Maquina raging and storming up the trail toward them with me behind him, trying to calm him down.

Call it spring madness if you wish, but my brother-in-law did not seem especially angry with his favorite Spuck. Nor was he angry with Jon Jay. No, he saved all his rage for his own nephew, Toowin. He roared and bellowed out at him, saying Toowin was trying to mount that girl against her will.

When I laughed at that, he turned and shouted in my face. Imagine my brother-in-law working his anger off on me! He swore I was no better than my sister, that I had been lying with that widow and had utterly failed to teach my son right from wrong. He accused me of turning Toowin over to my long-legged Hupa servant girl and allowing her to run him absolutely wild.

Naturally I got raging mad when my brother-in-law said that. I started shouting harsh words back at him. I told him he was not fit to be married to my sister and that I was ashamed to have him as an in-law and to live in the same house with him.

I admit that I, his usher, should not have said that to Maquina, for he turned pale and trembled in his rage. No one in Wolf Town had ever dared curse him or his father or his father's father. Toowin refused to come out of the water, and that girl, Spuck, stood beautifully naked on the bank, trembling with fright. The dagger maker was watching both our faces and understanding only some of the spiteful words that Maquina and I were hurling at each other. Let me tell you, this was more than just an ordinary family fight.

My brother-in-law stepped so close to me that my heart went tum-titty-tum-titty-tum. For an instant I was certain that both of us would draw our daggers. I am glad to say that did not happen. Finally, I turned my back on him and ordered Toowin to come out of the water. Sullenly he followed me as I walked swiftly back toward the Eagle house.

Kawskaws helped us pack up everything we owned into a dozen good-sized boxes. We rolled up our bed mats, took our wooden dishes, our weapons, and hunting gear, and we prepared to leave.

Maquina would not even look at me, and I could not tolerate the thought of remaining in the same house with that evil-tempered brute another moment. I ranted to my sister, saying she was welcome to come south with us and live among our decent relatives, that she didn't have to stay and suffer such a jealous fool. But she refused. She begged me to calm down and wait a few days, then decide.

"Let the usher go!" Maquina shouted at her. "I'll be glad to see the last of him."

I ordered my paddlers to make my whale canoe ready for the journey. Oh, I was furious! I heard my sister talking to Maquina, trying to soothe our troubles. But nothing she could say did any good. I heard him tell my sister that he never wanted to see my bear-turd face again—those were his very words!

My four paddlers carried my eight-man whale canoe to the water and piled in all that we could carry. Only my boldest friends came down to see us off. They looked as though they wished to support me, but the way things were, they dared not say too much. They secretly slipped three new yew-wood paddles and some useful gifts of food into my canoe.

It's truly hard to leave your friends and the household where you've been living almost all your life. But at that moment I thought of nothing save the pleasure of separating from Maquina—of never setting eyes on him again. There was only one person that I would badly miss in Wolf Town. I wondered how I could give her my copper bracelet.

My sister came down to my canoe, and she was weeping, which I've almost never seen her do. She gave me a big box of salmonberries packed in the most costly fish grease. Jon Jay came with her, looking sad and confused. He didn't have his skins folded between the two black cloth boards that tell him how to talk to us, so he counted on his fingers, trying to ask us how many days, or, I wondered, did he mean moons, that we would be away. The copper widow, fearing no one, came boldly down to see me off.

Toowin stared at her, and Kawskaws started weeping.

"Push off! Get going now!" I said to my four paddlers, and they did.

As they eased the whale canoe away from the beach, the copper widow, the dagger maker, and old Matla were the only ones who stepped out into the water to help us off. Jon Jay pushed with my paddlers into the cold salt chuck until they all three stood crotch-deep in the water. Then they pushed us off.

I looked at the copper widow and the dagger maker and wondered what would become of both of them and Tom Sin. I did not expect to see any of them again. I wanted to shout out to the widow, "*Chahko nika.* Come mine with me." She smiled at me and called out, "I'll be waiting for you here when you return." I saw her slip my bracelet on her wrist.

Jon Jay might have tried to leap into my whale canoe. But, of course, I had no right to encourage him.

When we were some distance from the shore, Kawskaws called out to Jon Jay in a high and shaking voice, "Gooo-bye! Gooo-bye!"

And Toowin, he also called, "Gooo-bye, Jonee."

Jon Jay just stood in the icy water, staring after us as we stroked away. Then he called out, "Good-bye!" And in Chinook he said, "*Mesika kelipi.* You return, return to me! Soon!" My sister too was weeping. I felt bad. He was losing us, and we were losing him—and I, that sweet-smelling copper widow. It was almost more than I could bear.

I glanced back only once. Oh, yes, Maquina had heard Jon Jay's words to us. My brother-in-law, naked except for the old cedar cape he had flung across his shoulders, was standing alone near the entrance to the Eagle house. There was something about the dejected way he stood that made me know he took no pleasure in our leaving Wolf Town. Nor did I. We three exiles set off sadly for the south to visit my other sister, whom I had not tried to see for years.

Suddenly I heard a single yew-wood staff start drumming violently against the wall of the Thunder house, resounding in the silence. I saw Maquina turn and stare toward that sound, as did everyone ashore. The ear-splitting noise of protest went on for some time until I heard the stern voice of the Thunder house chief shouting, "Stop that, do you hear me? Stop that!" He knew as well as I that it was his daughter Spuck's defiant way of calling out good-bye to my son, Toowin.

I guess Maquina knew that too.

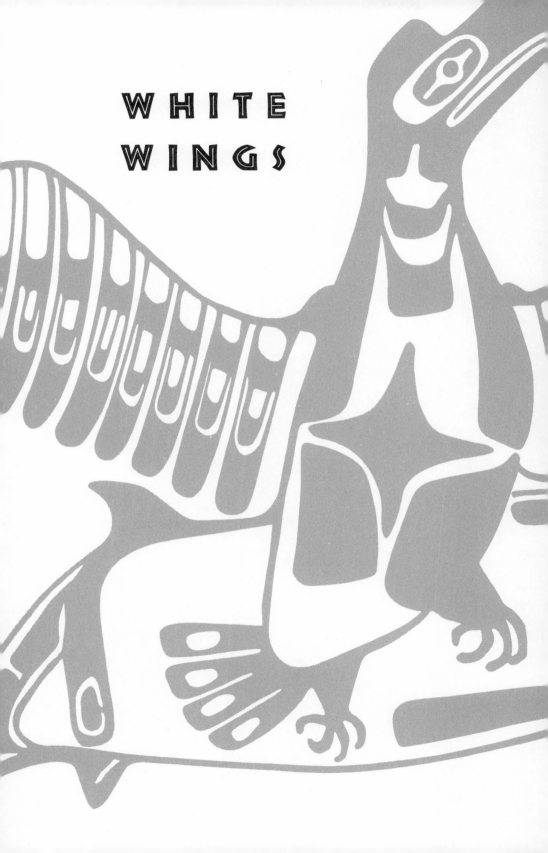

WHITE WINGS

 A s w e made our way south down the long fiord, unseen birds sent up a ghostly crying that was distorted and echoed into a heightened chorus, giving us a terrifying sense of loneliness. It was as though we were three persons drifting in a dream canoe, lost forever in an endless sea of fog. I hated that journey because my fight with Maquina was the reason we were going south, I had lost the widow, and I didn't want to see my other sister or her wretched husband. But what else could I do?

"There's a canoe coming out from behind that island," Toowin told me, standing up and shading his hawk-sharp eyes.

"Who is it?" I asked him.

He waited a while before answering. "It's her!" he said. "It's the dagger maker's wife. She's in my uncle's boat. Yes, it's Sea Star going back to Wolf Town."

I said, "Well, that's good. Jon Jay would be lonely with us gone and he will need somebody."

"But she won't need him," Kawskaws said bitterly.

"Humans do need friends," I told them. "Humans are not always of the kindly sort they used to be," said I. "In the beginning, when we ourselves were much more like the animals, we possessed their instinctive intelligence. We moved as smoothly as mountain lions, we could send our singing voices out as far as loons do, we were swimmers slick as seals. We were—well, we were animals. You need only look at the beasts to see how beautifully we appeared when cloaked with our own sea otter furs or gorgeously arrayed in brilliant-yellow puffin feathers. The costly blue-green abalone shells we treasure shine not one-half so brightly as the leaping silver sides of trout or salmon."

Toowin snorted at my words and said, "If the animals know more than we, why do they allow themselves to be so easily caught by us?"

"Only," I answered, "because we are their closest relatives—and being of their high intelligence, they pity us. Without their constant gifts of flesh and fat and warming furs, we would, when we left our mothers' breasts, be forced to lie shuddering in the darkness until we starved to death. All the troubles we have suffered in our village are not surprising," I told Toowin. "When the animals die and return in human form, life becomes much more difficult for them."

"Why is that?" Toowin demanded, and from the expression on his face I could tell that he doubted every word that I had uttered.

"Observe the animals!" I told my son. "Have you noticed that they rarely give themselves to the whites? Yes, that is why the shipsmen have to trade for the otter and the salmon. Do you see the animals trying to live mixed into one den as we do—mountain lions dancing with beavers, song sparrows housed with whales, loons feasting with otters, eagles sleeping with octopus? O, no! Never! The animals are much too wise for that. It is we humans who crowd all together regardless of our ancestors, then wonder why we disagree."

"The way I understand you," Toowin said, "the animals are on top, we in the middle, and the whites at the bottom."

"You've got that exactly right," I answered.

At dawn we paddled into Clamshell Inlet. It lay partly cloaked in drifting patches of white fog. In the distance we could see an otter hunter and his son, who sat low in their canoe, waiting. A light harpoon and tight-coiled line lay near the father's hand. The hunter's son had a white man's noisy musket, which I knew they hoped they would not need to use.

Gradually a big rock became visible to them and us. Around it we could hear the slow, sucking sound of the ocean's swell. Now the hunters could faintly see idling on the rock at least a dozen short-tailed sea otters with long whiskers shining on their blunt heads. Some slipped into the water and swam lazily on their backs, cleverly holding a stone against their bellies to help crack the mussel shells. The old man sniffed the morning breeze, waiting for his instincts to tell him how they could best approach their prey. Cautiously he craned his neck, studying various narrow paths of open water that meandered through the slithering kelp. How unwise of nature to have endlessly supplied these Clamshell with so much food and so many otters for their lazy taking.

Even from a distance, the appearance of the whole place was far worse than I had remembered—houses up on ugly stilts, totems and welcome figures, old and tilted at strange angles, boats atumble on their beach, everything uncared for, everything worn out. Toowin and I and Kawskaws had no choice but to languish down here in the south at my other brother-in-law's house.

We managed to hold out at that Clamshell house from the beginning of the egg-laying moon until the middle of the cleansing winter moon. I could scarcely bear to count those turning seasons on my fingers. Yes, we stayed ten long moons among the Clamshell. Each day was more depressing than the night before. Each day, from one moon to another as the seasons oh, so slowly changed, I thought I would surely die or go completely mad from boredom. Nobody knows how much I missed that hot-blooded copper widow. It rained steadily until it choked their sodden houses full of smoke and their roof boards sprouted green with heavy moss. It set their women screaming while it drizzled on and on. Oh, how I longed for our ceremonial house at Tahsis.

My sister's husband was a monstrous sort of chief who had somehow changed his wife from the laughing, cheerful girl whom I had known into a dreadful female image of himself. Queece had even taken on his greasy, treacherous ways of thinking, as if she was no kin to us.

Their village, where we found ourselves that spring, was small and unbelievably shabby compared to our large, lusty Wolf Town. Theirs was a mildewed huddle of collapsing ruins of houses half-hidden by the edges of a dripping forest. The people in those houses were lazy, thoughtless dolts when it came to entertaining visitors. We discovered that they scarcely knew the meaning of a feast.

The Clamshell were content to throw their rich belongings into a scattering of leaking dugouts and travel carelessly in any season to three separate places—one for berries, another for sealing, and this last place for otter, fish, and clams. It seemed unjust to me, but those few, clumsy moves provided them with such a rich abundance that they had always vastly more fat, seafood, skins, and berries than they could ever eat or trade. Toowin said he thought consuming too much greasy seal and porpoise meat was what had made their women's bodies cold and slippery and their menfolk thick and stupid.

The Clamshell people's slaves, those who had not run away from them, were half-mad human shadows who dwelt underneath their stilted houses, coming out to howl at the moon when it was full. These dangerous hidden people greatly frightened Kawskaws. Both Toowin and I warned her to be careful, to keep far away from all of them and always sleep near us.

While we were staying there, those Clamshell people were visited by the wildest tribe of humans I have ever seen. Never in my whole life had I imagined that there existed in this world such unkempt, crafty-looking people. The men wore long, shaggy, unplucked beards. Their hair, I think, had never known the knife. Their women I cannot bring myself to describe. Those people were dressed in tattered dog skins, and their fingernails and toenails were so long, they hooked like claws. Can you believe it? Those were almost the only kind of visitors they knew down there—except for us.

What a pity for Queece. "Poor thing! That's the way life goes," I told Toowin, "when one marries badly. Our parents made the great mistake of offering this daughter to a family rich in otter pelts and all the goods that they had gained from trade. Neither my father nor mother thought enough about the kind of in-laws and ghastly household my sister would be forced to suffer."

Twice that spring when we were living with the Clamshell people, shipsmen arrived to trade sea otter skins with them. Two ships traveling together were the first arrivals. I purposely did not go aboard them, but Toowin went—against my better judgment. He returned unharmed, saying nothing to me of his visit. Toowin was of that age!

The strange thing was that the masters seemed to like and trust my sister's greedy husband, and because of this he did very well at trading. While there, foreign shipsmen rowed in and walked fearlessly on shore. I tell you, that was rare for us to see. Shipsmen greatly feared Wolf Town, partly because of what the Spanish said had happened in the past.

Several times during each moon of our dreadful exile, Toowin, Kawskaws, and I would gather where our words could not be heard. There we would whisper fondly of those we had been forced to leave behind us up in Tahsis. We would usually mention Fog Woman first, and then we would speak of Jon Jay and, of course, the luscious Spuck. Then I would say I liked old Matla, and Toowin would laugh and wonder if Tom Sin was still lying each evening in his lonely hammock staring up at all those delicious fish. Kawskaws would recall wisdoms from the Salish weaver woman whom she liked very much, and we would speak of the carver, Ax Hand, and even the slave Knee Scars, and bad young Hoiss, whom we had seen so bravely save a man from drowning on the stormy beach. Toowin never failed to speak well of Maquina, who was, he reminded me, his uncle.

While we were rotting in the south, Toowin for the first time began to love his country and his own Wolf Town and his relatives. I also knew that Toowin came to love Kawskaws in every way he could. Yes, my son was growing up. He even started viewing me, his lonely father, in a slightly fonder light.

When our existence with the Clamshell had already reached the point of breaking, something occurred that made our lives far worse. Our first warning came when on a winter evening, just at sunset, the village children started screaming, warning all of us that they had seen a strange canoe. Such rare arrivals in this Clamshell village caused suspicion. I, like Toowin, Kawskaws, and the others, rushed outside.

My sharp-eyed Toowin told me that it was a twelve-man Wolf Town dugout paddled by our men. When they drew closer, I could see that he was right. For no other boatmen on this coast use their paddles in our way, stroking through the water, then turning the sharp-pointed blades powerfully inward in that swift, rhythmic style that we alone possess. Because they mistrusted strangers, the Clamshell people came slowly down to the beach and stood watching in silent groups apart from us.

There was only one person of importance sitting high in the center of that canoe. I could not see her face beneath the shadow of her wide-brimmed hat, but that did not keep me from recognizing my sister, Fog Woman.

When they were not far from shore, our Eagle house canoemen backstroked to hold the canoe offshore. Fog Woman turned and looked at me and all the others gathered there in the winter gloom. It seemed an age before that loutish brother-in-law of ours mumbled out the poorest kind of greeting—words barely civil enough to allow Fog Woman to order her canoe ashore.

My younger sister wandered forward and greeted Fog Woman as coolly and as casually as though she saw her older sister every day. My younger sister got a cold look on her face when she saw the large number of boxes and heard Fog Woman order all of them to be passed ashore. She and her husband looked at each other in horror when they heard Fog Woman tell the Eagle paddlers to leave without her early on the morning tide.

"I shall never return to Wolf Town," Fog Woman said flatly. "Brother! Sister! I will live here with you forever!"

Those were poorly chosen words, words my sister never would have uttered if she had known this dreadful place as we did.

Our loutish brother-in-law hunched his shoulders, grunted, and kicked cold gray gravel at a skulking dog, then turned his back on all of us and shambled up toward the houses. My younger sister refused to ask her slaves to carry up Fog Woman's boxes. No. Toowin and my four men were left to do that with some help from Kawskaws. What a horrible beginning for any visitor to suffer.

Fog Woman and our younger sister walked side by side in silence up toward the Clamshell houses.

"What's wrong up there?" Queece asked suddenly. "Is your husband, Maquina, dead?"

"Oh, no. He's alive," Fog Woman answered coldly.

No other word was spoken until Fog Woman had been shown a cramped space on the off-side of the Clamshell house where she would be allowed to sleep. My men lit her fire and stacked her boxes exactly as she ordered, so that they formed a small apartment. When Fog Woman was finally settled, Kaws-kaws brought our fish broth to her, and Toowin came and sat with us.

"What's happened up in Wolf Town?" I asked my sister. "What caused you to come down here to us?"

But Fog Woman simply put her fingers to my lips, for she had heard listeners move in and squat behind her walls of boxes.

Next morning, early, Fog Woman came to my apartment and whispered, "Brother, let us walk along the beach—alone."

When we were far beyond the ears of others, she said, "Everything turned very bad for me at Wolf Town, so bad I did not want Toowin or those back there to hear."

"What happened?" I asked.

"She came back!" My sister frowned. "Sea Star, Jon Jay's wife, came back to Wolf Town."

"Yes, we saw her being paddled north. What's wrong with that?"

"That brute I used to call my husband, he turned bad!" My sister stopped walking and glared at me. "He sent me off to see my cousins . . . said he had dreamt they needed me. They didn't need me!" she scoffed. "When I got back, Maquina had taken Jon Jay's young wife away from him. Oh, she was more than willing. Yes, my husband had allowed that useless snip of a girl to crawl underneath that otter robe with him." My sister started walking fast. "Not just by herself—the Salish weaver woman told me—but with all those others who are trying to get rid of me so that they can be the *hacumb*!" Fog Woman snorted with disdain. "Spuck! Kali! Those two sluts from the Whale house and the other two from the Otter and the Thunder houses. Yes, on the night that I returned from visiting my cousin, Maquina had all of those grasping females underneath his blanket. Your copper widow, she was in there with them too. Imagine! Eight women! I saw them with my own two eyes. He had four of Tom Sin's iron oil lanterns blazing high so that anyone could see the lot of them.

"Do you think that man had the decency to crawl out of there to greet me?" my sister asked me angrily. "No, he did not! Instead, he took his arms from around two of those naked sluts, and he pointed across the fire at your old apartment, and he called out to me, 'Woman, you sleep over there! And keep your mouth shut too,' he ordered. Just like that he said it to me.

"I could see by the way they looked that all of them had been drinking half rum and half molasses and there was no use my arguing with him. Without you and Toowin, I had no close relatives in that house to help me, and I was worried about my son.

"I stirred up the fire to give more light," she said, "and I went across to your old apartment. And who do you think I found in there?"

Fog Woman and I both stopped walking. "I found Jon Jay." She shook her head. "Poor boy, he was spying on them, propped up on one elbow in the shadows staring over into our apartment, just the way you used to do.

"I squatted down beside Jon Jay, and we started whispering together in Chinook. 'My husband and that young Otter Town wife of yours, they've both turned bad on us,' I told him very slowly so he'd understand.

" 'It's all your husband's fault,' Jon Jay answered me, and he pointed across the fire at the lot of them. His wife, Sea Star, lay curled up against Maquina with her arm across his chest. She must have known we would be watching her, so she pretended to be asleep."

My sister started walking fast along the beach again. "Have

you ever seen the dagger maker angry?" she asked me.

"No," I answered, as I hurried to keep up with her.

"Well, I have," Fog Woman said. "Jon Jay was raging mad that night. He mostly blames Maquina and not young Sea Star, who, he says, went with Maquina only because she was afraid to disobey him.

"I was just as mad as Jon Jay," said my sister. "But what could we two do? When Sea Star first arrived, I believed that girl and Jon Jay would stay together. Yes, and have children and become like any other family living with us. But even before I left, I saw that cunning Otter Town girl sitting up on the sleeping mats in my apartment, fawning over that brute, your brother-in-law."

Fog Woman stopped again and pointed north. "Now I know Maquina paid that huge bride's price and brought that Otter Town girl up north not for Jon Jay. No! He got her up there for himself!"

"Ssh!" I told my sister, for she was getting excited, and her voice was rising. "He'll get over that Otter Town girl the way he has with all the others. He'll be begging to take you back before another season turns around."

"Oh, no, he won't," my sister rasped. "Let him keep that horde of sluts. He'll never put his hand on me again."

"I wish you'd brought the copper widow here with you." My sister gave me an awful look when I said that. She started walking faster, kicking sand, until I took her by the arm and slowed her down. "What about your son?"

She looked at me, and I could see tears come into her eyes. "He will never let me have him. The Salish weaver woman is taking care of him."

"Who's taking food to Jon Jay?" I asked her. "Who takes care of him?"

"No one," she said sadly. "He and Tom Sin have got no one. Maquina no longer shares a scrap of food with them. They have to beg from others or find mussels and dig for clams when the tide goes out. I let them have my small canoe, but they know

very little about fishing, and they bring home almost nothing.
Maquina has forbidden them to wear any of their shipsmen's
clothing. They have to paint and dress like us, in capes and
kotsaks."

"What's going to happen?" I asked her.

"I don't know," my sister said. "I wish I had Satsatsoksis
here with me. Yes, and Jon Jay and Tom Sin too."

"Maybe it's just as well they are not here," I told her.

"Why?" she said.

"You haven't seen the worst of it," I answered. "It's so bad
here," I told her, "that if nothing changes, we will have to leave
in spring and find some other place to live."

"What other place is there for us to live?" she asked me.

I could find no answer, for our family had been destroyed,
and we had no other relatives, and in truth, there was no other
village in this whole world where we could go and live and keep
our rank as high-caste people. In other places we would be
treated like commoners or even slaves.

Together we walked slowly back toward the Clamshell
houses.

"Be kindly to our sister and her husband," I told Fog
Woman, "and be very careful of all these people living here.
Maybe you can help to smooth away the awful feelings that
have grown up between us."

I am sad to tell you that exactly the opposite came true. A
few days later, I heard my two sisters and my slovenly brother-
in-law begin a bitter argument that finally turned into a shouting match. The words that those two sisters flung against each
other ended forever our hopes of staying on with the Clamshell.

The late-winter rains hung on and on and on until I thought
spring would never come to us. But when it did, it brought a
fast canoe.

Toowin looked out over Clamshell Inlet and saw a sleek,
fast Wolf Town canoe stroking in toward us. I ran out with
Kawskaws when we heard Toowin shouting. Just the sight of
our Wolf Town men in that long, slim dugout made my heart

go tum-tum-tum. It was Man Frog with twelve of our strongest paddlers. What a sight! As they drew near, both Toowin and I wept with pleasure, seeing all those good familiar faces from our own village.

Man Frog smiled at us and said, "Our *tyee* sent me here to speak for him. Maquina forgives everything. He wants you all to come back home to Wolf Town. Our *tyee* says that everything is different now and he is lonely for his *hacumb*. Jon Jay's young wife, Sea Star, has gone back to Otter Town forever, and all those girls are gone."

My sister Fog Woman coughed when she heard that, and she looked at me and smiled triumphantly.

I nodded to her and said, "I was right; he wants you back. He wants all of us home with him."

"That's what I was told to say to you," Man Frog announced. "He wants you to come back with me."

"Why?" I asked, still feeling strong suspicions against Maquina.

"The *tyee* needs his head usher," Man Frog said. "Maquina is now preparing to give a real potlatch. He's going to ask the Black Fin and many other high-caste people to his feast. He says you and his *hacumb* must come home and decide exactly where to seat these people, not high above nor low below their proper places. He says you, Siam, know that best of all."

I didn't have to ask Fog Woman. She turned and ran up the beach and disappeared inside the moldering house that we shared with that loutish chief and forty-seven dreary Clamshell people and their children, whom we had never bothered counting.

"Toowin!" I yelled. "Quick, go and find our four paddlers! And you, Kawskaws, start packing up the boxes. We are going home to Wolf Town! Now! Today! Before this tide runs out!"

Man Frog turned and stared scornfully at the husband of my younger sister. He was standing on the beach but had not yet had the decency to invite Man Frog to step ashore. In spite of this, our war chief called out in a firm voice, "Maquina invites you and your wife and some others of your choice to come to Wolf Town in the lateness of the little-sister moon to feast with him."

Queece's husband stood there sucking on a seal bone, the marrow dribbling down his chin. Anyone could tell he didn't want to go to Wolf Town. But how could he refuse?

He scowled and grunted at Man Frog. "Tell Maquina that if we are alive, we shall attend . . ." He sniffed and blew out his lips. "Yes, we will join him at his little feast."

We flung everything into my whale canoe and pushed out on that tide. Fog Woman and I called back thank-you to Queece and her husband. We had never been so glad to escape from any place in all our lives.

Oh, we were all four overeager to see Wolf Town once again. But we were delayed by the power of the last of the winter winds. Man Frog's canoe, with its dozen paddlers, was much too fast for us. So he loaned me three strong paddlers and took almost all of our load. Still, they arrived in Wolf Town one whole day ahead of us. Perhaps that was just as well, for it gave Maquina time to prepare a splendid welcome.

Ax Hand had specially carved two welcome figures, which now stood on the beach. There was a male one for me and a female figure for Fog Woman. Almost everyone from Wolf Town was down all along the shore and smiling at us. Oh, what a welcome sight that was. Kawskaws joined us as we all wept with joy at being home again.

Maquina warmly greeted my sister as his only *hacumb*. He greeted me and Toowin as though we were his best-loved friends. The copper widow did not come down to greet me with the others. Instead she stood shyly in the shadow of the Thunder house. She smiled at me and made a secret gesture with her body that made my heart go tum-tum-titty-tum-tum.

Maquina was unusually excited, and in a moment he was telling us the many details of the feast that he had planned.

He looked at Toowin, then put his hand upon his shoulder and said, "Nephew, it is good to have you here again."

Toowin smiled and, looking up and down the beach, said,

"Uncle, where is the dagger maker? Is he not still here with you?"

"Yes, he is," Maquina said. "He's out there with Tom Sin in a clearing in the forest. They are helping Ax Hand build a small idea I've had. Well, if you must know, it's . . . a whale."

I heard Toowin shout. I looked and saw Jon Jay and Ax Hand running toward us along the Wolf Town beach, with big Tom Sin following not far behind.

Some will find this difficult to believe, but Jon Jay put his arms around me and Fog Woman and hugged us to him, and he did the same to Toowin and Kawskaws. We laughed and wept together, so glad were we to see one another. And strange to say, when Tom Sin came up to all of us, he turned up the edges of his mouth and said, "Haaaloo." Then I, proudly speaking my English language for the first time since I went away, smiled and said, "Harooo, Tom Sin, harooo."

When Toowin asked Ax Hand about the whale, Ax Hand held his hands against his face and said, "It's awful! That man up there"—he pointed to Maquina, who was entering the Eagle house—"has got me carving an impossible, life-sized whale. He says it's got to be finished by the time he gives his feast. He says this wooden whale has got to dive and rise again and blow. I tell you, I can't make it do anything like that!"

Ax Hand had spoken Chinook with his strong and unfamiliar Haida accent. I was amazed that the dagger maker so quickly answered him, having easily understood every word he said.

Jon Jay laughed. "Don't believe him. That whale will look wonderful gliding up and diving down through the water."

"It won't dive," said Ax Hand. "I swear, if it ever does dive, it will not come up again."

"You may be right," said Jon Jay. "But don't worry. Just floating on the inlet, your whale will astound the guests."

When we got up to our fire, Kawskaws smiled at Jon Jay and said, "Oh, it's good to hear you speaking such wonderful Chinook."

She too was a foreigner who scarcely understood our Wakashan language. It was a marvel of the Chinook trade talk that it allowed all of us—Ahts, Hupa, shipsmen, Salish, Haida, people from across this whole flat world—to speak together.

"What about you, poor you?" Kawskaws said to Jon Jay. "We heard that bad things happened to you after we went away."

"Yes, well, I don't want to talk about that now," the dagger maker said. "I'll tell you that some other day."

"After you left, it was bad around this fire for one whole moon," Red Tongue told me. "Oh, we missed you, Siam. Your sister would look over into your empty apartment and start weeping. That was before she went away. It was better when we were working, forgetting all the troubles while preparing for the feast. Since then, Jon Jay and the sailmaker have made two hundred handsome daggers for Maquina to give away. And Ax Hand has worked so hard. He's grown so lean it worries me. I work hard too," laughed Red Tongue, "but, as you see, it doesn't make me fat or thin."

That night, though we were tired from traveling, I could scarcely go to sleep. Everywhere I looked I saw beloved smiling faces or some familiar object I had known for oh, so long: the mountains, the inlet, the river, the houses, my old apartment across from Maquina's. Best of all was seeing Fog Woman once again the *hacumb* of the Eagle House. What a pleasure to lie down on my own mats among friends and look up at our small fish drying and feel that smooth-skinned copper widow lying with me once again.

I wish that I had been able to retain all those thrilling feelings of being back among my friends. But I was soon caught up in all our old house problems. Upon our return, Maquina gave me a slab of wood, rubbed smooth with sharkskin, on which he told me to draw a plan to show him exactly how I would seat all the important visitors and ourselves in proper rank.

As if that was not enough to occupy me, Maquina required my presence at a conference with his elder sister, whom we considered the wealthiest and most difficult woman alive on all our whole coast, for he believed I had influence with her. She arrived next day from Kelp Rock, and let me warn you, she is sharper than a fine knife's edge when it comes to making trades of any kind.

When Toowin and Jon Jay first came in the Eagle house, they scarcely noticed the two visitors who now sat by our fire.

Kawskaws whispered to them, "Look how tall Maquina's sister is. She looks just like him. She and her husband are certainly important people. You can see that by the way Fog Woman is waiting until Maquina comes before she really talks to them," said Kawskaws. "Look, Toowin, at the way your aunt makes her women run to serve them food. See how she herself carefully soaks everything she offers them in that best fish oil she got from Kitimat."

Maquina had been out instructing his carver, Ax Hand. He came into the Eagle house with an easy look of pleasure on his face. His expression froze when he recognized his elder sister and her husband. All good feelings seemed to fly away from him. His eyes narrowed as he peered at the austere couple, who sat high on painted boxes by his fire.

The man was small, with a face like a wrinkled knot of driftwood. He was dressed somberly in a single fathom of faded-blue blanket cloth undecorated except for a plain gray edging. Around his forehead he wore a small fresh twist of cedar bark, casual proof that he was a visiting man of rank. He pursed his lips and nodded coldly to Maquina, but said nothing, for he had long since learned when he should and should not speak.

Maquina's lean-jawed elder sister sat regally in the warm reflection of the fire, her naked feet drawn up beneath her. The blanket that she wore was faded to almost pink and held together by an elaborate clasp of hammered silver engraved with the form of Sisiutl, the double-headed serpent. Her wrists and lower arms were covered with costly brass and copper bracelets. She possessed an untold wealth of goods, and for this reason she did almost all the talking.

"Obviously we didn't visit them," Maquina's sister said in a cold and haughty voice, "because we enjoy those dreadful Black Fin people. We simply stayed with them because we had no other choice," she said defensively. "It was growing dark, and we were passing near the Black Fin narrows, with, as usual, too few paddling slaves, and those we had were nothing but a gang of weaklings." She threw a fierce glance at her husband. "The wind was rising, and this poor man here, who shares my house with me, has not the slightest knowledge of those dangerous waters." She snorted like an elk that senses danger. "We stayed only one night there with those Black Fin, or was it two?"

"Four nights," said her husband smugly, holding up that many fingers.

"Yes, well"—she scowled at him—"it was not what we could call a pleasant visit . . . nor a bad one either. They talk of little up there except how degraded you must feel after poor old Tall Hat and his son put you down forever!

"Naturally, the new Black Fin chief misses his old father. No wonder! Tall Hat proved that he was the most generous and powerful chief on this whole coast." She glared at both Maquina and her little husband, daring them to disagree with her. "Yes, there's no man left alive like him," she said, taunting her brother. Her dark eyes glittered as she thrust her firm jaw forward. "The Black Fin say there probably never will be another big gift-giver like their generous chief. All other chiefs on this coast are shaky, little men compared with him. It's true," she sneered. "With our father gone, there's not a man left on all these island inlets whose head stands high enough to kiss that Black Fin chieftain's scrotum."

Leering at her wizened little husband and then at her powerful brother, the lean-jawed woman hurried on without giving Maquina a chance to speak. "Now, my husband here is a noble from the Moon house. Naturally, he doesn't really care about the Black Fin people beating us, nor does your wife or her brother, Siam, who is sitting over there. They, too, were born in another house." She curled her lip, showing her long, narrow teeth to all of us. *"But me!"* she screamed. "My father was the great *tyee* Maquina. *I am your sister!* I was at that bloody feast! The shame of that Black Fin triumph over this Eagle house— my house—is smothering me."

"I was the one he went against," Maquina shouted at her. "I feel far worse than you do!" He closed his eyes and clapped his hands over his ears. No one except his sister dared to speak like that.

"Open up your head holes, brother!" she shrieked at him. "I've known you all my life. I used to carry you. Have you forgotten the meaning of the name our father gave you? Do you, the *tyee* of this village, plan to sit there like a helpless child, or do you plan to strike back? How did it happen that you allowed those mindless children from this village to murder all those shipsmen, the very ones who would bring you blankets, muskets, daggers, molasses, and southern abalone? Are you too miserly," she carped at him, "to feed some folks a trencherful of clams and salmon and give away a few spare blankets?"

Maquina thrust out both his palms toward his raucous sister. "Stop!" he bellowed. "It's late for you to come here screaming for revenge against that Black Fin house. Of course I am going to give a potlatch. I have been planning little else!"

"No wonder I am demanding revenge," Maquina's sister shrieked. "How long do I have to listen to other women gossiping about the splendid treasures that Tall Hat gave away to us even after he was dead? Oh, yes, that will never be forgotten. He was dead!"

"Don't you speak a word to her," Maquina warned Fog Woman as he kicked the fire with his bare foot and glared murderously at his elder sister. "You are, as you say, Eagle house born. But are you willing to help me go against those Black Fin people?"

Maquina waved his hand toward the wizened little Moon house man. "You two haven't potlatched for how long? Not since I was young. I can scarcely remember when you gave that smallish feast down there." He counted on his fingers. "Seventeen or eighteen winters past? Will you help me give a potlatch feast?"

The sullen little Moon house chief frowned at Maquina, turning down the corners of his mouth to show displeasure.

Ignoring him, Maquina leaned into the firelight, staring at

his elder sister. "Will you help me?" he demanded. "Will you give me sea otter skins? A hundred, two hundred—I'll need many more. Will you lend me all those trade blankets you've been hoarding? Those boxes full of carver's files and brass bracelets, and the masks? Good masks! Your dentalia shells, and southern abalone. Will you give me carved rattles? Will you share your wealth? If you want me to go against the Black Fin house, you'll have to help me."

Maquina's sister ground her long incisor teeth together. "Yes, brother, we will help you." She nodded sideways at her husband. "It's true, we have been hoarding treasures for one last potlatch. Yes, we will help you. But, later, you must let me speak to Siam about those who will and will not be invited to this Wolf Town feast. I want only the highest-ranking persons sitting near me in this house where I was born."

Without another word, Maquina's lean-jawed sister jammed her cedar-root hat upon her head and with a storklike motion hopped down off the painted box and strode toward the entrance. Her husband followed her without a look or a nod at any of us. They spent four days in Wolf Town. Then they left.

"I can't stand that woman—or her frightened little husband!" Fog Woman wailed. "I don't care how many potlatch gifts she gives you."

"She sits on wealth," Maquina said with pride.

"Like she sits on that Moon-faced little man of hers," Fog Woman said. "Did you hear her, Siam," my sister called across the fire, "insulting us by saying we two didn't care about this Eagle house?"

"Don't get excited," I said, trying to calm my sister down.

"Silence, woman!" Maquina shouted at his wife. "If I am going to give a truly great potlatch, I will need all their help and any more that I can find."

A few days later, Fog Woman and I journeyed two days east up Muchalat Inlet. There we visited with our dying aunt.

"Stay alive and watch us." My sister leaned close and spoke those words quite loudly to that dear old woman. "Stay alive, come feast with us and bring a thousand blankets. Stay alive,"

she called out. "Help us put those boastful Black Fin down forever. Stay alive and see us bury them in wealth!"

"*Eeh, eeh*, I will help you," our aunt answered in a weak
and quavering voice, then she gave a rasping, deathlike cough.
"I'll help you fight them. I'll give you all my blankets and the
two big dugouts. Yes, you can have them whether I am here,
alive, or gone up in my burial canoe. I'll help you go against
them—gladly!"

 ALMOST no one, except Ax Hand and his carvers, had been allowed into the forest clearing in the south cove since work on the wooden whale had begun. One day I walked there with Maquina and Red Tongue to see how the work was going. Two good canoe builders, together with Toowin and both shipsmen, were helping Ax Hand. When the morning sun pierced through the trees, it made the yellow cedar steam.

I heard Maquina say to Ax Hand, "If the whale's belly is partly filled with heavy stones, the men inside can throw them out at the very moment the whale should rise."

"Where are they going to throw the stones?" Ax Hand asked him.

Maquina thought a moment then said, "Give the whale a proper rectum and let them drop them out that way, or maybe they could toss them out its blowhole."

Ax Hand stared at Maquina in disbelief. "Don't you think the water might come shooting up through the rectum and drown everyone inside?"

Maquina laughed, "You worry about such small details! Come now," said my brother-in-law, "you can carve some kind of simple rectum plug so that the men inside can get the stones out of the whale without letting too much water in. And don't forget the blowhole. I want that whale to rise and blow out clouds of steam. Ask Siam how to do that. He's a whaler. Maybe he can help you figure how to work the spout."

As he walked away, Ax Hand punched both sides of his head in frustration.

Maquina laughed. "Don't worry about him. Most carvers are like that—high-strung, nervous, and not at all inventive. Present them with a new idea that has not been tried before, and they go all to pieces and swear it can't be done. Carvers have quite skillful hands, but they usually lack any originality or courage. We chiefs are the ones with great ideas."

Ax Hand swore that under no condition would he set foot inside that whale if it were in the water. "Even if I manage to complete this mess," Ax Hand complained, "as soon as it touches the sea, it will roll over. Not even a white man would risk his life inside that gross invention of Maquina's."

"You're wrong," Red Tongue said. "Maquina told me that both you and the sailmaker, Tom Sin, are going to have the privilege of riding in the body of that whale."

"Oh, no! Not me!" said Ax Hand. "Tom Sin and Jon Jay are just the right men for that task. They are shipsmen, after all, used to climbing around clumsy vessels. They should be the ones who first dive with that whale."

Jon Jay held his hands over his ears, pretending he had not heard the words the carver said. Ax Hand threw up his hands in disgust, then snatched up his long adze and ran inside his wooden whale's open mouth and started chopping at its blow-hole.

That night, Ax Hand came to Kawskaws beside our fire and explained his needs for paints, for she was good at mixing them.

"I want a rich black like that," he told her, raking fresh charcoal from the yew-wood fire. "Will you also make me a red from this trade ocher, and a brown and yellow from the dyes of the two cedar roots?"

"For the white," she said, "I'll burn clamshells into powder, and for blue I'll press some berries."

"Be sure to grind your paints smooth, then make them waterproof with salmon eggs and milt," Ax Hand said. "I will need all these colors as soon as you can have them for me."

In the morning, Fog Woman warned me, "Whales may not be all my husband is thinking of. He was up half the night under one of Tom Sin's oil lamps again, making drawings on that cedar board of his. He's determined to have more than one marvel at this feast, some original work of genius that will undo all his rivals and his guests."

I listened to my brother-in-law and was surprised to hear him ordering, of all things, an enormous wooden eagle. Yes, he had a small, crude drawing of it on his cedar board.

Poor Ax Hand. He turned pale when he heard Maquina's words demanding that he carve an eagle large enough for a man to ride upon its back and big enough for him to fly! Maquina sat there calmly telling that bewildered carver exactly how the eagle's wings should be attached by cedar cords, how they could be moved by pulling sinews, and just when the wooden tail feathers should be shifted to guide it during flight.

"Study the eagle's movements and you will see exactly how to build it," said Maquina. "That should not be difficult for you."

Ax Hand, almost weeping, asked him who would fly the eagle.

Maquina said, "Oh, you, if you insist, or Jon Jay. Yes, the dagger maker's the one who will know just how to make it fly. Oh, yes," Maquina said, "that reminds me, if you want iron claws for my eagle, the dagger maker will surely shape some for you from those long ship's bolts."

Ax Hand complained that the trouble with a wooden eagle was not how to paint it or the claws, but how to make it rise up off the ground.

Maquina told him not to worry about that, that with great lengths of ship's rope they could haul the eagle up into a tall dead tree and then just push it off and let it flap its wings and soar gracefully out over the inlet exactly like a living eagle. In fact, it might scarcely even need to move its wings.

When he heard that, Ax Hand leapt off the box on which he sat. He said, "Please promise that if I carve it for you, I won't be the one who has to fly it."

When I heard that, I said to Maquina, "Toowin can't do it either! He will be too busy helping me arrange the seating of the guests."

Our preparations for the potlatch continued at such a rapid pace that I suggested to Maquina that we take some time to think. During this period I, with Toowin and Kawskaws, led

Jon Jay and the sailmaker over to the Spanish gardens. The Spanish shipsmen had been gone for ten—or was it eleven?—summers. Everything was overgrown. If I had not known where they had once built houses here, I could not have found their garden.

I showed Jon Jay and Tom Sin the foundation ruins of the Spaniards' houses and where they had planted bulbous roots that still grew there each summer.

I want to tell you those two foreigners were starving for those round brown bulbs. They dug them up with their knife points and their fingers and rubbed the dirt away against their thighs and bit right into them and smiled and chewed and swallowed them. They borrowed Kawskaws's cedar cape and put a pile of those roots in it. Together we carried them back to the Eagle house fire and boiled them by putting them with hot stones in the water box. I tried one bite and found it quite revolting.

Tears ran out of Jon Jay's eyes when he was eating them. He spoke to Kawskaws, and she wept a little too. She said Jon Jay had told her that eating uuuneeuuns and the others he called hot poo-too-toos reminded him of being in his father's house, which he told us was very, very far away.

I advised those two shipsmen that the Spanish gardens were haunted by human shades and ghosts. I warned them against going there when it was dark.

Strange to tell, on that same night as I lay close to sleep, I heard an owl calling deep inside the forest. I listened carefully, then breathed a sigh. It was not my name it called. No, it wanted Hool Hool, the mouse man. It twice called his name. And then I heard it hoot for someone else. "Toowah, Toowah," the owl called, uttering the name of an old aunt of mine who dwelt at Ahousat. I was thankful that it had not spoken Toowin's name or mine, for to hear an owl call out a human's name means that person's soul is wanted. Yes, wanted in the other world. The copper widow gently ran her hand along the whole length of my naked back before she left me and I fell asleep again.

At daybreak a sentinel came whispering into Maquina's ear and mine. "Two of the Moon canoes are coming up the inlet," he said. "The second one is loaded heavily."

"Oh, what a relief," I heard Maquina say to Fog Woman. "I thought that hoarding sister of mine might forget her promise. Siam," he said, "will you go down and greet her? Welcome her! Tell her for me how much I need her gifts and that big canoe of theirs as well."

In the Eagle house, the whole of that day was spent arranging the countless gifts that Maquina had amassed, not counting almost half of the ship's treasures that we still held safely in the cave. We scarcely saw our village women or their servants, who were busy arranging all the food. Most of our newly made things were held in painted boxes. Now they were carefully taken out and arranged on either side of Maquina's Eagle screen.

I gasped in wonder, for I had never seen anything like this: dozens and dozens of exquisitely carved face masks, small clever boxes, unique wooden whistles, rare rattles of all shapes and sizes, graceful spoons made from the horns of mountain goats and rams, necklaces of white dentalia, huge foreign abalone cut into money pieces reflecting blue and green, elaborately carved halibut hooks and sacred salmon clubs, and woven Salish capes, and hats, and dozens and dozens of Jon Jay's beautiful long daggers laid out in fan shapes, their handles bound in leather, and ivory or abalone set in the hilts to form Wolf and Whale and Eagle eyes. Oh, what a sight! We in that house stood back in wonder, scarcely able to believe all we had made or gathered to be given away.

"Cover it! Hide these treasures beneath the mats," Maquina ordered. He clapped his hands together and said, "This is going to be my final feast. Help me to make it grand!"

Next morning was the fourth and most fortunate day following the appearance of the new-horned moon of spring. As the mists cleared from our cove, we could see half a dozen big canoes approaching from the north and south.

Yes, there were the rival Black Fin, who had just put on their potlatch finery. In the prow of their lead canoe they had a sorcerer dressed as the Hawk, wearing an enormous hook-beaked mask, his body clad from head to foot in feathers, waving his wings and dancing like a madman while the Black Fin chanted. What an outlandish sight for us more civilized folk to have to look upon.

Oh, well. We had to have them. We had to have all the chiefs and nobles of important households: the Bears, Otters, Ravens, Eagles, even those terrible Clamshell people, for a potlatch was made strong only by those who witnessed it and could later tell of the event. Upquesta was there from Otter Town, accompanying the high and mighty Wickinnish. Sea Star did not come with her family because they wished to take no chances with Maquina.

It was up to me, the usher, to decide exactly what rank and titles every chief and nobleman or noblewoman held. This was not easy because such persons often changed their rank for potlatches. For example, the parents of a child may rank number two in seating among the guests but decide to uplift their child's position by giving that child some of their songs and titles. In so doing, they lower their own position of importance to perhaps ninth or nineteenth in our ranking system. Births, marriages, deaths, and especially young people coming of age—all these affect the seating at a potlatch. Among these proud and jealous people, one cannot be too careful!

It is no easy task to give a feast like this. Certainly Maquina could not have done it by himself. He relied heavily on others such as me. A head usher is supposed to lead important guests up to greet Maquina and his *hacumb*, who both await them, sitting grandly in their house, then show the new arrivals where they'll sleep and, much more important, exactly where they'll sit while feasting. Paddlers and slaves, of course, throw up their own rough shelters or huddle together under their canoes.

As each big dugout neared our shore, I quickly ordered slaves to unroll the new cedar mats toward them. Our slave women had woven these mats especially for this feast. They were just wide enough for two persons to walk side by side. These mats created a long, clean reddish path from our landing beach straight up to the single central entrance to the Eagle house, whose whole front Maquina had had freshly painted with a splendid black-and-red design.

At first the Black Fin, Otter, and Clamshell canoes waited cautiously offshore until we sang the welcome songs to them and threw out eagle down. They replied with a scattering of down and a visiting song, then landed.

During all of this I had been watching from the shadows of the Eagle house entrance. The instant that their dugout prows touched shore, I gave a signal for the wind whistles to start calling one-two-three and the lucky number four. I nodded respectfully to the new-horned moon and, followed by Red Tongue, walked grandly down the mat to greet the dreadful Molasses Eater, who had inherited the highest titles from old Tall Hat, and his wretched son.

Molasses Eater returned with me, his son between us. His wife followed with a few of their most important people. The others came after them in two lines, but of course, none of them dared to put their feet upon that mat, which was reserved for oh, so few.

Once inside the Eagle house, these important persons went forward and greeted Maquina and Fog Woman and their son, Satsatsoksis, who waited with his parents before the grandly painted Eagle screen made from a large ship's sail and decorated with a huge, impressive Eagle design painted by a skillful Whalehouse artisan. Tom Sin had easily been able to sew the heavy canvas with his strong steel needles. Fog Woman had carefully watched his ways of sewing and was able to have her women help him with the work. She told Kawskaws that she had learned a lot from big Tom Sin.

For ourselves and guests to sit upon, we had placed wide split cedar planks around the Eagle house central fire pit, which we had prepared especially for this event. I was the one to usher each important family to their places. Many of them seemed determined to arrange themselves in positions far higher than their rank deserved. A few started complaining, until I stood back and looked at them with utter scorn, then led them to their proper places. To be an usher, one has to be firm. There was only a little pushing, shoving, and complaining as the high chiefs, war chiefs, and dance chiefs, and lesser noblemen and noblewomen seated themselves in the positions I felt their rank deserved.

Wickinnish, though he should not have done so, claimed his position in the first rank, sitting equal to the young Black Fin chief. Jon Jay and Tom Sin, acting as Maquina's two foreign bodyguards, were neatly dressed once more as shipsmen. Both of them had a pair of heavy flintlock pistols thrust into their belts, and each wore a newly sharpened cutlass, which they laid across their knees. They sat bolt upright at each end of Maquina's Eagle screen, staring out suspiciously at the gathering of guests.

Finally, when I had every person seated, I went and squeezed myself in between the dagger maker and my old uncle. Of course, that made a lot of persons angry, but there was little they could do. Red Tongue sat on the other side of Tom Sin. Next to him sat old Matla and Fog Woman in her new woven cape. Around the fire another fifty chiefs and noblemen and noblewomen sat according to their rank. Beyond stood rows and rows of commoners, who had little to lose and everything to gain from attending such a feast.

Ax Hand had supervised the carving of some wooden trenchers that were now carried in by slaves. These were the size of small canoes, large enough to allow a grown man to seat himself in. Each one was beautiful to behold, carved and painted to represent some animal: a wolf, a sea otter, a killer whale, a seal, a thunder eagle. These immense cedar dishes were filled to the brim with delicate steamed clams and tender little trout, with herring eggs on seaweed and octopus cut into mouth-sized chunks. All of this delicious food was richly drenched in eulachon oil of the highest quality, imported by Maquina from distant inland rivers.

"Save space for the main courses that are still to come," my sister whispered to the visiting noblewoman who sat near her. "I can't wait to see you get those teeth of yours into that octopus," she said to Maquina's wolf-jawed sister, who sat leering at her.

Slaves brought in more feast dishes: boiled venison cut into chunks, black-bear meat, which I had to be oh, so careful not to eat, sun-dried herring, halibut, pounded abalone, salmon and whale meat rendered soft in its own oil and surrounded by ripe duck eggs. Six of us sat cross-legged around each feast dish and dipped into the varied rich mixtures with large clamshells. I started to relax and enjoy the food. This was truly a tremendous feast.

When the meal was over, our guests were groaning either to show their appreciation of our generosity or to suggest our food had given them a bellyache. The big wind whistles sounded once again, and Maquina's all-important witnessing began.

Red Tongue rose and drove his chief talker's stick into the hard-packed earth beside the fire pit. "Maquina's son, Satsatsoksis, is now coming of age," Red Tongue called out in his most impressive voice. "Satsatsoksis shall be the inheritor of all the titles Maquina now possesses," Red Tongue shouted as he drove his staff into the hot sand. "Witnesses, these gifts mark Maquina's words."

Six slaves ran forward holding four muskets on each shoulder and they laid the forty-eight new muskets at the feet of Molasses Eater.

Molasses Eater nodded grandly.

"Satsatsoksis now has the highest Whale rank from his mother's people," Red Tongue proclaimed.

With those words resounding through the Eagle house, six slaves ran forward and placed a hundred German silver looking-glasses at the Moachat chieftain's feet, who nodded to Maquina, recognizing the Whale gift to his house.

Four barrels, two of molasses and two of rum, were rolled by slave men to the feet of the Clamshell chief.

"He has the Bear rank from his uncle," Red Tongue announced in a commanding voice.

The chiefs remained unmoved, each staring straight ahead, a scowl upon their faces. Just when this feast had grown most exciting, I was horrified to see the copper widow leaving our house leaning against Wickinnish. Oh, yes, I saw her run her hand up underneath his cape. I saw him stiffen, when he felt her fingernails. Well, I thought, a man can't really lose the copper widow. The rich musky smell and the warm feel of her will linger on forever.

"Forget about her," Maquina whispered to me. "Tomorrow you will have to help me give these guests of ours a wild surprise!"

The next morning, Red Tongue and I rose and followed Maquina out of the Eagle house. It was not yet fully light, and the distant mountains looked like still white wings above the forest and beneath the dark-blue morning sky.

The sailmaker stood by one of Maquina's cannons, and Jon Jay stood by the other. They both held smoking fuses in their hands.

"Are you ready?" Maquina asked me.

Before I had a chance to answer him, he raised both hands, then quickly brought the left one down. There was a little puff of smoke at the touchhole of Jon Jay's cannon, then a belch of yellow smoke and a tremendous *Boom!* that echoed along the inlet. *Boom-Boom-Boom!*

I held my hands over my ears as Maquina brought his right hand down and Tom Sin's cannon roared and blew a perfect smoke ring out before it.

"That ought to get them up," Maquina said, laughing richly.

As we turned to go, we saw a high geyser rise up in the water halfway to the opposite shore.

"I didn't tell him to load an iron ball inside that cannon's mouth!" Maquina frowned. "When I tell that sailmaker to do something, he will do it, but only in his own way. I don't trust him."

"Forget Tom Sin," I urged as every living soul in Wolf Town came dashing out of the houses, the women looking frightened, the men clutching daggers, fearing an attack. "That was a good start," I admitted, "but it's only the beginning. I promise you, I'm going to liven up this feast!"

My son, Toowin, came running down the beach and whispered to Maquina, "It's finished! Ax Hand says his carving of the whale is finished! Oh, you should see it! It looks enormous now that he's pegged that high fin on its back. It's oiled and fully painted, black with bright-red designs, ovoid eyes, and huge white teeth. Ax Hand says he'll help ease it on the rollers to the water, but then he says he's going into hiding."

"Nonsense," Maquina snorted. "Don't bother me with that nervous carver's petty quirks. I'm counting on that wooden whale to be the best surprise of this whole potlatch. A number of these little so-called chiefs from up and down this coast have sometimes tried to have a crudely carved salmon puppet flop along between their house beams. Remember that old wooden raven the Gitskan people traded here? The one we used to fly on strings at funeral feasts? Forget such toys! Wait until you see this whale of mine! And then the eagle!"

"How many warriors did you say will fit inside the whale's belly?" Red Tongue asked.

"Ten," Maquina answered, "and our two shipsmen. They're both handy seamen. Have you planned it carefully," Maquina asked, "so that all those gathered on the beach will have the best view of our warriors when the whale opens its mouth?"

"Yes, yes," said Red Tongue. "Everything has been arranged, but of course, there was no time for rehearsal."

We fed our guests another huge meal at midday, and they rested heavily until the sun was setting in the west.

"Wake them," I told Red Tongue. "Strike the Thunder drum. We're ready!"

At exactly the right moment, I led Maquina's guests out onto our gravel beach. Stuffed with food, they moved more slowly now, drawing their colorful capes around them against the afternoon chill. They had given up their earlier pushing and shoving, for at this feast each person's rank had been established. Maquina, too, seemed more relaxed now that the enormous task of preparation was over and the enjoyable parts were about to come. The wind was calm, and the sun came shining out through broken storm clouds, giving off long, lucky rays of light. Before us the waters of the inlet stood as still as new-formed ice.

"Here comes the war canoe," Toowin whispered to me. "These visitors on the beach, they think they're going to see some sorcerer's ceremony performed on its dancing board. They don't know that our paddlers are towing something . . . something unbelievable!"

"This part makes me very nervous," I told Toowin. "Here it comes out from behind the point." I shaded my eyes against the sinking sun.

"I see it!" gasped Toowin. "Look at the high fin on its back."

"Something's wrong!" I gasped. "That whale is riding over on its side."

I looked at Maquina, who was trying to hold his face expressionless. He had wanted the wooden whale to be completely out of sight at first.

"The way that thing is wobbling," old Matla said, "I don't think it's going very far."

Human voices have a strange way of carrying over calm water. Now from the belly of the wooden whale the audience that was gathered on the beach could hear the sound of our Eagle house warriors' muffled cursing. Some of the guests began to laugh in a way that could not be considered kindly.

As Maquina's whale was drawn forward by his paddlers, it jerked and rolled like a wounded beast in a heavy sea. The audience could hear more cursing from inside the whale's belly. Then suddenly the huge red-painted mouth flew open.

"Foockin' foools! Foockin' foools!" or some such words I could hear big Tom Sin shouting.

Then I heard Ax Hand's high, excited voice calling out through the whale's mouth, *"Hyak! Mahkh! Mahkh!* Quick! Get out! Get out!"

When I stood on my toe tips and looked into the creature's

mouth, I could see half a dozen warriors desperately heaving boulders out into the water.

"You're not supposed to do it that way!" Maquina shouted out to Ax Hand and his men inside, but of course, they couldn't hear our *tyee*. "That fool of a carver! They have bungled this whole whaling scene completely!"

As Maquina started pacing up and down the beach, the jaws of the wooden whale slammed closed. Then its whole black body tipped and rolled dangerously. The painted whale lurched through the water after the big canoe.

Maquina cupped his hands around his mouth and yelled loudly to his warriors in the whale, "Make it spout the way I told you to, you flatheads! Then make it dive! Go under! Do you hear me? Under!"

"Yooo moost be shittting uuus," Tom Sin's deep, foreign voice bellowed from inside the whale. "We're drowning in this turd-shaped monster."

There was a lot more thumping and cursing from within the wooden belly. Again the huge jaws flew open. Everyone saw Ax Hand and the dagger maker leap into the water, followed by two warriors and a second shower of boulders, just before its jaws clamped shut again.

Jon Jay was frog-kicking in the water and calling out to shore as the great painted tail fins of the whale jerked past him, still lurching toward the beach.

"*Tyee! Tyee!* Chief! She is going under!" Jon Jay yelled out to Maquina. "They can't stop her. Tell the paddlers to cut the line! LINE CUT! PADDLERS TELL! *Tsick mahka-ah-ah!*" Jon Jay was speaking backward, his language mixed with Chinook and with ours. It made him very difficult to understand.

Maquina shouted back, "No! No! Tell them to throw those heavy stones out through its rectum!"

The men inside the whale could not hear him, but, I believe, even if they had, his words came far too late.

A violent lurch may have caused one of the warriors inside the whale to sit down hard on the sealskin bladder, which sent a thick spout of water up out of the whale's blowhole. The audience let out their one and only gasp of admiration.

At that moment complete disaster struck. All of the remaining ballast of rocks slipped backward, causing the whale and its cargo to begin to go under—tail first. As it disappeared, the mouth jerked open wide and the panic-stricken warriors came leaping from between its teeth, three of them clinging to the floating sealskin bladder. The last to come struggling out was big Tom Sin. There was some undignified snorting from the audience but as yet no open laughter, except from the sailmaker. I'd never really heard him laugh before. It came out, "Cow, cow, cow." It sounded like a drunken raven's croaking.

"Those two foreign shipsmen ruined the whole thing, and my warriors didn't do it right," Man Frog whispered to me as Ax Hand, Jon Jay, Tom Sin, and the sodden warriors came straggling up onto the beach.

"You just wait until all these witnesses get home," I said, sighing. "They'll build up this story of Maquina's wooden whale until you'd never recognize what you've just seen. This whole event will soon become a ghastly legend that no one could possibly forget."

 I THOUGHT that dreadful day of the whale would never end, but at last it did. Oh, what a release it was to be in my apartment, and then in the oblivion of sleep. We slept late next morning, until we heard the sad, deep tones of the big wind flutes summoning the guests to join our feasting.

In front of the painted Eagle crest on the sailcloth screen Maquina sat high upon a large square box. He sat cross-legged with great dignity, for he was trying to wipe away all human memory of that awful whale performance. Our *tyee* wore his finest ship master's coat and hat. He had white eagle down plastered in his hair and a whole cloud of it hidden in the rim of his hat. My sister sat not far away from him, dressed in her finest *hacumb*'s costume, her arms and ankles ablaze with wide brass and copper bracelets.

As each important chief entered our enormous house, Maquina nodded his head to right or left as a sign of welcome, and each of his head movements sent a small snowstorm of down swirling into the air. It hung there, then floated gently upward, caught by the faint updraft from our central fire.

After eating, we were entertained by songs and drumming and a special masked dance. When one first lifts the lid of a storage box, our masks, which are usually in pairs, look like twin death's-heads staring up from little coffins. But fitted to clever dancers' faces, they immediately take on life. If a dancer moves well, twisting and turning in the flickering firelight, the eyes, the teeth, the hair or feathers of the wooden mask become alive. The mask becomes a part of the dancer, and he or she a part of it. We believe that if the ancient songs are sung exactly right, they act as an invitation to the spirit of the mask, who will then come inside the house and feast among our guests.

Totoosh, one of our best dancers, had inherited the Sea

Serpent song and mask. Those had always been his family's
prized possessions. From his grandfather, Totoosh had learned
the groaning words and monstrous movements of that dance,
which set children howling and young girls screaming shrill as
herring gulls.

At the very peak of the excitement in the Eagle house, the
Totoosh family monster moved in on the Black Fin chief,
crouching low before him, slowly opening and closing its heavy
lower jaw, turning its head to display the ancient wood grain
that spread across the mask like silver ripples in a stream.

Suddenly cedar mats on each side of the monster seemed
magically to slip away, revealing two enormous snakelike coils
of precious white dentalia. These exquisite finger-length white
shells, hollowed out by nature, are perfect for stringing into
priceless necklaces or other forms of human decoration. Certain
of our boatmen have become expert at reaching down with a
long pole whose end is thick with pine pitch, which sticks to
the dentalia. Sometimes a whole day's work may gain them less
than half a dozen shells or none at all. That is why these slender
treasures are so valuable in trade. When strung together end to
end and measuring exactly four times the length of a male slave,
they are worth enough to buy him. Little wonder that the eyes
of Maquina's rival Black Fin chief, Molasses Eater, had a ratlike
glitter when he saw these two long coils of precious treasure
lying at his feet.

"Take them!" Red Tongue called out as he drove his talking stick into the ashes of our fire pit. "My *tyee* gives both coils
to you."

Molasses Eater's jowls trembled as he rose and reached forward greedily to grasp the two white coils of wealth. Then he
snatched back his hands in fright. First one and then the other
coil uncurled like a thin bone snake and went slithering fast
across the earthen floor toward the Eagle house entrance.

Women screamed in fright, and the Wolf Town warriors
chuckled with delight as they saw the heavy-bellied Black Fin
chief bend low and run after them, trying desperately to grasp
his disappearing gift. Jon Jay and Tom Sin jumped up with

all of us and ran after him toward the entrance.

Outside in the darkness, we all watched the two long, bony lines of shells go snaking away across the sand. We could see that those two white serpents seemed to follow the outstretched hands of a strong young man who ran before them to the edge of the water, where he leapt into a small canoe.

"Stop him! Stop him!" the Black Fin people shouted.

But they were too late. Looking out along the pale moon's path, they saw the young man dig his paddle hard into the water. The heads of the two white snakes of rich dentalia followed him, plunging into the inlet, gliding beneath the surface. The Black Fin chief stumbled into the sea, clutching at their tails. The young man then cut the cords bound to his wrists, and the long lines of dentalia pulled apart and sank like skeleton finger bones disappearing into the deepest waters of our cove.

"Oh, what a pity!" Fog Woman said to the *hacumb* of the Black Fin chief. "My husband gave you two that lovely gift of all our very best dentalia, and now you have let it slip away from you and fall into the sea."

When the guests had gathered in the house again and had more or less composed themselves, an event occurred that surprised almost every person in the Eagle house except Maquina's family and me, of course, for I was in charge of protocol. Red Tongue, when he heard the news, drove his talking stick into the earth and announced before all those noble witnesses that Maquina's only son, Satsatsoksis, would on that very day be married to the mighty Wickinnish's daughter.

A murmur of gossip ran like wind among the guests. Not because Satsatsoksis had seen only eleven winters and his bride was not yet six years old. Oh, no! Our guests were worried at the thought of two such mighty households joining together. They knew that that was how our high-caste families arrange to have the power stay among themselves forever.

After those two noble children were pronounced man and wife, their dances performed, and their songs sung, the girl's mother would, of course, take her back to Otter Town and raise her carefully until she was ready for the marriage bed. The important thing was that Satsatsoksis now had an influential wife.

Maquina looked at my sister and at me and across at Wickinnish and his *hacumb*, for he had now done everything he could to assure that the might of the Maquinas would continue making this Eagle house the most powerful human dwelling in the world.

Next day we could see that the food was running low, but Maquina and my sister were not worried. We had lots more stored away. Fog Woman went out early with the servants to bring it down.

"While your sister's away, let us take a walk together," Maquina said. "We can go to the cave and have our men sort out the best of everything. Your sister's up there at the smokehouse by the river. We'll surprise her. We'll eat some fish while we're up there." He slapped his lean belly. "We must see if they are smoked the way we like them for this feast."

I followed him up the narrow winding trail beside the river, silently admiring the deadly red-and-white-spotted toadstools that had sprung up through the lush green moss edging the path, listening to scarlet-headed woodpeckers hammering high above us in the trees while ravens called harsh insults to a mated pair of eagles. It was good to be away from all those crowds of envious people. We could see the dark course of the river dappled in warm sunlight. The first smokehouse was sending hazy plumes of blue into the young spring air.

Maquina was halfway past the second smokehouse, with me following him. As I drew near that place, my eye caught the slightest hint of movement. I turned my head, and there to my surprise I saw my sister. She was crouching in the shadow of the hut, alert and watchful as a hunted mink. Her cape hung open, and her arms were tight around the hairy-chested Tom Sin, who was kneeling close beside her.

My shock at seeing them so close together was suddenly blown to large proportions by the thought of what might happen if my brother-in-law turned his head and saw my sister clinging to the sailmaker. That very idea caused my heart to go tum-tum-tum so loudly that Maquina must have heard it, for he stopped and turned around.

"What's the matter?" he asked. "You look pale. Have you seen a ghost?"

"Not ghosts," I said. "Keep going. Keep going." I placed my hand against my throat to keep my heart from leaping out.

"You sit down right here," Maquina told me. "Catch your breath. You're not as young as you once were. Sometimes I think you overdo it with that copper widow."

We sat together, almost beside my sister and Tom Sin. They remained as still as though they had been carved from wood. I could scarcely wait to rise and move away.

But Maquina put his hand upon my shoulder, saying, "Rest, friend. Rest. Don't be in a hurry on this beautiful day. Just look around and enjoy yourself."

He turned his head and glanced toward the smokehouse, and I stood up just in time to block his view.

"Let's go upriver," I suggested, "and tell them what to take out of the cave."

Maquina and I set out again, moving slowly up the river path to where my sister was supposed to be ordering food for feasting instead of teaching foreigners our most joyful ways of life. I glanced back at the smokehouse, and my sister raised one finger to her lips and smiled. Big Tom Sin slowly turned his head and closed one eye at me, which perhaps may have had some secret foreign meaning.

After that evening's feasting, Maquina himself stood up and shouted to his guests, "Tomorrow, rise up early!"

When the last of them had gone, he looked up at the roof and smiled. "I'm going to sleep," Maquina yawned. "I didn't close my eyes last night. Fog Woman talked and talked—I don't know what's got into her. I've never seen her so bright-eyed and excited."

Everyone knew that the next day would be important. Early that morning, to start things off right, Maquina ordered young Toowin and three other of his closest nephews to stand up on the roof of the Eagle house. Slaves removed some boards and passed blankets up to them. Our guests gathered outside the house.

Following Maquina's wishes, his nephews threw down more than three thousand red wool and nearly one thousand of the poorer blue wool blankets as gifts to be shared by all important guests, who could now see that Maquina was determined to give his son a strong beginning. Even I did not guess how far he was prepared to go.

Later, in the midday, the guests were not surprised when they heard the drum and whistle calling them to gather in the Eagle house.

"Now! Do it now!" Maquina bellowed out to Red Tongue.

Maquina's chief talker rose and spoke for our *tyee*. "The right to fish the Tlupana River every spring—I give that to my son, Satsatsoksis. All the berry-picking ground near Muchalat— I give them to Fog Woman's nephew, the one who wears his uncle's cape."

The gifts went on and on, as Maquina gave away clam-gathering bays, duck marshes, and river estuaries and huge portions of the ocean that his family had held, they said, since the creation of mankind. Our noble guests nodded to one another. This potlatch, they agreed, had a very good beginning.

Not long after sundown, I myself went outside to make sure that all was in readiness, then gave the signal. The wind flutes started calling. Everyone left the house.

Four great bonfires had been lighted with dried driftwood that sent bright crackling tongues of flame licking hungrily at the cold night air. To our visitors' surprise, the kelp and seaweed had been cleared away to expose the burned ship's hull, half-buried on our beach. Three straight cedar masts had been lashed erect. Its deck had been replanked, and many bright flags now flew from the imitation rigging. Jon Jay and Tom Sin shouted when they saw it, scarcely able to believe their eyes.

Thirty of our warrior canoemen, naked except for their short cedar capes, stood beside Sea Spear, Maquina's grand canoe. Maquina, of course, was there in full regalia, dressed not as a shipsman but as a Nootkan *tyee*. Jon Jay and Tom Sin, again clad as shipsmen, were standing beside Maquina, and Red Tongue and I took our rightful places one on either side of them.

At Maquina's signal, his paddlers pretended to dip and stroke together in imaginary water, chanting our most terrifying war song, giving it the strongest voice that I had ever heard. Our sorcerer began dancing wildly, flinging handfuls of gunpowder into the roaring flames. The gunpowder made a beautiful *poof* that turned gray smoke billowing into the darkness.

What an awesome sight our Wolf Town pageant was. Surely all jokes about the folly of the wooden whale would be forgotten. Our jealous visitors who now stood before our houses could never erase the grandeur of this scene.

Suddenly, when it was least expected, dozens of our young warriors came leaping up out of the shipwrecked vessel. Screaming and yelling, "Yep, yah, oooh hoooy, maaateee, looor de booom, readyyy-aimmm-fireee!" they shouted in the most perfect imitation of foreigners' voices. These men of ours, all with faces masked or painted white to look like shipsmen, were completely dressed in white men's clothing, using all the many costumes we had discovered in the ship's hold. The men imitating shipsmen had on very special costumes. Oh, they did not look exactly like the ordinary shipsmen you see walking on a deck, though each one held a musket and a sword. Maquina had talked about that with Red Tongue and with me. Yes, we three had decided that these brighter clothes must be what the shipsmen wear when they are feasting. After all, we reasoned, they, like us, must save their very finest costumes for grand events like this. Jon Jay told me later that because they had not asked him, many of them were wearing women's hats and dresses. Some had chosen to wear long colored or striped skirts as scarves around their necks or pulled women's stockings onto their heads like lovely dangling caps. Jon Jay admitted that he and Tom Sin laughed very hard throughout that first part of the pageant because our pale-faced shipsmen were not dressed at all like any shipsmen they had ever seen.

Maquina and his *hacumb* sat high on painted boxes on the

cross planks of the mighty Sea Spear. Both were so excited that they were bouncing up and down. I must say that my heart, too, was pounding double-time as I looked out and saw our splendid multicolored pageant bursting all around us in the flickering yellow firelight. Fifty of our most powerful paddlers, their faces painted red and their cedar capes flung back, made their muscles ripple as they pretended to be stroking through the water toward the flag-hung ship.

Just at that moment, big Tom Sin decided to fire a cannon, which by luck alone was aimed above the heads of all our guests. It so surprised them that even our grandest guests fell flat down on the sand. That set the exact mood that Maquina wanted. Most of our own Wolf Town house chiefs climbed aboard the ship and started dancing wildly on the deck, and many others joined them. I was proud of Toowin dancing wildly in our family's Chilkat cape.

Another interesting, if slightly different, version of the ship-taking pageant was soon to be enacted. Instead of those slave girls smuggling aboard the daggers, those same slaves were now played by our high-caste Wolf Town daughters. So I suppose I must admit the legend will be just a little different from the way it really happened. But that doesn't matter. You'll agree it's far more fitting that Wolf Town's high-caste women, instead of slaves, be remembered for performing such courageous deeds.

Of course, our noblemen and hunters have all fired guns before. But what Jon Jay and the sailmaker did not realize was that many of our paddlers and commoners were firing muskets for the first time in their lives. Most held the musket butt plates in the sand, screwed up their faces, turned their heads away, then pulled the trigger. What an exciting roar! Fortunately the muskets were loaded with powder and chewed cedar root—but not with ball—which surely saved a lot of lives.

After that, a great sham battle occurred between our brave warriors and those who took the part of the whites aboard the ship. It was not at all the way that I had seen it happen. But I wonder, does that really matter?

Following Maquina's incessant directions, Jon Jay and Tom

Sin rushed out and drew back two great curtains made of sails, revealing Ax Hand's enormous carving of the painted eagle. When its beak opened and shut and its huge wings moved, Maquina's guests reeled back in awe.

My brother-in-law turned to me and said so others would not hear, "Isn't it a pity that that fool Ax Hand couldn't make it fly?" Nevertheless, I could see by the way Maquina clapped his hands in glee that he was utterly delighted.

At that very moment the two sailors leapt back and held their torches to the touch holes. The two cannons thundered, spitting fire and belching out two rings of smoke. Our guests held their ears and went running and screaming up and down the beach. That signaled the battle's end. The ship was ours!

A roar of victory went up from every throat, and some of our women and our children set up a tremendous din by pounding with their yew-wood staffs against the drumlike Thunder house. Oh, what a grand event it was!

Maquina became so excited that he would not wait for me or his chief talker. He ran back to his house and climbed up on the roof with Jon Jay. From that height, using the large brass talking horn that we had taken from the master's cabin, he called out to everyone, "Come inside! Come inside and feast with us, *amigos!*" (He loved using foreign words.) Of course, our *tyee* should have allowed Red Tongue to make this announcement. But when Maquina gets excited, he rarely follows any rules.

So elated was Maquina that I could see his legs had grown weak beneath him, and he laughed so hard he looked drunk and had to be supported by the dagger maker and Tom Sin—but, Jon Jay assured me later, Maquina had not been drinking rum.

After our guests had stuffed themselves and thought that all was finished for the night, Maquina, Red Tongue, and I followed by my sister, marched toward the special holding house that Maquina had ordered built. He and Red Tongue told the slaves to pull away the front house boards, exposing the contents of the building. There, packed tight, were row upon row of red woolen blankets and blue blankets—six thousand of them—and buckets and buckets of blue Chinese beads and chest

Toowin dancing in the
family's Chilkat cape.

upon chest packed full of bright pearl buttons. Maquina called in his helpers and gave away every single thing. The gift-giving seemed without end. When we returned to the Eagle house, Maquina suddenly, without warning, had Red Tongue wave his hand. A dozen slaves ran down at this command and heaped before the Black Fin chief two hundred new greased shipsmen's cutlasses.

I looked around me and could see a look of pleasure on the faces of all the visiting chiefs. But Maquina was not content for the evening to conclude so peacefully as this. I saw him whisper to a young slave who sat at his feet. Without others noticing, the boy slipped away and was gone.

Slowly at first, with increasing volume, a few drips, then a dribble, then a continuous stream of clear white sperm whale oil came downward through the smoke hole, falling directly into the fire. It only sputtered and flared up white at first, but as the flow increased, the fire began to spread and make a spitting, roaring sound. Now the whale oil fell in a thick, heavy stream. I inconspicuously drew my heavy goat-wool cape across my knees, for I could no longer bear the heat. Maquina drew his thick sea otter robe around him, as did Matla and the Thunder house chief. Their suspicious natures had caused them to wear their heaviest robes, which would keep out heat should Maquina try to roast his guests.

Poor things. It was not long until most of our guests had to admit their weakness and squirm back from their rightful places or simply sit in that blinding heat and suffer, which the proudest of them did, but with dark and murderous looks upon their faces.

I watched the whale oil continue falling until the heat was so intense that the white sparks leapt from the fire and landed on the capes of the front-rank chiefs and noblemen. You could smell the burning goat hair and, that most costly odor, singeing otter robes.

I saw small sparks land on Jon Jay's thin blue trousers, and I flipped one side of my heavy goat-hair cape across his knees. Beneath that covering, I could see his hands rub out the painful sparks. Then I forgot about Jon Jay and Maquina, as did all the others sitting in the Eagle house. Our eyes were on the ram-rod figure of Tom Sin, for he sat there, chin up, his face and body stiff. We watched the glowing sparks fly onto his thin blue shipsman's trousers and smoke and burn against his legs. Still he did not move or flinch as much as others, prepared for the worst tricks that their host could do to them, who had come heavily dressed.

Somewhere behind me I heard a sharp cough from Fog Woman, which always means enough's enough! Instantly, the stream of whale oil ceased to fall into the fire, and I could see the smoke board narrow in the Eagle house roof. I knew the feast was over.

"Tell that boy to come down off that roof," my sister called out, "before some chief's son flings a whalebone club up there and brains him. Those proud old *tyees* sit without complaining, but still, they greatly hate a potlatch roasting."

After the guests returned to the other houses, Fog Woman called out to a slave girl, "You! Go rub some bear grease on that poor sailmaker's legs. And hurry! I don't want him ruined!"

Maquina said to me, "That sailmaker is a man as hard as iron. People here could easily learn to like him, but Tom Sin will not let us know him. Have you noticed that he will have almost nothing to do with our men and is absolutely scornful of all contact with our women?"

When Maquina said that, I tried to catch my sister's eye. But she was ladling out some thick clam broth and was careful not to look at me.

"Tomorrow," Maquina told me, "is going to be the biggest yet. I'm going to pay off all old debts. You'll see. Blow the welcome whistles early. We'll have so much to do."

Next day it didn't matter what their rank. Maquina had everyone searched for weapons as they came through the Eagle house entrance, for he sensed that his fireside roasting on the previous evening had not gone down well with all his guests. The left side of Molasses Eater's face was so swollen from the heat of that fire that he could scarcely talk. His upper and lower lips were puffed up on one side like a fat pair of salmonberries.

The Black Fin chief leered sadistically at Maquina as he said lopsidedly, "I'll remember this fiery little feast of yours—forever!"

Red Tongue rose, thumped his chief's talking stick into the soft earth near the fire, and shouted, "Maquina leaps over the fires of his enemies. Maquina soars like an eagle over his mountains of blankets. Maquina gives muskets to the ones that he is owing, first to the Black Fin chief. All here today have come to witness this."

There was a pause. The Black Fin chief talker mumbled through his swollen lips, "I see no muskets. Where are these muskets? I hate such idle boasts and lies."

"All of you come outside," called Red Tongue. "Witness what Maquina gives this poor and needy Black Fin family."

Once outside, most persons clapped their hands to the sides of their heads and shouted, for no one there had ever seen so many muskets: long muskets, medium muskets, short bell-mouthed scatter guns, weapons in numbers beyond their wildest dreams. Spread out on the beach before them were two thousand of the best new English military muskets, each laid flat on the sand, impressively arranged in huge fanlike circles, their thin, sharp bayonets twinkling in the sunlight.

Jon Jay started running up and down, shouting words we could not understand. Kawskaws told us he was doing that because he, like us, could see that a strong tide was coming in. Indeed, the big moon tide was fast creeping upward, its waters already touching many of the rifle butts.

Jon Jay said, "That salt water will rust those locks and barrels and ruin those muskets, that is sure."

Maquina laughed and whispered to us, "You tell Jon Jay that I have already given every one of them away to the Black Fin chief. Tell him I won't mind if they all get spoiled. I wonder"—Maquina chuckled—"if we will see Molasses Eater sacrifice his noble dignity and go rushing down to save his muskets from the tide."

"Well, look at that!" I said to him. "Not one of those Black

Fin folk has moved to protect your gifts to them. I suppose they think themselves too grand for that."

"See Molasses Eater's *hacumb* grind her teeth," Fog Woman said. "Poor thing, she's just got to stand there like her husband and the others and watch the tide ruin all those fine new muskets we have given them. Have you ever seen such foolish pride?"

When the last of the muskets had disappeared beneath the water, everyone went back inside the Eagle house, and Red Tongue continued to announce each special gift Maquina presented to his guests. He now seemed more careless with his treasures, giving them out to any nobleman or noblewoman who had come to watch him overwhelm the Black Fin chief. He began giving even commoners and children gifts of small spoons, woven hats, short lengths of colorful calico, small hollow bulbs of seaweed filled with rum mixed with molasses—anything to reward them and remind them that they had been a witness at this, Maquina's overwhelming potlatch. Fog Woman was keeping Kawskaws close behind her, as though she feared that Maquina might foolishly try to give her away in this, his most expansive hour.

Yes, this was a truly memorable potlatch. To enjoy all of the greatest thrills of life, a man needs a worthwhile rival. Maquina was a man who secretly valued his enemies almost as much as he did his friends.

Maquina drank a long draft of thick molasses, then in spite of his wife's frown, he rinsed his mouth out with some strong ship's rum. He told her he had to swallow quite a lot to cut the sweet taste in his mouth. It made him gasp, and suddenly he desired to dance again.

But no, Maquina wasn't finished yet. He gave the Clamshell chief ten bolts of indigo-colored calico and four barrels of gunpowder, but no balls at all or swan shot. To Wickinnish, the high chief from Otter Town, he gave a lovely pair of pistols and a brand-new cutlass and three barrels of trade beads for his women. You could tell that he respected him—as a rival, not a friend.

It was now dark outside, and just to change the scene, Maquina called in the northern wha-wha cannibal birds who clacked their long, cruel beaks and performed a violent Kwakiutl dance that set everyone's nerves on edge.

Maquina had Red Tongue take a small model of a war canoe and give it to Molasses Eater's son, the highest-ranking Black Fin, whose sneering mother, as though by accident, knocked it from his hands.

"What is that little broken thing?" the Black Fin *hacumb* screeched.

"Little!" Maquina shouted. "I'll show you what it is. Bring it here to me," he bellowed to his paddlers.

"We can't do that," Red Tongue exclaimed.

"Send all our paddlers down and bring it here to me. I'll not have this poor ignorant child insulted!"

As they heard the sound of grunting men running up the beach, Red Tongue warned Maquina, "You'll never get it through the entrance."

"Tear the planks off the wall," Maquina bellowed to the Eagle house slaves.

The visitors stared at one another in open glee, unable to imagine how this excess would end.

The wide cedar planks were ripped and battered away from the west wall. As the last one fell, Molasses Eater and all the guests were forced to rise and draw back, stumbling over one another. The enormous prow of the canoe came thrusting into the very center of the Eagle house.

"Keep coming! Farther! Farther!" Maquina shouted, until his paddlers laid the beautifully carved bow of my canoe amidst the guests. Its great keel lay in the center of the blazing fire pit. Soon there was a crackling roar as flames blistered its painted sides, then bit into the dry cedar hull.

"It's over!" Maquina shouted. "For me it's over. I have given away my titles, my songs, my masks, my rivers, and my part of the ocean to my son." He turned to me and said, "Siam, I have even given that Black Fin boy your big canoe, and now everything is ended!

"All you slaves of mine—you are free!" he yelled. "Hear me, witnesses! All my slaves are free men! Ax Hand, I forgive you for that awful whale. You are free to stay here as a free man or to go back to your Haida people."

Maquina took off his small Wolf-head frontlet and placed it on his son's head, saying, "It looks handsome on you."

"Husband, you've really decided to go all the way!" Fog Woman laughed as she snatched her hat of rank off her head and handed it to my son, Toowin.

"I knew you'd go down with me," Maquina laughed as he jerked his beautiful goat-wool cape from his shoulders and flung it carelessly toward the rising fire and all his fleeing guests.

"Not like that," my sister said, and taking off her finest cape, she hung it generously over Kawskaws's shoulders. "There!" She laughed. "Now that it's all done, I feel much better. I'm not a *hacumb* any more. I have nothing now. I'm completely free—no more potlatches, no more worries—not a single one. Let that little girl become the *hacumb* when she's ready."

"Brother, you really gave a feast!" Maquina's long-toothed sister called to him.

Maquina laughed. "I told Ax Hand I forgave him for that dreadful whale he made for me," Maquina told her. "I knew he never should have tried it—being a northerner. Flying the eagle would have been much better. They can mount that eagle on the whale beside my funeral tree."

Taking Fog Woman by the hand, Maquina said, "Come on, old wife of mine, let's go and find a place that's quiet where we can catch some salmon. We two are through forever with witnessing and giving feasts. We're going to live a simple life."

My sister smiled at him and giggled like a shy young girl. "Well," she said, "at last we finally gave a party, and I think it was a good one. Anyone who wants to outdo us will have to ruin himself."

NEXT DAY, we in the Eagle house were exhausted. I cannot tell you how relieved we were to see our guests depart. I didn't care what they did, what they took, or whom they insulted, so long as they got out of Wolf Town—fast.

The only regret I had was when I saw the copper widow climb into Wickinnish's big canoe. I heard the Wolf Town women near me sigh with pleasure, and I also heard Wickinnish's *hacumb* and her women snarl and spit like female cougars when they realized that she was going back with them to Otter Town.

Cheepoke sklickeryek reached down between her breasts, took out my dead wife's ivory pendant, and waved it at me. "I'll remember all the good times," she called out to me. "Farewell, Siam, farewell." I could not help but notice that she was wearing Tom Sin's best neck scarf.

Following that potlatch, we Wolf Town folk had a great feeling of triumph and relief that it was done. That lasted us for one whole moon. One night, when I lay thinking of the widow, I heard an owl call in the darkness, calling for some human soul. That left me with the ominous thought that our triumphant feelings all too soon might end.

Not more than six days passed before Maquina and my sister were back, tired, I suppose, of their lean-to on the forest's edge and the simple life that they had chosen. Maquina and Fog Woman began advising their powerful young son, Satsatsoksis, how to run his village and preparing him for married life.

On the very morning that the new summer moon was to have appeared, it rained. When that was over, a dangerous rainbow arched across a storm-dark sky, stretching across our whole inlet. I didn't look at it, of course, but you may be sure that some foolish Wolf Town person did. That brought violent times upon us.

It began three days later when a light summer fog had drifted across the whole of Yoquot Sound. The first one to suffer was the halibut fisherman, who was kneeling out there in his small dugout canoe, baiting his wooden halibut hook with a tough white piece of abalone. He said he touched it to his nose for luck, then lowered it until he felt its weight stone hit bottom. Only then did he begin to jig the line with a quick, rhythmic motion of his hand.

Suddenly he felt a violent tug upon the line, and his small canoe lurched as he set the hook. Oh, it was a heavy one. He could feel it fighting with that curious swaying movement as, hand over hand, he hauled it up toward the surface. Peering anxiously down into the blue-gray waters, he finally saw the flash of its flat white belly. It was a huge fish, he told us.

He glanced around to see if he could call in another fisherman's canoe to help him. As he did, he almost died of fright. Through the morning mists, he saw a huge ship come bearing down upon him, silent as a pale white-winged ghost. Its heron-like beak came thrusting straight toward him. He held fast to the halibut, his mouth agape with fright, as he heard the groaning sound of hemp ropes stretching and saw the creature's enormous wing bones spread out wide. He could hear human voices coming from the deck.

Snatching up a knife, the halibut fisherman slashed the thin twisted-cedar cord that held him to the halibut and at the same time accidentally cut his wrist. Frantically grabbing his paddle, he stroked away from the ship's path and headed in to shore. This was no dream. He could see silhouettes of several men climbing in the lower rigging, their arms and legs spread wide, working as busily with their ropes and lines as spiders on a web.

The halibut fisherman stroked away with every ounce of strength that he possessed, grateful to be out from beneath the great ship's prow. When his canoe finally touched the beach, he came running up to tell Maquina all that he had seen. Licking his bleeding wrist, he scurried to our fire pit.

"It'll be . . . anchoring off . . . that point, *Tyee*," he gasped. "That ship tried to slice me into two, and it would have done if I hadn't cut my best fishline. You should have seen the halibut I had to let away," he told all those who had gathered around him. The short fisherman stood on his toe tips and raised his arms into the air. "I tell you, brothers, that halibut was at least as long as me!"

"That's a nasty cut you've got on your wrist," said Fog Woman. She reached into a box and took out a tobacco leaf. "Bind it tight to stop the bleeding." She sniffed his breath to see if he'd been drinking rum.

I myself only half believed the story the halibut fisherman told until, like all the others, I jumped in fright. For at that moment we heard a great *boom* that echoed and reechoed on the points and islands out beyond our bay. That ship's first cannon thunder had not died away before a second heavy blast came rumbling in across the water.

"Are they coming here to fight us?" our war chief, Man Frog, shouted.

Villagers came running into the Eagle house, calling, *"Tyee! Tyee!"*

I didn't bother about Maquina at that moment. I ran outside, for I hate being inside a house when I hear cannon fire. My eyes were busy searching for Toowin, Jon Jay, and big Tom Sin. They had been working together at their forge, hammering out some daggers. Where were they now?

As we saw the ship rounding the point, Toowin came running to me. I walked fast, hurrying straight toward him. The Salish weaver woman's white dogs were yapping madly. Children were running everywhere. I could see Man Frog's warriors stripping the protective covering from the fighting canoes and Maquina's two iron cannons. The women stood together in tight flocks, staring at the ship and whispering to one another.

Hearing no more cannon fire, I went back inside the Eagle house. Maquina sat himself upon a box beside our fire pit and called to Jon Jay and the sailmaker, saying, *"Chahko nika.* Come to me."

Everyone fell silent as they watched the two shipsmen come and stand in front of him.

Maquina peered straight into the young dagger maker's eyes. Jon Jay stared coldly back at him, for the ship that sailed so close to our village seemed to have given him new power.

Before another word could pass between them, a paddler came running through the entrance to the Eagle house and wormed his way through the crowd around Maquina. *"Tyee!"* he gasped. "The fog is clearing. The men on the point see only one ship. We believe it has come here alone."

"One, two, three ships—it would be the same." My brother-in-law sighed. "Siam!" Maquina called to me in an unsure voice. "Should Satsatsoksis tell all the Wolf Town people to run away and hide or to stay and fight?"

"Let's run," I counseled. "If those shipsmen start firing their cannons at these houses, people will be killed."

"Perhaps they only fired those cannons in the fog," Maquina said, "to let us know that they were near, hoping we'd come out to greet them." When I did not answer, Maquina said, "I believe my son should not hide from them or fight with them. We want to trade."

Because he was excited by his own idea, Maquina called to Kawskaws, asking her to help him speak to Jon Jay. "You tell him," Maquina said, "that I do not want trouble with the foreigners. Our people want to trade peacefully with this ship. You ask Jon Jay how I am going to make those shipsmen understand that so they won't make any trouble here."

When Kawskaws translated that, Jon Jay looked up at the Eagle house roof and did not at first answer my brother-in-law. Then the dagger maker nodded toward Tom Sin and said, "We two could go out there and tell them that you want only trade."

"Oh, no!" Maquina scowled. "I can't let you two go out together. Even though you are a son of mine, I don't know what you'd say to them, and I'm not sure you would come . . . back here to us."

My brother-in-law turned his head and looked at all of us

who stood around him. "I myself am going out aboard that ship," he said. "I am not afraid of them. I will be the one to go and make the welcome sign. If trouble comes, then it should come to me."

"Don't you do that," my sister scolded her husband.

Red Tongue joined her in warning him, for neither could imagine my brother-in-law carrying out such a dangerous plan.

"They'll seize you and whip you and hang you from those high wing bones," my sister told him.

Maquina sat staring into our fire, not listening as we all opposed him. "Jon Jay, if I go out there . . ." he asked the dagger maker, "are they going to kill me?"

Jon Jay shifted his gaze from Maquina's face. I saw him glance at Tom Sin and then back at Kawskaws. He said, "*Wake memaloost mesika*. They will not kill you. *Nika kiatawa kopa mesika*. I will go with you. They will not kill you."

Maquina thought about Jon Jay's words. "No," he said. "You two must stay on shore." Maquina turned and looked at me, saying, "If someone does not go out to that ship, I believe those shipsmen will fire their cannons at us. Siam," he said, "do you think I can trust this adopted son of mine to squiggle something good about his father, something for me to give to those shipsmen waiting out there?"

I did not answer quickly, for I was thinking about his twice saying "son of mine." I looked at Jon Jay, then I answered truthfully, "I don't know what marks he will make, but he has always been faithful to us. It is the foreigners I do not trust. You should send young Hoiss out there," I said. "Let them do what they wish with him. He caused us all our troubles; let him repair them."

Almost every person around Maquina echoed my words. "*Tyee*, send someone else. They will kill you . . . kill you!"

"Am I to sit here on this empty box," he asked, "and send mindless fools to do what I myself should do? Shall I allow those shipsmen to sail away? Is Wolf Town never going to trade with foreigners again?"

That was a bitter thought, and no one answered him except my sister, who said, "You stay here with me. Wait and see what happens."

Maquina snorted at her words. "Go and bring the dagger maker's narrow squiggle box," he told Toowin.

Toowin hurried into Maquina's apartment and returned, carrying the box as though it were as fragile as an eggshell. He handed it to Jon Jay.

Jon Jay drew a small knife from his pocket and very carefully sharpened the point of his raven quill, then dipped it in the little pot of berry juice mixed with charcoal and began to make his long, broken squiggles on the flat, white skin.

My brother-in-law spoke slowly to Kawskaws and Jon Jay, using simple Chinook words. Anyone could tell from the quick way Jon Jay nodded that he easily understood Maquina's meaning. Anyone could see that Jon Jay was eager to follow Maquina's finicky instructions.

Jon Jay did not write easily or quickly, for Maquina demanded to know the meaning of each word after it was written. Several times big Tom Sin mumbled something to Jon Jay, but the dagger maker only looked away and shook his head, saying, "No, no, no!"

It seemed to take forever, but finally Jon Jay sprinkled some beach sand over the wet words and then waited before he blew out his breath across the skin, then said, "It is finished."

I glanced at the veiled look that had come over Jon Jay's eyes and the wooden expression on Tom Sin's face. As we rose to go outside, I wondered if they were hiding thoughts from us deep inside their bodies. Was it because they were creatures without mothers—was that what made it so difficult to understand these foreigners?

The breeze that had been blowing since dawn had almost died, and low clouds were drifting lazily through the treetops. The birdlike vessel rested out before our village, its wings half folded, and the shipsmen who lined its side were watching us. I could see it flew no flags. The ship made no further sound, as it watched and waited, deciding perhaps whether it should stay and trade, or fight, or sail out on the midday tide.

Not knowing who they were, I looked at Jon Jay's face and saw him cast a triumphant glance at Tom Sin, who nodded back to him. That made me feel that they believed this ship was not one from King George, nor was it the Oui-oui men, or Spanish, this was a Boston man, one of their very own.

Clutching Jon Jay's message, Maquina hurried into his apartment, shouting excitedly to Fog Woman, demanding fresh paint and a mirror. He told me he wanted to borrow my otter cloak because he had long since given his away, and he asked that Kawskaws sew my gift to him of southern abalone all along its outer edges. Does that sound to you like a man who shuns all power and truly wishes to live a simple life?

Suddenly Maquina raised his hand and said, "No, I don't want the paint. I want that grand captain's coat, and those uncomfortable trousers, the hat, and my half-boots as well, and don't forget that beautiful blue sash. I'm going to wear them all when I go out to greet the master of this ship."

Fog Woman was too horrified to speak or move. Red Tongue stepped closer to Maquina and said earnestly, "It is very dangerous to go aboard that ship no matter what you wear."

"Why?" Maquina demanded.

"Because you do not really know what squiggles the dagger maker has marked down on that skin."

"That is true," Maquina said, and he called Jon Jay to him again. This time Maquina took the white skin in his hand and pointing at each squiggle, he made Jon Jay repeat exactly what it said.

"Look at it! It's good!" said Jon Jay, holding it up for everyone to see, though none of us could read a word.

I could not make out anything on the dagger maker's skin except Tom Sin's mark. It was a big X with two dots. When I saw this, I smiled and nodded my approval to Tom Sin, for his mark I recognized.

Jon Jay pointed to his own mark. It was a little bolder than the other squiggles, but it meant nothing to me. The rest of the message, I guessed, was just Jon Jay trying to help Maquina.

"You all heard the words yourself," Maquina snapped at us. "And Siam is right. Jon Jay has never lied to me. I'm going." He held up the mirror and examined the beautiful shining buttons on his dark-blue uniform. He flung my otter cloak loosely across his shoulders. Maquina was dressed far finer than any foreign ship master I had seen. Then he looked at me. "Bear Man, do you think it right if I go aboard that ship alone?"

My sister sucked in her breath, making her disapproval known to all of us. What could I say? I sat in silence. Certainly I did not wish to go with him.

"I would like one other person as well as a strong paddler to come with me. Who shall that person be?" Maquina asked.

Toowin was the first one to jump up. He stepped straight toward his uncle.

"You sit down," I ordered him. "You're too young to go out there." But Toowin's brave actions had forced me to say, "I'm the one . . . who's going out there with our *tyee*."

Maquina smiled at me and nodded his approval. "You can both come with me," he said. "Toowin will be the first to climb aboard. Grease him, and if they grab him, he can jump away and shout out a warning to us. We two will try to pick him up in our canoe. We'll take Knee Scars with us," Maquina added. "He's a strong paddler and one who will keep his head if we are caught by trouble."

I watched Maquina fold Jon Jay's message very, very small, then place it carefully up inside the dark crown of his elegant ship master's hat. I, Siam, felt like a grizzly bear that walks knowingly into a deadfall.

"I want four of the best sea otter skins placed in that box," he told his wife, "and I want you to fill all my pockets full of eagle down. Get ready," he told me and Toowin.

I dressed myself as a proper nobleman, wearing the splendid goat-wool cape that my wife's father had given me. On my head I wore my finest woven whaling hat. I had Kawskaws lightly paint the left half of my face with red ocher. Toowin wore a short cedar cape that was trimmed with a band of otter fur. He always looked fine to me no matter what he wore.

"Don't either of you bother to wear a dagger," Maquina warned us. "They'll only take them from us when we step aboard."

As we walked down to the beach, a huge crowd of our villagers stepped aside to make a path, staring at us as though we three were already dead. We got into my slim white seal canoe, and Knee Scars pushed out from shore. Maquina and I sat properly in mid-canoe, while Toowin paddled in the bow. In this way we went out toward the silent ship, which seemed to watch us coldly with its cannons' eyes. The sun-yellowed wings of this unfamiliar ship hung slack, perfectly reflected in the smoothly undulating summer waters.

"I can't believe that we are doing such a thing," I told Maquina as we drew near the vessel's side.

The tall masts and bulging, black hull of the ship towered high above us. Maquina himself seemed nervous and threw out a welcoming flurry of eagle down. But there was no breeze at all, and it did not carry on the wind the way it should. My brother-in-law eased open the box between us, and taking out a pair of sea otter skins, he stood cautiously in the canoe and held these pelts high for all to see.

"They don't want to hurt us any more than we want to hurt them," Maquina whispered, knowing how well human voices carry across still water. "They're here for otter trading, nothing else. They probably know nothing of the troubles we had with that other ship." All that he said to steady up our nerves. "How could they know?" he continued. "No one went away from here to tell them."

I turned and looked at him in sheer amazement. "I think going aboard this ship is madness. You are begging to be killed."

Those words annoyed my brother-in-law. He slung the pelts back into the box and spoke no more to me.

We were now very close to this strange ship. We needed only to look up to see the shipsmen climbing in the rigging and the grim faces of those who were lined along the ship's rail. All their cannon ports were gaping open. But of course, we being only four in number, they had no need to haul their rope nets up against us.

"*Yukwa!*" a voice shouted down to us in Chinook. "Come this way!"

We saw a rope ladder with wooden cross steps unroll as it came tumbling down the ship's enormous side. Toowin took hold of it.

"Go!" Maquina ordered him.

Toowin climbed as I stretched out my hand and held the ladder, trying to steady it for both of us. The oily, black paint on their vessel's side had a mean, sharp, sickening smell.

I am ashamed to say it, but my legs were trembling as I climbed up after Toowin. Yes, I had warning feelings grabbing at my guts. I felt something terrible was just about to happen.

I was roughly searched for weapons as soon as I placed my foot upon that deck. I was glad they found none to snatch from me. All those strange, foreign eyes made me feel that here and now our lives might end.

Maquina came up after me, and a score of shipsmen crowded round the two of us. These foreigners did not smile or frown. They just stood there, pale-eyed, motionless, staring at Maquina in his splendid ship master's uniform, his otter cloak draped grandly from his shoulders.

My brother-in-law hesitated only for a moment to see if all seemed safe, then he stepped back to the railing and ordered Knee Scars to throw up the cord that was attached to the painted box that held the otter skins. Carefully my brother-in-law drew the box up over the side. Knee Scars reliably remained in our canoe, holding the ladder ready until the moment we would need him.

I was pleased with the special way these shipsmen looked at Maquina, not just at his wonderful, high ship master's uniform with its huge shining buttons. No, they were admiring Maquina's size, his wide, clear cheekbones, his flashing eyes, his elegant plucked mustache turning smoothly down around his lips. Let me assure you that before a single word was spoken, every shipsman on that vessel knew Maquina was our *tyee.*

These new shipsmen had a man with them who spoke quite good Chinook. I saw that he had a long forehead that had been elegantly flattened when he was a child, which on this coast could only mean he was a highborn person.

He said, *"Kwann mesika chahko.* Glad you've come."

We answered, *"Nesika kwann weght.* We're glad also."

Those words seemed to mark a good beginning. But we saw the interpreter squint upward and move ever so cautiously away from us to avoid startling the two scatter-gun men who stood in the rope webbing, aiming down at the three of us.

This ship appeared slightly larger than the one that lay upon our beach. This ship's scrubbed deck was so large it made me think that I was standing on an island of white sand. I could feel it swaying slowly with a stomach-churning motion right beneath my feet. I truly hated being on that foreign ship because of all the dreadful memories it brought back to me—the loss of my dear wife and then that ghastly slaughter at Abooksha.

I eyed every shipsman carefully to see if I could recognize their master. Out of habit, I was looking for a red-faced, heavy-bellied man. But I was wrong. I did not recognize him as he came in sight. He was a thin, hunch-shouldered youngish man with a nervous, pock-marked face, a jutting nose, and a narrow pointed chin. He was dressed in a costume most ordinary except for a gray-white collar with a black kerchief tied carelessly around his neck.

Ignoring me and Toowin, he walked slowly up to Maquina, then cautiously stepped back more than an arm's length from him, even though he knew that we possessed no weapons.

"Is he this ship's *tyee?*" Maquina asked in disbelief.

"Yes, he's the captain," the flathead told him in Chinook.

Maquina reached up very gently and removed his three-cornered hat. Feeling inside, he withdrew the neatly folded skin that bore the squiggles from the dagger maker. This he held out to the nervous-looking master, who, afraid perhaps that Maquina had concealed a dagger, took a long step back. Then, seeing the white square of skin, he leaned forward and awkwardly received this harmless offering from our *tyee*.

We were the ones to feel nervous when the master put his right hand inside his pocket, where high shipsmen often hide a dangerous small pistol. Instead of that, this man withdrew a small brass box from which he took a pair of little mirrors held in place by metal wires. These wires he hooked behind his ears, letting the mirrors rest one on either side of his bony nose. He looked over the top of his mirrors at Maquina as he quickly unfolded the small square of skin until it lay full-sized in his hands. He held it far away from his face, then drew it in quite close. I watched his eyes moving from left to right and back, and left to right again, and back again, going faster and faster until at last they stopped. He sucked in his breath and quickly handed the skin to the tall, thin nobleman who stood beside him. He too commenced to make his eyes go roving back and forth along Jon Jay's curious squiggles.

To the Captain of the Brig anchored before this village.

Sir: The man who will deliver this letter into your hand is Ma-Quin-na the chief who is to blame for the burning of the ship *Boston* and the murdering of Capt. Jon Salter and all his crew save two of us who are now ashore.

When this man gives you this letter, I trust that you will seize him and chain him under watch so that he can in no way escape from you. Only after that has been done may we hope to bargain for our release.

Respectfully,
John R. Jewitt armourer
and for John Thompson
X his mark.   sailmaker

When the master's second chief had finished looking at the skin, they both stared at us once more. Their eyes narrowed. Then the master smiled at Maquina, and I thought, Yes, the dagger maker has done exactly what he was asked to do. He's made good marks upon that skin, and now this master will forget any old bad feelings with our people and start to trade with us.

At that moment, Maquina bent, removed the box top, and shook out four prime sea otter skins, and these he handed grandly to the master, saying, "*Cultus potlatch mesika.* These are a gift for you."

I, like Maquina, felt that all was going well.

The master snatched the otters from Maquina, then folded up his little mirrors and put them in their box, which he dropped into his pocket.

Then, leering at us hatefully, the master leapt back and shouted words we could not understand. In an instant, dozens of his shipsmen came crowding in on us. Five of them grabbed me before I could even hope to jump. I was forced onto my knees with both arms twisted painfully behind my back. I could feel my heart go tum-titty-tum-titty-tum as I waited for their knives to strike.

I managed to look sideways and saw that they had done the same to Maquina. A lot of them had forced his face onto the deck, and some of them had trampled on his beautiful master's hat. Toowin was the only one to slip away from them because of the seal grease. But a moment later I saw them fling him to the deck and kneel on him. It was over.

In such times before a slaughter, it is our warriors' custom not to make a sound. Remembering this, we three held our breath and waited, each as silent as a stone.

To our surprise, we were not murdered and beheaded instantly, but instead we felt our arms being tightly bound behind our backs. When this was done, we were once more forced to stand. I looked at Maquina sadly, and at poor Toowin. My son smiled back at me to try and cheer me up.

The master glared at Maquina and said, "Ma-quinn-aah?"

My brother-in-law nodded proudly and answered him in French. *"Oui, Mon capitaine. Moi, Maquina!"*

The master sent a man scurrying down below the deck. He returned, his arms loaded with heavy iron bracelets attached to chains. These they clamped upon our wrists and circled around our waists so that we could not possibly escape. Seeing my son caught shamefully in iron chains caused tears to blur my eyes.

Some of the shipsmen ran barefooted up into the spider webs of rope above us and tied three neck nooses to the lowest wing bone. They called down to the master in excited voices, yelling rough words impossible to understand. They laughed hatefully as they swung and dangled the noose ends against our faces. We three stared out proudly past them at our beloved Wolf Town.

The master's face turned red as he yelled up, demanding that the shipsmen come down onto the deck. Then he read aloud the dagger maker's squiggles so that all those listening could understand the words that Jon Jay had written.

When he was finished, most of the shipsmen shouted out in anger, and many came and shook their fists before our faces.

Maquina looked at me and said, "I guess he did write something wrong."

The master ordered two strong men, each carrying a curved sword and a club, to protect us from the angry crewmen, many of whom were eager to do us harm. At midday we watched the shipsmen squatting on the forward deck, eating their midday meal and glaring back at us.

"Well, this is how it goes," I said to Toowin. "A man lives the best way he can, then suddenly it's ended. You should think of the animal you would most like to be," I told him, "when you return to this world another time." For my Toowin's sake, I tried to sound accepting of our fate. But my heart cried out at Jon Jay's treachery. Oh, Maquina had been right to worry about the squiggles, but in the end, it was Jon Jay—not the squiggles—who had hurt us.

"Your father's right," Maquina said to Toowin. "Pay attention to the things he tells you now." Maquina was silent for a while, then said to me, "I've lain with a lot of women, but none that I liked half so well as your sister."

"I always knew that," I said to him.

"I hope she'll be all right," said Toowin.

"She'll look after Satsatsoksis," I said.

"I hope they don't fire cannons at the houses when our women and the children are inside," Maquina said.

Thin rain began to fall, and summer fog drifted to us from the ocean. Far away I could hear the slow regular thunder of the surf, the last gasping of a passing ocean storm.

Maquina did not speak another word as he stood near me, hatless. His light-blue sash had been torn away from across his breast, and his lovely uniform looked poor and sodden in the rain. He stared out across the waters toward Wolf Town, with its long, low houses sprawled just above the beach. He probably believed, as I did, that we would never live to reach that shore again.

When the rain ceased, the skinny master came up from below. He had one shipsman of rank walking by his left hand. He was still carrying Jon Jay's squiggles in his right hand, and he looked angrily at us three. Crewmen crowded round, urging him, I think, to do the worst to us.

The master started talking excitedly while pointing his bony finger in Maquina's face. I guess he thought it safe to do so because Maquina was in chains. However, I watched closely, wondering if Maquina would lunge forward and bite that finger off, for he was a wily, well-trained Nootkan fighter.

The interpreter said, "My captain understands the marks that were made on the thin skin you gave him. He says he is very angry with you three dogmen"—he pointed in at Wolf Town—"and all the other murderers hiding in your houses on that shore. That letter says you put the daggers to some shipsmen, killed their captain, then burned their boat. The letter also says you still got two." He held up two fingers. "Is that true . . . you still got two shipsmen in your house . . . alive?"

There was a pause. Then Maquina said, "Yes. They are our friends. They live with us. Those two I saved from getting killed.

One of them is now my son. On the thin skin does it say that I came out here to trade with you?" Maquina asked.

"No. Those words said nothing about trade," the interpreter told him. "The skin says you, Maquina, are a murdering man."

The master and his man of rank whispered together, and the Chinook talker listened, then stepped forward and began translating the master's words. "That man," he said, pointing over the side at Knee Scars, who still bravely clutched the bottom of the ladder though he knew that we were all in deadly danger, "you tell him—in Chinook so I understand you—to paddle to the village and tell the people to send those two shipsmen out to us alive—not hurt. You understand? Or shipsmen here are going to kill you. My captain says if those two stolen shipsmen not brought out here quick—damn quick—he's going to hang you three up by the neck." The interpreter pointed to the nooses high in the rigging. "Everybody in that village will look out here and see you three swinging, slowly dying in the wind." He made a crude pantomime of how we would look with a noose around our throats, letting his eyes roll back and his tongue hang out.

I could feel my heart go tum-tum-tum, for after drowning, the death that our people fear most is hanging. If either of those happen to a man, it is said that his soul never finds a place to rest.

"That little flathead talker needs his neck cut," Maquina said to me in our own language, slurring the words so that the Chinook talker would not understand.

"You are not to speak together!" that little seal turd shouted at us as he snatched up a knotted piece of rope and struck Maquina in the face. "You tell that paddler to go back to your village. Tell him have your people bring those two shipsmen out here. Quick!"

Knee Scars let go the ladder only when Maquina called down to him in Chinook, saying that he should go ashore and tell Man Frog to send Jon Jay and Tom Sin to the ship. We watched Knee Scars stroking steadily toward Wolf Town.

Not long after he arrived, we could hear hundreds of yew-wood staffs drummed wildly against the houses as our people thundered out their anger and confusion. Could this mark the end for Maquina, Toowin, and me? Our people on the shore had only Knee Scar's brief account of what had happened. When the master heard that violent sound come rolling out across the water, he ordered his shipsmen to mount two swivel guns and load them. A man went round to see that every shipsman had his musket primed and loaded.

Slowly the beating on the houses died away, and in a while we saw a small white seal canoe put out from the village with three paddlers. The sailmaker sat erect in the middle, wearing one of our cedar capes and hat. His face was painted red. In my opinion, our paint and dark cape did nothing to disguise that great hulking Tom Sin. I was amazed that there was only one shipsman instead of two and that these foreigners could not easily recognize their own kin. At first, the master paid little attention to this small canoe that came toward us, because he did not realize it held a captive shipsman.

As the dugout neared the ship, Tom Sin took off his woven hat and shouted out, "Ahoy, mates, ahoy!" Oh, yes, they knew him then, and they called loudly back to him, and after much scrambling on the deck, they lowered the ladder.

The muscular Tom Sin came leaping up over the ship's side with a look of triumph on his face. He leered wordlessly at Maquina and at me and at Toowin, then shook hands warmly with every shipsman near him. He stood stiff and straight and touched his hand to his forehead when he saw their skinny master.

Knee Scars was one of our three canoemen, and he shouted up, "The *hacumb* says that she will send the dagger maker only halfway to the ship, and when shipsmen bring the three men halfway to meet them, only then will she allow the exchange."

The master paused, then spoke to his first ranking shipsman. He had his flathead call out to our three paddlers, "Yes, you go in and bring that other shipsman halfway to this ship, and we will send these three in our small boat to exchange them."

Our three paddlers called back that they understood, then stroked hard away for shore.

After they had spoken for a little while, the master led Tom Sin down below the deck, and they were not long gone before they reappeared. To my surprise almost all the red ocher and black eyebrow paint had been wiped from Tom Sin's face, and he was wearing shipsmen's clothes that seemed too small for him. He wore new pants, a new canvas shirt, a stiff blue scarf tied around his neck, and a shiny flat black hat upon his head. In his arms he carried the rolled-up cedar cape and woven hat that we had given him. These he flung violently over the ship's side.

He turned and walked toward Maquina, stopping only when he stood face to face with him. Tom Sin, a scowl upon his face, said some thick, harsh words to Maquina that I could not understand, but I know that they were bad. I had the feeling that Tom Sin might have struck Maquina with his heavy fists, but at that moment the master came up to us, with that little flat-headed Chinook talker trailing close behind him.

There was no beating on the houses this time, nothing but an ominous silence after the small canoe touched shore. It was not long before that same dugout left the beach again, this time holding four. The master watched them carefully with his bring-near glass, but I didn't need a long brass tube to see that one was Jon Jay. He was sitting in the prow of that canoe, his back to us as he faced the paddlers. Toowin said he thought that odd.

The master called out words that caused some shipsmen to lower their small white boat.

We watched the seal canoe come closer, and I believe our guards were getting ready to unchain our wrists and put us in their white boat when suddenly I heard a shout go up from the shipsmen who lined the rail.

Looking out across the water, I could see that Jon Jay had drawn the two pistols that he usually carried and was pointing both of them straight at the heads of our three canoemen, who had ceased to paddle.

The shipsmen now were silent, watching. Then the paddler closest to Jon Jay took one stroke, and we saw the red-pointed paddles of the other two dip reluctantly into the water. The dagger maker ordered them toward the ship. Jon Jay had won. The shipsmen hauled their white boat back onto the deck again.

Maquina groaned and looked at me. I was as worried as he was, for I realized that our chance of being exchanged was gone.

The shipsmen around us waited until they saw Jon Jay come climbing safely up the ladder and step onto their ship's deck before they sent up a roar of triumph.

The first thing Jon Jay did was to grab a rag that was offered him and wipe away the red and black paint from his face and the Eagle crest from his shoulder. For the first time I realized that he too had hated the smell and feel of our *kotsaks* and our handsome painted decorations.

The master welcomed him with a hearty clap on the back and sent a young shipsman to his cabin. This boy ran back carrying a board with a jug of rum, three horn cups, a knife, a huge chunk of hard bread, and an evil-smelling wedge of cheese.

Tom Sin gladly joined the dagger maker, and together with the master, they took a drink of rum, then stuffed their mouths with bread and cheese until their cheeks stood out like those of gluttonous children. They smiled at one another, and with their mouths still crammed full of food, they drank their rum cups empty.

Yes, anyone could tell that they were happy with life, grateful to be the victors. Jon Jay's squiggles on the white skins and Maquina's allowing him to keep a pair of pistols had changed everything for him and us. I looked up at the nooses hanging just above our heads and thought, Now we are all three going to pay for my brother-in-law's kindnesses to those two men.

Sneering angrily, the crowd of shipsmen ran and laid violent hands on the three of us, and I truly felt that these would be my last moments in this world. My heart went tum-titty-tum-titty-tum as I heard the shipsmen's angry shouts and laughter all around me. I watched them hop and skip before us with murder in their eyes.

One of them, a small brown man with a face like a tight-clenched fist, went scurrying up the rigging, agile as a squirrel. Looking up, I saw him tighten the knots, then once more fling down the three rope nooses. They came swaying like live snakes before our eyes.

"Now you're going to die," the flathead told us without any sign of pity while he eagerly helped the shipsmen fit the nooses round our necks.

TOGETHER we three stood bound like slaves in chains to that ship's mast with rough rope nooses already rasping against our throats. I felt dismayed, and ashamed, that, with the help of Jon Jay, these new shipsmen could so easily have conquered all of us.

I watched Jon Jay going round and having his hand shaken by almost every shipsman on that boat. I know he felt bad, because he avoided even glancing at the three of us. It must have been hard for the dagger maker knowing that Maquina, his father who had saved his life, and Toowin, his best friend from our village, were now about to die because of him.

When the people of Wolf Town saw their small seal canoe heading back to shore without Maquina or me or Toowin, an awesome stillness seemed to rise between this strange ship and our village beach. It took them some time to understand that they had been deceived. Then we heard our women wailing, our paddlers and our warriors and young people drumming hard against our houses with their yew-wood staffs, pounding out their wild frustration as they realized that through trickery they had lost their *tyee*.

Suddenly the harsh pounding ended as abruptly as it had begun, and all was once more silent. Our people lined the beaches, staring helplessly at the ship that held us prisoner. The master had anchored his vessel so that four dark eyes of the ship's cannons pointed threateningly at Wolf Town.

Darkness fell and cloaked the ship in starless night. We three prisoners waited. What else could we do? It was easy enough for us to work our heads free of those nooses, but we were forced to stay standing on our feet, our arms and waists still bound to the mast by chains.

Next morning I watched big Tom Sin and Jon Jay getting used to life aboard this ship. They carefully avoided coming near the three of us. It was almost as though they had never known us. Though they both remained barefooted, they had washed their hair and knife-scraped their faces free of any lip or chin hair. Every sign of our red and black paint and seal oil had been scrubbed away. Jon Jay was now dressed in new ship's clothing: a stiff, clean canvas shirt, new blue trousers, and a dark neckerchief. Both he and Tom Sin had their long hair tied tightly back with dark ribbons and each wore a stiff, black-tarred hat placed squarely on his head. They now looked like two unfamiliar humans we had scarcely known before.

Big Tom Sin smirked at Maquina as he carried Jon Jay's Wolf Town clothing to the rail. With a look of disgust upon his face, Tom Sin flung all of it far out over the side. I saw Fog Woman's gift of a beautiful goat-wool cape spread itself like a bird, its fringes rippling in the breeze like white feathers, as it fell into the water. Jon Jay's bulbous whaling hat, which had been given to him by Maquina, sank slowly. The shipsmen laughed and spat tobacco at it.

After their morning meal, Tom Sin came toward us, followed by Jon Jay. Both of them were still chewing, so delighted were they to have shipsmen's food again. Tom Sin stood directly in front of Maquina, his muscular arms perched on his hips, a vengeful look in his eyes. Maquina stared coldly back at him but did not speak.

The dagger maker must have feared that Tom Sin might strike him, for he stepped forward quickly and pressed himself against Tom Sin's strong right arm. The sailmaker frowned at Jon Jay, then shrugged and walked away. Jon Jay might have followed him, but Maquina spoke out in English, saying, "Jon Jay! Me . . . I speak you."

The young dagger maker turned back to hear Maquina. All the cheerfulness, the laughing, and the singing seemed to have flown out of him, leaving only a cold, clean-scrubbed young face that stared at us as though we three were strangers to him.

"I am ashamed of you," Maquina said to Jon Jay in Chinook. "I believed you when you said you didn't make bad squiggles on the skins."

When he understood his words, Jon Jay glared angrily at Maquina. "I wasn't going to stay a slave to you forever," Jon Jay answered, using our proper word for slave, *kak-koelth*.

"You were no slave to me. You were my son!" Maquina said indignantly. "Slaves are not allowed to marry. I bought you a chief's daughter just to be your wife."

The dagger maker clenched his fists when my brother-in-law said that. "You took her away from me," Jon Jay shouted at him. "I loved her. I wanted her. You stole her away from me. Then you sent them all away." He pointed at me and Toowin. "You sent my friends and Kawskaws and, later, Fog Woman away. I had no one." I saw tears come in his eyes, and Jon Jay said again, "No one! You took Sea Star away from me, and you used her, and then you forced her to go away. You sent away every friend I had!"

"I trusted you like a son," Maquina said. "I let you keep the little guns with you to protect yourself. Why? Because you are my son."

"I am not your son," said Jon Jay. "Am I his son?" Jon Jay asked Toowin.

"Certainly you are his son," Toowin answered.

"*No! No! No!*" Jon Jay shook his head. He was weeping when he turned away from us and walked toward the Master's cabin. He turned and called back to Maquina, "Does a father steal the wife of his own son?"

My brother-in-law looked down at the chains around his waist and did not answer Jon Jay. Oh, what sadness we four shared together.

Jon Jay was gone for some time, and when he returned, he was with the Master, who had that little flathead with him.

That was the one and only time that I had been tied or chained in my whole life. I felt terrible! We three stood there helplessly while these foreigners, aided by their little Chinook talker, casually decided what they would or would not do to us, planning, perhaps, exactly how they would murder us—hang us by the neck or something worse. Maybe it was just as well we did not understand their words. But I tell you, not understand-

ing the way foreigners move their tongues can make a man feel
very helpless. I suppose that's how Jon Jay and the big sailmaker must have felt when they were made to stay with us. Yes,
I realized then that they had stayed with us against their wills.

Maquina interrupted their words by saying to Jon Jay, "You
wrote bad words against me on that skin, but you are still my
son."

Jon Jay looked down at the deck between his feet, then
nodded his head up and down, which we know is the foreign
way of saying yes.

"I trusted you," Maquina said. "We three trusted you.
That's why we came here." When Jon Jay looked up, Maquina
asked him, "Are they going to hang us from that wing bone for
Fog Woman and all our relatives to see?"

The Master's talker laughed again when he started to interpret that, but Maquina gave him such a murderous look that he
did not finish speaking.

Tom Sin scowled at us three prisoners, saying nothing in
our favor.

"Haaang dem!" we heard some sailors shouting. "Haaang
three of dem!"

The squirrel man above us swung the neck nooses back and
forth until they struck our faces.

"Stop that!" Jon Jay shouted up at him, and he caught the
nooses so they would not hit us. His hands trembled, and his
face seemed sickly pale. The dagger maker turned and said a lot
more words directly to the Master.

Even as he was talking, I heard a buzz of words like angry
bees come out of all the shipsmen gathered along the rail. Coming across the water, I could see a medium-sized canoe stroking
straight toward us. The paddlers paused at a safe distance from
the ship and waited.

The deep voice of my old friend Matla came booming across
the oily stillness. Haltingly, in very bad Chinook, he said, "Give
back us our *tyee* . . . also other men . . . you understand? We
give you some things good."

I watched the ship's talker lean close to the Master, whis-

pering to him the words that Matla had shouted. The Master
made a sign, and a little curly-headed ship's boy came running
to him with a short, wide-mouthed brass horn, which he handed
to the ship's talker, who climbed a little up the web of rope.

"We know you got lotsa ship's stuff hid away on shore,"
the Chinook talker hollered to old Matla, who stood fiercely
straight in his canoe. "Johnny here, he say you got two ship's
cannons. Johnny here, he say you got a big ship's anchor.
Johnny, he say you got lotsa, lotsa muskets, lotsa looking-glasses.
Johnny, he say you got lotsa blankets, lotsa everything from off
that ship you stole. Thompson, he say you people got some otter skins as well. Now listen to me, old man. Hear me? You tell
people, bring all of those things out to us *mui pronto*—quick,
you understand? Or we is going to hang your *tyee* and these
other two and then start shooting through your houses with the
cannonballs. Did you hear me good, old man?"

There was a pause. Then Matla shouted, "*Ah-ah nika kumtuks.* Yes, I understand. We bring two cannons, anchor, musket,
everything to you . . . you let our *tyee* and other two come
home."

"That's right!" the interpreter shouted. "You bring everything you got quick, quick! Then *mui pronto* we let these three
go!"

I worried that Jon Jay had not told this master that Maquina had lost half by fire and had given almost everything else
away at potlatch.

Matla sat down, and his paddlers turned the whale canoe
to take him back to shore. In a short while, we could see our
people stripping the coverings away from our two largest jour-
neying canoes. I watched them pull some wide wall boards off
the Whale house to build a platform between the two canoes.
When these had been strongly lashed together, a swarm of men
and women helped load the heavy cannons onto that floating
platform. It took about forty paddlers working together to ease
the enormous iron anchor into place.

When they left the beach, every one of all those forty paddlers seemed to be stroking hard, and yet it took some time

before they reached the ship, so heavy was the load.

Ropes and slings were lowered from the wing bones, and the shipsmen easily hauled each cannon and the anchor up onto their deck. Jon Jay and the sailmaker leaned against the ship's rail, looking on in silence, never once glancing at us. I wondered, what were Jon Jay's feelings.

The double canoes returned to shore again, then came back out with an enormous pile of musket boxes and blankets and many other items from all the other Wolf Town houses. These goods the shipsmen also hauled aboard.

Matla and the paddlers shouted, *"Tyee* come with us now?"

But that flat-headed little dog turd who did the master's talking laughed and shouted, "Oh, no, not yet! You bring us every damn last thing that you got from any shipsman." He pointed at Jon Jay and at Tom Sin, saying, "They got it all marked down in squiggles on the skins. We know everything you stole. You don't bring it all back, we going to hang these three men by their necks. You understand?"

"I would like to get a dagger inside that treacherous little piece of cheese before I leave this world," my brother-in-law told me in Wakashan.

The interpreter must have partly understood the words, for he leapt forward and stamped upon Maquina's naked foot with the hard heel of his leather boot. Maquina did not flinch but smiled disdainfully and, flicking out his foot, spattered blood across the trouser legs of the interpreter and the master. The master jumped back in dismay.

Our canoes turned once more away from the ship's side and went back to Wolf Town. They returned with another huge load of trade goods, including seven good-sized barrels of gunpowder. The shipsmen hauled it all on board and laughed with glee, for these were free items that their master could trade up north for otter pelts. One of the returned items seemed to fascinate the master. It was the elegantly chased, double-barrel swan gun that Maquina had been given, the very weapon that had in the beginning caused us all this trouble. The master examined it with care, pointing out the clever designs carved in its silver side plates.

"That's mine!" Maquina exclaimed. "Why did they send that out?"

"Fog Woman must have sent it," I said. "She told me that musket has caused all our bad fortune."

"I don't believe that," said Toowin.

Maquina, refusing to use the master's talker, called to Jon Jay. "You tell them we've got no more anything. You tell them every Wolf Town house is bare."

Tom Sin and the dagger maker nodded in agreement. "That's all," they told the Master. "They tell the truth. We know of nothing more."

The interpreter smiled when he heard the master's next words to him.

"Now the captain says he's ready to set you three dogmen free." The ship's talker laughed. "But only after you have given him a gift of sixty sea otter skins and all their tails. Remember that . . . he want every one of them goddam otter tails! You understand me? *Taghum-tatlehum*—sixty . . . otter skins . . . and tails!"

I could not believe what I was hearing. Sixty otter skins! I once was told that fewer than one hundred otter skins would trade in value for the entire ship on which we stood.

The Chinook talker said, "Captain says we are leaving on the morning tide. If he don't get his sixty otter skins by then, he will hang you or perhaps take you far up north and trade you to some Tsimshan chief as slaves. But if my captain gets the sixty skins, he says he'll set you free!"

"Is this true?" Maquina called out to Jon Jay.

The dagger maker said something to the master, then answered, "Yes, it is true. If you give him sixty otter skins, he says he will let the three of you go home."

Speaking in Wakashan, Maquina called down to old Mat-la, saying, "Ask my wife to try and collect sixty otter skins and tails and send them out here in a small and fast canoe. Do not bring them right on board," he warned, "but stand off beyond their musket range. Wait there until I tell you what to do."

The awkward double canoes were cut apart, and turning away, they set off toward the shore. By the time they arrived, it was dark, and we could see warm lights that seemed to beckon to us through the entrances of our houses.

"I don't believe there are sixty otter skins in all of Wolf Town," Maquina whispered to me.

"If anyone can find them for us, it will be my sister," I said proudly.

Toowin agreed. "If there are sixty skins in there, my aunt will find them, though she might hold back the tails."

When Toowin said that, Maquina and I both smiled a little.

A shipsman came with three bowls of food and set them on the deck. He quickly turned and walked away. I do not know whether he meant this as an insult. We did not touch the food until long after dark because, with our hands tied behind our backs, we had to kneel and lap and gnaw the food like dogs.

I slept soundly through this second night even though I, like Toowin and Maquina, remained chained to the mast and could not lie down.

Not long after dawn a new boy came on guard. He smiled in a friendly way and without our asking, offered each of us a wooden dipper full of cool, clear water and kindly held it while we drank. The wind rose slightly with the coming of the morning, and high clouds drifted like gray sand cranes across the summer sky.

The Chinook interpreter came out on deck alone and said in a rude voice, "Where are your otter skins, Wolf people?"

Maquina answered with a rattle of his chains, then said to the flathead, "You make noises to us only when your *tyee* speak Chinook through you."

This made the talker mad. He searched around until he found a length of tarred rope knotted at the end and leapt forward and whipped this at Maquina, leaving two white welts across his face.

Fog woman paddles her
canoe to trade sea otter skins.

I called out an insult that would make the flathead take his thoughts away from Maquina. He turned and struck me so hard that blood gushed from my nose. I was grateful that he didn't bother hitting Toowin.

The sight of two canoes coming out from shore caused him to throw down the rope and call out to the master, who came up quickly from his cabin.

"Here they come!" he said. "If they haven't got the sixty otter skins, we're going to hang you high."

There were only four persons in the whale canoe, and I could see four large painted boxes resting in the middle. They towed a small woman's canoe behind them.

As these two dugouts were still quite far from us, Maquina said in a low voice, "I believe Fog Woman is sitting in that first canoe."

Toowin, who has eyes like a falcon, whispered, "Yes, that is my aunt, and Matla is in the stern."

"I wonder if she found that many skins?" I said.

The two paddlers slowed their progress and waited cautiously just beyond the shipmen's musket range.

"Tell them to being the otter furs to us," the Chinook talker yelled at Maquina even before the master spoke to him.

"How many have you got?" Maquina called out across the water.

"As many as you asked for," his wife answered, "and two more."

She had her paddlers pull up the canoe that trailed behind them and load two boxes inside. Then she, herself, climbed in among them and took up her woman's paddle.

"What are you doing?" Maquina shouted to my sister.

"Husband, I am going to bring two boxes holding thirty skins. I will count them out for the foreigners. Only when you climb halfway down their ladder will I exchange these skins for you. Then I will take you to Matla's canoe and return with two more boxes full of fur. *Comprende?*" she shouted up in Spanish to the shipsmen.

I could tell that my sister had this worked out neatly in her mind and knew exactly what she was going to do. "No use arguing with her," I told Maquina.

The interpreter explained my sister's words to the master, who shouted to Fog Woman, "*Si! Si! Yo comprendo!*"

Jon Jay called out greetings to my sister in Chinook, and Tom Sin called to her in shipsman's language, which surprisingly she seemed to understand.

Quietly the master spoke to his second officer, who came and unbound Maquina. Then he and another stronger man kept a hold on him until my sister's canoe reached the ladder. She opened the two big boxes and showed them the otter skins.

I could not see her, and neither could Toowin or Maquina, but all of us could hear her counting in an angry voice, "*Ikt, mokst, klone, lakit . . .*" until she had shown them twenty-eight, twenty-nine, thirty skins.

"*Bueno!*" said the captain. "*Bueno, Señora.*"

"Before he lets you go," the Chinook talker said to Maquina, "you give my captain your sea otter cloak." He laughed. "Just a little present that you gladly give to this good man."

Maquina looked murderously at the interpreter as he pulled off the full-length cloak, which he had borrowed from me, and flung it carelessly upon the deck.

The interpreter reached for his sea knife, and suddenly big Tom Sin surprised all of us by stepping in between them to defend Maquina.

The master was not proud. He stooped down and snatched up the precious sea otter cloak.

The two shipsmen beside Maquina unchained him and rudely pushed him forward as the two fur boxes were hauled up over the ship's side. Maquina climbed down the rope ladder into his wife's canoe.

"Dagger maker!" she called up in Chinook to the deck, which she could not see. "You take care of my nephew Toowinikinnish and my brother, Siam, do you hear me? You tell those shipsmen I'll be back again."

I felt sorry for Maquina. He looked like nobody in his crumpled ship master's uniform with no hat and no proud paint upon his face. As my sister paddled him safely out to Matla's canoe, I saw her lean forward, and I tried to imagine what she must be whispering to her husband.

It was not long before Fog Woman returned with two more boxes and counted out another thirty skins. In exchange for these, they unchained me and Toowin. We were free! I wore a modest Chilkat goat-wool cape, and Toowin a cedar cape. They did not bother taking them from us.

"Now I give you thirty skins for that man and his son," she said, pointing up at me. "And I will give you two more"— she held them up—"if you give back to my husband that swan gun, which was a gift to him."

"Tell her I agree to that. Send up the otter skins," the master said.

The master mumbled something else to the interpreter, who took Toowin roughly by the shoulder and turned him around, saying, "You go with captain. He's gonna give you that damn two-barrel gun."

I was worried about Toowin. I did not like him going out of my sight, and yet it would be important to Maquina—I mean, getting back that gun.

I went and placed one leg over the ship's rail, ready to go down the ladder. But I couldn't make myself move. Not without my son. While I waited, I tried to rub the tight chain marks from my belly and my arms, and I wondered what was taking him so long. Maquina was free, and Fog Woman was waiting nervously below with the last two trade skins in her hands.

She whispered to me, "You tell that boy to hurry. I want to get away from here."

The bow of my sister's small canoe was touching the last rung of the ladder, and the shipsmen's hauling net went down to take the skins. Fog Woman looked up and saw me watching her. She whispered, "They forgot to ask me for the tails. Don't you say anything about the otter tails." In a much louder voice she called up to me, "Where's Toowin?" Then she shouted, "Jon Jay, you tell Toowin, hurry. Hurry!"

At that moment I heard a dull explosion somewhere in the

ship. It made me jump and I could feel my legs tremble and my heart leap to my throat. Every shipsman was looking back toward the narrow passageway.

The master came out, his eyes looking wild. He yelled something to the Chinook talker.

That flat-headed man, he turned to me and said, "He says . . . he shot your son . . . he says . . . didn't mean to do it. But he did shoot him! Come you now with us."

I ran along the deck after the master and the Chinook talker into the lower cabin, and there through the reeking musket smoke and gloom I saw my Toowin. He was lying with his head on the table, shuddering and coughing blood. His eyes were still half open, but he wasn't seeing anything. The two-barreled musket was still lying on the table.

I took Toowin in my arms and tried to lift him up. He was so limp it frightened me. There was a dark-red patch still spreading on his right side, where he had been hit from just across the table with a charge of heavy shot from one barrel of the swan gun.

"The captain says to you . . . he's very, very sorry," the Chinook talker said, and he looked sad at me. He whispered, "I am sorry for you too. Such a nice, strong-looking boy to lose. I know how bad you feel. I lost a son."

I shook Toowin when I heard that Chinook talker tell me that I was going to lose my son. Toowin moaned, and his head sagged back against my chest.

"Father, is that you?" he asked me in a voice that was choked with blood.

When I said yes, he gasped, "It's dark in here . . . what happened?"

"The master shot you. He says he did it . . . by mistake."

"I'm not mad at him," said Toowin. "You tell him I'm not mad at him." He held his hand against his wound, then took it away and tried to see his blood-soaked palm. "I feel better now," he said. "I can walk. You help me."

Toowin put his left hand on the table and tried to force himself to rise. He could not do it by himself. I had to help him.

A dozen foreign faces were staring at us through the master's narrow doorway. The only ones I knew were Jon Jay's and Tom Sin's.

Toowin looked better standing with his hurt side turned away, and I felt hope come flooding over me. Inside myself I pleaded, Don't die, Toowin. You're all I've got. Please . . . try to stay alive. I'm getting old, Toowin, I whispered deep inside myself. Please don't go, Toowin—not before I get a chance to die.

"Can we leave now?" Toowin asked me. "I want to lie down in my aunt's canoe."

"Yes, you go," the ship's talker said. "Both of you . . . go now!"

I took Toowin by the right arm, and the little flathead took him very gently by the left arm, and together we helped him out of the master's cabin and up the narrow stairs. Every one of the shipsmen was standing back in silence, watching us.

The master said something to his crew, and the interpreter said softly to me and Toowin, "He tells them he feels very bad."

The master reached out and offered me a horn cup full of rum.

I said thank you, but I could not drink it or even hold it in my trembling hand. It just fell to the deck. My eyes were dry as dust, and I thought, Just keep on living, Toowin. Keep on walking. I want to get you back to Wolf Town.

My thoughts were interrupted by Jon Jay, who came running to us. He had with him two fathoms of white trade cloth. He knelt and laid four tobacco leaves crisscross over Toowin's wound, and with good help from the little flathead man, we three drew the clean white cloth round and round Toowin's body until no blood showed through.

"What happened?" Fog Woman called up to me.

"Toowin got shot," I answered in a shaking voice.

"Shot?" she echoed. "Shot! Those bad buggers! And I gave them all the skins. Make those *hijos de puntas* stop—sons of whores!" She cursed them using words she had learned from earlier Spanish shipsmen. "I hate them tricking us like that!

Old Matla warned me not to trust them. He was right. They're awful, awful buggers!"

"The master says he didn't mean to shoot Toowin," I called down to her. "He said the gun just went off by itself."

"You tell him he's a *hijos de puntas,* too," my sister shouted up to me. Then she called out, "Brother, you bring poor Toowin down here. I can see the blood coming through that white cloth on his side. He's weak. Be careful he doesn't fall!"

"I'll be all right," Toowin told her. "The shot has not gone through me. It's only on my ribs."

Just as we started down, the ship's talker said in a quiet humble voice, "I'm sorry to tell you this . . . but the captain says if that woman doesn't send us up those last two otters in our net, then you are never going to leave this ship. That's not what I say. It's what the captain says."

I saw the ship's talker staring down at the patch of dark blood that was widening on Toowin's side. Suddenly, I liked that Chinook talker. I would have gladly killed him in the morning, but now he seemed to me like Toowin's only other friend aboard the ship, except maybe Jon Jay, who stood looking at us, worried.

I called down to my sister, asking her to get the two skins ready for the hoist net, telling her that we were coming down.

I was very careful on the swaying ladder, and as we reached the small canoe, Toowin was gasping for breath and bleeding from the mouth again. I saw the small net that held the otter skins go slithering up the vessel's side and disappear.

"Hurry! Hurry! Paddle hard!" I heard old Matla yell.

"Where are those goddamn otter tails?" the master shouted.

The little flathead called out in Chinook, "Keep going! Paddle fast!"

We were only a house length away from the ship when Maquina shouted, "They've got two men at the swivel gun. They're getting it ready. They're going to fire at you!"

"*Hyak! Hyak!* Hurry! Get away!" I heard Jon Jay shouting out to the three of us in the small canoe.

"Gooo-bye. Gooo-bye," Toowin called back to him in the

shipsmen's language. "Gooo-bye, my brother."

"The swivel gun man!" we heard old Matla shout. "He's aiming straight at you!"

Then we could hear Maquina's voice yelling to us, "Duck down! Duck down!"

I saw a wide blast of shot come lashing through the water all around our small canoe. It was a moment before we heard the sharp boom of the gun.

At first I felt nothing, but my ears were buzzing, and there was numbness near my spine. I saw my sister straighten as she took several heavy pellets in her back, almost in the same place I had taken mine. Only Toowin they had not hit, for he was slumped below the gunwales, protected by our bodies. Three small new holes sent water spurting into our canoe.

"Buggers! Buggers! Awful foockin buggers!" Fog Woman screamed, using the foulest words that she had learned from shipsmen. "Jon Jay, you make them stop!" she yelled back to him in Chinook.

Together we paddled hard. I could see blood running out of her left ear, dripping on her cedar cape.

"Give me the other paddle," I said to her. "We have got to get away before they fire again."

"Brother, rest yourself. You're hurt," my sister said, and I could tell that she was weeping. "Look at the blood," she said, "it's running all along your arms."

I took a dozen strokes with the paddle, but they did not fire a second blast of shot. "I saw Jon Jay stop them," she gasped just as we were out beyond their range.

"Hurry, woman! Hurry!" Maquina bellowed. "They're getting ready to fire at you with the cannon. Tom Sin is helping them with the cannon. They have handed him the fuse. Paddle hard, I tell you. Zigzag the canoe."

Those thoughts drove terror deep inside my heart, for I had the feeling that Tom Sin had held all the anger in himself for two long years and now he held the power he was looking for. I felt that if he wished to kill us, he would kill us now.

"Duck down! Duck down!" I heard Maquina shout again.

What's the use, I thought, No thin cedar wall of this canoe is going to hold out the heavy blast of ball or chain shot that the sailmaker must now be aiming at us.

Fog Woman looked back at the ship. "Brother, I promise you," she gasped, "Tom Sin will not let them fire that heavy gun at me."

I paddled as hard as she did, not believing a word she said. We two stroked completely out of rhythm. Toowin was unconscious now, and I could see that the white trade cloth around his ribs was completely soaked with blood.

I could scarcely believe it when Maquina reached out and caught the high slim prow of his wife's canoe.

"I watched him," Maquina said. "Tom Sin struck one of their cannon men with his fist. He didn't let them fire at you! Tom Sin and the dagger maker, they wouldn't let the others fire at you!"

"I knew he wouldn't try to kill me," Fog Woman gasped as Maquina and old Matla gently helped us lift Toowin into the big canoe.

It seemed to take forever before we reached the Wolf Town beach. So many helped us to get Toowin inside our apartment. Poor Toowin could not hear or speak, and I lay on my belly wishing that my wounds would make me die instead of Toowin.

Old Kula, the healing man, took a long time to dig the round shot out of my back and my sister's, using that curve-tipped knife of his. Kawskaws carefully dressed the wounds with a hot poultice of seaweed and sticky salmon paste that draws out all the poison and covered each with the bits of healing tobacco leaf that had been saved. I was exhausted from our ordeal and fell asleep and dreamed most awful visions.

In the morning, when I woke, Kawskaws told me that the ship was gone. Toowin looked deathly sick and very small, as helpless as an infant sleeping on his mother's breast. Kawskaws sat beside Toowin with a wooden trencher full of steaming clam soup. Its perfume filled the air. I guessed by looking at Kawskaws's eyes that she had not slept but had been watching Toowin through the night. I felt so sad for Toowin that I could not bring myself even to taste the rich broth that Kawskaws offered me.

"Where is Jon Jay?" Toowin asked us in a weakened voice.

"He's gone," I said. "He called goo-bye to you. Don't you remember?"

"No," said Toowin, and he tried to force himself up on one elbow to drink the broth, but couldn't. Toowin lay back against Kawskaws, who supported him. They looked so splendid together, like brother and sister—or a young husband and his wife.

"How is my sister?" I asked Maquina.

"Oh, she, like you, is feeling better. They dug the lead out of her back. Only the bleeding from her ear goes on," Maquina said. "She has got a piece of shot deep in her head, and the healer says he is afraid to try to pick it out."

"My sister will get better," I said to Kawskaws. "And Toowin is young and strong. I believe that he is going to live. I will buy two powerful amulets for both of them. Yes, Toowin will get better."

Toowin did raise his head and drank a little water. I held on to my good thoughts about my sister and my son as I stretched out on my belly and let my shot holes pucker as I slept again, still plagued by frightful dreams of that iron cannon's single eye and of our canoe slowly filling with blood and sinking.

I awoke and looked at Kawskaws's face. It was pale and tear-streaked, the faint fernlike tattoos trembling at the corners of her mouth. "I am so afraid," she said. "Something is wrong with Toowin. I can't wake him." Kawskaws stared at me in horror and said, "He's hardly breathing. I think . . . that he is dying."

"Dying!" I cried out as I crawled on hands and knees to look at Toowin's side.

The blood patch was enormous, fresh dark red in the center and brown on all the outer edges. All the hot salmon poultices and the tobacco leaves and the ship's clean white cloth had not helped him. His young face was gray in color, his eyes were partly open, their pupils rolled back so I could not see them.

I spoke softly, then in panic I shook Toowin and called out to him. No, he could not hear me, for his mind and his soul were wandering in some distant place. Kawskaws held a looking-glass to his mouth. Yes, he was breathing fog, but oh, so very faintly.

Kawskaws laid her face against his hands. Being Hupa, perhaps she knew that Toowin had already moved too far away, that he was never coming back to us.

Again I called the shaman, who tried to blow the life back into Toowin. But he failed. Yes, I just sat there watching Toowin go. There was nothing I could do. Kawskaws started weeping, clinging to me like a daughter. Tears ran down my face and mixed with hers.

My sister, the highest ranking woman we had ever known, when she heard that Toowin was gone, she came limping to us not at all like a *hacumb* but like a simple servant woman. Saying nothing, she offered Kawskaws and me food and laid her warm, strong hands on both of us to show her feelings. My sister took her most costly pieces of abalone from a small box and laid them on her nephew Toowin's eyes and mouth and placed others in a neat row on his belly and his chest.

I left those two women with him, and I went out of the Eagle house and walked along the beach by myself, for I cannot stand the sight or sound of a grown man, once a fighting man, who cannot keep himself from weeping like a woman. Yet my feelings for my poor lost son were so strong that I could not control my sobbing. I tore my hair and garments, and I cut my cheeks with a sharp-edged clamshell. But these were only small things to show my Toowin how bad I felt about his going. Still, I knew that nothing I did then would bring him back to me.

I'll just lie down, I thought, and wash out with the tide. I don't care how I die. I have no one to haul my burial canoe into a tree—no living son to sing for me.

A cold blue eye opened in the sky, then slowly misted over and closed again. It began to rain. After a while, my shot wounds pained me so that I rose from the wet sand and slowly made my way back to our fire in the Eagle house. It was nearly out. Beyond the walls I could hear the sad sound of the whistles and the sorcerer's rattle opening a path for Toowin's soul.

I tried to present a braver face to Kawskaws, who had already sprinkled the red ocher over Toowin and laid young deer horns near him, which is a Hupa way of saying farewell. Seeing those little antlers made me start to weep again, for they seemed to mark the end of everything for me.

I had believed that every last sea otter skin in Wolf Town had been gathered to pay the whites for our release. But I was wrong. When I awoke, I saw that a beautiful death robe of otter skins had been sewn together by the women of the Eagle house, and on this they had placed my Toowin. Toowin's body rested there until Ax Hand carved a new high prow to attach to my son's burial canoe.

My sister and Kawskaws and the Salish weaver woman carefully wrapped Toowin in his robe of otter skins. I helped lay him in the small canoe. Slowly we drew him up with cedar ropes until his body rested in the green boughs of a cedar tree. I knew that Toowin would soon be on his way.

Inside that canoe I placed some small but useful things that any traveler would wish to have: some fishing gear, a seal harpoon, a strong, new, well-painted paddle, my warmest goat-wool cape, and a cedar box containing food enough, I hoped, for Toowin's unknown journey.

I waited in that quiet place beyond Wolf Town until all the others had gone away, and then I looked up into Toowin's tree and I wept again and called good-bye to him. What more could I, Siam, a poor old childless father, do?

NIGHT rain ran soft as mice across our Eagle house roof. Everyone inside was sleeping. Everyone, that is, save me, for I was plagued by nightmares. The dampness in Maquina's house caused smoke from the fire pit to sink and move above the sleeping platforms like phantoms from my past.

My hand groped cautiously beneath the goat-hair covers, feeling for a wife who used to share my bed. But, like another, she was gone, leaving me a son—he, too, was gone.

After all the violence at Abooksha, Maquina had promised me that he would be careful about going aboard any ship again. He, like me, had lost his trust in whites and had thrown his shipmaster's clothes away. Maquina did not let his anger die, as I did. Man Frog, the war chief, told me that the two of them had secretly devised a plan to avenge our village by going against the next ship that came into our inlet. But they never did.

Because of her gunshot wounds, my sister limped quite badly during the winter rains, and it was clear to all of us that she could not remember things, perhaps because of that one small piece of shot that lay hidden somewhere in her head. All memory of that trouble with the second ship had entirely gone from her, but she still spoke wistfully of the dagger maker as though he had truly been her son and would soon return to her.

All the troubles, we agreed, had started when that drunken ship master insulted Maquina by throwing his broken swan gun down the stairs. We know now that weapon carried some kind of a double curse within it. First it had caused the deaths of all those earlier shipsmen. Then that vengeful, two-barreled gun had turned itself around to take poor Toowin's life.

Later, I told Kawskaws that I would help arrange a marriage for her. I suggested Ax Hand. But she wept and said she would not have him. Kawskaws said she wanted only to stay

and care for me, as a daughter does for a widowed father. I was
not sorry to hear her say those words. She steamed fish for me
in the delicate Hupa style and wove thick sleeping mats and told
me her people's curious myths and legends from the south. It is
true I would have suffered greatly if Kawskaws had gone away
from me.

Summer at the salmon grounds at Coptee passed too
quickly, as all summers do when one grows old. In autumn we
journeyed north again to Tahsis. It was almost a year after Tom
Sin and the dagger maker had sailed away when another master
sailed his ship into our bay and boldly dropped anchor. This
man did not aim his cannons in at Wolf Town. No.

His vessel, like most other ships before it, flew no flag, but
by this time we did not need to see their colored flags to recognize the differences. Boston men, the King George's men, Spanish men, not one of them was like the other. These were French
shipsmen. They were the easiest of all to tell because they said,
"*Oui, oui,*" and were much less suspicious than the Boston or
the King George's men, and the clothes they wore were good in
color but not so handsome as the sharply bearded Spanish men's.

These Frenchmen did not nervously pull up their fighting
nets or place grim-faced crewmen with scatter guns above us in
the rigging. No. When our people went aboard, they were welcomed like old friends. The Oui-oui men's kindly gestures may
have saved their lives—or ours—for it was then that Man Frog
decided on his own that we would make no trouble with them.

These newly arrived French shipsmen, I was told, had some
pipes that they could play far better than birds could sing, and
they had a three-stringed fiddle that any man would wish to
own. A few days later I went out to them and before long I was
drinking their thick, sweet, fiery brandy and bee's honey and
joyfully circling hand in hand with them around the deck, all
dancing to their pipes. Oh, yes, life goes on, and I could not
help but like these Oui-oui men. I liked the way they laughed
and joked and made sad love eyes at our youngest girls and
secretly gave them tasty bits of sugar tit.

Even on the second and third day of the Frenchmen's visit,

Maquina refused to come out in the canoes with us. He said he never wanted to see another foreign face again. He sat somberly on his bentwood box beside our fire, not listening to the good we spoke of them or looking at their clever trinkets we had brought to him. That was because the foreigners had shot his wife and spoiled her cheerful way of thinking. He could not forgive them that.

On the fourth night, I went to see Maquina, and I said to him, "These are not at all the same kind of shipsmen who did those earlier bad tricks on us. These shipsmen out there are good-hearted . . . like we ourselves. Come with me tomorrow," I said, "and see how nice they are. You'll know just what I mean when you see them laughing, dancing, singing, being generous with gifts, mixing brandy, and handing out the sugar tits."

Maquina did come out with me next day, but his face was painted blue with white tear stains beneath his eyes. The French master greeted him with a lovely gift of a green coat that had huge brass buttons and red and white and pale flowers finely sewn all over it. Besides that, the master gave him a small yellow bottle of something smelling flowery that the Oui-ouis said was not for drinking but putting underneath your arms and between your legs and in your hair. Their ship's talker told Maquina that the smell drove young girls wild with passion. Maquina couldn't help but laugh at that and quickly put some on himself and me, and when the fiddling started, he rubbed the sad paint off his face, and we both joined in dancing with the others. It had been a long, long time since I had danced so joyfully. The perfume set me thinking of the sweet musk of the copper widow.

After dark, when the shipsmen lit their lanterns, I heard Maquina warn young Hoiss and his wild companions, saying, "Don't dare try any of your tricks aboard this ship!" But there was little chance of that, for we could see that Hoiss, like all his friends, enjoyed these shipsmen every bit as much as we did.

Maquina invited them ashore to walk freely about our village, visiting any house they wished in Wolf Town, eating and sleeping anywhere they pleased. It gave us pleasure to hear these other traders saying, *"Oui, oui, oui,"* instead of the Boston men's quick "Yup," and "Yah-yah," or the King George's men endlessly saying, "Coomeer, dolly—Ello, whatcha got theer?"

The Oui-oui master and his two high men came and feasted with us in the Eagle house. And when we were laughing and feeling all like brothers, Maquina rose and pointed at the master and said, "I give you my name—Ma-quinn-na. You will be as safe as I am in this village."

Then, when the master heard that from his Chinook talker, he too rose and, spreading both his arms, said, *"Je vous donne mon nom, Capitaine Gaston Dupont,"* then embraced Maquina by touching his cheeks to Maquina's, first one cheek and then the other, very lightly.

Maquina was delighted when he heard that the master had exchanged names with him. He repeated the words *Capeetan Gassa Doopon* over and over again, changing the sound only slightly to fit the rhythm of our language. Capeetan Gassa Doopon—it really is a lovely name.

In the end, these French shipsmen stayed and traded with us for more than half a moon. They got just as many otter skins from us, and we got no more trade goods in return than from any other ship. But we had a truly friendly time together. When that ship pulled up its anchor and prepared to sail away, highborn folk from Wolf Town had to go out and search below the deck to find the slave girls they had loaned these foreigners. Most of those young ones had hidden themselves in the dark places where the shipsmen slung their hammocks. So well did these girls enjoy the Oui-oui men that they wished to sail away with them.

During the autumn moon, both Maquina and I talked of whaling again, though I admit that we had both grown somewhat old to withstand the hardships of the chase in the fast eight-man canoes. As you know, with whaling first should come vigorous fornication, then complete abstinence from all those lush bodily pleasures women offer. Only with this preparation, as well as sacred songs and early-morning bathing, may a whaling chief strive to assure good fortune in that most dangerous form of hunting. That good Kawskaws helped me perform each ritual exactly right.

My canoe left Wolf Town for the whaling grounds with all our women singing on the beach. On the second morning out, using Jon Jay's knife-sharp harpoon head, I struck a huge sperm whale, and the dagger maker's iron held fast. My heart went tum-tum-tum, for it was the first whale that I had taken in six long years.

I am more than proud to tell you that, in answer to our women's sacred chanting, that mighty sea beast rose and turned toward our beach. I held back and did not lance him until the whale towed us very close to shore. That grand animal did not breathe his last until I humbly helped him with my killing lance just as he touched against the gravel beach at Wolf Town. You should have heard the chanting of our people as they sang to him before and during our long feast. I gave one of his flippers to my sister, Fog Woman, and the other to Kawskaws, which made a lot of older women gossip.

After the whaling, we paddled north once more to our winter home in Tahsis, and saw no other foreigners until the following summer, when Wolf Town returned to Coptee. At that time anyone could see that my usually thin-waisted Kawskaws was about to have a child. For this reason she was confined away from other humans in the farthest corner of the Eagle house, which was hung with tattered cedar mats. Kawskaws was warned by older, wiser women to eat no animal's flesh and above all no berry that was fresh. Most especially they warned her against eating salmon. A woman in her condition can be oh, so harmful to the fishing and the hunting. One wrong act by a woman in confinement can easily wither countless berry patches.

I, Siam, was counseled as the father to do as little work as possible, to rest quietly by my fire and think good thoughts and eat only well-smoked salmon. That, I was assured, would make the birthing easier.

I was advised to think powerfully against Kawskaws giving birth to twins, for if that disastrous event occurred, neither she nor I could eat fresh meat of any kind for several years, and we would have to live alone in miserable seclusion. When twins are born to humans, which is rare, it is understood that one of them is a spirit from the Salmon people and must quickly be returned to its rightful place beneath the water.

Fortunately we had no twins. Kawskaws gave birth to one fine son. Oh, yes, I knew that he was mine, for had she not helped me with the sacred rights before the autumn moon?

I gave a present to the midwife and another to the sorcerer for laying his hands upon my child, to ensure for him a long, strong life and to infuse in him the special gifts of a carver. To make certain of this, Ax Hand carved a small pair of deer antlers for him, and Kawskaws performed some Hupa magic over our new child. I gave a modest feast in honor of my son Chickaminny and that fine sperm whale.

My sister, whose right it was, chose for him the name Chickaminny, which means he was born with the coming of iron. Fog Woman sewed a splendid hat of otter tails that she said she had saved for him. Anyone could see that our son looked just like Toowin. Kawskaws said it was his way of coming back to us. Maquina himself tried hard with all his girls to have another son in imitation of my famous feat, but, poor man, he had no success.

As the years passed, fewer and fewer foreigners came and anchored off our beach. Perhaps that was because the sea otter trade was dying. Because of our greediness, those gentle, glossy-coated people of the kelp beds who had once so gladly given themselves to us were now fast disappearing from their floating homelands in the bays.

Some said that most shipsmen now avoided Wolf Town because word had spread among them that we Yoquot were sometimes very dangerous. Some admitted that we were made that way only after shipsmen had twice fired cannons at us. But they kept away, believing that we, like themselves, would be eager to seek revenge.

With time, our bitterest feelings toward the whites grew smaller. Only the sight of my poor sister, Fog Woman, who had lost most of her hearing and her thinking, made me sad. When

I saw the young dagger maker's rusting bolts and hammering stone, I remembered that we had loved those two shipsmen who had once lived here.

Maquina gave only one more small feast. It was nothing at all like the great one he had given against his Black Fin rivals and the mighty Wickinnish, who, like my brother-in-law, had later given all his power away. After his great feast, Maquina had nothing left, for he had given away his canoes, his house, his masks and songs and dances to his son, and almost everything else he owned to others.

Even his famous name, Maquina, he had given away. He now called himself Capeetan Gassa Doopon and would answer only to that name. The name seemed to make of him a gentler and more kindly man. With most of the sea otter gone and his great wealth in canoes and slaves and blankets and abalone given away, Capeetan Doopon relaxed and lay back comfortably, basking in his age and legendary fame as the greatest party-giver in the world.

Always, when we knew the whales were passing south in early autumn or going north again as summer came, Capeetan Doopon would have a woman come and wake me before dawn, exactly as he had so often done in our old hunting days. He would walk with me to the mouth of the small river, and together we would squat in the ice-cold water with green boughs of hemlock knotted in our hair, scrubbing our naked bodies and our faces free of paint, and we would sing grand songs to the whales and beg help from the southwest wind. Then we would take my old whale canoe—for Maquina had given his away— and six young paddlers, and order them to take us to Sea Lion Rock. Once there, we two alone would help each other climb to the highest ledge. Adjusting our bulb-topped whaling hats dead straight upon our heads, we would sit together and watch the midday sun spread its golden light across the mighty western ocean, remembering that all the waters we could see had once belonged to Maquina, the *tyee* of Wolf Town.

I could feel my heart go tum-tum-tum when we saw the great whales breach and blow. Capeetan Doopon would whis-

Siam Gauges
the weather
before the
whale hunt.

per, "Steady, men, steady," as though he were commanding his
paddlers in upon the whale. He would bend forward and silently lay down his invisible paddle. Then he would stand up on
the rock, with his left foot forward, bracing himself as though
he were in the bow of his whale canoe and moving in to strike.

I would watch as Gassa Doopon cupped his strong hand
around the end of his huge harpoon, which still had its old-
fashioned clamshell point. He would take careful aim along its
shaft, swaying his whole body back, and make his imaginary
thrust. Only then would Maquina call out in his strong voice
with triumph and respect. And so we would begin the magic
Eagle song to the Whale. I, Siam, gladly joined my brother-in-
law in this one, last incantation that he himself possessed.

> Aw, ha ya ha ya ha,
> Whale! I have given you my best harpoon.
> Please, Whale, turn toward the shore.
> Joyfully our women will come down to greet you.
> What a great whale you are, they'll sing.
> What a fat, strong whale you are, they'll sing.
> Please, Whale, turn toward our beach.
> Our men will spread blue duck feathers on your back.
> Whale! Look upon us, Whale.
> We are the very men you have been searching for
> Along the watery edges of the world.
> Rest now, mighty Whale,
> You are home with us at last.
> Ha, ha wo wo wo.

When his Eagle song was sung, I stood studying the vastness of the western ocean. The whales had now passed far beyond our view. There were no white-winged ships, no dangerous rainbows anywhere that I could see, only the undulating
ocean shimmering gold, then turning blood red as the sun walked
slowly down along its ancient path.

"The sun is like we ourselves, a traveler wandering forever

≽ 3 5 9 ≼

through the sky," I told Capeetan Gassa Doopon. "To die is but to leap into a new beginning."

He did not respond when I said that.

"What shall we two be when we return?" I asked him. "An eagle? A fish? A wolf? A bear? A tree?"

"I do not know." He laughed, then paused. "But I do believe we shall go on and on forever."

I T   I S an historical fact that at midnight on Sunday, March 13, 1803, the ship *Boston* moved in from the Pacific Ocean, searching for an anchorage in Nootka Sound on the Northwest Coast of America. The ship's captain, smelling woodsmoke "from some savage habitation," dropped anchor, hoping to trade sea otter pelts from this Yoquot village, the very place that Captain James Cook had so recently named Friendly Cove.

Nootka Sound is scarcely one hundred and fifty nautical miles north of Canada's modern city of Victoria, on the southwest tip of Vancouver Island. The still-remote village of Friendly Cove remains without roads or air strips, inaccessible except by sea—here Northwest Coast Indian memories are long and outside contacts very few.

On Friday, July 19, 1805, the young armorer, John Rodgers Jewitt, and John Thompson departed from Friendly Cove aboard their rescue ship, the *Lydia*, of Boston. They left the Northwest Coast and sailed for Canton, China. After a voyage of 114 days, Jewitt arrived in Boston, Massachusetts, still in possession of his carefully kept journal.

John Thompson, the sailmaker from the *Boston*, had been born in Philadelphia. An orphan, he had run away and become a cabin boy and sailed to England at the age of eight. There he was impressed aboard an English man-of-war. He saw much action with the British Navy during his twenty-seven years of service and became a bare-fist boxer of renown. Tom Sin died in Havana during their long sea voyage home.

Upon his return, John Jewitt settled in Hartford, Connecticut, far from his birthplace in England. He received assistance in writing his *Adventures as a Captive* from Richard Alsop, satirist and poet, a Hartford wit, and one of the few millionaires in early nineteenth-century America.

Wearing a tall stovepipe hat that only partly concealed his dreadful head scar, Jon Jay would roam the main square, pushing a small wheelbarrow loaded with slim pamphlets. There he would stand and sing several choruses of "The Armorer Boy," a song he had composed about his own adventures. Then he would attempt to peddle his books. The short account sold for ten cents; the longer account, for twenty-five cents.

John Jewitt married on Christmas Day, 1809. He died on January 7, 1821, at the age of thirty-eight, almost sixteen years after his harrowing adventure at Nootka ended. He lies buried in a quiet cemetery in Hartford, Connecticut. On the other side of the continent, beside Maquina's burial site near Friendly Cove, there was for many years an enormous carving of a wooden whale surmounted by a giant painted eagle.

James Houston

Queen Charlotte Islands
British Columbia, 1982